MEN LIKE SHADOWS

DOROTHY CHARQUES

MEN LIKE SHADOWS

★

LONDON
JOHN MURRAY, ALBEMARLE STREET, W.

First edition 1952

Printed in Great Britain by Butler & Tanner Ltd., Frome and London
and Published by John Murray (Publishers) Ltd.

" Men are most like shadows
That move with the great sun,
Show fair, and then do falter,
Come, and are gone."

For the background of the story I have gone to the Chronicles of Richard of Devizes and of Geoffrey de Vinsauf. The latter's *Itinerary of Richard, King of the English, to the Holy Land*, and the History of the Holy War by Ambroise have been my chief source books.

Among other books, I am deeply indebted to Kate Norgate's *Richard the Lion-Heart*, to Oman's *Art of War in the Middle Ages*, to von Hammer's *History of the Assassins*, and, for the Assassin country, to the writings of Miss Freya Stark.

With the exception of the principal characters in the story, all the persons mentioned bear authentic names and titles and play the parts assigned to them in history. I have allowed the knight Hugh de Winton the title, still a courtesy title in the twelfth century, of Sir.

CONTENTS

vii

CONTENTS

PART ONE

THE PRIDE OF THE MORNING

1

I, JOHN OF OVERSLEY...

WHEN King Richard's Holy War was first proclaimed in the month of December, in the year 1189, I laughed and said, I think to Robert of Kinwarton, with one of those bursts of rhetoric that Robert never approved : " I would as soon go on a voyage to the Unattainable Mountains." I had no sooner spoken than the word " unattainable " teased me and lured me on and the desire to join King Richard grew until it outpaced all the objections in my mind. I went to King Richard's Holy War and lived through all that came to me in the land of Outremer, which some men call Holy Land though I do not, and returned.

Since my return I have thought much, as all men must who lie inactive for long spells of time, of the hidden key to each separate life, and the mystery that shapes our lives. There are times when I lie on my couch as I lie now, racked by the fever that like a bad conscience never leaves me quite, and watch the mad sport of the shadows in our great hearth. This watching of shadows is an old habit of mine learned during my first eight years when, sickly and weak, I was not much more than a long thought on a bed in a cool shade, before Raymond, my dead father's brother, returned himself from the Holy Wars and took command of my mother and of all our house, and, according to his own model, re-fashioned me. Sometimes, as I watch them now, the shadows take form and substance and become men and I myself am once more a shadow chasing shadows. Not things, I tell myself then, nor the substance of things, though we pursue both, shape our lives so much as all that comes before each event, that follows after, and lies between.

It is scarcely an hour since Sir Hugh de Winton left me, riding hard down our great avenue of limes. Kinwarton village will know now of King Richard's death, and Bearley and Aston, and Henley beyond. So the news, ill news travelling fast, will spread from every manor and market town in the shire. And still, though the April dusk turns from blue-grey to misty dark, and the fire, crackling and noisy enough before, burns white-hot and clear, I have not stirred from my couch. Only my mind, as though a sudden wind ruffled the page, turns back nine years to the green youth I was at that time, and to King Richard the Lion-heart whom I loved and served. And I am astonished again at the way in which my

3

fortunes, which seemed no more than those of any other poor esquire, crossed at last with those of that great king who now lies dead at Fontevraud, and the adventures that came to me in body and spirit, and to Robert of Kinwarton also, when we two set out with Sir Hugh de Winton for the Third Crusade.

As I lie and the wind stirs the leaves of the elder tree against our manor wall to a mad riot and quickly passes, and the grey ashes stir upon the hearth, it seems to me for the first time a good thing that I should write as Father Andrew and my mother have often urged me to do of the time from our setting out until my return, that I should tell how I crossed the seas and fought at Acre and Arsur, how I fell prisoner to the great Sheikh Sinan, chief of the murderous sect of the Assassins of Syria, in his fortress of Massiat in the mountains of the Nosairii, and escaped; and finally, in what manner I served King Richard and failed to serve him, and of the suspicion that like another shadow fell upon me. In the greater part of this I must speak not of myself only, but of Robert of Kinwarton also. In remembering him, and in grief for King Richard, I, John of Oversley, who never thought to turn chronicler for any purpose under the sun, write now for my wife Elfrida's sake, and for our son and all those who will come after him.

2

THE SETTING OUT

IT was not among mists or shadows that Robert of Kinwarton and I set out, but in the pride of the morning, on a day in May when the sun, distant yet, burned in the sky, and the air was moist around us and cold, like dew falling. Our purpose when he and I were met at Kinwarton was to join company with Sir Hugh de Winton and Everard Mortebois and the rest of the muster of the Midland shires at Avon Bridge at Stratteforde. From Stratteforde we were to make our way to Dover. From that port we of England would take ship for Normandy. Once there, our intentions were to ride with all the speed we could to the great Abbey Church of Vézelay where King Richard, we were assured, would be waiting for us with his army of Normans and Angevins and his men of Poitou beside the armies of King Philip of France.

This was no ordinary adventure upon which so many different minds were set. It was to win back for Christian men the city of Jerusalem and the shrine of Christ and the Holy Places lost three years ago to the great

Sultan of Egypt and worshipper of the prophet Mahommed, Saladin. After the many disappointments and despairs of these three years, during which many men had fought to save Jerusalem and died, Jerusalem still unsaved, men's hopes were once more high. The name of King Richard, who was to lead us and all Christendom in this Holy War, was on all men's lips, and if there were some who spoke of him as a rebellious son and impious in other ways, there were many more who could not think of him without turning ardent in praise.

All that happened to me on that first day of our setting out comes to me now through a bright blur of colour, a roundness about it as though our hill and the valley through which we rode were enclosed in a green globe of light. I was much above myself; I felt not only elated but curiously alone; my thoughts like my own feet scarcely seemed to touch earth. I know that the dew had a frosty shine, that the sun thrust up through the clouds like a new world on fire, and I was on fire too for hazard or profit or for sacrifice, for anything that was different from being my mother's son, my uncle's chopping-block at Oversley. I was eighteen; I had stayed too long at home; at all costs, now that my decision was made, I wished to be abroad. I thrust my head from my turret window. From every church in the valley, from Wixforde, from Arrow, from Alyncestre, the cross of St. George waved; from our own tower of Oversley the dragon standard of England flew. I cast my eyes below to our courtyard: there was Giles, our smith, going very ponderously as he always did on his flat feet, putting my new horse, Tristram, through his paces. A little way off, holding the other two horses, Brand the shepherd stood, looking heavenward for weather signs. My hands trembling from the chill air of the morning and the excitement in my mind, I wondered as I put on my new surcoat of orange over my shirt of mail what sort of men-at-arms Giles and Brand would make for me when we were abroad, and how Brand's great nose would sit under a cap of steel and whether my new hound Seagrim would be grey before I returned. And as I fastened my sword girdle I remembered my father's sword and shield that my mother would shortly bind upon me, that came home without him with my uncle Raymond from the Christian victory at Tiberias against this same Sultan Saladin.

But now my sister Eleanour came running up the narrow stairway that led to my turret room. "Are you ready, John? They—mother and Raymond are waiting." For so, she and I, always secretly to each other, spoke of my uncle.

"They are always waiting before it is time for me to be ready," I said.

I took care not to hurry. From now on, I assured myself, my time, if it were not my own, would no longer be theirs.

"You are mistaken to-day. To-day they think only of you," my sister said. "You will see. But wait." She came nearer and whipped out a hand from the linen wallet she carried at her waist. "I have made this for you. And this for Robert. Will you give it to him?"

Two small cakes of white bread stuffed with dried plums and marked with a cross lay in her hand.

"With your love?" I said. "But Robert has little thought of love."

"I know. But he will like the white bread nevertheless." My sister turned her back inelegantly, then facing me in the next moment, said: "Our mother has been on her knees half the night long praying for you."

I answered her callously. "Then must her knees be cold." Taking a small comb from the lid of my oak coffer, I gave, which I did not often do, a middle parting to my hair.

My sister watched me and sighed. "Your hair is stiff and crinkled like mine. I wish it were straight and fair."

Except that a hair sat on it, it was on the tip of my tongue to say that since I was Eleanour's brother I could not very well be Robert of Kinwarton also, when she said again: "You should not pretend so much. You are not so unfeeling as you would have people believe, or so hard."

I smoothed my hair. "It is Raymond's fault," I said, "if I pretend, just as it is Raymond's fault if I have turned hard. Did he not harden me?"

I bent to straighten my shoe-ties. As I did so I remembered, with an odd and familiar mixture of gratitude and resentment, with what severities of food and discipline, with what harsh Templar rites of flagellations, of cold water douches, of sleeping in my shirt on the bare stones, Raymond had hardened me; I remembered also how my mother had wailed at his attentions but permitted them nevertheless, except that she would steal out from her room sometimes to where I lay and bring me a rug of fur for my feet. I remembered how I would scarcely thank her on these occasions, lumping the two of them together ungraciously in my mind. I remembered again why I had hated them—Raymond that he should assume such power over me; my mother, who could have resisted him easily, I told myself, if she had wished, for having made herself in every way his slave.

I straightened my back. "Sometimes I do not know," I said, "whether I am as Raymond or as God made me."

"Well, you will know soon," Eleanour remarked. "When you are alone and in the battle you will know everything."

I was silent as perhaps Eleanour had intended me to be, for I had not yet seen myself clearly in any battle.

My sister turned to go down the stairway. As I made ready to follow, she swung round once more. "John!"

6

" What now ? " I waited, wedged uncomfortably against the cold stone, looking down at her, at her cheeks, pink with earnestness at this moment, at her mouth, a pursed Cupid's bow of a mouth which would have interested me enough in any other face.

" Why do you always say odd things and make yourself believe them afterwards ? " she asked.

" Move on," I said.

She said again anxiously : " You will tell them that I am not to marry until you return ? "

I answered, my face solemn : " You shall wait for Robert. I have told our mother. I will tell Raymond also."

My sister declared valiantly : " I do not think of Robert of Kinwarton or of any man."

" Do you not ? " I followed her down. " What do you think of ? " I asked. I added : " You shall do one thing, or perhaps two in return for me."

" I know," she said again. " Keep our mother from the cloister if Raymond should die. And see your hawks, David and Bathsheba, are trained."

" And I," I promised, " will not turn Templar as Raymond did and in a fit of piety for a lost skirmish vow away half our lands and your dowry."

" That is an old story now," my sister said.

" You would have everything at peace between the four of us now that I am going away ? " Almost I accused Eleanour.

" Why, yes. Would not you ? " She looked at me.

" My going away alters nothing," I declared, and I slipped in front of her where the stairway widened to a turn and went on alone into our great hall. I was resolved to be flinty-hearted, to continue the opposition to Raymond and my mother which was almost second nature in me by this time.

My resolution weakened when I saw them. My mother waited for me at the far end of our great hall in her gown of blue cloth furred with ermine, a cross of jewels upon her breast. To-day, though her face was grey—it had been grey for years from fret and grief—her look, like that of someone whose torment is past, was tranquil and still. She had prayed until she no longer had any grief left, I thought. On the other side of the heaped fire of logs that burned between them, my uncle waited for me, leaning, for all that he could not stand without pain, only lightly upon his sword. He was clad, as I had seldom seen him clad, in the full armour of a Knight Templar : the white surcoat over his hauberk, the red girdle and shoes, in the long white cloak marked with the red cross on the right shoulder. White for chastity, red for the blood they would shed, I remembered, and a shiver of something like sympathy—for was I not also pledged to the Cross?—ran down my spine. I drew nearer. My uncle's armour hung loosely upon him, his face was not more hollowed and dark than within my memory it had always been. But his eyes, like my mother's eyes, were tranquil as they rested upon me. Was he glad to be rid of me, I wondered, or, more likely, was the old love working in him for the old Cause? And contentment also, that I, the only hostage he had left in life, should stand in his and in my father's place? I went on one knee to them and kissed hands, and the heat from the fire, I remember, struck at my face. I stood up before them and waited. My mother—I had not expected so much weakness from her—leaned her head on my shoulder. I stroked her hair. It smelt of incense and the wax candle she had no doubt burned for me all night. She wept and I kissed her cheek and felt, not tenderness yet—that was to come—but pity. In the next moment I surprised myself. Poor lady, I thought now, too late, she had been in need all these years since my father's death of some other kind of love than Eleanour's or mine, for at its best, I thought, ours could only have been a kind of clamouring.

I turned from my mother to Raymond. As always, he straightened and hardened under my gaze, and this was comforting to me since at least it was not new. I said with an authority I had never yet used towards him : " Sir, I will not have my sister Eleanour given in marriage until my return." His face lightened ; he appeared astonished for a moment, and then almost amused. He said : " So the two of you are agreed upon this also ? " I said—as I spoke I heard Eleanour, who was standing a little behind me, swallow hard, then cough to hide her swallowing— " We are agreed that she may not marry without her own or my consent."

" Then we are all agreed," my uncle said.

He and I looked at each other. There was, I thought now, something like pleading in his eyes. Feeling struggled in me. I remembered again what cause I had to be grateful to him. Because of him I could play the man's part I had always dreamed and often despaired of playing ; because of him I was whole and strong, fit in all ways to ride out as he and my father had done before me in the service of Christendom. For all this I was grateful. But because of him also I was possessed, as it were, of two separate selves, the one seen by all the world, shaped and hammered after his fashion, the other malleable and secret and my own, full, I knew, of timidities and hesitations and qualms, full of fancies and odd quirks of spirit, of selfishness and dreaming and unsatisfied desires. How the two would work together in harness in King Richard's war I did not know. Well, habit and time must decide, I thought, and I looked away from my uncle and wondered what secret hungry self lived still unquenched in him. I knew that he was full of pride, that all his life he had appeared a man of stone. Yet I knew also—none better—how much passion was hidden in him, what bewilderment and angry pain, all of which he had in some unspoken fashion conveyed to me when he beat me, when he was silent with me as now, or when he talked to me sometimes harshly, sometimes not so harshly, for my soul's and my body's good. While I gazed at him in this neutral fashion a muscle twitched as though at some sudden twinge of thought or pain in his cheek. I pitied and did homage to him then willingly, and received his blessing.

" God keep you," he said, a softening about his lips.

" That will be as God pleases, sir," I answered.

Afterwards my mother fastened my father's sword on me and I took his shield and kissed her again. Drawing off from me, her face working strangely from grief, she said : " Come back, only come back."

I answered her simply out of what I momentarily felt to be knowledge :
" I think I am one of those that always come back."

" If it were true," my mother said, her tears flowing now.

I answered her hastily. " I do not know. How can any man know ? "
For I had caught my uncle's look and seen how he had turned away. It was plain that he was displeased. He, Raymond of Oversley, would never have spoken so of himself in a war from which it was impious to return, from which few indeed, maimed or well, ever returned. On another occasion I might have laughed to think how easily once more without meaning to do so I had offended him. But this time I was sorry ; this time I would have pleased him if I could, I would have taken the whole and not merely a part of his blessing with me.

We parted then. While the two of them watched from the open doorway of our great hall, I went out into the courtyard where the house servants and Brand and Giles were waiting. My sister Eleanour brought us wine : Giles and Brand tossed theirs off as if it were harvest mead. Sitting my horse, I drank more slowly, looking out at the green valley below, filled with faint rainbow mists, and the low line of hill and the dense green ruffle of forest ahead of me, and thought soberly again that I was for more burning suns and stranger fields. Then Oswald, our steward, a fat, soft, dim and creeping sort of man, who would no doubt have ruled my mother if Raymond had not, stepped forward, unasked for all that I knew, and blew two loud blasts upon his hunting horn. I doffed my cap and waved. Somewhat ridiculously we were off then, the servants running beside us down our hill ; our oak trees, their trunks like Lyons velvet in the light, came with us too, I thought, but stepped more lightly. A pack of barefooted children, the half of them, I think, closely akin to Giles, the other half, I had no doubt, to Brand, came splashing through the Willow Brook at the bottom, hallooing as they came. I gave them all the small coins I had ; silent and gaping they stood to one side. The gates were opened, then clanged to behind us ; once more we waved farewell. Now the sun burned out, filling the open doors of our great barn, as I had seen it do a thousand times and more, with dusky splendour and flame ; for a moment the outline of our castle of Oversley showed up thin as a worn knife blade, then the clouds moved, the light changed, and once more it fell away into shadow.

As we drew near Alyncestre Giles belched miserably, and said : " I know not if it is the wine that is to blame, but my stomach, that was so hot for the Cause before, is turned cold, and to tell the truth, friend Brand, now that I am started I do not feel so brave by a haycartfull. If you will believe me, friend, I have as much heart for going after hares and conies as after pagans and infidels, nay, more," Giles said. " But now that we are begun it must be as it will be, amen."

" Amen," said Brand.

" I know that poor men must always follow their betters and do as they are bid," Giles said, " and go to the wars and get nothing from them but wounds and sorrows."

" And a horse," I put in, " and good wages, and a hope of plunder. And always, good matter for grumbling."

" Yet, master," Giles continued, " I do think now I would rather be in Oversley. Only this morning my wife, a soft silly woman, master, begged of me before cockcrow that I would give leave to Jim the Penman to go in my place though he is not one half so good a smith as I. For if I escaped the pagans, my wife said, I should be devoured of the sea serpents and the little monsters that hide in the desert sand. And, master, I like not these sea serpents."

" I'm certain sure," Brand declared, " I know nothing of monsters. As for these she serpents, if they be women they can be dealt with in the way o' women as every man knows."

" Sea serpents," I interrupted him. " Sea serpents, man."

" Ah, I know nothing of them then," Brand continued. " I only know, master, that with the rubbing of this plaguey steel cap o' mine I am like to lose all my hair for King Richard before I clap eyes on his face. Let us hope," Brand said, " King Richard would do the same for me. Though I do doubt it, sadly." Brand shook his head.

" This is vagabond talk," I said. " And Jack's as good as his master and always was." The better to silence them, I spurred my horse.

We rode at a smart trot into Alyncestre, past the Unicorn Inn on our left and the Tavern of the Bell on our right and on again past the Inn of the Circlet of Gold—Alyncestre was a market town sewn thick with taverns and drinking houses, the needlers and smiths who abounded there being thirsty folk. To-day they came out to stare, little men in leather aprons and flat caps, men that were shrunken and dry, having bushy eyebrows and shining pates and beacon-like noses. They were not hostile, but not friendly either, for in general the townspeople had no love for our castle of Oversley since they must pay us rents and dues and tolls. Only one or two of the women, plump and comely in their kirtles of scarlet and blue, wished us God speed ; only when I saluted the women in thanks did the men turn courteous in return and doff their caps. From the west door of the church of Saint Nicholas, Father Andrew, who had bestowed upon Robert of Kinwarton and upon me also all the learning that was ours, came out to meet us, bearing the crucifix before him, his choir (lads trained for the choir of the great Abbey of Pershore) stepping two by two behind him and singing like young linnets as they came. They sang the Children's Song which Father Andrew, who had spent some years at Gothenburg in Germany, had translated from the German not six months past, and which Robert of Kinwarton, who had a gift for the stringing of verses, had put into English rhyme. The words, which seemed made for the day, came very prettily from the children's lips. We bowed our heads to listen as they sang :

> " *Fair are the meadows,*
> *Fairer still the woodlands,*
> *Robed in .the blossoming garb of spring :*
> *Jesus is fairer,*
> *Jesus is purer,*
> *Jesus makes all our sad hearts to sing.*
>
> " *Fair is the sunshine,*
> *Fairer still the moonlight*
> *And the sparkling, starry host.*
> *Jesus shines brighter,*
> *Jesus shines purer*
> *Than all the angels Heaven can boast.*"

The singing over, we took our blessing of Father Andrew and our leave of them all and went on between the new gabled houses of the merchants, beside the Market Hall to the Deep Ford, and thence, having passed it safely, to Kinwarton.

Bidding Brand and Giles go on, I rode alone down the long lane to Kinwarton. The doves as I passed the manor dovecot, like nesting birds, seemed half asleep. The manor house when I came to it appeared asleep also : two swans sailed upon the moat ; the May wind ruffled their feathers and the green water, and sent the blossoms flying from the may trees. Robert rode slowly across the meadow to meet me. From excitement and pleasure mixed I cried out to him and urged my horse on. Like a man surprised out of some secret mood he greeted me only coolly, I thought. Somewhat chastened I fell in beside him. We were alike or we could never have become friends, and yet unlike, or we might never have arrived at so deep a misunderstanding finally as to appear almost enemies.

Robert was stiff with reserve and pride ; I was not so assured nor so quiet within myself as he was, nor so rooted in purpose. I was uncertain of myself, as I have said, and besides that, over-demonstrative at times and over-bold, and given, out of the timidity which pricked me now and then, to a harmless sort of boasting. For the rest we were English and Norman, and in England English and Norman were not then, nor are they yet, truly mixed. And Robert, I would think sometimes, could never quite forget that we of Oversley were newcomers, and that of the Kinwarton lands all but his own manor of Kinwarton had passed in the gift of the Conqueror's brother Odo, Bishop of Bayeux, to us, his Norman followers, at Oversley. So if there was love between us there were the seeds of a little enmity as well.

Robert turned to me. His cap hung at his saddle bow, his fair hair shone, his surcoat was no bluer than his eyes. He said, smiling : " You were offended just now. Why ? I meant nothing."

I answered : " Then I was a fool to be offended." In sudden affection I took note of him. He carried his lute on his back, his crossbow slung over one shoulder, a short sword hung at his belt, a Book of Hours thrust out of his wallet. There was an ease and grace about him that I envied ; there was a carelessness about him also that scarcely belonged to war. I said, laughing : " You would pass for Saint George on your white horse, but you must be more orderly when we come up with old Sir Wisdom." For that was the name all his esquires had for Sir Hugh de Winton.

" Sir Wisdom shall correct me himself when we come up with him." Robert laughed back at me. " I have always heard," he said, " that there is great ennui in war, therefore I have brought my lute."

I said regretfully : " I have left my chessmen at home." As I spoke I remembered how Robert had come to Oversley first, a tall thin lad in a green leather jerkin, in search, he said, of a falcon called Diane, which had flown from Kinwarton. The falcon was lost for ever, it seemed, but Robert came again, repeatedly, to play chess with me or to sing to his lute, while Eleanour, silent and secretly worshipful, twanged—it is an instrument I have never liked—upon her harp, and Raymond took himself off to his tower room or some quieter place, and my mother, not far off from the three of us, hovered fondly. From chess and playing upon the lute Robert passed to sharing lessons with me under Father Andrew. When I walked almost for the first time he encouraged me like a brother. In those days we had no differences. It was chiefly due to Robert that I learned to ride, to use the lance and the short sword and shoot with the crossbow, and swim and dive. We tried tilting together also ; we played at fisticuffs and quarter staves, while Raymond, which almost spoiled my pleasure, looked on and approved us silently.

" You must make a new song of King Richard," I said, " on the lines of the Lay of Bohemund." And I went off day-dreaming again.

" I was thinking," Robert interrupted, " when you called to me, that I would rather the Sepulchre were won by gentleness and peace than by the sword."

I came back with a start to myself. " Gentleness and peace are for monks," I declared, perhaps stupidly.

" Then I am half a monk," Robert answered, " since one half of me thinks of peace."

" Turn back now," I begged him, " if I have over-persuaded you."

" Even you could not over-persuade me," Robert said.

I remained uneasy. It was certain that Robert, burdened as he was with the care of a younger brother and sister, would not have volunteered for King Richard's Holy War if I had not pressed him to do so ; it was certain also that without the help of Sir Hugh de Winton he could not have borne from the revenues of Kinwarton alone the expense of his passage oversea. I remembered how all the talk the year before at the Warwick Tournament had been of King Richard's oath to recover Jerusalem, and of the company of esquires and men-at-arms which Sir Hugh de Winton would take with him upon King Richard's Crusade. My own mind had been clear for days before the tournament. I remembered saying to Robert on our way back from Warwick, " Why could you not come also ? " For secretly, even then, I was unwilling to venture so far alone. Robert had answered me quietly : " I cannot leave Oscar and Elfrida. I cannot from the rents of one manor find funds for arms and the journey." I had pressed him again. " Would you leave Oscar and Elfrida if arms and service money were yours ? " He had waited for a moment. " Yes," he had answered at last. He had spoken so quietly I had known that he would keep his word. I had gone secretly to work. It was April when I spoke again. The cowslips were scenting all the high fields and king-cups gilding all the low water meadows. Robert and I had swum in the river at Kinwarton for the first time that spring and dived again and again into the deep pool ; having rubbed ourselves dry with a switch of grass, we were so full of the delight of it all we were in the mood to agree to any adventure. "Will you come now?" I asked over one of Eleanour's cakes of white bread, eaten crumb by crumb from our palms. I had gone on to tell Robert how Sir Hugh de Winton had found room for him and for several more in his company, and armour and weapons also. I told Robert he had only to find a horse.

"And serving men," Robert said.

I told him again: "You shall share Brand and Giles."

"I shall go in poorer state than any other of Sir Hugh's esquires," Robert had objected.

"Why care so much for that," I asked, "when there are rewards to be had and land and prizes to win? And also—or so Everard Mortebois declares—glory."

"I am not one for rewards so much," Robert said, and spat out a piece of grass as he spoke. "But I am for Jerusalem, and perhaps for glory."

I was beginning to wish he would show more zest for the Cause when suddenly, as if gladness brimmed over in him, his mood changed. He tossed his jerkin in the air and caught it again, half-dressed as we both were and in our shirts. "Penniless though I am, see if I am not the greatest leopard among you all." He laughed at himself, then sobered suddenly.

In order to test him further, I asked after a moment: "Do you not hate the Turk?"

"Why, no," he answered. "As yet I hate no one."

I thought for a moment. "I hate no one either," I said, "unless it be Raymond." We had looked at each other and laughed again and felt the lighter for it.

We rode on in silence for a time. Where the meadow joined the lane once more we paused. In the wilderness on the far side Elfrida danced in and out of the shining trunks of the silver birches, over the short turf that was blue with dog violets and starred white with the wild strawberry flowers, a tall child, thin and fair, dancing to herself in a rose-coloured gown. Absorbed in her game she did not turn or speak to us.

"I have told her only that I have gone to join King Richard," Robert said, "and that if I may I shall come back a knight."

"You desire that?" I looked at him.

"That is one of the things I desire, yes," Robert answered.

I could guess the rest: my sister for a wife and his own land, or part of it, for her dowry again. His own land, I thought wryly.

"And you?" Robert enquired.

I did my best to answer soberly. "I desire to prove myself, to be Raymond's equal and my own master." I turned extravagant in the next breath, and sobriety fled. " I desire to be gay and loved. I desire everything."

" Presently I shall desire my breakfast," Robert said. He reined in his horse and turned to face the flat fields. " Here is Oscar," he declared, " and I must wait for him."

We had not long to wait before Oscar came splashing towards us, stumbling from one tuft of marshy grass to the next. He carried a bent withy stick looped with thread for a fishing rod ; a leather bag, bulging with bait, jolted and bumped against his side as he ran.

" Oscar has no desires," Robert said, watching him, " except to catch a pike half as large as himself."

" And afterwards ? " I laughed.

" One twice as large, of course," Robert said.

Oscar jumped the full ditch and arrived, panting, almost at our horses' feet. He was a little plump lad, fiery-faced and blue-eyed. He had a blunted knife in his belt, a linen cap of grey shaped like a crusader's helm flapping loosely about his ears.

Robert lifted him on to his saddle bow and held him there. Together and in silence they rode on. Where the high road to Stratteforde showed Robert lifted him down. " Farewell," he said, and bent over him. Oscar raised his face, smudged with tears and angry now, then ducked his head and plunged once more across the wide ditch. Though Robert called after him he would not turn nor look back, but ran on blindly, like someone astonished and angered at his own grief.

" He will not forgive you, or me either perhaps," I said.

" Elfrida and he will comfort each other," Robert said. He turned as he spoke so that I should not see his face.

By the dovecot we paused for the last time and crumbled our cakes of bread, tossing the last morsels to the doves. They were about us at once in a sudden whirr of Pentecostal wings. " Let this be a good omen," Robert said. I looked up at the arched ceiling of wings over our heads and echoed his thought. Once more we rode on. The road to Stratteforde lay open before us. A short distance ahead Brand and Giles waited patiently, their heads bent and nodding like sleepy thistles under the may trees. We caught up with them. At Alne Bridge Everard Mortebois joined us with others of our small company. We had scarcely greeted them when Sir Hugh de Winton himself swept down on us from the dark fringe of the woods on our other side. The old knight had his old armour on, but a new pot helm, as near as possible in size and shape to King Richard's own, half smothered his head. There was not an esquire among us who did not long to titter at the sight, and not one who dared. Sir Hugh roared a greeting at us ; meek as maids we fell in behind. Together, knights and esquires and archers and men-at-arms, we rode on. The sun burned out, the cuckoo called and mocked us from the young oaks along the way, the larks soared dizzy as our hopes over the stripes of green corn.

3

VÉZELAY

IT was not until the first day of July, many days later, that we rode into Vézelay. We were in time, but only just in time, for our rendezvous with King Richard. For to-morrow, the Kings of France and England were due to meet and make solemn promises one to the other in the great Abbey Church of Vézelay ; on the following day the armies of the two countries would set out on the long road that led through Lyons-on-the-Rhône to Marseilles, and thence over the Great Sea to the land of Outremer, and on, by deserts and ways unknown to us as yet, at last to Jerusalem. Unity, brotherhood, love were to guide us ; Christ's name and charity were to govern all. In this first flush of our journeying we believed that God was with us, that even if every circumstance should prove contrary we could not fail. More than one motive was present in our minds : a true piety, a restlessness that sent us adventuring, a hope, rosy and comforting when all else failed, of gain. We sought first the Sepulchre and the Holy Places. But beyond Jerusalem, we knew, lay the treasures of Damascus and Baghdad, and all the fabulous wonders of the East. We were to experience strife and despair greater, it may be, than any army yet had known, but to-day, for a little while, our dream, so much vaster than the sum of all our lives, united us and drew us on. The flints on the steep road of approach to Vézelay were sharp under our horses' feet ; the dust was a white cloud that moved with us, that burned our eyelids, that parched mouth and tongue ; we were saddle-sore and armour-sore, and hungry and thirsty besides, yet excitement was an extra life in our veins ; the hundred small delays, the mire and sweat of our long journeyings, even the fearful sickness, which I had dreaded most, caused by the hump-backed waves of the sea, were almost forgotten ; and to me at least our journey across England through London to Canterbury to Dover, across the sea through Normandy to Champagne to Burgundy, seemed not a great deal more than the long road I had travelled first as a boy from Oversley to Warwick for the Tournament. I had never been better pleased with myself nor more content. The small round hills, the blue valley mists which had enclosed me so softly all my life at Oversley were gone ; before me, or so I believed, was this small hub of strife that was the world ; beyond, so I had been told and so I believed, chaos and thick darkness lay, and a tideless creeping sea. But to-day and for many days and months afterwards I did not think of the dark, nor of the tideless sea.

On the brow of the hill that led by a steep ascent to the town we paused to look around and to take breath. Through the thinning cloud of dust we saw that a vast city of tents filled the green hollow of the plain and invaded even the vineyard-clad slope of the hills. There were few houses to be seen : it was as if the tide of the two armies had flowed in and covered them. High above the many white peaks of the tents, above the scarlet, the yellow, the purple and gold of the pavilions, the great Abbey Church could be seen and, distant from it a little, the castle of Vézelay. Around lay the mountains, streaked at this sunset hour with darkness and shadow. Even now, as we watched, the sinking sun filled the valley with a fiery dust-diffused light and a little sudden wind blew, lifting and setting in motion the many drooping pennons and banners that hung from the tents, until indeed the plain itself seemed in ripple and movement like an inland sea.

" The pennons show like wings," Robert said.

" No, like water," I returned.

From my other side Giles licked his lips with a dry tongue and enquired earnestly : " Master, do you reckon those thirsty pilgrims that went on before us over the field-ways will have left any ale in the town ? "

" If they have not," said Brand, " we will drink wine. In foreign parts I am one for wine." Then, looking around him in the vast simple way he had, and nodding towards the tents, he said : " Master John, we shall meet Sodom and Gomorrah there."

" Ay, fellow, ay," old Sir Hugh said, " ay. What of it ? "

Sodom and Gomorrah, I explained hastily, were twin brothers of Brand, named, so his mother, poor dame, believed, after two saints recently come out of Ireland.

" Ireland, oh, ay, Ireland," old Sir Wisdom said. " God's feet, I would believe anything of King Dermot's country," and he clapped his helm, under which he had twisted and sweated for many a mile, once more upon his round close-cropped head. And Brand, addressing all the company with so much gravity even the silliest esquire ceased to laugh, declared : " Your worship, and Master John, our Morrah is no laughing matter, sirs. Our Morrah, I did hear, is sergeant of crossbowmen, sergeant of the King's own company of crossbowmen, sirs."

Old Sir Hugh sucked his teeth loudly and thrust out his lower lip as he did when he was much amused. " On then, gentlemen," he said, " to

17

Sodom and Gomorrah. Sodom and Gomorrah "—here he guffawed outright—" indeed."

As we drew nearer the town so the press of people grew. Squadrons of knights and esquires and serving men could be seen threading their way down the steep slopes of the hills ; companies of men-at-arms, marching compactly, filled the roads ; baggage carts rolled and trundled behind, while bands of pilgrims carrying staves and waving banners, diligent as ants and more active than monkeys, swarmed between. One such band, preceded by a tall striding goliard-like fellow in a brown cassock, a viol slung over one shoulder, pressed close upon us. At the foot of the hill carts and horses and mules and pilgrims and foot soldiers were held in the vilest confusion. No fair, or bear-baiting, or hanging and quartering, no saint's day, ever produced such a spectacle. Men—and women also —of every condition except the poorest were here, all wearing the Cross, all bent upon pilgrimage. They were of every race and people, from the unknown regions of Dalmatia to the sandy lands southward beyond the mountains of the Pyrenees. Without discipline, without leaders, each one bent upon his own way, they were hard to move, impossible to command. Sir Hugh chafed and swore by every oath of his own and by more than one he had borrowed from his late master King Henry. " By God's eyes," he swore, " by God's feet." In all that crowd while we waited, and we had no choice but to wait, only one man appeared at ease : our goliard, who by this time had climbed a bending sycamore tree and was sitting astride a pliant bough, twanging his viol among the dusty leaves. Everard Mortebois called to him : " Give us the Lay of Antioch, Sir Goliard." A part of the crowd took up the plea : " The Lay, brother Goliard, the Lay." The goliard leaned out dangerously from his branch and answered them : " Can a song-thrush sing without showers or a goliard without wine ? " And he went on plucking his viol strings.

Presently there was a stir among the company of crossbowmen who had halted immediately before us. A fellow who appeared to be in some authority over the crossbowmen mounted a baggage waggon and, after vainly roaring out his orders in rough English and rougher Norman-French, began to blow furiously upon a horn. In the same moment the small company of French notables who had arrived only a few minutes after our own arrival, and who were held as we were, almost crushed between the edge of the crowd and the steep slope of the way down which they had come, pressed forward. They advanced only a foot or two and were held again. I looked at them curiously. They were not dusty and travel-stained as we were, but fine and new-fashioned in all their armour and gear, in the trappings of their horses, in their blazoned surcoats and the nodding plumes on their helmets. Only one of their number, an esquire no older than Robert or myself, was bareheaded. He wore a surcoat of white linen over a black coat of mail ; he sat a fine Arab horse that was piebald too, his dark straight hair swung free as a girl's and was almost as long about his ears. I had stared hard at him for an instant and caught his look, smiling, but arrogant as well ; then, shame-faced but curious still, I had turned away. He called out now to the sergeant of crossbowmen : " Make way there, make way, fellow, for His Grace the Most Noble the Duke of Burgundy. Shields out, press forward, I say." Sir Hugh de Winton, not to be outdone by a company of Frenchmen, called out in similar terms, but a shade more courteously : " In the name of King Richard of England, sergeant of crossbowmen, make way, I command you, make way."

" I heard you, both," the sergeant of crossbowmen answered, glowering first at the Frenchman, glowering next at Sir Hugh de Winton, but obeying nevertheless.

The brave curve of the sergeant's nose, the glint in his little pig's eyes, even the cumbersome quickness of his large frame were marvellously familiar to me. I turned, and in the next instant the truth jolted me like the sudden dig of an elbow in my ribs, and Brand, leaping in his saddle beside me like an unwieldy tadpole, cried out, " 'Tis Sodom. No, 'tis Gomorrah. By my soul, 'tis Morrah. How dost, lad ? How art now ? Sweet Morrah, tell me, where shall we meet ? "

In between roaring out his orders and cuffing and cursing anyone who came in his way, Gomorrah answered Brand : " To-night, by the Tavern of the Little Sisters.—Back, there ! " he called out. " Back ! Make way, good masters, or be trod upon. Hard by the Market Hall, good brother Brand.—Forward, Shields," he roared, " forward, I say, in King Richard's name.—Ask for Dame Lilias, brother Brand, a plump yellow-haired wench. —Press on, press on, crossbowmen. Steady there, steady.—Out, Sir Bob-o-Link, out, my cock chaffinch "—here Gomorrah cuffed a pilgrim with a dulcimer off the road. " Forget not, brother, the Tavern of the Little Sisters, this night.—Press on there, crossbowmen, press on, I say."

Behind locked shields the crossbowmen thrust slowly forward ; foot by foot the crowd yielded, or were forced back, or trampled upon. With difficulty at first, then more easily, the horsemen, both French and English, forced a way through. The thing was not well done on all our parts— Robert and I were afterwards agreed upon that—for many pilgrims, both men and women, fell and were trampled underfoot. But the press was broken, we were moving, though at a snail's pace, and the Frenchman who had first given the order to make way rode beside our company.

I looked back. Our goliard was peering down at us from his branch. " Let us meet again, goliard," Everard cried out to him as we moved on.

"I am Ambrose, Ambrose. We shall meet again, brothers, depend upon it," the goliard answered, and quick as ever he shinned down from his sycamore tree.

The French esquire who had just given the order to move on laughed and shot a glance towards us. "Ambrose is no goliard nor even a trouvère. He is a poet," he said, "a writer of flat rhyming tales, and, for all that he rhymes so well, he is a melancholy fellow."

"You know him?" I spoke in surprise.

"I have often been in his company." The other spoke carelessly again. "He is English, I think. Or Irish, it may be. Truly, I forget which, but from your islands. And you, of course, are from England also?"

I gave him my name. "Heir to Raymond of Oversley in the county of Warwickshire," I said. "And on your right is Robert of Kinwarton, my friend, of the same county."

He bowed in his saddle towards first one, then the other of us. "Guy de Passy, at your service," he said.

We were of Sir Hugh de Winton's company, I informed him.

"And I," he returned, "serve His Grace the Most Noble the Duke of Burgundy." As he spoke he bowed so low I thought he almost mocked the Duke.

While I wondered why an esquire of the Duke of Burgundy should care to mock the Duke of Burgundy, the Frenchman spoke again. "Sir Hugh de Winton wears as vast a pot helm as I have ever seen."

"After the fashion of King Richard," Everard cheerfully said.

"But Sir Hugh is not made after the fashion of King Richard," de Passy countered.

"No." I laughed. "Sir Hugh is short and thick and tough and red-headed where he has hair at all, after the fashion of the dead King Henry."

"And does King Richard bear him no ill-will that he was once King Henry's man?" de Passy enquired.

"King Richard seldom bears ill-will to any man," Robert answered. He added, which he need not have done, I thought: "Both his allies and his friends traffic too much upon the King's failure to remember an injury."

"Surely there is a certain arrogance in so much forgetfulness," the Frenchman said.

"I do not call it forgetfulness," Robert returned.

We were silent for a while, then de Passy spoke again, differently. "The English camp is most pleasantly placed, under a hill, hard by a stream. But we of Burgundy, since we are no strangers to Vézelay, have our quarters in the castle." He went on: "Tell me more of King Richard. We speak of him often. We say, for instance, that he is a great captain, perhaps even, though we are not certain of that yet, a great king. For the rest, we of France who acknowledge King Philip are inclined to be critical of King Richard. That is not, I think, to be wondered at in us, since beside your King ours must seem of small importance even within his own country."

"King Richard, it is true, has inherited more of France than the King of France," I said. "But surely you would not blame King Richard for what is no more than his good fortune."

"Say we are envious, then," the Frenchman returned.

He talked as confidently, I thought, as if we were alone and riding at our ease, as if we were not surrounded by a press of people and separated by only a few crossbowmen from our respective masters, Sir Hugh de Winton and the Duke of Burgundy.

He appeared to read my thoughts. "Never fear!" he said. "These pot helms are useless for eavesdropping." With one look over his shoulder, he went on : "I was about to say that men fall into some sort of bewitchment before members of the House of Plantagenet. The bewitchment springs, I have heard it said, from the demon blood of Anjou."

"There is too much talk of demons," Robert declared, "among those of us who worship Christ."

De Passy regarded him curiously. "I cannot agree. Who is not aware," he asked, "of the demon within himself?"

"Surely that is not the same thing," Robert said.

I spoke hastily. "You know much, de Passy, of our affairs."

"I have studied in the schools of Chartres and of Notre Dame," he returned. "One meets all sorts there, one discusses everything, the darkness of the world, the flux of faith and the brutishness of life, and the astonishing affairs of the House of Anjou also."

"Now tell us of King Philip of France," Everard said.

"I shall be indiscreet again," de Passy replied. "But, as Robert of Kinwarton has no doubt observed "—here he looked at Robert—"I delight in indiscretion."

"Why?" Everard asked bluntly.

The Frenchman laughed. "Do not invite me so early to speak about myself." He continued : "King Philip is subtle, I would say. I like his subtlety. It will serve him, I think, better than any mere force of arms. For the rest, it is reported of him that he desires to leave behind him a great power and a great name. He, also, if you like, is dangerously in love with greatness."

We went on to talk in general terms of the way French and English would travel to Outremer.

"King Philip plans to go overland to Genoa and take ship from there to Acre," de Passy said. "But yours is a voyage without parallel since you plan to go all the way from Marseilles by sea. It is true your fleet is large."

"It is in all ways fit," Robert said. "For all that"—here he looked at me—"I pray we meet no storms."

"If we do," I said, "my poor Giles will dream of sea serpents and die of fright."

"When our ships pitch in the waves as they do," said de Passy, "then I most abhor the sea. At night it is a monstrous creeping thing, so many heaving fathoms deep; by day there is so much of it, a man longs for land." Half in earnest he shivered. "For one who has crossed the sea twice," he joked, "I am deadly afraid."

"Do not think of it." Robert spoke seriously. "It is always," he said, "of the next moment that a man is afraid."

I looked from one to the other of them. They were to be rivals and bitter enemies, but as yet I saw nothing of this. That day I saw only that they liked and yet disliked each other, were drawn together as in this moment, only to be thrust apart in the next by some deep current of feeling in them both.

A silence fell on us then. Whether it sprang from discretion or fatigue or even from some faint foreknowledge of what was before us I do not know, nor do I remember who was the first to speak. I only know that soon, in spite of the slow pace at which we moved, we were in Vézelay. Before us, as far as the eye could see, was an unbroken line of men and horses and baggage trains winding between the low walls of the houses. All Vézelay was out of doors to greet us : every house was garlanded with flowers and vine leaves. Gifts of flagons of wine, dishes of fruit and cheese were pressed upon us. There was no staying to enjoy them, for we knew that every man among us must be encamped before nightfall. Already the sun was a round Saxon shield of gold above the hills, and dusk, rose-dark like a bat's wing, was tender about us, and the shadows of roofs and trees were long and still. It was then that suddenly, and for no reason, I saw not the streets of Vézelay, but the grey boughs of our apple trees at Oversley, and the spring dusk, tender as this about them, but filled with catkin gold.

Robert pulled at my arm. "Look, man ! "

I rode beside him.

"Look," he said again.

Through the triple portals of the great Abbey Church of Saint Mary Magdalene as we approached the procession of Vespers came : another moving stream of banners and silken vestments and gold. As it paused before once more entering the Church, the Abbey Cross held on high, the dun-coloured throng of pilgrims that crowded the many steps of the Abbey moved and swayed and bent their heads as I have seen a field of barley ears move and sway just before harvest time when the wind passes. Our own Archbishop, Baldwin of Canterbury, was there, men said, and the King's half-brother, Geoffrey, Archbishop of York, but at this distance we could not distinguish them. We saw only the triple portals as if indeed we were at Heaven's gate, and the splendour and the holiness within.

Robert looked at me. " Now indeed we are in Vézelay."

" I could wish we were at Acre and the fighting begun," I said.

" Why so impatient," de Passy asked, " unless indeed you hope the sooner to be home again ? "

" For the moment I did wish it," I replied.

" Every place alike is home to me who belong nowhere," de Passy said.

" This is no time," Everard declared, " for a man to desire anything more than his supper and his bed. As I do desire both," he added almost piously.

Brand and Giles could be heard now, both of them talking in loud tones. " Here, friend Brand," I heard Giles say, " is the Tavern of the Two Sisters or the somesuch-named tavern of which Gomorrah spoke." I turned my head. Brand, who had been staring about him, grunted and dropped his gaze, but did not speak. Close on our left, a house with a painted sign on which two women, as alike as two peas and pretty well as round and bare, sat astride one horse, leaned against the Market Hall. From the casement window that seemed to glower out of the thatch hung a stout dame who could be no other than Dame Lilias. She was as soft and overflowing as a down pillow put out to air.

" I declare," Giles gulped and admired, " this is as fine a tavern as any in Alyncestre."

" I like not these vast-bosomed dames," Brand declared.

" How so ? " said Giles.

" Why, for this," Brand answered. " A juggler told me his life under a haystack one day in April when it rained. With the female sex, this juggler said, all goes by opposites. If a woman be stout she is often niggardly ; if merely fat, cold. But a lean woman has often the most overflowing heart. A man must have a rule for dealing with all that are female, this juggler said." Brand paused and looked at Dame Lilias again. " Truly, I think she is too abounding for me."

Giles was inclined to argue. " If this dame be friend to Gomorrah she will be friend to us. But if she be like Jael to King Sisera we shall not be well served."

" As Jael to Sisera ! " exclaimed Brand. " Holy Saint Martin ! Of all the deaths a man might die I would wish least to die of a tent peg."

I interrupted him. "I'll listen to no more foolishness of women or of tent pegs," I said, laughing but red-faced.

Giles grumbled. "We are not foolish, master." And Brand answered me stoutly as I might have known he would. "Master John, we spoke of matters private to ourselves as any men might do."

"Your fellows are over-ready with their answers," de Passy observed.

"They are free men," I said, "and have followed me freely, and have a right to speak."

De Passy rode nearer me. "How many of your English here are free?"

"All who come with King Richard on this crusade are free; none are forced," Robert and I, both speaking in chorus, said.

"I believe as many come in hope of gain as for any reason of Christian piety," de Passy said.

"Have you so little faith left?" Robert asked, half laughing for the first time.

The Frenchman was serious. "I no longer dream, that is all. Our dreams destroy us, I think."

No one answered him.

We moved on. Lights flowered out, one by one, in the Abbey Church; the smell of incense hung in the dust-laden air; from the slopes of the hills came fresher scents of leaves and flowers.

Beyond the Abbey a narrow road turned off to the castle of Vézelay. Here once more we were held in an infinite confusion as those horsemen and men-at-arms who were for the castle tried with shouts and oaths to separate themselves from those others who were for the French or for the English camp. While we waited I turned over in my mind how best to part from Guy de Passy. There was much in him that on a better acquaintance I might dislike. Yet he seemed to me to be of the world, and I, who knew myself rustic and untried, wished to be of the world also. It seemed to me that I might learn from him. At least, I told myself obstinately —for Robert, I felt, would not be with me in this—at least I would see more of him if I could.

While I was turning all this over in my mind de Passy himself spoke to me. "Your King goes hunting to-morrow, they say. Will the three of you be there?"

We looked at each other. We believed we were for Lyons-on-the-Rhône, I said. "But if King Richard goes hunting," I added, "then the three of us will certainly be there."

"We shall be well in the rear," Everard grumbled. "I know these hunts of ceremony. All the coxcombs are there, but no quarry." He stopped short; he rubbed his eyes, then shaded them with one hand. "By all that is gentle, see what comes."

We shaded our eyes and looked also. Winding down the slope of the opposite hill in the last glare of the sun the oddest procession of all that we had seen that day met our eyes. First came a half-dozen or so mounted men-at-arms in steel caps and leather jerkins stamped in silver and blue, led by a stout fish-faced fellow stuck in an embroidered tabard; behind them a plump dame rode astride a white palfrey. A horse-drawn litter followed, closely curtained in silver and blue and hung about with little tinkling silver bells. Nor was this all. On each side of the litter a great shaven mastiff ran, on the top a small brown monkey held by a silver chain chattered and clung. Two serving women in grey habits and another half-dozen or so of mounted men brought up the rear.

" My Lady Worldly Vanity herself, I think," I said.

" They are the colours of the des Préaux," de Passy declared.

" King Richard's friends? Holy Saint Anthony! The man knows everything," Everard said.

The procession halted before us and the fish-faced fellow in the embroidered tabard addressed us peevishly: " Is this, good sirs, the castle and town of Vézelay?"

At once the curtains of the litter parted, the silver bells tinkled and shook and a small imperious voice sang out: " Stupid! Can you not see the church?"

" Melisande, Melisande!" The plump dame on the palfrey wailed and beat her hands.

" But, Aunt, I stifle in here. May I not breathe?" the voice cried and a face brimful of laughter was turned towards us for a moment, then withdrawn behind the blue and silver curtains again. With more tinklings of silver bells the litter creaked past us and moved on.

We eyed each other. " I am in love," de Passy declared.

" What colour were her eyes? I would drown in blue eyes," said Everard.

" I would drown in any eyes that were bright enough," de Passy returned.

" Her eyes are blue," Robert said.

I alone at first said nothing. I saw again the quick small turn of her head, and her cheeks, coloured so softly, and her hair, primrose-fair and shining about her face.

" Perhaps I am in love too," at last I said.

" If some monster came foaming out of the hill, and the men-at-arms fled, and if the monster would have none of the plump dame—and I would not—we would spur forward," said Everard, and he tossed his lance in the air and caught it again.

" The monster would not wait for us. Why should he?" Robert very drily said.

"And there would be no rescue. See, she is gone." De Passy, standing up in his stirrups, snatched at his cap and waved it. "Farewell! Farewell!"

But the lady was out of hearing, and presently even the last of her men-at-arms was out of sight.

At the end of the town where a trampled waggon-way led to the English camp, de Passy turned to us. "To-morrow," he said.

We parted then.

I questioned Robert afterwards. "You do not care for the Frenchman?"

Robert was cautious. "I do not know him."

I spoke firmly. "I would know him better."

Old Sir Wisdom and Roger de Furneval of Yorkshire charged past us in that moment. "The Duke of Burgundy," we heard old Sir Hugh grind out between his teeth as he passed. "Who *is* the Duke of Burgundy? By God's eyes! By God's feet!"

We laughed at them. "Unity, brotherhood, love," we said, "where are they now?"

Laughing still but full of wonder also, the heralds riding forward to greet us, we rode in after Sir Hugh de Winton into our camp at Vézelay.

4

THE KING'S HUNT

THE horns, more shattering than the last trump to such heavy sleepers as we were that first night at Vézelay, roused us soon after dawn. King Richard—the chase was as dear to him, his enemies said, as his Holy War—would be out early hunting the boar in the woods round Vézelay, and King Philip of France and many Frenchmen, together with everyone of consequence in the English camp, were commanded to hunt with him.

Before the time for our assembly at the hunt arrived Sir Hugh de Winton sent us word that he would inspect all those who were of his company and would speak with us afterwards for our souls' good and for the good of King Richard. To old Sir Wisdom, the two things, as we all knew, were the same.

Some hundred and fifty of us, esquires and sergeants and men-at-arms, waited for him therefore in the still morning mists. While we waited we joked and laughed together irreverently. I said: "To-morrow, when

26

we set out in earnest—unless we go hunting once more—would have been a better time for a sermon."

"It will be of wine and women, and of being tempted," Robert said. "Do not ask me why."

"I am not tempted," I declared.

"If I were a witch of Satan I would tempt old Sir Wisdom in his bath," Everard said, "then we might be spared a sermon."

"If old Sir Wisdom were tempted and fell," Robert said, "then we should pay for his sinning with two sermons."

Hardly had the titters that followed this solemnity died away than the old knight himself appeared from his steaming tent, looking like red meat newly boiled, and wearing, though it was a hunting day, his pot helm and coat of mail. He came out stamping his small blunt feet and blinking a little in the light, his head lowered like that of some old bull, his small round eyes upon us all.

He moved down our lines, tweaking a buckle here, a jerkin there, now standing off to get a better view, now coming disconcertingly near, and talking in snatches all the while. "You are not dragon-flies, nor cocks in mating-time—no, colours and feathers are not for you. Yet you must go fine and neat for all that, and you must be ready before the time. For King Richard is a true son of his father, as many sons are that quarrel with their fathers and repent after, and King Richard, like King Henry, will not wait. For the rest, he is not like King Henry, for that King was the most restless man alive. Awake or asleep, there was a demon of no peace in him, God rest him now."

He halted before Robert at last and addressed us in earnest, his sword belt creaking, his great belly thrust forward. "To-morrow were indeed a better day for a sermon—I will not differ from John of Oversley there. But to-morrow there will be such a ha-ha in all the camp, such a confusion in every place, such short tempers and long oaths as if all Christendom were in motion. To-morrow there will be neither time nor breath for a sermon.

"So"—here he paused and looked at us from under his pot helm again—"first I would have you remember that though Kings may have little care of their own safety, it is for captains and esquires, and sergeants also, to keep guard. Of the King first; next, of those under the King, and last, last always, of themselves.

"For the second matter, do not throw away safety. Remember that the infidel Turks are more numerous than we are by a hundredfold—do they not have more wives than we have, two or three to our one, and in the same hour, and marry earlier? Because they are more numerous than we are I will have no dangerous competing between knights and esquires, and no exercises in early dying between French and English. If a Frenchman call you to your face ' the tailed English,' do not hear him for the first time, but on the second time fell him to the ground. Do not kill him or be killed. Remember you are two men for the Sepulchre, two men against the infidel.

" For my third matter. I advise you, be on your guard with all strangers whether in your own camp or outside it. If they question you, rather mislead them than lie downright. I would not have you err in this, for the giving away of secrets spells treachery and death and it is not you who die first but your fellows. You must have the greater care, for just as King Richard, and King Philip of France also, have their spies, so the Sultan Saladin has his, and the old Sheikh of the Mountains also.

" Fourthly, I command you, except in courtesy, that you leave all women where they belong. You are young yet and landless. If women are of ill-fame they will only serve you ill. If they are virtuous they will bind you with chains of virtue and you may not be bound except to King Richard. As for wine, drink chiefly at night that you may sleep your-selves sober. And as for grumbling, do not grumble too much. Be thankful that you serve King Richard, a captain unmatched in all Christendom for skill, one who will have great care of the least one among you and of every detail of the march and the battle.

" I have almost done. I have said that you must be guarded and temperate. Be so. But when you come to battle, whether with the devil and his evil counsels, or with the infidel Turks, those servants of the devil, then, by God's Holy Cross and Passion, remembering only Christ and your soul's salvation, fight. Having done so, you will be better on the day, and thereafter."

Sir Hugh finished abruptly and stood off from us. " May God prosper us," he said, " may God deliver us from all evil and yielding." Raising his hand in salute while we saluted him again, he turned, and mounting his horse, which his man had ready and waiting for him, he rode slowly away.

In the next moment, in order to hide from each other what we thought and felt, for there was not one of us, I believe, who was not moved in some way by the old knight's words, we were talking and laughing together again.

" Leave women in their place ! " Everard exclaimed. " What in these days, noble Sir Wisdom, is their place ? "

" It is where we are not," Robert slyly said.

" All women seem alike, and all are beautiful to me," Everard sighed.

Then he was in great danger, we were all agreed.

" I would not be distracted by women," said Robert.

Then you are in greater danger than Everard, we declared.

We scattered and made ready for the hunt. As we rode out an hour later we could see in the light of the summer dawn how well-ordered the camp was and how vast. Around us were green hills for shelter from the winds and green woods for comfort and shade. Every commander had his own place marked out for him by his helm and shield. In the midst, in a green open space, the dragon standard of England drooped mast-high in heavy folds, but from the King's own tent hung only the leopard banner of Anjou. The King's pavilion of ceremony was crimson and gold, turreted like a castle and large enough to hold all the King's own knights and esquires and the musicians and minstrels whom he loved, but his private tent in which he slept unguarded was as simple and plain as Robert's or my own.

The King's companions had first place about him. Among those whose blazonings we knew were William de Stagno ; William, Marshal of all England ; Robert Trussebot of Yorkshire, the King's banner-bearer ; Gerard de Furneval of the same county ; Bertrand de Verdun, Sheriff of our own county of Warwick, and Ralph Taissons, that sweet singer, with Blondel de Nesle to keep company with him. Here also were the three brothers des Préaux, Jean and Pierre and William des Préaux. The last the King was said to love somewhat better than a brother, but as to the truth of this at this time we knew nothing. The Templars under Robert de Sabloil, and the Hospitallers under Garnier de Naplouse kept an inner circle about the King. Some distance from them and apart, though in a privileged place for all that, Sir Hugh de Winton was lodged and our own small company. Beyond and all around the rest of the encampment lay.

We were early yet. We rode slowly, therefore, missing nothing as we passed of the many sights and sounds and smells of the camp. As I write the sounds come back again to my ears : the ring of hammers from the farriers' anvils and the armourers' shops, the clanking of bridles and bits, the braying of mules, and, suddenly, the scream of a warhorse, battle and madness in it, I thought, shivering. I can hear again the voices of men calling to each other, in rough English, thick German, smooth Norman-French ; and other voices still, calling to each other in languages we did not know ; and last of all, a boy's voice singing from a closed tent, as if a grounded lark sang unseen, a song that was of nothing but love, while at some distance, faint as voices heard in sickness or in dreams, the chanting of the monks of Vézelay came to us, an undercurrent of prayer and praise that did not cease. I remember a red rose of Provence blooming against a wall and how Robert picked it and held it to his lips, and how, curiously, I envied him. Of other sights I remember best a cook trolling a drinking song of the night before, while a scullion, knee bent, tied his

blue apron on him from behind ; a dark-haired page sitting alone, stringing red roses (perhaps of Provence also) into a chaplet feverishly, and a
tall striding monk who passed us like a lost wave of the sea. I thought I
saw a swift passionate despair upon his face. We smelled rich mingled
smells of sheep and oxen roasting whole on the turning spits, of savoury
stews simmering in round cooking pots, of herbs and garlic freshly chopped
on boards, of cool cucumbers newly-sliced, of burnt horn from the black-
smith's forge, and hot iron sizzling in the armourers' vats, and the smell
of loaves baking. As I write I can see again the azures and crimsons
and gold under the pale sky, the lift of the pennons, the sluggish stir of the
banners and the camp like a world to itself, consecrated and remote, and
in some way strange.

We rode on, no longer alone but part of a long procession of horsemen
and foot followers. The sights and sounds of the camp diminished, then
fell behind. Sweeter airs came down from the hills, small birds sang from
the thickets, and the day grew fair. As we had expected, the company
at the meeting-place was too numerous by a half. This was no hunt, as
Everard had prophesied, but a parade of notables before a crowd, and
Robert and Everard and I were of the crowd. The French, with King
Philip and the Duke of Burgundy, were everywhere to be seen, pricking
about now here, now there, on their light palfreys, as many and as gay as
a shoal of bright fish in a clear stream. The English, only less gay than
the French, moved so closely around King Richard as almost to hide him
from our sight. At the spectacle of so many knights with hawks and
hounds, so many falconers and huntsmen, I wished I had my two hounds,
Pallas and Dion, with me and my two falcons King David and Bathsheba
upon my wrist, so that the three of us might have gone hunting or hawking
on our own account. We were on the outskirts of the crowd ; among so
numerous and important a company we could scarcely, I thought, be
missed. When finally I complained Robert laughed at me. " What did
you expect ? " he asked.

Later I grumbled again : " We shall lose the hunt completely if we
move no faster than this."

" We have lost it already," Robert said.

As he spoke I noticed for the first time that in addition to his hunting
spear he carried his crossbow slung across his back. I suspected this was
another odd careful quirk of Robert's, for he was careful over many things,
and particularly careful, perhaps because of his lack of means, of his arms
and gear.

He read my thoughts. " All camps are full of thieves, and I, if you
like, am full of too much carefulness." He tossed an arm in the air.
" Besides, who knows I may not meet with an assassin ? "

I scoffed at him. "It is well known," I said, "that Sinan, the Old Man of the Syrian Mountains, does indeed send his young men from Massiat and elsewhere to murder in Burgundy. It is not far."

"His young men find their way everywhere," Robert said, "or so I have heard."

I took up the tale. "They make a craft of murder. They kill coldly and exactly, at a command. They obey; they ask nothing on earth, for all their hopes are set upon Paradise."

"Only a fool would laugh at them," Robert said. "One of their number recently pinned a warning note from Sinan with a dagger to the Sultan Saladin's pillow while he slept, and escaped unseen even though the guards had been doubled about the Sultan's tent.

"The sect of the Assassins is feared everywhere, I grant you," I said. "But still I will not believe more than two-thirds of the tales that are told of its members."

"They say," said Everard, "that the Old Man of the Mountains has a great white beard divided into two parts, each part held up by a black slave. I would set eyes on Sinan and his beard and his two black slaves if I might. I do not care so much about his murdering."

We went on to talk in a desultory fashion of this and that, of the chances of the campaign before us, of King Richard's plans and of all the gossip we had already gathered of the King himself and of those who stood closest to him.

By noonday we had ridden far, not caring very much that we had lagged far behind the rest. When the sun was high we came out at last from the long ride of the woods which had confined us until now into a wide open space set with young birch trees and dense thickets of bramble and thorn. Tall thistles with leaves like swords grew as high as a man here and there; in between the thickets where the short grass grew were cushions of thyme jewelled with bright-eyed sleepy bees, and carpets of some small creeping yellow flower. The air was heavy with scents and still. We tied our horses to a tree, climbed a small round hill and waited, stretched out in the shade, our hunting caps over our eyes. We waited for what we scarcely knew, for the day to go or the hunt to return. Before us was the wide stretch of the glade, and the drive out of which we had come; all around were the hills.

"If I were looking for a boar I should find him there, I swear it, in that chalk pit." Everard pointed to where on our left a disused chalk pit showed behind a thick screen of trees. Scarcely visible from the glade it was yet plain enough from our hill. Beyond the pit lay rough country once more and a dense growth of young trees.

"The hunt will come back this way, I promise you," Everard said again.

"Heaven forbid." Robert sat up and lifted his cap from his eyes. Replacing it, he lay down again. "If you are expecting your goliard, Everard," he announced, "here he comes."

Ambrose himself, mounted on a small ass, came riding, as we had done, out of the woods into the glade. We called to him; he looked about him, then came trotting gallantly towards us, in and out of the thickets, round the tall thistles, over the tussocks of thyme, as if he and his ass were treading the maze at Warwick Tourney. He wore his brown habit still, his feet all but touched earth, his pilgrim's hat protected his ass's head.

"Why do you not lend your ass your gown also?" Everard called down to him.

"Our Lord rode upon an ass. Do not mock me, or my ass," Ambrose returned. And he tied Melchior (for that, it appeared afterwards, was his ass's name) to a different tree and was soon seated beside us on our hill.

"This is a famous hunt," Everard sighed once more. "We have had not a sight of the boar, scarcely a glimpse of King Richard."

"Then am I disappointed. I had come in the hope of seeing the King of England." Hugging his knees, his long chin pressed against them, Ambrose went on: "I have seen this place, as it is now, under this sun. I have dreamed of it. I do not often dream."

What to reply to this we did not immediately know.

Robert said: "We were speaking of the sect of Assassins just before you came."

"I have flat feet. I could not be a member of the Assassin Brotherhood," Ambrose said. "Every one of Sheikh Sinan's young men must be as perfect in body as he is perverted in mind."

Still uncertain of his meaning we stared at him.

He informed us: "De Passy says so."

"Who *is* de Passy?" From his tone of voice Robert might have been old Sir Hugh, I thought. He was both impatient and peremptory.

Ambrose answered carefully. "There is some secret about his parentage. If a thing is secret, I let it lie. I am not curious."

"I have invited the Frenchman to our tent to-night," said Everard. "And now I am reminded of what I had almost forgotten. I have some news for all of you who are love-struck. She is gone from us. She is off to the port of Marseilles in the train of Queen Eleanour. I mean she whom we saw when we came in to Vézelay, sister to the King's friends."

"The Lady Melisande des Préaux?" Ambrose spoke questioningly.

I repeated what he said. I found a curious pleasure in speaking her name.

"I wish she had stayed," Everard declared. "I had a mind to be joyful, and capering and in love."

" Love does not last. I have proved it," said Ambrose, " many times."

" Why should it last ? " Everard enquired idly.

" Richard the Chronicler saw Queen Eleanour when she rode beside King Henry in the streets of Rouen," Ambrose began. " He saw her but the once. He was in love then. She was like a small blossoming tree, he said, like a fine May morning. She was a sight to live in a man's eyes for ever."

" The students made songs for her and sang them," Robert said. " There is one from the German that I know. In English it runs like this :

> " If the world were all mine
> From the sea to the Rhine
> I would give it all
> If so be the Queen of England
> Would lie in my arms."

" And now," Ambrose continued, " no one looking at Richard the Chronicler would think that he could dream of love. And Queen Eleanour has forgotten all the love between herself and King Henry since she and all their sons made war against him in such bitter hate."

" They quarrelled over Alois of France, this King Philip's sister. Or so it was whispered everywhere, though with what truth I do not know," Robert said.

" The Lady Alois was King Henry's ward and King Richard's betrothed also," Ambrose explained. " King Henry took her for his mistress though she was his ward and sister to the King of France also, and had four children by her, or so again it is said. It is for this reason that King Richard will not take her for his wife. And it is for this reason also that King Philip feels himself deeply injured."

" In King Richard's place King Philip would not marry her either," I declared.

" But King Philip is not reasonable, and in his place you might not be reasonable either," Ambrose said, smiling. " More especially as King Richard sees no reason why he should not marry where he pleases."

" With Berengaria of Navarre, for instance," Everard said. " She has a little shape and a little nose, they say, and a vast dowry. And King Richard has already provisioned his fleet with the half of her dowry."

I must confess we laughed at that, for this mixture of romance and bargaining on King Richard's part seemed to match all that we had heard of the King.

Ambrose had his head resting upon his knees once more. " I care not whom the King marries, nor when he marries, but if French and English do not agree how shall we win back Jerusalem ? "

I stirred uneasily, remembering too late, I confess, old Sir Wisdom's warnings. Ambrose appeared to read my mind. " I would not speak so frankly to a Frenchman," he declared. " From that, John of Oversley," he said, " you may guess I am not much more French than you are." " I am Norman," I replied, " though Norman and English are not in truth so different from one another."

" One day," Robert said cheerfully, " there will, I think, be no Normans in England, only English. And English land will be divided again." Here he looked at me.

" The French are beginning to dream something of the same dream," Ambrose said. " They dream that the English shall hold no part of France, and that all Frenchmen shall one day live under the same French king. My own dream is further off still, though I can remember when it seemed within every man's hand. I would have all Christendom one country, one brotherhood of Christian men." He paused, and we waited. It was plain that there was more to come. He went on. " I myself am a poor scholar-poet, a wandering Irishman of no country, but of God. Though I have lived much in France I was bred in England and born in Ireland, my mother an O'Daly of Munster. The O'Dalys, you should know, are one of the great poet families of Ireland. With us the making of verse is a craft handed down from father to son, for the O'Dalys have been poets for five hundred years. My own father was a crossbowman in King Henry's conquering army in Ireland, himself the son of a master weaver of Ipswich. I do not remember him, but my mother has told me how he took her for love and charity and to keep her safe when every other soul was slain at the sack of Cork. My father died of his wounds, my mother of a fever at Bury St. Edmunds where my father had brought her. At her death the monks of the great Abbey of Bury took me when I could scarcely talk, and bred me up and taught me in the Abbey School, I do not know why, unless there was a monk of Ireland among them there who would not willingly let an O'Daly starve. In all the county of Suffolk there was nothing to compare with the Abbey for beauty or greatness. I was lost in the brotherhood, a mite in a vast lively cheese. Brother Helvetius was my tutor and bedfellow. He taught me much besides an *Ave* or two and a little Latin and Greek. He taught me the lute and the viol. He was one of those, and there are still many of them, who love the old songs better than the new canticles. It was he who sang all the old songs to me of love and battle, of the sea and of women beautiful and false and satin-fair. We would go fishing, he and I. When our basket was full—and that was soon, for he was a good fisherman and the fish came to his bait as if he charmed them—he would play upon the viol which he hid at the bottom of his basket. So he charmed and taught me. In time he died also and I grieved for him. After that I was sent to the Abbey School and there I worked hard and a little against my will at Latin and at Greek, at rhetoric and all the lore of the schools. But I did not forget the old songs ; I longed always to sing them better than he did and to make new ones for myself. And always I kept his viol." Ambrose touched the viol at his side. " It is here," he said, and was silent.

We begged him to tell us more.

" I have almost done," he said. " From Bury, while my voice was still uncracked, I went to Canterbury—they were in need of sweet singers there."

" And saw my lord Archbishop Thomas à Becket, surely ? " I said.

" And served him," Ambrose answered. " When he was slain I fled, again I do not know why, except that all vows seemed broken then, though as yet I had taken no vow. From Canterbury I fled to Paris and Notre Dame, where a Brother of Bury was. The city, perhaps because of some quality in the air, held me. From novice I turned scholar and poet also. All my words were songs and rhyme. Now poesy is no longer a gift with me, but a vice like the rest. A man should abstain sometimes from poesy and from love."

" What will you do now, Ambrose ? " Robert asked.

" Now," Ambrose answered, " I intend to make what in Ireland we call the white martyrdom of pilgrimage. If I return, if the perils of the seas, or the heathen Turk, or sickness, or reptiles, do not prevent me, or my own folly, I shall make a story in rhyme of all our adventure from the first setting-out of King Richard and his host until the end—I will not say until Jerusalem. And perhaps my story will live like those stories of Ireland that have come down to me from my ancestor, Colman mac Lenine."

" But you will write in French ? " after a moment's silence Robert said.

" In French, for I have not enough Irish," Ambrose returned.

Robert leaned forward, and as he spoke he, too, clasped his knees. " Ambrose, I am curious to know why you should come so far to see King Richard when it would appear easier to look for him in the camp."

" For this reason," Ambrose answered. " Last night I dreamed of the King ; I dreamed that he was in great danger in this place. The nature of the danger was hidden from me. Only the place where we are now and this glade before us and this chalk pit beyond were clear. Because of my anxiety for the King I followed the hunt. I do not often hunt or dream."

We looked at each other uneasily, for there is something a shade terrifying in every warning dream. Of the three of us Everard was the least impressed. " Keep watch if you must," he told us, " but let me sleep."

Stretched out beside me, pink-faced and peaceful as a child, his head pillowed conveniently upon my arm, he was soon asleep.

Ambrose leaned his long chin upon his hands and seemed to dream again. I had thought his face merry when I saw him first, now in shadow it appeared melancholy and dark. Robert, his arms crossed beneath his head, lay removed from us a little, and did not speak. The sun burned down, piercing the small interstices of the leaves. So drowsy was the quiet, so warm the sun, I too slept. I woke to hear Robert say, " In moments like this, Ambrose, is a man nearest to content ? "

I heard Ambrose answer : " I am asleep."

I said : " I am awake. I dreamed that I betrayed King Richard and turned Mahommedan and entered Paradise. Even in Paradise I was not content."

" You should have burned in Hell for ever if you denied Christ," Robert said.

Ambrose spoke absently. " An infidel said to me once before he died, ' God has a hundred names.' "

Everard rubbed his eyes and scrambled to his feet. " I am cramped," he declared, holding one foot and hopping upon the other. " By Beelzebub and all his devils," he cried then, " here, if you please, is old Sir Wisdom of all men gone astray."

Ambrose was on his feet also and shading his eyes. He spoke, a sudden tremor in his voice : " I think all the hunt is returned."

" The boar ! " Everard cried. " Oh, Holy Virgin, the boar ! "

He had scarcely spoken when we were all upon our feet. Well within sight and not more than two hundred yards from our round hill the boar broke cover.

" See him," Everard cried, pointing, " see him. He is spent, and angry as well. Soon he will turn on them. Can you not see him ? Holy St. Martin, already he hesitates, already he moves more slowly."

Horns sounding, horse and foot broke cover from both sides of the glade. The boar was nearer now, a small moving shape, solitary, hard-pressed, men and horses and dogs hard after him.

Ambrose spoke quietly. " All this is as I saw it in my dream."

I looked for King Richard. " Two men leading," I cried out. " One wears the cap of Poitou. It is King Richard. William des Préaux, I think it is William des Préaux, rides beside him."

" No, King Richard leads," Robert contradicted me.

" Why are we not with them ? " Everard flung up a hand and began to plunge down the steep slope of our hill towards the horses.

" Christ, oh, Christ turn him," we heard Ambrose pray.

We looked again and understood at once why Ambrose was afraid.

The boar, with the cunning an old boar often shows, was leading straight towards the chalk-pit's edge, and King Richard, William des Préaux following, was riding hard after him.

We watched, held motionless, while the boar turned and, moving slowly, seemed to skirt the fringe of trees at the pit's edge. An instant later the hounds leapt forward ; in a flash their leader, poor beast, was carried over the chalk-pit's edge and gone. A second hound followed him.

" The King's horse is in a frenzy. No one can check him," Ambrose quietly said.

So indeed it seemed. For though the King reined him in hard, though we shouted until we could shout no more, the Spanish horse, as if the Evil One and all his train were after him, came on, and William des Préaux was still a length or two behind. My brain moved sluggishly at first, then more quickly.

" Could you not shoot, Robert ? " I cried then. " Shoot to turn the King's horse, not to kill."

I could not look at Robert as he took aim. I remember only how the arrow flew curving, then straight, cutting low across the path of the King and perilously close to the great horse as he drew upon us and passed. I know only that the horse snorted and reared and was cruelly checked ; I saw only this and the arrow half-bury itself in the grass on the other side. It was a feat simple enough to perform, yet it seemed like a miracle to me and, I think, to every one of us then.

On occasions like this there is no movement and no time ; we are held in the moment ; the sun himself stands still. As we ran down the hill the King had dismounted. Cap in hand, he was standing beside his horse, and the hunt was pressing about him like bees about to swarm. And to all the hubbub of voices raised suddenly Melchior, Ambrose's ass, added his, making a louder and more fearful din.

" I would not have lived," Ambrose spoke tremblingly at my elbow, " if harm had come to the King—I, who was warned of the danger and the place, and had not wit enough to speak."

" There were many more than you," I said, " who knew the dangers of this place and did not speak."

We moved nearer the King. William the Marshal stood nearest him. On the other side William des Préaux waited, his hand on the King's horse, his fair hair sweaty and damp about his face. I saw the Duke of Burgundy come up in the press of knights and lords, and de Passy following him at a distance with the other Burgundian esquires. As we watched, old Sir Wisdom thrust forward through the crowd towards William the Marshal and the King. Sir Hugh beckoned to us where we waited, moving both arms like windmill sails so that once more, solemn though the moment was, I wished to laugh. I remember that Robert and I, both our names having been called, moved forward together down the narrow aisle that was cleared for us, towards the King. I was aware of the cushioned fall, as if I were drunk, of my own feet on the soft turf, and the silence as we advanced, as inquisitive, as sharp as though a myriad eyes looked on us through a million leaves. Robert moved, I fancy, with an equal blindness. Once more, and oddly in this instant, I envied him his height. He was lifted above the crowd ; he could look over them. The moment held interminably, it seemed to me, then broke suddenly. The King's companions closed in about us, we were through the throng and standing before the King.

Old Sir Wisdom whispered urgently in the King's ear again. King Richard spoke to us then, his eyes, blue and frosty and unsmiling at first, moving from Robert's face to mine and back again. " I have to thank one of you gentlemen for my limbs, perhaps for my life, and certainly for my horse. Which of you must I thank ? " he asked, smiling now.

While he spoke I looked at him. Capless, in a jerkin of azure, he stood head and shoulders taller than any who were about him except only William des Préaux. But his length and grace of limb were not so memorable as the passion and power of life one felt in him. Beside him all other men—even William the Marshal, even the handsome Geoffrey, his half-brother—seemed dwarfed and dim. While I looked and worshipped a little, Robert answered : " It was nothing, sire."

" Nothing to save my limbs and perhaps my life, Robert of Kinwarton ? " the King said, and I remember how he and everyone else laughed and how Robert changed colour, then steadied and spoke. My blood leapt as I heard him say : " Sire, it was John of Oversley who bade me shoot."

" You were together in this ? " The King looked directly at me.

I said swiftly : " Sire, we have been long together ; we would not be separated." For it was in my mind that the King might wish to honour us, and in doing so might thrust us apart.

" You speak out of your turn—that is a Norman vice," the King said and laughed again. He enquired after my uncle then.

" My uncle will never be healed in this life of the wounds he had at Tiberias," I answered, discovering for the first time a great pride in my Uncle Raymond.

It was Robert's turn after that. " You are English, I think, Robert of Kinwarton," the King said.

" My fathers held three manors before Domesday, sire," Robert answered.

" And you would have them again ? "

Robert hesitated. " Once I did desire them, or others like them, sire."

38

" And now ? " The King waited.

Robert spoke simply. " My desire is that the cross of gold should wave once more over God's city, sire." Having spoken, he flushed and was silent.

" That is all our desire. Have we not sworn it, gentlemen ? " the King turned to us all and said.

In the silence that followed, that was no more, I thought, than a passive and obedient silence, King Richard spoke courteously to us again : " I thank you both, John of Oversley, Robert of Kinwarton."

When we had kissed his hand old Sir Wisdom came forward once more and led us all but captive away, muttering in our ears all the while : " He will see more of you ; this is something you must not miss. Nevertheless do not count upon it ; the Almighty could not have more prayers and beseechings made to him for favours than King Richard, nor be more forgetful of them than the King is. So have patience, wait. Be assured I will keep him in memory of you. Yet do not expect earldoms or baronies ; you do not deserve so much ; you have been ready at the moment you should ha' been ready and that is something and worth a little something again. Now patience and expect nothing." Abrupt and nodding, Sir Hugh left us. But his promises or rather his half-promises stayed in our minds.

I cannot speak for Robert, yet for myself I know that as we rode back to the camp my shoulders carried no burden. I was exalted a little, even a little light-headed. At the least invitation I could have talked nonsense, or sung, or laughed ; in short, I could have been as mad as King David. I was aware of the many voices and the many people around me, yet I myself seemed far away. I told myself only one thing repeatedly, that this that had happened could not but mean good fortune : I had spoken to the King, I had been noticed. The sun beat mercilessly upon my head, yet I did not feel it ; the air was leaden with approaching storms, yet I felt it not. I saw little of the road, almost nothing of the sights around me ; in my mind's eye I saw only King Richard again, standing and stooping a little beside his horse, the light colouring and warming his hair, that was neither gold nor red, to the shade of the dancing leopards in gold upon his sleeves. I remembered the fret of leaves like a forest of lance heads about him and the light quiver of shadows, as if earth were fluid under his feet. I saw again the trembling—something humbled and pitiful about it in so proud a beast—of his Spanish horse, and William des Préaux's hands, sunburned and tapering and fine, like a physician's hands, stroking and soothing him. And I was happy, when I remembered all this, to think that I had been of some slight service to the King.

I was alone, for Robert had fallen behind and Ambrose had moved on, when de Passy's voice brought me sharply out of my day-dream. He said many flattering things of Robert and myself and of the day's events. It was to be regretted, he said at last, that Robert of Kinwarton and I must share to-day's honours between us, since clearly King Richard would not reward two as he might have rewarded one.

"I should be happier if Robert's state were mended rather than my own," I said, and meant what I said.

De Passy laughed at me. "Forgive me, I do not know whether to call you a simpleton or merely magnanimous. If, that is, you are sincere."

"I am sincere." For a moment I was angry.

He spoke quickly if somewhat too smoothly. "Do not be offended. I had more thought for you than for your friend and, it seems, more thought for you than you have for yourself."

Leaving me to digest this as best I could, he saluted me and, apparently in the best of good humours, rode off.

I looked after him. Almost as if he were a woman he attracted and vexed me also. There was, that is to say, much about him that tickled and astonished me, much that, without any great liking on my part as yet, drew me on. I began to suspect that he was one of those who might use me for his own purposes and afterwards, when my usefulness was past, discard me. Well, I would use him also, I resolved, I would equal him in worldliness.

When Robert caught up with me again, as he did presently, I related what had passed between the Frenchman and myself.

"He has always a sting in his tail for you," I said, "and sometimes for me also."

"Poor wasp," said Robert. He was merry. Before long we were laughing together and content. Of all that we felt and saw that day, it is the contentment we had together that I remember now. Yet both contentment and fame were brief.

5

CONTENDING VOICES

SIR HUGH DE WINTON's messenger, a pert lad with chestnut locks and a pointed face like a girl's, waited on us a few hours after our return from the King's Hunt. Old Sir Wisdom, he said familiarly, had news for us from the King. Would we make ready therefore? And he crossed his legs and put a rose between his lips.

While we made ready Everard teased us from the open flap of his tent where he sat cross-legged like a Turk, scratching a name industriously upon his dagger's hilt and looking, I feared, somewhat downcast for all his wit. "You will have fat manors bestowed upon you, or else baronies," he prophesied, "and both in turn will wed the Lady Melisande. For we shall not last long," he declared, "none of us, in this Holy War."

The page boy uncrossed his legs. He spoke eagerly, twirling his long-stemmed rose. "The Demoiselle des Préaux, ah, what a veritable fleur de lys!"

Robert checked him. "Sir, you speak impudently."

Everard looked morosely at the boy. "I have gone fishing for trout with things like that. Tell us, Sir Dragon-Fly, what is it like to be in love?"

The boy was gay and full of flourishes and quite unperturbed. "It is, Sir Ox"—here he bowed low—"may it please your Rusticity, both sweet and bitter. I have known it like ecstasy, or like brine in the mouth, or a white tongue after a feast, or sleep that will hover but settle never. But it is soon over, your highnesses, this love, soon cured and forgotten and all to begin over again."

Everard spoke more cheerfully. "I will wed a Saracen dame and keep her close within walls and obedient. Here, Sir Impudence, is her name carved on my dagger hilt." He held up the knife and spelled out the name: "F–A–T–I–M–A."

It was a vile name, we declared. Only afterwards did I remember the name.

Robert and I went with the page to old Sir Wisdom, and in a short while returned. King Richard would have us both as esquires in his own company, Sir Hugh had said. It was for us to prove ourselves in the King's service and the service of the Cause. Meanwhile the King's debt to us would not be forgotten. Would so much content us? the old knight asked. If we were indeed content we might choose another esquire from among our friends to serve with us.

Robert and I exchanged glances. "There is Everard Mortebois, sir." I spoke at once and eagerly, for I could guess in advance how Everard would joke with us on our return and for all his joking show the same downcast face. Sir Hugh turned to Robert. "Are you for this Bogis, this Short-Nose also?" Robert answered earnestly: "Sir, we three shall be able to serve the King better together than apart."

It was dusk when we returned. The sky, blue in the west as a sparrow's egg, held even now a glimmer of the day's gold. Beneath it the wide sea of tents stretched away to the hills, and the camp, that had appeared so noisy before, seemed silent. A scullion mocked us as we passed and bowed low, a basting spoon in one hand: "God bless your greatnesses!" Rapt in our own thoughts we did no more than stare at him.

41

Everard had prepared a feast for us in our absence. There was wine in flagons of thick green glass, small hard apricots set among their own leaves, spiced meats on platters, flat cakes of white bread, and, for sweet-meats, sugared violets and rose leaves which the French cooks had learned to make since the First Crusade, the whole set out most nobly on the grass within our tent on one of my best embroidered shirts. I stared down at it.

" Are you Barons yet ? " Everard asked, coming in and stooping and helping himself to a sugared violet.

" You will see," we said darkly.

De Passy came in. " You are to be esquires to King Richard, all three of you, I swear it."

" Not I," said Everard.

" We asked for you, man," I said.

Robert spoke to de Passy. " How did you guess ? "

" Why, is it true ? "

I nodded. " Quite true."

But Everard displayed a surprising stiffness. He thanked us, but we could have kept our kindness ; he had no wish to be grateful to Sir Hugh or to us ; he wanted no honours he had not earned, and so on.

Think of it over-night, we urged him. His face cleared surprisingly at that. Everard, I realised for the first time, would not be hurried into anything.

Ambrose was the next to appear within the door of our tent. His face glowed darkly in the light of our two torches ; a lock of wild hair tumbled over his forehead, he had a leather bottle of wine under each arm, and a long twist of bread not unlike a parchment roll in one hand. He stooped lower and came in. A little mouse-like man, bent and grey, though he was not old, followed him and stood a little to one side of him like a small shadow. " I have brought Richard the Chronicler," Ambrose announced. We greeted them. And our muster of friends appeared to be complete.

The wine and the company, I think, loosed all our tongues that night. I can see again my embroidered shirt, stained now with fruit and wine, stretched like a rough cross upon the trampled grass, and the flare and smoke of the torches against the canvas walls, the broken meats and bread, the full cups of wine, and the circle of faces, eager and intent. From outside the cool air blew in ; through the opening of the tent we could glimpse the vague shapes of men passing and re-passing. We talked long and late. I leaned on my elbow ; Guy de Passy, turning a little towards the open flap of the tent, leaned on his ; Robert, his face half-hidden, clasped his knees. I could observe the Chronicler at my leisure. He was no mere shadow of Ambrose as I had thought at first, but a small man with eyes of so deep and tranquil a grey that, having seen them, forgot the great listening ears, the mouse-like disappearing chin.

We caught each other's eye in the same moment and laughed. Leaning forward, Ambrose spoke merrily : " Do not think you can observe Richard the Chronicler and not yourself be observed. He listens and enquires and notes down constantly, for he is Scribe Richard, Chronicler Richard. All is sober prose with him ; he has not a line of verse in his head. It is fortunate that he speaks so seldom, for there are times when my rhymes, like my good aunt's butter, will not come, when even my thoughts turn sour and fretful, when I would be anything, tapster or tadpole, rather than the rhymster I am. There are times when I would quarrel with Apollo that he was beautiful, or God that He is good, or my own feet that they do not fly. When I turn upon my good friend Richard the Chronicler, and revile him, how does he answer me ? ' Oh, aie,' he says, ' so it is, so it is. Worms are meant to be trod upon. Everything passes. This, too, will pass.' "

" It is for that reason that I write," the Chronicler said and looked amused. " Since everything will pass and be forgotten, I say to myself, ' Write, Richard. Write ! ' "

Robert leaned forward. " What will you write now, Chronicler ? "

" While I live," the Chronicler said, " I will write of deeds of valour, I will write of both good and evil."

" But who," de Passy asked, " shall know for a certainty what is evil and what is good ? For a certainty, I say. If you answer that the things that belong to God are good and those that belong to the devil evil, I say this is no answer. Are not good and evil mixed in men as they are in life ? "

" I have lived much in monasteries," Ambrose said, " and I have learned how dangerous it is to meddle much with things we cannot understand."

" Do you warn me ? " Guy asked softly.

" Brother Joachim was not warned," Ambrose answered, " and he is to be tried for heresy since he spoke against King Richard's Holy War."

" A tall striding monk—I saw him," I cried. I stopped short ; I remembered the despair I had seen written upon his face.

" He questioned whether this war were indeed holy," Ambrose continued. " And was reported upon. I think he will burn in the market place."

" I spoke among friends," Guy said. " And truly I am certain of this, that from thinking too much a man may come in time to believe nothing."

" Of the hundreds that speak unwisely," the Chronicler said, " only one burns."

self. " Why should we not speak ? There is great
ween Jew and Turk and Christian on this same matter

most logical that we should do so," de Passy said, " to
argument."

m. " Why must you speak so dangerously ? "

us. Did you not know ? " he asked. " I think at times
I would ra   serve the devil himself than the Duke of Burgundy."

" I have noted him down," the Chronicler said, " as stout and vain
and choleric and proud, and not unduly brave."

" That is my master." Guy turned over abruptly and beat a hand for
a second time upon the ground.

" Where was Bernard, the King's Spy," Everard enquired, " that he
did not know there was a chalk-pit plumb in the track of the hunt ? "

De Passy appeared interested for a moment. " Who is Bernard the
King's Spy ? "

Robert and I answered, I think together. " We joke about him and
scarcely know that in truth he exists."

" A most efficient spy." De Passy spoke drily.

" Though Saladin has his spies we never hear of them either," Ambrose
said.

" I would set eyes if I might," the Chronicler spoke dreamily, " on this
Sultan Saladin."

The Sultan was a little man and not worth the seeing, de Passy assured
him.

The Chronicler continued : " I would also view Baghdad, the City of
Peace, and hear the one hundred lions that guard the palace steps roar
in concert on their golden chains."

Ambrose shook his head deprecatingly. " When men travel they see
as many wonders as if they were in love."

" And yet," the Chronicler pursued, " some travellers' tales have been
proved to be true. There is indeed a river which runs through this land
of Egypt which comes from the terrestrial paradise. It is full of spices,
of cinnamon and ginger and cloves, all of which are blown down like
twigs from the trees of spice in the terrestrial paradise."

" When we have won Jerusalem," said Everard, " we will visit this
paradise. But first, I say again, I would be face to face with this Old
Man of the Mountains of whom we spoke before, this Sheikh Sinan and
his sect of the Assassins."

" I have a note of their rule," the Chronicler said, " but I have mislaid the note. I have mended my sandals with it, perhaps. That is
unfortunate."

We began to laugh at the Chronicler, but de Passy said irritably : " The Chronicler has mended his sandals with the Assassins' rule ; he has taken the Knowledge of the Calling, for so the Assassins describe their rule, for so much shoe leather ! "

" What is their Knowledge ? " Ambrose spoke so coolly I was made aware for a moment of an odd current of dislike between these two wanderers.

" Much of it is secret, the rest you might not comprehend," de Passy answered. " The Assassins are Mahommedans, but they have cast off morality and truth. They have even cast off Mahommed himself in favour of their Lord, Sinan. Those who are found proficient in the Knowledge of the Calling are known as the Fedavi, the Faithful. It is to Sinan only that they are faithful. For them nothing is forbidden, obedience is their only law and it must be blind. They have no scruples, and I think little of either hope or memory. They are dedicated ; they will dare all in the interests of Sinan and his dominions." Guy paused. " There is much more," he said, " but perhaps that is enough."

Everard, who had been playing with his dagger, looked up and spoke jokingly : " I believe de Passy knows more of these murderers of Sinan than he is willing to say."

Guy was on his feet at that, so full of anger that he could scarcely speak. Everard, on his feet also, was confused and loud in distress. " I meant nothing. I meant nothing, I say."

" Bogis' tongue is too long, just as his nose is too short," Robert calmly said.

" Take Everard at his word," I said.

De Passy grew quiet then.

I looked at Everard. There was a goodness about him that was obvious to all the world. There was a thick-headedness about him also. At this moment, looking sulky and shame-faced, he was trying the point of his dagger against his finger. The point drew blood ; like a boy he wiped the blood guiltily away and began to trace the name Fatima once more upon the hilt.

I was not alone in observing him. " Why Fatima ? " De Passy, who had returned to his place, leaned towards him and appeared amused. " In Syria Fatima is a name for she-camels and she-asses."

They drew together. I excused myself. I left them and sought out Brand and Giles. I found them, though the night was warm, stretched out beside a fire vast enough to keep wolves away. They were as good as alone, for the scullion who had mocked us this evening snored in a drunken stupor at their feet.

" What now ? " I came nearer and stared at them. I might well do so. Giles had a scarf swathed so tenderly around his neck the hangman might have been busy upon him ; Brand could look at me out of one eye only, and that was watery and as though shaken in his head.

Brand lumbered to his feet. " Why, nothing, master." He sat down heavily again.

I scolded them. " From drinking and brawling you will die of apoplexy if you do not perish of the sea."

. Giles spoke in a weak and laughable croak. " If we were going by land only I would drink only water from the blessed Jordan, master. But I do greatly fear these sea monsters, and do drink in part, master, to drown the thoughts of them."

" You are cunning and you lie," I said. " You have been brawling with Gomorrah at the house of Dame Lilias, at the tavern of the Little Sisters."

Giles hiccoughed gently. " Not brawling, master. We did no more than take part in a most valiant combat in which Sergeant Gomorrah carried off the glory."

" You cheapen me, both of you," I said. I heard my own voice. It rang only childishly in my ears. I sat down and leaned my head on my hands. " If you were two strangers," I said, " I could discipline you. But because there is so old an acquaintance between us you shame me." I looked at them. Out of one queerly disturbed eye Brand miserably regarded me. In another moment he would answer, I thought ; in another moment I, and not Brand or Giles, would be rebuked. I addressed Giles. " Why tie up your neck as if it were a hambone ? " I snatched at his scarf, then paused. His throat was livid and swollen, and here and there black also.

" A pious pilgrim did that to me, master," Giles said. He spoke smugly.

Brand reproached me, as I had foreseen. " Would you have us of Wixforde and Oversley swallow all insults, master ? "

" I will not have you drinking and brawling." I spoke obstinately and weakly also, I knew.

" Brand did promise to wed Dame Lilias on his return." Giles sniggered, then laid a hand tenderly to his throat.

" I did not." Brand was firm. " I swore By Jacob, and By Jacob is nothing of an oath. Therefore the promise is nothing either. Come to think on it," Brand said, " the Dame, though she is as big as a hogshead, is also nothing. But this eye," he touched his damaged eye as tenderly as Giles had touched his throat, " master, I do now veritably believe, is something."

I rose to my feet. I wished to tell them to take more care of their good name and mine; I wished to command them to speak less rustically. But now that my fit of temper was past I was unwilling to offend them. I remembered that they had come far for my sake, and were likely to travel further; that I was rustic myself and likely for some time to remain so.

I looked at them. They were taller and stouter than I was. Standing up and almost sober now, they looked steadily down at me. There was a patience about them, a kindness that I could feel, that I needed among so much strangeness, that weakened me. By instinct I knew them; by instinct and by knowledge also they knew me. I found words at last: "I will not disgrace you. Do not you disgrace me." We parted then.

I returned to find Robert alone. We spoke once again of the Frenchman.

"You are still impressed?" Robert said. "I think I know why. He is cynical in matters where we have scarcely begun to be wise. We accept what we have learned; he seldom accepts; he is forever restless, forever probing and questioning. It is this manner of the great world about him that astonishes and charms you. I am not so easily charmed. I think that just now he pretended more anger than he felt. Do not ask me why. I think he rates us lowly: Bogis he considers a brave fool; myself discontented and half a monk; you a staunch simpleton. In part he is right, of course, though he may blunder badly. If I were asked, I would say he is one of those people who may perish of their own cleverness, as you and I, it may be, will perish of our stupidity, or, if you prefer it, of our simplicity."

"The two of you are not so unlike. He would make speeches too and talk needlessly of perishing." I spoke sulkily.

Robert laughed. "That, no doubt, is why I understand him so well."

I stood outside the tent. After a moment Robert joined me. A faint mist rose from the ground, the hills were withdrawn, the sky was thick with stars. We spoke in undertones, not of Jerusalem nor of the Cause, but of each other and of our return. My resentment vanished; I acknowledged what there was of truth in all that Robert had said. "When we come back," I declared, "you shall marry my sister Eleanour. And if you agree, I will have Elfrida for my wife."

"That must be as they wish," Robert answered.

"A woman marries, and loves too, where she is commanded." I spoke somewhat too manfully.

"That is not how I would marry," Robert said.

"If King Richard should keep his promise everything may be different for us when we return," I declared again.

"Even if he does not . . ." Robert began. Our voices trailed off. Like two people on the edge of sleep we fell silent. As we watched, a star fell in a sudden curve of gossamer light, spun out like a spider's thread, then gone. Another followed and another, like swallows, like arrows curving into space. For a moment I thought I saw the heavens move ; for a moment I could believe the stars themselves were glad.

We turned and went in. We had scarcely done so when de Passy once more stood before us in the opening of the tent. Surprised out of our mood, we stared at him. He crossed over to us and spoke tensely :
" I was a fool to take offence."

" It was momentary only," I said.

" Leave it, man. See how uncomfortable you make us," Robert said.

Guy spoke differently then. " I came to make my apologies. I came also to tell you what you may not know, that from Marseilles you will sail first to Messina in the island of Sicily. French and English, and you and I among them, will meet there."

He laid a hand on my sleeve for a moment, then turned from me and bowed once, deeply, and I thought a trifle ironically, to Robert, and left us.

" He has told us no more than we knew already," Robert said. We watched him go, a slight figure moving lightly between the long lines of tents, then gone.

All over the camp now lights were burning and tossing as men came home and lit a way to their beds. From the King's tent until far into the night came the sound of recorders and viols, then the sound of a lute plucked softly, and a man's voice singing, very practised and mellow and full.

Stretched out upon our pallets we listened. " That is Blondel de Nesle's voice, I swear it. That is his song," Robert said.

I was to hear the same song many times afterwards. As I write I remember the words :

> The heart, ever desirous,
> Cries for peace
> And for solace.
> Of joy of my true love
> Is all my complaining.
> If her heart be torn from me,
> If from her I am sundered,
> If in dalliance
> Too long she hold me,
> Then death, I'll embrace thee,
> Nought else is there left to me.

With the first touch of lips
Love's dart
Pierceth the heart.
Much anguish and pain, methinks,
Might be spared me again,
But why do I vaunt?
All my complaining
Is unavailing
If love's sweet dart
Come not again
To my lips,
To my heart.

I remember how Robert's lips moved to the words. Was he stirred by them or by the singer? I wondered, looking at him, too sleepy myself by this time to be moved at all. After a fashion Ambrose's ass answered me. As if, like the ass in the fable, he were jealous of any other music than his own, he set up a fearful braying, and every other ass and mule in the camp answered him. We laughed into our pallets of straw. " Love and longing, and an ass braying," I said. Robert, still laughing, sat up and, as if he would wipe all ecstasy away, passed a hand comically over his face.

The singing had ceased abruptly ; the consort of asses and mules, too, was over. Presently I slept and dreamed. I dreamed that I sought endlessly for Robert over burning sands, that when at last I found him he would not speak to me. I dreamed again. This time I thought I told Robert of my dream. " I dreamed the same dream," he said. " In my dream I answered you."

I woke. Robert slept beside me, the light full and tranquil upon his face. The pattern of the stars, the sleeping camp and the hills alike seemed beautiful to me. I dismissed my dream and was no longer afraid. Like dew on the grass peace with its certainty fell on me and I slept again.

PART TWO

THE LONG DELAYS

1

MESSINA AND THE LADY

HAVING set out from England for the port of Acre and the Holy
City of Jerusalem I wish I might write that we arrived at the
coast of God's Holy Land without delay. For then the greater
part of our hopes might have been fulfilled, and the story of the
East and of the West have been changed. But delays, more faithful than
any ally, followed us from the first step of our journey until the end ; and
delay is part of the truth I have to tell. I know that in every high romance
love comes after war, but here again truth is something different from
romance. Here love, and the changes of love, come first with the delays.
Now that I look back, with that after-breath of wisdom that comes too
late, upon the chain of events from our setting-out until my return I cannot
help but grudge most bitterly the time our armies spent at Messina in
the island of Sicily. The seven months we spent there were in many ways
the best of all my life, and yet this long postponement of our plans assisted
greatly, I can see now, in the ruin of our Cause.

At first our intentions had been to put into Messina in order to rest
and re-victual the King's ships and collect and take on board the treasure
bequeathed to King Richard for purposes of the Cause by his brother-in-
law, the late King William of Sicily. From the beginning all things went
contrary. King Tancred, who had succeeded King William, withheld not
only King Richard's treasure, but the dowry of the King's widowed sister,
Queen Joan, also. And King Richard, who was not to be put off by any
obstacle under the sun from claiming what he felt to be his by right, was
determined to secure both treasure and dowry before continuing on his
way. In this manner the fates laughed at us as they so often do, and all
history and all our lives were changed, as in some old tale, by, among
other things, a gold bed and a few golden goblets and a golden chair. If
it had not been for them the web of circumstance spun so closely around
us at Messina might have been no web at all but a straight road over the
Great Sea to Acre and thence to Jerusalem, and so many men of our own
time, and it is likely also of other generations to come, might not have
died for that city.

But the treachery and quarrelling and all the folly that were to come
were hidden from us still when King Richard's fleet, having paused most
lightheartedly to liberate the city of Lisbon in Portugal from the Moors,

sailed in at last to Messina, Robert and Everard and I on board. To me that twenty-third day of September is among the most memorable of days. A warm sea mist at first hid the shore. Behind it Messina waited for us, a white city glistening behind white walls. A great throng of pilgrims of all nations, among them our own people of England who had gone before us and many French and Genoese, together with a fair sprinkling of Greeks and Lombards, those two ancient peoples of Sicily, waited for us. A vast array of sea birds waited too, treading as though impatiently upon the shore with their pink webbed feet.

We came in more proudly than swans to the creak of sails and the dip of a thousand oars, to the shouts of the onlookers and the notes of innumerable horns and trumpets echoing with strange dissonances from ship to shore, to the beat of the gulls' wings about our ships and their harsh screaming cries. The straits seemed filled, the seas boiling with the King's fleet : the painted galleys pressing forward, laden with their still ranks of waiting men ; the buzzas, or transport vessels, following them, heavy and slow like draught oxen ; the light dancing smacks flocking like sea-birds between. On the surface all was glitter and movement ; beneath it one could sense the expectations and the fears of many men, and the great onward surge and press of the sea. The King's scarlet galley leading, Alan Trenchemer at the helm, King Richard himself in the prow, we came in.

King Richard leaping first from the ship, the rest of us following, we were soon ashore. Presently, mounted on horses that were waiting, the crowds pressing closely about us, we rode slowly up the steep track that led from the harbour to the town. Our hands were clasped ; we were kissed and garlanded ; it was small wonder that we felt the town and the townspeople also were on our side. All the world knows now how mistaken we were. The old crow that separated itself from the white ranks of the gulls and flapped and cawed overhead was a truer omen of what was to come to us at Messina than the garlands or the outstretched hands. But to-day we were gay ; our adventure was at its beginning ; we were in good company. We had no fears any longer for the safety of the King's ships, no misgivings and scarcely a thought for the events of to-morrow.

Robert and Everard and I had taken easily to our new circumstances. Indeed I am astonished now to remember how comfortable and how pleasant it was to serve King Richard. We served him as all his men did, without flattery, without an eternity of doffing of caps and bending of knees, without intrigue or jealousy. His friends were closest about him, that was all ; and any one of us might become his friend. We had spent the time waiting for the King's ships very pleasantly. We had sailed with the King to Genoa where King Philip of France lay ill and had spoken with him and kissed his hand. Unused to courts though we were we had noted the peevish air of greatness that King Philip wore, and how almost uncivil he showed himself in response to King Richard's courtesies. William des Préaux had made excuses for him : King Philip was sick, his fever had not left him, he was unfit for company. Unfit indeed, Robert and I thought, for the bearing of the King of France seemed to us to be like that of a man who has quarrelled with a friend and hugs his quarrel still. From Genoa we sailed on towards Messina, past white-walled castles and cities, past broken stumps of towers and ruined porticoes, past vineyards and cypress trees and grey-green olive groves, under skies so vaulted and so blue my eyes longed for lowness and clouds again. We went ashore where King Richard pleased, at Baratto and Ostia, at Naples and at Salerno, and hawked and hunted, riding whatever horses, or even mules, the country could provide. When we tired of sport we went sightseeing. At Ostia the Pope's Eminence sent a cardinal bishop and other notables to the King to bring him for audience to Rome : the King preferred to make excursions round about Ostia instead. When it rained as it did now and then even on these coasts, we played at games of chance, at backgammon and at chess, which King Richard loved. William des Préaux and I had wearied of chess : we played draughts instead, always if we could the losing game, in which the player who loses all his counters wins. I do not remember who was more skilled at that, William or I. Everard played no games of chance at all. He ate and rode hard ; he slept often. In between he kicked his heels and looked out to sea and seemed to dream. Of what he dreamed I had no notion, except that once he sighed and said he wished he could play upon the recorder but he had no breath. I did not believe then that he thought at all : instead I believed he was content to grow in breadth and height, as he did prodigiously. It was a joke with us that we could see him grow as if he were an apple on a bough.

In the evening, whether on sea or on shore, the King's musicians played to us on the flute and the viol, and Blondel de Nesle sang in the language of the South, songs as passionate and as beyond our understanding as the nightingale's. When Blondel sang Robert was rapt and lost, and Everard stole quickly away and slept. Sometimes, if he had eaten too much pork (the pigs of these parts were good) or drunk too much wine of the country, he snored. We kept a small silken cap, given to us by King Richard himself, with which to muzzle his snores.

The pleasantness of that time fresh in all our minds, we rode to a fine clatter and noise up the narrow streets of the town, past the long flight of steps that led to the palace, where King Philip, who had arrived unheralded before us, had taken care to lodge himself, on between the white walls of the shuttered houses to the lodging outside the walls of the city among the vineyards which had been prepared for us. Some little time was to pass before we could recapture the pleasantness or the sense of freedom we felt then. Much was to happen meanwhile. We were to take part, on King Richard's orders, in the assault and capture of the city of Messina ; we were to be members of an embassy to King Tancred ; more important perhaps, we were to learn from a dozen different signs and actions something of the French envy and dislike of us, and not a little also of the hatred of the Sicilians.

Hardly had we arrived at our quarters than the first complaints reached us of the ill-treatment dealt out to our men who had arrived before us by the people of Messina. They had been denied food though they had been willing to pay for it, shelter though it had been courteously requested. Though they had offered no provocation they had been set upon and stoned ; some had had their throats slit most secretly, others had been set upon and stabbed in broad daylight. Though the King issued proclamations, though he tried offenders of all parties with an equal justice and hanged no man higher than another upon the gallows he had erected upon the shore, the insults and the provocations of the Sicilians increased. From the beginning the enmity of the townspeople was directed against English and Normans much more than against French or Genoese. Indeed, every Frenchman went about in these days with an air, insupportable to the rest of us, of being holier and more beloved than we were. The truth is that while the Sicilians resented the presence of every armed foreigner among them and wished to possess their island to themselves— and who would blame them ?—they remembered the first Norman conquest of Sicily and feared that King Richard, since he was both King of England and Duke of Normandy, had come with his Normans and English men to conquer them a second time.

It was only when all attempts at peace between the citizens and ourselves had failed, and when indeed it appeared that they were resolved to drive us back into the sea, that King Richard ordered an assault of the city. With no more than twenty of us at his back he drove the townspeople before him with the flat of his sword all the way from the shore, where they had besieged us, to the postern gate in the west of the city. On foot now, once more following the King, we took by storm the hill of Messina, which the Sicilians had believed we could never scale, and drove its defenders down, for all their darts and arrows, in fearful flight. In less than five hours from the first onset, the city was taken and our banners, much to the anger of the French who had held aloof from the struggle, hung upon the walls.

Scarcely had Robert and Everard and I recovered from the excitement of this, our first occasion, than we were engaged upon another and quite different affair. Messina was in our hands, but King Tancred remained unrepentant at Palermo. He had returned Queen Joan, King Richard's sister, to the King, together with her bedroom furniture but little more. Kings do not care to take delivery of their sisters like pedlar's parcels, and King Richard was angry. I do not know which angered him the more, the insult to Queen Joan or the gift of bedroom furniture. Our orders were to offer peace but not too much peace to Tancred, and, unless he made amends, to promise him war.

I remember, as we rode to Palermo, how Robert and Everard and I joked of the treasure of the dead King William that King Tancred must still deliver to King Richard for the Cause : the golden table, twelve feet long and two and a half feet wide, the hundred galleys, the twenty-four cups and dishes of gold, and the gold chair.

"I would have the table and sell it to the Jews," Everard said, "and buy three manors, and a fine French bed, and sleep in it too."

"I would sleep in such a bed also, if it were mine," Robert said. "After that I would take the hundred galleys and sail with them."

For my part I swore I would put Elfrida in the golden chair, and take her to Oversley, and never ride out a second time.

Everard stared. "Why, the chair would suit her well."

Ours was an odd embassy : we resembled most a dismembered insect whose hind parts go one way, whose head and forelegs go another, for sometimes the Duke of Burgundy led for the French, sometimes Robert de Sabloil, Grand Master of the Templars, for the English. Even on the road we were divided, the Burgundians, among whom was Guy de Passy, going off in one direction, ourselves in another. Our reception was markedly different also. To the French, King Tancred gave costly gifts and a welcome, to us only coldness and short answers. The equivalent of Queen Joan's dowry had been paid, Tancred said ; as for the rest, our King must know that the King of Sicily would do what he ought to do and no more. King Richard would know, and answer, Robert de Sabloil replied. Except for compliments and courtesies, the Burgundians from first to last said nothing. Whenever the treasure was mentioned they turned stiff as wood, as if for all that they were our allies and the treasure was for the Cause, they were not concerned.

When we had taken our leave and after several days' journey were once more within sight of Messina, de Passy caught up with us. He was apologetic. "I could not greet you before," he said.

I answered him shortly, for this was the first time he and I had spoken since our first arrival in the island : "Why greet us now ? "

He laughed at me. "Why, out of friendship."

therefore, lightly armed, taking only our food in our wallets and a horn on our saddle bow with which to summon help if we should meet with too many Greeks or Lombards at once.

Never, I think now, did sea or skies show so blue, nor October sun shed more benign a light on white walls and grey-green olive groves, on terraced vineyard slopes, on broken towers and shadowed rocks and firm shining sands. We kept on our way. The road, still bearing westwards, climbed steadily among rounded hills set thickly with gardens and vineyards. Here and there orchards and white houses with pillared porticoes could be seen, and rough old statues standing about very solidly by cypress trees. We climbed higher to where a brown hillock thrust out a desert patch among a waste of green.

We grew sleepy and easily content, resting there in full sight of the harbour and the sea and the King's ships. A small green lizard blinked warily at us, then vanished again ; a small wind that had come with the lizard vanished too. We slept and were wakened by the faint rattling of a chain. We looked at each other, expecting we scarcely knew what. The sound came again, unmistakably. While we still waited a small sand-coloured monkey leapt into sight. He lit on a rock facing us, and stayed there, mopping and mowing, and holding out to us both small dusky hands. From one leg dangled a broken silver chain. We tempted him with bread and dried figs (cold beans and bacon he despised) and caught him by guile at last. A silver disc hung from the broken chain : " I am Melisande's," the lettering on the disc read.

We had suspected as much. " But where ? " Robert fell back and shut his eyes as if he could think better that way.

I held on to the monkey. " Let this creature lead us," I said.

We tied a leather belt to the end of the chain and followed where the small animal led.

I never knew until that day why leading apes in hell should be so fine a torment for the damned. I know now, for this small ape, chattering to us and encouraging us, as it were, all the while, led us precisely nowhere, down narrow paths, up steep slopes, over rocks and boulders and prickly shrubs in senseless crazy pattern like some small prince of demons recently come to Sicily from Hell. When our breath, and our patience with it, were spent, the creature paused and scratched itself revoltingly and nibbled at a secret flea and chattered again.

Robert leaned sideways and cut a bent wand from a bush with grey leaves that grew near. Having tried it with both hands as a schoolmaster tries a birch rod, he applied it like a birch rod to the buttocks of the small ape. Yelping, the creature set off to some purpose now. Helpless with laughter, we followed. After some twenty minutes more hard scrambling, we were obliged to pause at a rough track, dusty and well-trodden, which skirted the slope of the next hill and undulated out of sight. Robert raised his switch again. At an even hotter pace we went on, doubling and turning with the track until at last we fetched up at an ornamental gate set in a dense wall of yew.

His hand on the gate, Robert laughed. "Remember it was I who caught him."

"Remember how you beat him also," I said. I followed Robert in.

On the other side of the yew hedge all was quiet. We trod on velvet there, on turf that some miracle of watering had kept soft and green as a nunnery lawn, past tall late lilies and dark cypress trees, down tiled paths between beds of yellow and red roses, at last to a colonnade of white fluted columns, the earth between set thick with violet leaves. No sound came from the garden or the house. As we came nearer even the small ape grew quiet and tense, leaning forward on Robert's shoulder as if he would urge us on. Halfway up the wide flight of steps leading on to the pillared portico of the house we paused again. The Lady Melisande—it could be no other—faced us there, seated on a curved alabaster chair, whose sides were shaped in the likeness of two swans. Her arms rested on the long curves of their necks, her turquoise-coloured gown fell in deep folds about her feet, her hair under the stiff white veil, under the falling head-dress of azure, shone yellow-gold ; the long sleeves of her gown lined with rose touched the tiled floor.

At sight of her the small ape jerked and chattered upon his chain. Startled, the Lady looked at us. Though her colour changed she stayed composed and still. Only her hands that were lying upturned and empty in her lap came together suddenly. She stood up and waited for us then and an apple that had been hidden in the folds of her gown rolled a little way towards our feet.

Robert stooped and picked it up and tendered it to her.

"This is yours also, I think," he said.

"You have found Aziz. Where ? " she asked. There was a coolness about her that made me think of flowers.

We told her where we had found Aziz. While we spoke the small ape leapt on her shoulder. She removed him, I thought, fastidiously. She was no longer listening to us. "Poor beast," she said. " I would not have him too near me, and yet I torment him with my love."

"We beat him about the buttocks so that he might show us the way. Will you pardon us ? " Robert said.

"I have never beaten him. The Lady Isambeau, my aunt, beats him," she said, the colour changing in her face as she spoke.

Lady Melisande spoke roundly. "I have rowed in King Henry's royal barge with William to Westminster in May, and fed the royal swans, and then the sun shone upon us so fiercely we were burned scarlet as the King's red banner or the King's face."

"Ah, perhaps in Westminster," the Dame conceded. "In Westminster perhaps it is different."

"What foolishness!" Melisande began, and Robert, as if to keep the peace, said : "I was wondering who it was that played upon your viol."

"Blondel de Nesle," Melisande answered. "William brought him." She clapped her hands. "If you play we will have a Broken Consort, or, better still, a Consort of Two Viols. Though Blondel "—here her face fell—"like King Richard himself, plays best alone."

We would bring Ambrose, we said. We spoke of Ambrose when, abruptly, the Dame interrupted us. "The harp has a soul and is played in heaven. Therefore the harp is to be preferred to all other instruments."

"This is more foolishness," Melisande declared indignantly. "For all angels carry trumpets as every Christian knows, and, it must be presumed, play upon them also." She stamped her foot. "I will have the viol, I say, and afterwards a Consort of Two Viols, but not the harp, never, never the harp."

"You are wilful," the Dame said, "and will have what you wish, always, even if afterwards you come to despise it." She held up her long hose and examined it severely.

"Truly, messieurs, I am not wilful," the Lady declared, two bright spots of colour burning in her cheeks. "Truly I wish for nothing except to be gay and happy and skilful in all good pleasures. And I do love music and dancing and flowers and fine weather and good company. And I do love to love my friends and keep from quarrelling with them. But my aunt will have me chained to her side as Aziz is chained, with a silver chain, or most deeply married, or walled most closely in a cold nunnery, or kept as a favoured prisoner in this villa and in this place."

"If you speak of the Lady Alois," the Dame calmly said, "in my judgment no man should wed her, least of all King Richard."

"I spoke of Aziz and of pleasure," the Lady Melisande said.

"For my part I never admired the Lady Alois," the Dame continued. "She is pock-marked, and that is most unappetising for a man."

"Truly," Melisande said again, "the deaf are fortunate, for only the deaf can speak of what they please." She looked at me not over-kindly, I thought. "You shall play chess with my aunt, or draughts, messire. I will arrange it."

The Dame began very nimbly to roll her long hose into a ball. "I do love," she said, "to play the losing game."

" There is this about deaf people also," Melisande resumed. " They are not always deaf." She turned to us. " Truly, messieurs, what a life it is I lead ! Silence all day long and a long grey stocking. All silence, I think sometimes, is no more than a sea view and a long grey stocking." She took a step towards us, for we were on our feet now, preparing to take our leave. " Messieurs, will you not come again ? Bring Bogis with you." Here she curtsied deeply to us both. " William shall consent to your coming, I promise you."

We gave her our word that if it were permitted us we would come again. We kissed her hand ; we made our obeisances to the Lady Isambeau. We bowed low and left them then, and the small ape, chattering still, sheltered from us in the Lady's skirts. As we walked once more down the pillared colonnade, past the fountain, between the close beds of violet leaves, one of the Lady's hounds bounded silently beside us all the way.

" The Lady is well guarded," Robert said. He closed the gate while the hound pressed near and watched us silently from the other side.

" And rebellious," I added.

" And spoiled," Robert, laughing, said.

The way that had seemed so long when we set out appeared short on our return. Whether we talked much or were silent I do not remember. I know that every sight that met our eyes held some special grace : the dark-eyed Griffon children standing silent by the track as we advanced, fading bunches of flowers tightly clutched in grimy hands ; the moving pennons of the King's ships ; the rustle and sway of the withered grasses that smelled, I thought, of dust like harvest fields. I know that for a space the daylight earth was as full of unheard music as a sky of stars. But suddenly our peace splintered and broke : the horns, summoning and shrill, sounded from every ship in the harbour, from every outpost on the shore. As suddenly our mood changed. Loosening our short swords we ran on. But this that awaited us was truce, not war. In the town the citizens were calling the news to each other in the streets and laughing from their doorways ; a group of soldiers outside a tavern were cheering and throwing their daggers in the air and catching them again like jugglers ; in the gutter a mangy dog and a ginger cat ceased their feud and licked their wounds. Peace, the heralds began to cry throughout Messina ; Peace, gentles and commons, between the most noble Tancred of Sicily and Richard of England—Peace, Peace. A rose flung from a topmost window and aimed, I did not doubt, at Robert, struck my cheek. The thorns drew blood. Like a man in a dream I hurled the rose away. Peace, my mind echoed, Peace. But I saw only the Lady Melisande's hands, upturned and curled, empty, waiting hands they seemed to me again, and in all the my mother's letter, brought to me surprisingly by a shipman from London, had been of the plump capons she had fatted for the Christmas market at Alyncestre, and of the new carol, so pagan and so sweet, Father Andrew had ordered to be sung upon Christmas Eve, and how red the holly berries were, and how she feared it would for that reason be a hard winter. Here in Sicily the sun shone yellow and pale in a turquoise-coloured sky and the sea, all milky-blue, moved gently as if it were asleep. Though a great brazier of charcoal burned indoors, casting small sooty-coloured shadows on dark tapestries and pale stone walls, the cold flowed uncharted like the currents of the sea over the tiled floor, beneath the wolf-skins at our feet.

His lips conning the lines silently now, Robert lay outstretched beside Melisande's chair. Her chin on her hand she watched him thoughtfully. Then suddenly she said, " Too many songs are made of love." Robert laughed at her and moved his viol. " What would you have them made of ? " he asked, and lay down again. Though he loved her he treated her, mistakenly, I thought, as if she were still a child. The waiting-maid came in, laid more charcoal upon the brazier, went out again ; I was conscious of the movement of her gown, of the upright carriage of her head ; as she passed she came so close her hand brushed my sleeve. The small curling charcoal flames sent flickers of light over Melisande's claret-coloured gown, over the green cloak furred with miniver that she wore, over her blue-clad, furred and slippered feet ; the two hounds on her other side stretched and yawned, and Aziz, the small ape, muffled and hooded like some child prince from Tartary against the cold, shivered where he crouched, folded and half-hidden in the Lady's gown. And suddenly, in a fresh spurt of flame, the green glass eyes of the swans in Melisande's swan chair seemed for a moment to look sideways, as a swan's eyes do, and come alive.

As suddenly the Dame said : " Messire John, you have a heart of gold."

I started. The Dame continued imperturbably : " In truth, messire John, my niece stands in no need of kindness from a husband, or from any man, but much in need of correction and the rod."

I said, to speak the truth (since it would not be heard) and to give myself some small pleasure also : " No one should be beautiful. It is always an offence."

The Dame, as if I had not spoken, said : " Adversity will school her, though she will meet adversity with the same high hand. For she has been brought up by men, messire, and has been much loved, and has always lorded men. She is one who melted even the heart of a Cardinal-Archbishop on a Visitation and set a houseful of nuns twittering for years." The Dame paused.

"How, madam?" I asked idly, watching how Melisande's head and Robert's came together again, and how lost they were to everything but themselves.

I knew the Lady Melisande was not for me. I had told myself so a score of times, for I would never allow myself to dream as Robert did. I could never bring her, or one like her, to Oversley, to feed the pond geese, and scold the serving maids, see the butter churned and the cheese pressed and fresh rushes strewn. I could not see her in homespun, kirtled high, treading the wet miry leaves. I could not fill those hands, so empty, so upturned and curled. Therefore, it is true again, I hoped for nothing. I was never one to look for hopeless quests and desperate deeds, though both, out of an odd contrariety of fortune, came to me. If in these last few weeks I felt some of the twinges of love I had remained stoical under them. A man suffers and loves many more times than once, I held. I did not think of love in terms of passion as some men do, nor as a oneness of mind and spirit, as Robert did. For me love was part of the peace I sought. My peace was at Oversley, and I did not seek it yet. For all that, there were times, as in this moment, when I would willingly have stood in Robert's place, when most angrily I pitied myself for the part I had to play, and envied him.

"Messire John, you are not listening." The Dame was large-eyed and aggrieved.

I begged her pardon. My mind had flown to my own county in England, I said. If I had learned one thing in King Richard's Court it was to be courteous and quick in speech.

The Dame said, nodding: "I was speaking of my niece, the Lady Melisande. I was about to tell how once the nuns were vexed with her, with good cause, I am certain, and took away her clothes. But she was not to be quenched. She climbed the steeple of the nunnery, and showed herself most plain, naked as the Holy Babe, to monks and nuns and to any who passed. The Cardinal-Archbishop, coming on a Visitation to the place, saw her and stopped his horse. 'From Heaven, surely,' he said, and clapped his hands, 'for though she has lost both wings and robes the halo holds.' But Melisande climbed down a little way and hailed him irreverently: 'My Lord Bishop, bid the nuns give me back my clothes.'" The Dame paused and shook her head. "My niece, messire John, like her father, would order St. Peter at the Gate to let her in."

I laughed, though my cheeks burned.

The Dame checked her talk and looked solemnly at me. "You also," she said, "messire John," and nodded again. "But this is your green sickness," she declared, looking gravely at me.

I agreed, or half-agreed. I begged her to go on.

" Your green sickness, and it will do you good," the Dame said. As if to oblige me she continued : " You must know my niece in no way repented of what she had done. The nuns, who always enjoy a whipping —to be sure, what pleasures have they in their lives ?—begged the Cardinal-Archbishop to order her chastisement. He would not. He laughed at them, for great clerics, as you may guess, messire John, will have their jokes. They should, he said, since they had robbed the lady of her clothes, have locked the door, for then the devil which they declared had possessed the lady could never have found his way in. It was on account of this that her brothers took away the Lady Melisande and made me her keeper," the Dame said. Dropping the ball of wool into her bag, she sought for and found another skein.

I sighed sharply then, and the Dame looked up and spoke reproachfully : " I am deaf, messire John, but I am not blind."

" Madam, truly I did not mean to sigh," I said and blushed. For suddenly I remembered how de Passy had called out to me a week ago, loud enough for all his Burgundian men-at-arms to hear : " How goes your wooing, John ? " And when I stared at him, " Your wooing," he had added, " of the Lady Isambeau." In remembering what he had said, from vexation I blushed again.

At that moment Ambrose and Everard came in. The Dame curtsied to them grandly—she would never have us forget that she had been much at Court. The Lady Melisande gave her hand first to one, then to the other. " Why have you not kept your friends company before this, messire Bogis ? " she enquired.

How it happened I do not remember, but in the next moment we were all talking of dreams.

" Last night I dreamed of deserts," Melisande said, " and in my dream I was driven, oh, monstrously, by whom and to what purpose I cannot remember. And when I all but died of thirst and of being driven so against my will, a cool wind blew." She laughed. " As if," she said, " messire Everard came in and brought a different weather with him into the room."

Bogis was confused. " I do not dream. Or else I dream of horses," he said.

" And I, last night," Robert said, " dreamed that I died and walked upon the seas to England again. I think nothing of dreams," he added, " though I should miss them if none came."

" Messire Bogis," Melisande said, " are all your skills of the same sort, at horses, and bows, and throws ? " She paused.

In the laughter that followed I heard Bogis answer simply : " I do what I may."

She considered him, I thought, very sweetly for a moment, then said : " Messire Everard, will you be my friend ? "

Everard flushed and spoke slowly : " I think all who are here are your friends."

" No, no," Melisande said. " I have something different, messire Everard, in mind."

She moved away to where Ambrose stood, fingering his viol.

It was, I think, some childishness in me that persuaded me to lie as far as I could from Melisande and the two viols, and yet within sight and hearing of them. I was not part of the concert ; I had, I felt, more especially since the arrival of Bogis, been forgotten by the company.

I know nothing of music. The sounds that filled my ears were beguiling and sweet. I was at first transported, then in a different manner cast back upon myself. In the long gallery above the music chamber, the waiting-maid flitted silently here and there about her work. She was like a dragon-fly that takes a long stitch, then stays poised, then a long stitch again over the flowers. She looked down at me and I looked away.

The Consort of two Viols over, Robert sang then, a song which Blondel de Nesle had made. It was the same song we had heard from King Richard's tent on our first night in Vézelay.

I listened and gradually my soul, as though outlawed, lost all benevolence. Why was I here ? I asked. This music and these songs were for Robert and for Melisande only. They were not for me. I was moved, and yet made discontented by so much show of love in which I could not share. I had half a mind to go after the maid. The music continued Robert sang :

> " All my complaining
> Is unavailing
> If love's sweet smart
> Come not again
> To my lips,
> To my heart."

I sulked and ceased to listen. I cast some ill-conditioned looks about me. Since no one observed me, I set myself to observe my companions While Robert played his viol Ambrose cupped his long chin with even longer fingers and gazed far off, as if, I told myself, he had loved and lost a lady leprechaun from Ireland. She was primrose-fair ; she had stepped out of a green hill—all hills in Ireland, I told myself, like so much else, are green. Everard, like a shepherd after too much piping, lay stretched out upon a bearskin as rosily as if he slept under a may tree. Dame Isambeau's lips (her eyes were closed) were puffing and pouting like a carp's. And Aziz, that small melancholy ape, looked as mournful as Ambrose and cupped his chin also. And the Lady Melisande was rapt, though in what I did not know, unless in that clouded world of mist and rose in which she lived in love with love and with herself.

I got up. I went after the waiting-maid. I found her in a dim tapes-tried room, her hands full of vine leaves, busy about a dish of fruit set on the long trestle table there. She waited for me, her body straining in the tight bodice of her gown, her kirtle falling about her legs and thighs in heavy folds. I spoke harshly, for I felt an excitement and a trembling that was like and yet unlike fear :

" Have you an apple there ? "

" Messire, yes," she answered. " I have two." And suddenly she laughed and caught up two apples from the dish and ran from me.

I went after her. I believed she thrust them in the bosom of her gown. We struggled and I sought for them. Only her breasts were there. I held and kissed her then. She bit my hand with sharp pointed teeth. I grew angry, and, after I had possessed her, ashamed. This was an old trick she had played upon me. Below us, in the hall, the singing and the music still wound on as though in the Courts of Heaven, endlessly.

I drew off from her. " You know too much of love."

She stood up and smoothed her gown and drew her kerchief over her shoulders once more and spoke composedly : " Love is the chief of all pastimes."

" This that is between us is not love," I said.

She almost spat at me. " It will serve."

Murmuring childishly no doubt, I prepared to leave her. She called a soft challenge after me : " I told my lady she would have more joy of you than of your friend."

I turned. Motionless, she waited, her face showing as though it were oiled in the taper-lit room. I went on. But still in my mind's eye I saw her standing and looking after me. Odd, I thought, odd that one woman should so fill a room.

As no one had seen me go, so no one, I was convinced, marked my return. Piqued at being missed so little, I waited once more. In the room it was taper-light, outside a glow that was neither green nor blue lingered still. Ambrose was singing in fine goliard-fashion, with many flourishes of head and gesture, a song of his own composing :

> " Gentle heart, could you love true ?
> Heart to whom my love I've tendered.
> Day and night I think of you . . ."

I listened still—it was all a sword's length too sweet for me. At last

Ambrose laid aside his viol. After some small desultory talk during which I stayed obstinately silent ; after Dame Isambeau had opened her eyes and covertly wiped the corners of her mouth, and yawned, and sought in her bag for a sugared violet, and, brightening, found one and popped it into her mouth—when, after all this, we rose to go, Melisande begged us to stay and looked at Robert as she spoke.

Ambrose was the first to answer. The Chronicler waited for him, he said. Melisande turned to him. " You will bring Richard the Chronicler with you, I beg, when next you come, messire Ambrose ? " Everard, one side of his face patterned like a child's from the embroidered cushion upon which he had slept, declared that he had duties to perform, new harness to inspect for the King's Spanish horse. " I will go with Everard," I answered Melisande. Here Robert, who had been silent, looked at me. I read his look ; I loved him and cursed him in the same breath and stayed.

All this while the Dame, her confit box open, went from one to the other of us, offering each one a sugared almond or the sugared petal of a rose. Ambrose alone, I do not know why, refused. Like many bachelors he felt a disgust for women when they were not young. The Dame was tart. " Do not despise such sweets, sir clerk," she said. She made her goodbyes to us. " There are enough of you to guard each other, I think." Munching happily, she made off. The others took their leave also, and presently only Robert and I remained.

Looking at the Lady, Robert said : " I wished to speak with you."

Melisande answered him so compassionately I pitied him : " Do not speak to me now, messire Robert."

" I would ask you," Robert said, " will you indeed marry Gavin Fitzgerold ? " He waited, since she did not speak. " I have no right to ask," he added, too humbly, I thought, " but I would know."

" William and Jean and Pierre wish it," at last the Lady said. " But " —she took a step forward—" I, Melisande, say they may marry the knight, for I will not." There was such a concentration of childish venom in her voice I laughed. She caught my hand. " It is no laughing matter, messire John."

She turned to Robert once more. " Truly there are several more who profess love for me. But, truly again, I think it is not love they feel. Who among them will give all that he has to me ? And yet I, Melisande, must give all—my body, my lands, my time that is so free now, even my private self. Who among them will change his sweet life for me ? None," she said. " With every one of them it is as though I were an apple on a bough to which each one of them may stretch out his hand. If you will forgive me, messire Robert, and not think me discourteous, I am a little

73

tired of so much talk of love. It is no more than fashionable talk. Here in Messina I myself am in the fashion. I am famous, I think, as a little hill might be in a flat country. And it is difficult for me to know true from false when all profess the same."

Robert's colour changed before he spoke. " I would serve you always," he said. " I would give you all that I have."

Very slowly she bent her head. " You would love me, I know. But have you nothing, Robert, beside your love ? "

" Only my manor of Kinwarton. So little as to amount to nothing," he said.

" One manor is not enough." Melisande looked at him. " Even your love, Robert, is not enough."

Almost as if she were pleading with him she continued : " Forgive me. I say I am out of love with love and yet I have never loved. Jehane, my sister, who was twin to me, loved an esquire also but was set to marry an old knight. He was fifty if he was an hour, and grizzled, and shaggy like an old boar. When he was with her Jehane would shut her eyes and think of her esquire. For all that she was dead in nine months of the old knight's son. When my sister died, he wept. I hated him that he should weep for her out of his little fierce boar's eyes. So my sister loved and married and lost her love and her sweet privacy and all her life. And it was not necessary, for already the old knight had four sons. Surely four sons are enough."

We did not speak. There was that in the lady that confounded speech. I had felt compassionate at first but now feeling hardened in me. My sister Eleanour, indeed all marriageable women, I thought, would, if they dared, talk like this. Perhaps I felt some pity for the old knight, who, after all, was not so old.

" I am lonely without her," Melisande continued, with a quick glance towards me, " and I have grown over-scornful, it may be, for her sake. My brothers will marry me, too, if they can—it is that which makes me afraid—to some old knight, if not to Fitzgerold then to some other. For I may not refuse all those who ask."

Robert spoke gently : " I did not think there were so many old knights."

" Do they die too, then ? " Melisande asked. " I had thought only the old lived on for ever and the young died. I think," she said, and shook back her hair, " the young die of youth and chivalry."

Robert moved a hand as if he would brush all extravagances and all irrelevancies also aside. " Until you choose another I will serve you and ask nothing of you."

They faced each other. " If William or King Richard betroth me to the knight, I will not marry him, I promise you," Melisande said.

Robert took her hands and bent over them. " No one can force you to marry against your will."

I turned my back. I stood off from them a little way, but still I could not help but hear.

" Blondel de Nesle said he would make a song for me if he might kiss my lips," I heard Melisande say, and Robert answer, " I make no bargains even where I love."

I waited, and presently I heard him say again : " All the songs I shall ever make will be of you."

This was love indeed, I thought, and beyond my reach, for it was mountains high. I moved further off.

3

THE KING'S FEAST

I THINK the fates were uninvited guests at the King's Christmas feast. Certainly half our sorrows, Robert's and Melisande's and mine, dated from that day, and all or almost all the suspicion I had of de Passy, of which from lack of certainty and the indecision of my own mind more than from any love of him I did not speak. But if the fates rode with us we were deaf and blind.

The Christmas chimes had just ceased ; only the anchorite's bell jangled yet from her cell under the rock. That, too, died away. The sun shone red, the air was brisk and still, there was a smell of horse-dung in the streets, the clouds were filmed with grey, and Robert and Everard and I, part of a merry peacock-coloured throng, rode out, King Richard's guests, to his castle of Mate-griffon. To-day was the Feast of the Nativity ; for to-day all quarrels between French and English were forgotten ; even our more private discontents, of which I had my share, were laid aside. To-day we took fresh heart, we saw Jerusalem again. Even now the public criers went about the streets and the camp calling on all men of Christendom to unite with King Richard this day in joy and gladness.

Through all the weeks that had followed our Consort of Two Viols I had continued with what grace I could to play third or gooseberry to Robert and Melisande and had chafed at my part in this sour-tasting game. Their fineness towards each other in these days had seemed to breed a coarseness in me. While Robert wooed the Lady, as if to console myself I loved the waiting-maid. And she, in something of the same spirit, I think, for she was of a satirical turn of mind, loved me again. If we did each other no harm we did little good. I had travelled a long way, I would think not over-thankfully sometimes, from Oversley. For his part Robert appeared content to do no more than look and worship the Lady Melisande, as if he were indeed the mortal who in some ancient tale gazed at and loved the lady moon. Melisande was never so full of delicate fancies as now : homage, I told myself, would always fall as prettily as primroses into her lap. Yet now and then, when I observed Robert's strange and courteous ways with her, I wondered if the flesh did not turn in her sometimes, if in mind and body she did not weary of her part. For this was a game they played, it seemed to me, in which they were, not Robert and Melisande, but two lovers in a high fanciful romance. One might not love, I thought, and keep so very fine. But to-day, in common, I believe, with all King Richard's men, I put discontents and fears and disapproval also behind me. A little suffering, I told myself, became a man. Let them fall out of love and in again, how and with whom I did not at this moment greatly care.

Before us on the round hill upon which the castle was built we could see gaily coloured litters, small troops of men on horseback, bent figures carrying burdens and sturdy upright groups of marching men making their crossing to the summit by every path and zig-zag track. Never since Vézelay had I seen so vast a throng. The people of Messina looked down on us as we passed from their walls and windows, as the people of Vézelay had done, but without friendliness or courtesy. With what arrogance we looked back at them, with what pride of arms we rode past I can imagine now. I remember how their mangy dogs ran in and out and snapped at our hounds and were disregarded by them. And that, no doubt, was arrogance too. De Passy hailed us and afterwards joined us with a number of his Burgundians. As at Vézelay we turned off down a narrow way in order to avoid the worst of the throng. The track led us, a rabble of Griffon children running and bouncing before us like a flock of lambs, to the foot of the castle hill. When the children halted and stared at us one of de Passy's companions scattered sweetmeats to them. Wherever the sweetmeats fell the children, more like wolves than lambs, fought for them. From pride or simply from fear one child held back, then, too late, dashed forward recklessly. In the same moment the horses moved on. I saw where she lay between Guy's horse and mine in a smother of moving hooves and shadows, face down, her arms shielding her head. Guy's horse, a stallion kept for war, screamed and reared ; I saw his small sharp hooves come down. My stomach sickened ; when I looked again de Passy had stooped and caught her up—she was small and light enough—and laid her on his saddle bow. With that the stallion, like some young bull cheated of his kill, tore off. Man and horse were like two devils now : de Passy flogged the horse with the flat of his sword, scourged him with his spurs and brought him back humbled and distressed. Except for a deep gash in her skull from which the blood oozed over her dark curls, the child appeared unhurt.

De Passy bent over her, a bright smiling curiosity—no more than that—upon his face. "What do they call you?"

The child's eyes opened ; her lips stirred.

He stooped lower, then spoke triumphantly. "Beata ! That is good fortune, surely." He bent to the child again. "But what can be done with you?"

I looked at Brand, not in any hope of help but because Brand's face was broad and solid and good to look at in an emergency. Stolidly Brand said : "Master, let Giles and me take her to the infirmary woman at this Convent of the Holy Anchorite." We handed the child over most willingly and rode on.

On the last steep slope of the way our small company drew to one side to allow a long line of litters and outriders to pass. Among them a litter hung with purple and claret first caught, then outraged my eye : some dowager, I told myself, grown colour-blind, grown obese also, I thought, noting how the mules, white with trappings of green, sweated and strained. "You will not escape her." Everard laughed silently and pointed to where a thread of wool was tightening round the hub of an offside wheel. Until that moment I had forgotten Isambeau. The thread was grey. A horse-drawn litter followed at a smoother pace. A voice sang within, piping and small, like a willow wren, some ditty I did not know ; Aziz chattered on the roof, the Lady's two hounds ran beside.

We doffed our caps ; we cried out a greeting. The blue and silver curtains parted ; Elinor the maid looked out in blue and silver too. That was not kind of Melisande, I thought, for the colours were ill-suited to so dark a face. As if I were a stranger the waiting-maid's look slid over me. Since our first encounter she would, with one hand, as it were, flutter my conceit ; with the other humble me. I greeted her and laughed as I did so. I think I laughed at this first essay in love on my part much more than at any scorn she cared to show towards me. The maid withdrew and straightway I forgot the maid, for now the curtains parted a second time, a hand thrust out, a scarf spangled with silver stars was waved and withdrawn again. The outriders whipped up the horses, and the blue and silver litter passed on.

"The same," de Passy murmured.

"The Lady Melisande des Préaux," I said. For my life I could not hide the satisfaction that I felt.

De Passy inclined his head. "Betrothed to Fitzgerold?"

"Not yet." I spoke quickly.

No feast, I think, unless it were that of some Prince of Tartary or Sultan of Baghdad, was ever more magnificent than this. Next to plainness in war King Richard loved magnificence in peace, and in Messina for to-day for him at least, this was peace. All the treasure of Anjou was here in gold and silver plate, in jewelled cups, in rich carpets and silken hangings, all the tribute of King Tancred besides. The great hall that ran the full length of the King's castle of Mate-griffon was filled with perfume from the trunks of apple and cedar wood that burned in the wide hearths ; every table was lit with wax candles set in branched candlesticks of Byzantium ; the shadows of the flames and the smoke from the fires drifted like ghosts in the dark rafters ; beneath our feet were fresh green rushes and herbs—rosemary and bay and marjoram and lavender, and fleabane also ; rich carpets of Egypt and Persia decked the walls. The details escape me now ; the magnificence remains. I know there were trumpeters and heralds, and much coming and going, and a restless shifting of benches and of feet ; I remember there was silence at last as Queen Joan and her ladies came in. They made no sound except for the faint rustle of their gowns over the strewn earthen floor. They seemed cool and indifferent as flowers ; they had that deceiving flower-like air as they came in. Melisande came last in some pale-coloured gown, a fillet of pearls in her hair.

Perfection never holds. One of her great hounds followed, and bayed and looked for her. She spoke to him ; she laid a hand upon his head ; together, with scarcely a pause, they came on. I saw de Passy's look grow keen, Robert's eyes soften, his colour, that was apt to come and go in his face, change. My own pulse beat fast ; only Bogis, as if to discourage himself quite rightly from too much worship, muttered beneath his breath, so that I alone heard : " I tell you, she knocks her knees."

Presently we were seated, Archbishop Geoffrey of York, the King's half-brother, having said Grace, like a Plantagenet, briefly. Robert and Bogis and I were close enough to each other, far enough from the Lady Melisande. She sat at the King's high table at the end, her brother Pierre on one side, a French lord on the other. On the far side of Pierre, where the Duke of Burgundy's table joined that of King Richard, was de Passy. One dish followed another, the courtesies and the wine flowed ; the feast went on. The smoke hid the rafters, perfumes were not so fresh, the ring of ash widened round the fires, and Melisande's hound withdrew his head from her lap and crouched a foot away. Beside me Robert made polite but heavy weather with a French dame ; Bogis, to my delight, was to be seen not far off, cross-answering the Lady Isambeau.

I struggled differently. I had much to say, I felt, but small means to say it in. My lady was French and dimpled ; her English, I think I may say, was French and dimpled too.

"You are dimpled," I said. I made so bold, Bogis and Dame Isambeau regarding me with astonishment, to touch her cheek.

I glanced at Robert. He was silent, his eyes on Melisande. His lady that sat next to him had a sweetmeat bulging in each cheek. She appeared content. Had she fared better with Robert she could not have done so well with marzipan.

"M'sieu, you do not pay attention, ah, m'sieu," my lady reproached me.

"No, no," I comforted her and held her finger fast in mine ; Everard covered his eyes, and to the sound of horns and trumpets the jugglers came in.

I never cared for jugglers or for minstrels : they made, I always held, a feast stretch out too long. I watched a magician swallow knives and draw them, bloodless, from his ears, and was not at all amazed ; I saw Salome dance, a head between her hands, and marvelled only that her legs should be so supple and so short. I saw Pierre des Préaux leave his seat beside Melisande and go off to carry the King's instructions to the magicians in the long gallery and Guy de Passy slip very softly into his empty place. I saw all this and from the heat and the fumes of the wine I was not astonished at anything that I saw. All the while my French lady slept curled up like a plump child—she was little more than a child —her head upon my knees, and the scullions, redder than their own barons of beef, ran about with new dishes tirelessly.

The jugglers returned while the minstrels rested. One man threw red and white balls in the air and kept them moving for long minutes on end ; another threw knives and caught them marvellously, to the astonishment, I think, of every guest. From boredom or too much wine men threw him their own knives : the juggler performed as well with these. Next he begged for alms. As tribute men gave him purses or scarves, or what they had, quite recklessly. Though I parted with nothing, and Everard fingered his knife Fatima, and looked at it affectionately and put it back in his pocket again, de Passy threw the juggler his scarlet scarf. The fellow took it and with an expert flourish wrapped it round his waist, his eyes, or so it seemed to me, seeking de Passy's eyes meanwhile. Astonished and wondering, I looked away. How could any man be certain of seeing so slight a thing as this in so much heat and smoke and murk ? I looked for the man again, but the jugglers had withdrawn and the buffoons had taken their place.

Before their pleasantries began Queen Joan and her ladies curtsied to the King and took their leave. And Melisande's hound rose and yawned and stalked out beside her again. I laid a finger on my French girl's head. She started up. "Ah, nom du nom, par mon Saint Martin," she cried and ran off, ruffled and shaken, like a little hen. While King Richard gave gold and jewelled cups to King Philip and all his French guests of note Everard came over to me. " Are you drunk ? Or asleep ? " I was awake, I said. I rubbed my eyes and looked about me with astonishment once more. Had King Henry, whose treasure was being squandered in this fashion, been present he would have done more than yawn. I remembered the Chronicler's words, before we came to the feast, when it was known that King Richard would give his jewelled cups away, that like Titus, the great Roman, the King of England counted the day lost on which he made no gifts to those whom he called his friends.

We rode back under the first stars, though we had sat down to feast at noon. At the foot of the hill Brand and Giles waited for us with news from the Convent of the Holy Anchorite. The waif might stay, the Infirmière had said, until her wound was healed. But, the treasurer had added, would not the French knight—" meaning you, sir Esquire," Giles put in—give one gold besant to the Holy Anchorite in alms for the Griffon child's care and keep ? De Passy, with more violence than was necessary, swore he would not, swore a Sicilian waif was not worth a hundredth part of so much. He would have her in his own charge, he swore again ; he would keep her for himself.

Would he make a slave of the child ? Robert asked. Many of her kind, I knew, were indeed slaves at this time in Sicily.

" Why not ? Would it not be pleasant to be worshipped ? " de Passy returned.

His manner grated upon us all ; even at this time I can scarcely say why. We had learned much since we set out for Vézelay ; we were not, I am certain, over-squeamish by this time, and yet there was not one of us who was not in some way offended. Robert drew his cloak about him and withdrew under it like Jove under a thunder cloud ; Bogis looked stolid, in order, I suppose, that he should look nothing worse ; Brand and Giles fell behind so that they might discuss the rights and wrongs of the case virtuously and endlessly all the way to the camp. For my part I was silent, uneasy now not so much for the sake of the child, for by this time I was refusing to take de Passy's threat seriously, as for this fresh cause of difference between Robert and the Frenchman. Silence between friends can become so leaden no man can break it successfully. I spoke on an impulse. Could we not all meet in my tent later and continue the feast ? De Passy shot me a glance which I felt rather than saw to be ironical, and said, " I am all for feasting." Bogis said, " I am half asleep, but I am all for feasting too." His cloak lined with a felt of silence, Robert said nothing.

It was some time later that I went off myself in search of de Passy while Brand and Giles bestirred themselves under my orders. I had never known until this moment how quick the two of them could be. Brand, who had not hurried up our hill when his own house burned—" Master, it will be all the better for burning "—now, like a draught horse grown skittish with ale, came in at a trot, bearing faggots and a vast log for our fire, while Giles whom I had sent out to forage—he was a fruitful forager —returned brimful of slyness, the front of his jerkin of leather stuffed with straw.

" Eggs, master," he said. " Eggs make good meat." The blessed St. Josephine, he declared, had laid them in his way.

" Is the blessed St. Josephine a hen ? " Brand asked and stared.

It was then that I left them and came after de Passy. I enquired of his whereabouts of one of his Burgundians. He was in his tent, the fellow said. I thought he favoured me with an odd look as he spoke.

De Passy sprang up as though in alarm when I entered, then threw himself indifferently down again. Coming nearer I saw he held a wounded pigeon between his hands. " A most practised falcon. One of King Richard's own," he said and spoke bitterly. I looked at him in amazement. " Flown by one of your falconers," he explained, " and an English sergeant of crossbowmen. A burly fellow boasting a vast claret-coloured beak of a nose."

Gomorrah, clearly, I thought. I did not speak.

De Passy looked down at the bird. " Bah, it is dead already," he said. With sudden sharp violence he flung the bird, dead or half-dead away.

I found my tongue. " Who ordered their killing ? " He answered me : " I am told simply : ' No man must own pigeons and fly them as bearers of messages in all Sicily excepting only King Richard.' " He cursed fluently. " King Richard," he said, and a strange spasm of anger quivered for a moment in his face—" to whom I owe neither service nor loyalty."

" To-morrow," I answered, " you will see that the order is reasonable."

The flying of carrier pigeons was indeed expressly forbidden, whether in the French or the English camp.

De Passy said : " To-day I see nothing except that the birds were mine, that all six are dead, tossed back at me not half an hour since like so much carrion." He spoke passionately. " I ask you, what messages should I send ? ' No man loves Guy ? ' ' Guy loves no man ? ' " He was so beside himself with rage that for a moment I pitied him, for a moment also I felt a queer sense of shame that he who normally showed himself so unmoved should all at once exhibit so much rawness under the skin. I watched, fascinated, while he picked up the bird and began stroking its feathers. He was like a woman stroking a cat, I thought. No, he was like a great cat himself. I looked away. For the second time that evening I scarcely knew what to think or to believe.

Still not looking at him, I said : " You play with fire, I think you do so deliberately. Why ? "

He mocked me with a return of his old manner. " Perhaps I enjoy the fire." I did not answer.

We went out together and I remained disturbed and silent. At last de Passy said—I had been waiting for this—" Must I tell you again I sent no messages ? Do you not believe me ? "

I was moved in spite of myself. " I believe you," I said, " though I do not pretend to understand you."

With that, most thankfully and most fatally also, I put suspicion out of my mind. Together we returned to my tent.

There Brand greeted me. " Master, it is the innkeeper's daughter Giles has robbed. It is she who is his blessed Saint Josephine."

I dismissed them.

To look long into a fire both soothes and empties a man's mind. De Passy and I were silent for a little while.

I spoke foolishly then out of my own thoughts. " I wish Robert and you were better friends."

" How full of sentiment you are ! " De Passy turned on me. " Would you have all the world love one another ? "

I thought for a moment. " Would it not be simpler then ? " I asked.

" To you everything is simple, to me nothing," he returned. " You are not wise to love me. I care nothing for friendship, and very little for love. I care only for myself, and how much profit there is to myself in caring so much for myself I do not know. Keep away from me, John of Oversley. I shall use you if it suits me, and be rid of you if it suits me, I warn you now."

This was strange talk indeed and I was as incredulous as any man might be.

He looked at me. " I do not always lie."

I spoke cheerfully. " Nor do I always believe."

Without any further words between us we busied ourselves about the fire. We laid eggs to bake in the hot embers; we brought out wine and white bread, and sweetmeats, and goat's milk cheese. Presently Robert returned, bringing with him Ambrose and Richard the Chronicler ; Everard followed, whistling, a sprig of mistletoe in his cap, his pockets full of marzipan. As we ate and drank, warming our throats and burning our fingers at the same time, and the sea mists rolled up like a white carpet for angels and hid the shore, the constraint that had settled upon us lifted ; talk sharpened between us once again.

Richard the Chronicler observed drily that the King of France had appeared almost offended at the magnificence of King Richard's gifts. The Duke of Burgundy, Bogis said, had gone home in a litter. That was proof, de Passy insisted—for he had recovered his spirits—that even pork could not stomach His Grace the Duke of Burgundy. I said, one of Giles' straws between my lips, that I had again heard rumours that King Richard was about to marry his sister Queen Joan to the Sultan Saladin's brother, Saphadin.

"False again. A French rumour once more," de Passy declared. Though Saracens, he conceded, had their charms.

"There was Robert of St. Albans," the Chronicler began, and afterwards was silent.

Ambrose took up the tale. The knight of St. Albans, it appeared, though a Templar, had turned Moslem in the Second Crusade and married the Caliph of Baghdad's daughter. Afterwards he himself had led the Turkish forces most brazenly against his countrymen and former comrades-in-arms in the Holy City of Jerusalem.

"What moved the knight of St. Albans to so much treason?" de Passy enquired.

"Why, love," Bogis said easily. "Surely." He yawned. "Love will move a man to anything."

"Treachery moved him," Robert said.

"Yes, yes." Guy was impatient suddenly.

"A love of his own safety, it is more likely," Ambrose declared.

Everard turned serious. "But this knight of St. Albans had always been counted brave."

I was uneasy for some reason. "Could not a brave man," I asked, "suddenly become afraid and act according to his fear, and, having done so, be unable to turn back?"

"Let us be reasonable, as Abelard taught, rather than passionate," de Passy said. "Like all other errors treachery begins in the mind."

"What does it matter where treachery begins?" Robert asked. "I would follow reason as you bid me and as Abelard taught, if it were not that emotion, like the sun in my eyes, blinds me now and then. But truly I think what is evil cannot be justified by what is reasonable. Truly I think a man must choose."

"The great Abelard," Richard the Chronicler observed stiffly, "is greatly misunderstood."

We spoke of trifles after that and heaped more wood upon the fire. There was something vaguely disquieting to me and perhaps to all of us in so much talk of treachery. We were silent and suddenly Bogis asked, his voice no more than curious, I thought : " How did this Robert of St. Albans end ? "

" The Sultan himself ordered his death," the Chronicler said, and was silent.

There was no more argument. We stayed as we were. Guy's head was bent, his face hidden. All over the camp now the priests' bells rang out, summoning us to rejoicing and prayer. I thought I heard the anchorite's bell again and the bells of Messina echoing hers.

A moment later we were hailed by William des Préaux, by Robin de Herdecourt and the rest of their company. We went off with them. I was noisy and roistering, but beneath all its surface hilariousness my mind remained unquiet. The pattern of the day's events, intricate and strange as it seemed, eluded me. I saw the child Beata again and the dead bird between de Passy's hands and the sudden passionate anger upon his face ; once more I heard him say : " For you everything is simple, for me nothing," and my mind, as if in some strange prescience of what was to come, stayed troubled and confused.

4

SPRING FEVER

AFTER the King's Christmas feast there was little left to us but to wait as patiently as we might for spring, when the waves would be calm enough for us to attempt our perilous crossing of the Great Sea. No month is so long as January, none so unprofitable. We grew stale with waiting ; the seas did not change, it seemed to us, nor the skies ; even our thoughts seemed grey. While we chafed like children—for when has spring failed ?—earth changed once more. We saw and marked its change in the hastening flight of birds through bluer skies, in the quickening of everything. Our preparations for departure quickened also ; our minds and our expectations kept pace. Grumbling and discontent, quietened at Christmas, broke out again. The nearer our season for departure came the less willing men appeared to be to wait the last short stretch of time that remained.

Every week more ships came in from the ports of England and of France bringing stores of flour and bacon and cheese, of honey and wine ; jerkins of leather and felt, steel helms and every weapon of war, siege engines and battering rams, and canvas and pitch and tar and hides, from which to make " tortoises " (under cover of which our men might advance in comparative safety against the walls of fortresses) ; tall scaling ladders of elm wood clamped with iron, great kegs of Greek fire to pour upon the Turks, and casks of vinegar and boxes of saltpetre which, when mixed together, would, it was believed, put out the fire the Turks would undoubtedly pour upon us. Many great coils of rope were unloaded also, and warm cloaks of lamb's wool, many thousands of skin water-bottles, and huge bundles of oaken walking staves for covering the many miles our men must march between Acre and Jerusalem. Every month new ships able to fight and carry men-at-arms were added to the King's fleet. Stephen Turnham of London, captain of all the King's ships, arrived also about this time and not a few other famous sea captains and masters of ships with him. All day the unloading and checking and loading again went on, and all along the shore, like autumn congregations of swallows, a vast crowd of pilgrims waited, shifting uneasily upon their staves.

If the men-at-arms and the seamen were busy the priests were busier still. The ringing of bells, the singing of masses, the sounds of intercession and prayer scarcely ceased from dawn till dusk. Some men saw God and died raving ; others contended publicly with the devil and died raving also. All men are different, and yet I think there was not one of us who did not feel the pressure of the hour. The high-spirited among us sought fresh excitements everywhere ; when these failed we turned contentious and unreasonable ; quiet minds turned quieter and prepared themselves with fasting and prayer.

It was King Richard himself who called a halt to this spring fever. All his men, he commanded, should keep holiday for three days from the fourteenth to the sixteenth of February ; during all that time only the most necessary labour was to be done, the most necessary prayers said. And upon the fourteenth of February all men were to hold a St. Valentine's Day feast of rejoicing for so much work accomplished, so many dangers passed. In this way, though the tension was lifted most healthily from us all, more time was lost to the Cause.

St. Valentine's Day dawned thick with mist and cold, pierced with the sharp cries of mating birds. We were up early and saw the mists rise too, withdrawing gaily like dancers to the hills, and the sun thrust up among them arrogantly on golden ways of light. Robert and Everard and I had a rendezvous at the des Préaux villa on the hill. Queen Joan and others of her train, de Passy and a few of his Burgundians, William and Jean and Pierre des Préaux and many others of the King's company had agreed to meet there. Together with the Lady Melisande and the Lady Isambeau, we planned to go on beyond the villa to an open space between round hills called in the Sicilian tongue the Place of Blue Shadows. Here the main company would gather for games and dancing while the

85

King and all those who wished would go hawking and hunting in the country beyond. Everard and I were for the hunt ; Robert announced that he would remain with Ambrose and the Chronicler. Both Ambrose and the Chronicler, I knew, were set on observing the games and the dancing.

I rode out alone, for Robert and Everard had gone on before me into Messina, Robert to seek out a musician who would fit a new string to his lute, and Everard a blazoner who would blazon the device of his house, an oak tree alight with birds, upon his shield. We considered this a piece of new-found vanity on the part of Everard and teased him on account of it. It is true, we said, that you have a right to be grander than we are, since you are all Binton and all Grafton besides, not to speak of Kingleigh. " I wish to be known in battle," Everard said. " I do not wish to be smitten down by a friend." He had laughed cheerfully in his fashion as he spoke. He was in advance of me : even yet I had not seen myself in the midst of the battle.

De Passy was waiting for me at the foot of the hill outside the town. Though on the whole we saw little enough of each other, our friendship by this time was well-known. For reasons I did not understand then, he who professed affection for no man, who had been at pains to warn me against himself, courted me. Secretly I was flattered, as who would not have been in my place ? For, penniless though de Passy was, he stood high in the opinion of his fellows and there were others among the esquires who courted him and envied me. The old attraction he had for me held : he remained skilled where I was uncouth ; he was worldly, and I still wished to be wise in all the ways of the Court and the world. But this was not all. I was aware, as I have said, of something complex and secret in him which aroused my curiosity and my sympathy alike. He remained a stranger to me. His strangeness was apparent in his talk, which was sometimes glittering and often dangerous, but never, I believed then, quite insincere. It was to be seen in his sudden outbursts of bitterness, in his occasional, and quickly checked, fits of violence. Clearly he was not rooted, as Robert and I were, to one country and one place, perhaps not to one set of values or to one loyalty either. At first this singular disattachment of his had its charms for me. Mentally he was free in a way I had never known. By contrast with the extremes of fanaticism around me, his mind, at once temperate and cool, delighted me. It is true I would ask myself now and then what so roving a mind sought, true that I could never find a satisfactory answer to my own question. I had never, I think, any notion that our friendship would be lasting, nor did I imagine that there was any bond between us comparable to that between Robert and myself. The friendship de Passy and I had for each other was by contrast an impermanent thing. I held to it all the more jealously, therefore, taking from it all that I could of stimulus. What I was to de Passy I say again I do not know : a more faithful admirer than most, I would think sometimes, or perhaps no more than an audience.

To-day he was in the mood for confidences. I listened idly, asking no questions, riding on beside him under the warm sun over the bright shadows, thinking my own thoughts. Like any horse or cow, I told myself, a man would seek almost any company rather than be altogether solitary.

His had been an odd roving life, he said, always progressing—though it was not progress—from one place to another, from one stage to the next. " Now, suddenly," he declared, " here in Messina, time is mine. And suddenly, though Heaven knows the camp is full of smells unlike sweet garden smells, I feel like a traveller who has arrived at a garden and rests there, contained and yet free within its walls. I do not know why I should feel so, but the feeling is strong in me sometimes and brings with it something your Robert or your Ambrose would call peace. Though it is a sentimental word and I do not care to use it even in this sense. A man's life, I have always held, should be restlessness between long periods of rest : action, then for a long while inaction again. Not striving always. To enter the garden on the hill for me has been to find on every side the perfection of which I have always dreamed. All of it is formal and fabulous. Do you not find it so," he said, and laughed—" the fountain and the steps, and the trained apple trees, and the Lady Melisande in the garden, and the two hounds that guard her, and the three brothers and the Lady Isambeau ? The flowering and the imprisonment," he said again, " and the sound of the lute or the viol, and the sway, as though a green spirit lived in them, of the cypress trees ? "

I spoke out of an impatient kind of jealousy. " There is enchantment in all rich gardens. And whatever she may declare to the contrary the Lady Melisande is not imprisoned."

He laughed at me. " When I speak of the Lady you bristle at once. But since I am in the mood for talking I will continue if I may. Shall I confess to you—or did you guess it ?—that I have been inferior to other men in wealth and station all my life and have smarted for it ? I have smarted all the more since I knew myself to be superior to those whom the world considered superior to me."

I looked incredulously at him. " Yes, superior," he repeated. " Can you deny it ? All this has tended to make me arrogant and uncivil." He paused. " In order to be civil one should, of course, be as simple as you are."

I believed he spoke out of a sudden sharp fit of malice. I answered him warmly : " There is only this much to be said for cleverness, that it is for a short while more amusing than mere dullness."

"Why, that is very clever too." De Passy mocked me and yet appeared surprised.

I went on to say more than was just or courteous. "Brand and Giles," I declared, "know better how to live than you."

"I doubt it," he said. "Though I do not doubt they will make a better ending."

"Why do you speak of ending?" By this time I was ready to be a little ashamed of my outburst, particularly as it had once more put me at a disadvantage.

"Why indeed?" De Passy mocked me again. "There is so little, you will agree, of death to be seen and heard and smelt around us, in agues and camp fevers and plagues great and small. We shall certainly outlive Methuselah and enjoy as many loves, or be disgusted with them—perhaps the same thing—as King Solomon." He yawned, one hand over his mouth. "When you are simple, John, brother John, you keep me awake, when your wits work, I yawn. Why?"

I answered him swiftly. "Because when you listen to yourself you are one of those who never yawn."

He laughed back at me. We were in sight of the bronze gates now and the tops of the cypress trees.

"We shall find her," I said, "talking to her good monkey or listening to her dear deaf dame, or eating last season's withered apples out of boredom and throwing them, half-eaten, away."

De Passy heaved a mock sigh. "I sometimes feel like one of those apples where the Lady is concerned, except that I am determined not to be thrown away."

I was astonished and spoke carefully. "You have seen much of the Lady then since the King's feast?"

"As much as she would allow me."

We were silent for a while, then de Passy, pausing, his hand on the gate, said again as if he had been thinking of the Lady Melisande all this time: "She is all things, is she not? And yet she remains only herself. She is fair and fickle and loves beauty and greatness and praise and indolence. And longs after goodness and holiness, and believes she would enjoy a plain face, yet spends half her day beautifying her present one."

We dismounted and went in. "She is like a child without playmates," I declared.

"No young woman is like a child," de Passy observed. We came on, between the tall pillars, beside the rose bushes and the mulberry trees, our feet making scarcely a sound.

At the foot of the steps leading to the house we paused and listened.

We could hear steps and the sound of Melisande's chair being moved impatiently, and the light clank of a chain, and Melisande's voice, impetuous and high : " No, I will not. You may tell him so."

" Why ? Why ? " we heard the Lady Isambeau's voice.

" Because he has a bull neck, though you may not tell him so," we heard. " Because he has bowed legs and his helm has rubbed off all the hair from his head. Because I do not like his hands or his eyes."

" I cannot hear the half of what you say," we heard the Lady Isambeau answer crossly. " What," she enquired, " have hands and eyes, I would know, to do with marrying ? "

" A great deal, though you would not understand that," the Lady replied. We came nearer and now we caught the sound of an apple being bitten into and Aziz scampering. " I would as soon wed Aziz here," the Lady said, " if he were somewhat enlarged and wore a coat of mail. For reasons good and bad I will not have the knight, I say. I will stay virgin first. It would be more comfortable, and it is a state I am well used to. For in ten minutes this lord would get me with child, in ten days he would make me a widow, for he is a great slayer of Turks and most clumsy upon a horse, and in ten months he would make me an angel. In short, aunt, if I must die of matrimony I will mix a little pleasure with my dying. For it is well known," Melisande said, and here she sent a half-eaten apple flying over our heads, " that women do commonly die of matrimony and men of war."

" And pray, how shall I say one half of this ? " the Dame asked crisply.

Melisande appeared to pause for a moment.

We advanced a step or two and heard her say slowly : " Yes, well, yes, I will be serious. Yes. Then tell him I love him not. Say my heart is given to another who is lost to me. Say "—here she paused again and turned reckless once more—" say I am too young and would rather play ball. Say I have no health and am a secret leper. Say anything, good aunt, sober aunt, sweet sensible aunt, but deliver me from him. For truly," she added, " he has a monstrous mat of hair upon his chest and it is all the worse since it is red. Elinor has seen it and told me."

" Elinor ? " the dame said stiffly.

" Elinor ! " my mind echoed. I looked at de Passy. His face was full of mischief and delight.

" It had slipped, Elinor said, from his chin. It is not I who say so." Here Melisande paused once more. " So spare me, dear aunt. Or I will ask William to deliver me, and that will make Pierre angry. William would wed me himself, I believe, if he were not my brother. And truly I love him most of all men. So, aunt, be busy and diligent, and find me a husband like William, and I will marry him providing he thinks as well of me as I do of my dear William."

"You will bring us all to grief," the Dame declared.

"I care not, oh, I care not," we heard, and the shrill chatter of Aziz again, and one of the hounds barking. In the next second a ball came bouncing down the steps towards us. Melisande came running after it.

"So you heard?" She laid a finger on her lips. "You listened, both of you?"

"We could not help but listen," I said.

"We were happy to hear every word." De Passy bowed to her.

"What a life it is!" the Lady declared and tossed her ball in the air. "Never any talk but of husbands and marrying. Why must I marry?" She caught the ball again. "I am not in any danger of burning."

"It is we who burn," de Passy said. His eyes laughed at her.

"No, I do not believe you." Melisande sobered all at once. "I have told you so before." She turned once more towards the house and we followed her. The Lady Isambeau had gone. Her chair, all wound about with grey skeins, I noted nervously, waited for her, and perhaps for me also.

Melisande seated herself and, spreading her skirts, spoke almost guiltily. "When my aunt is gone I have only the kindest thoughts of her. When she appears, at once she vexes me. 'I must'; 'it is my duty'—why does she always lecture me? When she does so she looks a little like a grey horse, and I no longer feel half so kind to her as I did once to my old Grizel. Truly it is an honour—I expect it is an honour—that so great a lord, great in so many ways,"—here Melisande looked at us wickedly— "should wish to make me his wife." She leapt to her feet. "Except that I am now full of honest remorse, I do not deserve that any person who is not of my age should honour or be kind to me."

"When you are not of your age they will no longer be kind to you," de Passy said.

"When I am older I shall not need them," Melisande returned. She faced me. "Why did you not bring Robert of Kinwarton with you?"

"Robert of Kinwarton is not like William. Do not think it." De Passy shook his head.

"I think he is more like William than any other man in the King's company," Melisande replied.

De Passy teased her now. "You love gaiety too well to match with one who is so full of dreams and piety."

"I do not like your wit, messire Guy." Melisande flushed and turned away.

" It is you and I who are alike. Do you not feel it ? " he asked, coming after her.

" I do not feel anything long," she said.

" That is what I meant," he returned.

I prepared to leave them. " I will go meet Bogis and Robert," I declared.

" No. I will go. Keep messire de Passy company," Melisande said. She went off slowly down the steps, down the pillared walk, one hound running beside her, Aziz following, dragging his silver chain.

We watched her return with Robert—Everard, it appeared later, had not yet finished with his blazoner. Robert and she came on slowly, their hands touching, their heads bent, laughing together. Dame Isambeau, her hands jerking nervously, sent me after them.

I went unwillingly. When I came up I excused myself to them. " It is as if the Lady Isambeau feared you would suddenly mate like birds," I said. Robert flushed. He was queerly delicate for a man.

We came on together. Melisande had her face in a bunch of violets. She looked up at Robert. " I could wish it were always spring with the first flowers and the small birds singing." She broke off. " Messire Robert, why are you so solemn suddenly ? "

" I am afraid of this match with Fitzgerold," Robert said.

She spoke confidently. " I will never marry that one. He has no hair on his head."

Robert was wry. " And if he had ? "

" Then of course I would marry him. Of course. To-morrow." She tossed up her hands, held her skirts before her and ran from us. I marvelled that Robert did not go after her.

" She needs chastening," I said. " I would chasten her for you, most gladly. I love her well enough."

" She needs marrying," said Bogis, who had come up behind us. " Or leaving. Or both."

We laughed at him. Long afterwards I remembered what he had said.

Presently, when the rest of the company, including Gavin Fitzgerold, was assembled, we rode out. Melisande rode first between her brothers Jean and Pierre. Fitzgerold rode on Pierre's side. He was not so old, not more than forty, I judged, though forty to sixteen—and Melisande was no more than sixteen—may well appear old. For the rest, he was broad and almost as thick as a wall, his eyes, small and yellowish and intent, set wide apart in a heavy face. He watched Melisande, I thought, appraisingly. Her glance slid off him ; she talked and looked only over his head.

She called to us : " Messire Robert, messire John."

We drew parallel with them. Melisande chattered gaily to us of this and that, of the flowers by the way, the birds overhead. " I would go hawking," she assured us, " but to-day is St. Valentine's Day, to-day I would kill nothing." Guy, who had joined us, told her of his Sicilian waif. He made a long tale of it all, longer and more pathetic also than I would have thought possible. " I will take care of her," Melisande promised. Some of her warmth of feeling spilled over from the child Beata upon de Passy, I thought.

Fitzgerold fell behind with the brothers des Préaux. Under the Lady's chatter I could hear his voice murmuring on of weightier matters : of how necessary it was, for instance, that King Richard should hold the island of Cyprus. It was our larder, he declared, and our granary. With Cyprus in our hands we could be independent of the food promised, and often withheld, by the Marquis Conrad of Montserrat. " If we march to Jerusalem, we shall march on Cyprus," he declared. He laughed heartily at his own wit, then brushed a great hand across his eyes. He went on : " If the Emperor of Cyprus hinders us we shall take his island. And his yellow horse, Fauvel, which King Richard has long desired. There is no horse to match it, they say, in all Christendom." He dealt, for the most part, in short sentences, in small reiterated words. A mallet of a man, I told myself, and wooden at that.

" The conquest of Cyprus will mean more delays," Pierre des Préaux observed gloomily.

Everyone echoed his dismay. The knight hammered on, of necessities, and barons of beef, and wine, and grain, and how many and how much of each were required to feed three hundred thousand men. But the day was too pleasant for so many hard facts, our minds wandered, Cyprus and the possible conquest of Cyprus seemed many miles of sea away.

The Lady clapped her hands. We turned to her in relief. There was a famous tree, she declared, in the place to which we were bound ; we would dance round it as the Sicilians did, and hang garlands upon its branches also. " No one," Pierre grumbled, " shall see me dancing."

It was close on mid-day when we arrived in the valley. The mists were there, blue as the night sky between the small hills. It was a sheltered place ; the winds ran roundabout ; the pebbles in the clear waters of the stream showed bright as flowers ; there was no sound except that of the grey hill sheep cropping. Towards the far end and a little to one side stood a great solitary tree, an oak, I think, though as yet no leaves were to be seen. Withered garlands hung from its boughs, its trunk was knotted with age and deeply scored with strange marks and lines. Here a rough outline of a hound's head showed, here, more plainly, a stag's head and antlers could be seen, and below that an old man's bearded laughing face. I had seen ash trees in my own county of so wide a spread a herd of cattle and half a field could lie under one of them ; I had never seen so vast and gnarled a tree as this. A tree such as this might have been worshipped in its time ; as in some old headless idol there was, I thought, a strange quality of worship about it still.

We waited for the rest of our company to appear. They were not long in coming : Queen Joan and her train riding at a smart canter on their palfreys to the sound of trumpets ; King Richard and the French at a gallop to the sound of hunting horns. I bade farewell to the Lady Melisande and, as I believed, to the tree and went off, together with Everard, with the King's company.

The day, that had begun so strangely with cold mists and the sharp cries of birds, continued strange. I have never known a day so full of humours and sudden sharpnesses and fierce unreasonable flourishes of display. Almost it was as if St. Valentine slept, as if great Circe had passed too near and touched us with her wand.

We of the King's party enjoyed little sport. What birds there were stayed in the lower reaches of the sky or kept upon the ground. And our falcons moped. No doubt great Circe was upon them too. On the King's suggestion we decided upon a mimic tournament with bulrushes, which we bought from a countryman whom we chanced to meet. It was then, as all Christendom knows, that King Richard challenged the French knight, William des Barres, to a mimic combat and, to his own amazement and the amazement of us all, was repeatedly unhorsed by the Frenchman, then that the King's astonishment turned unexpectedly to fury. The rest of us crowding the steep banks of the lane, the King banished William des Barres from his company and from Messina.

I remember even yet to our shame how quietly the Frenchman, after his sentence of banishment, turned his horse, how slowly, his shoulders bent a little, he rode away. It was said afterwards in excuse of King Richard that William des Barres had recently broken his parole to the King and been pardoned, much against King Richard's will, and that the King had been provoked to fresh fury on this occasion partly from his own discomfiture, and partly from a recollection that rankled still of the French knight's previous offence. I only know that our Cause paid for this affront to the French, and that the new-found amity between our two armies was once more spoiled. We returned to the games and the dancing, French riding with French, English with English, while the King, like a man heartily sick of himself and therefore of all the world, rode on ahead.

The feast in the valley was at its height when we returned. Small parties, hands clasped, were going off in companies of two into the woods and coverts that lined the outskirts of the place ; we could hear laughter and whispering from the hollows ; a youth twanged a lute to a sleeping maiden under a birch tree ; confirmed bachelors, or those who had been crossed in love, slept here and there alone, a flagon of wine beside them, and snored not very pleasantly. The merriest noise of all came from around the tree. All the court, except Queen Joan and the Lady Isambeau and a number of the more elderly among the French and English dames, were there, dancing to the sound of flutes and rebecs. Here were no stately steppings or stiff posturings, but the plainest of May Day gambollings. Couples lined up, faced each other, clasped hands and whirled, separated, turned, sought each other again.

We dismounted and drew near. I found myself beside Ambrose. The Chronicler, a skin of wine beside him, his long nose twitching, was mousily asleep. The tune changed. A round dance followed. I saw Guy de Passy take the Lady Melisande's hand. I do not know how to describe her as I saw her then in her kirtle of green, her petticoat of yellow and lavender. To me all the flame of the spring seemed in her, all the quickening. I stood dismayed. I had thought her well-matched with Robert. To-day I saw, or thought I saw, an impatience in her, a wildness and a restlessness also that would go ill with Robert, that in truth went better with de Passy. I said as much to Ambrose. He answered me shortly: " These two will not do either. They have divided hearts."

I did not guess his meaning then, though I have caught it since. I watched the dance. Not a woman there but had thrown her head-dress on one side, not one who was not, in some rakish and antique fashion, garlanded. I looked about me. Queen Joan watched a trifle anxiously, I thought, although she smiled ; the Countess of Leicester, who was heavy with child, had her hands tight clasped before her, and looked both weary and envious ; the Lady Isambeau—she would always do both—primmed her mouth in disapproval and at the same time folded her hands. It was then that I caught sight of Robert. For a moment I saw him as clearly as if he had been a stranger. His viol slackly in one hand, he watched the dance, a great deal of England about him, I thought, and something else, a simplicity and a greenness also that belonged unmistakably to Kinwarton. I was aware that the French popinjays were nudging each other and whispering and pointing to Robert. I became alarmed for him. The French, I feared, might be in the mood for some revenge upon those of us who were English, however petty it might be and however small.

While I hesitated, growing first warm, then cold, the circle of dancers closed up. De Passy, one arm round the Lady, whirled past. While Robert continued to watch, his love like a green sickness on his face, Melisande called out to him, " Do not watch us. Do not." He turned away, white-faced, and the laughter, held back until this moment, tittered and broke around us then. A young Burgundian whom I had seen often enough with de Passy struck an attitude sufficiently like Robert's to be recognisable and put on a grotesquely sick and jealous face. I crossed over to Robert and spoke roughly to him. " Come away ; they are making fools of us both." He looked at me uncomprehendingly. I spoke again amid a fresh burst of mirth. I said : " They are too many for us to answer. Come away."

What happened after that I never exactly knew. I heard people clapping their hands ; I saw Melisande's garland tossed by de Passy upon a low-hanging branch of the tree and heard Robert's voice raised in anger : " Will you make offerings to the devil ? " And the Lady's answer, swift and pert, and childish as ever, " No. To the tree, the tree."

There had been a momentary lull in the whisperings when Robert spoke. It held as, our hands on our dagger hilts, we made our way together through the closely packed crowd. No one called after us, no one laughed any longer. A mob is quick to feel any change of mood, both good and bad. The crowd were silent : I think the passion that in these last few moments had burned all the simpleness from Robert's face silenced them. I remember Richard the Chronicler sitting up under his flowering tree and blinking at us as if the light on a sudden were too much for him ; I remember how Ambrose, out of pity, turned away. We collected our horses. Presently, joined by Everard and Ambrose and the Chronicler, we rode back.

Ambrose kept pace on his mule beside me ; Robert fell behind with Everard. I spoke to Ambrose of what had passed. He answered me : " I do not think Robert of Kinwarton is made for the love of women." I answered him sharply, for I thought he spoke out of his old clerkly habit of mind. " In all ways," I said, " Robert is what a man should be." Ambrose said : " He is in all ways what a man should be, except that there is more of worship in him than love or desire. He is one of those who are most fit for the service of God."

I did not answer. There were times, and I judged this to be one, when even a contending angel would not argue with Ambrose.

That night I spoke to Robert. He had been heavy and quiet, making an effort to speak, then falling silent once more.

" You have de Passy under your skin like a louse," I declared.

" He burrows deeper," after a moment Robert said.

" In your place I would challenge him," Everard declared. " In your place I would have everything over between us and live pleasantly."

Robert threw himself down beside the fire of sticks which Giles had built for us outside our tent. With one part of his mind he appeared to dismiss de Passy. " I think our stars have crossed," he said, " though what I, who am a Christian, mean by that I do not know." He fled into remoteness, I thought, watching him, as another man might take refuge in anger or revenge. "It is true," he went on, "that I hate the Frenchman; it is true also that I do not wish to hate either the Frenchman or any other man. I know nothing of him, I say. I know little even of myself. There is such a darkness about each one of us that we know nothing." He looked at us. "If I speak too much in metaphor, forgive me."

After a moment Everard returned obstinately to the subject of de Passy. "Why not challenge the Frenchman?"

I said hastily to Robert: "If you were to kill him you would be obliged to answer for his life to King Richard."

Robert read my fear. Turning away from me, he said: "I shall not challenge him."

From that day my anxiety for them both grew. It was from that day also, I believe, that Robert began to misjudge me.

5

NEWS FROM ABROAD

IT must often happen that wars and alliances designed to achieve one purpose end by achieving another and different purpose. Out of wars and the gathering of great armies thoughts long buried in men's minds quicken into ideas at last; new forces take shape. So, at least, it was with both French and English in these years. Ours was a dual identity; we suffered from a double rather than a divided loyalty. We were part of Christendom and aware of the unity of Christendom as a man looking at the night sky is aware of the concerted movement of the stars. But a new loyalty was beginning to take hold of our minds. An awareness of ourselves, a pride in our own identity, our separate achievements, was stirring in us both. With every day that we lived encamped, united by oath in the service of Christendom, this sense of separateness took firmer shape in us; English grew nearer to English, French to French.

At the time little enough of all this was clear to me. I felt hotly partisan one day and vaguely troubled and confused before the disunity of our two armies the next. For the greater part of the time I remained intent upon my own affairs. Ambrose and Richard the Chronicler were in a more constantly disturbed state: they took counsel together; they made separate notes and compared their different versions; they went about from one person to another in both camps. In the end they decided, as they might have done at the beginning, that the tide of affairs was too great for them to exert any influence upon it, and too mysterious for them to understand.

The arrival at Naples soon after our St. Valentine's Day feast of Queen Eleanour of England, King Richard's mother, and of the Lady Berengaria of Navarre, King Sancho of Navarre's daughter, made it plain that the King was resolved to break for ever with King Philip's sister, the Lady Alois of France. Old scandals—scandals to do with the Lady Alois and King Henry of England, and not only with King Henry, but with John Lackland, King Richard's brother also—put on morning faces and looked bright again. It was expected that the French would sail for Acre and the Holy Land in March : it was reported that King Philip had sent a summary message to King Richard : " By the blood of Christ, either sail in March or wed the Lady Alois." To this message, it was said, King Richard had answered in the next breath : " By that same oath, Sir King, I will neither go in March nor wed, at least not with Alois." And then, Everard said, the doves of peace once more fled the island.

The rumours entertained us all as they were meant to do. They left nevertheless a sour taste behind. Men thought of home and wondered why they had come so far to endure so much quarrelling. And the news from the port of Acre cast a shadow over us all. The Christian besiegers of the city under King Guy of Jerusalem were themselves besieged by the heathen Turks under Saladin. To all the torments the sun and the enemy might inflict upon the besiegers famine had been added. With famine came madness and strange dropsies, and at last death. Knights who loved their horses better, and needed them more also, than their wives slew and ate them to save themselves. Not only plain men-at-arms, but men of gentle nurture also, ran about the camp like dogs and in the extremity of their hunger, like dogs again, ate grass. Others, madder than dogs, snatched up bones the dogs had gnawed for days and licked them, not in the hope of finding meat upon them, for none was there, but in order to remind themselves once more of the taste of flesh. Many who were called upon to endure so frightful a torment denied Christ and turned to Mahommed ; others ate human flesh and sought forgetfulness in this and in other abominations. Before the spectacle of so much evil among Christian men the more tender among our people sickened in spirit and wished for death. Upon these, as upon Baldwin, Archbishop of Canterbury, God indeed had pity, and presently they died. Small wonder that the message brought to the two kings and to every one of us in Sicily from the besieging army was this : " Come quickly, or we perish." There was scarcely a man among us who was not moved, who would not gladly have departed at once for Acre if he might.

The siege, begun in August of the year 1190, was now in its eighteenth month. Throughout February we waited, anxiously and to no purpose. Presently, since nothing was asked of us in the way of sacrifice, our compassion, white-hot before, cooled ; the port of Acre, that had come so near to us in mind, receded again ; we busied ourselves once more, as men will when they are idle, with discontents and quarrelling and affairs of love. While I continued to see much of de Passy, Ambrose and Robert were much together. They had tastes in common : a love of romance and rhyme, a love of music and a practice in it also. It was with an unaccustomed pang of jealousy, quickly over, that I observed how well the two of them understood one another. It appeared almost as though Robert in these days wished to avoid me. There was, I had always known it, an immense pride and solitariness in him. However deeply offended he might be, he would make no complaint. He made none now. Instead he cut me off, not so much from his company as from all our former intimacy. He withdrew, not into himself so much as into some misty island-place, where his mind, hermit-like, followed its own bent and kept no pace with mine. Where the Lady Melisande was concerned I could not measure his hurt, nor the oppression of spirit that sprang from it. For the quarrel that had sprung up so unexpectedly between the Lady and Robert on St. Valentine's Day had hardened into an apparent permanence by this time, and all the talk of the Court and some of the talk of the camp also was of the success de Passy was having with the sister of the brothers des Préaux. Talk was one thing, truth another. Nevertheless it was plain that the Frenchman was as often at the villa as at one time Robert and I had been, and the Lady as much and as lovingly in his company as ever she had been in ours. And de Passy wore the look, unmistakable in a Frenchman, of one who was conquering and in love.

On other counts than this Robert was not, I think, over-happy. Besides Ambrose and myself there was no one to whom he could turn for diversion or for company. Everard he loved, as all the world did, but Everard Mortebois and he were two minds and almost two worlds apart. Outwardly there was an aloofness about Robert, almost a coldness. He was not rich ; he pretended nothing. Where everyone aped fashion, he scorned to be fashionable ; in a Court where we were all in some degree braggarts and peacocks he made no boast, he scarcely showed a bright feather ; his gifts for archery and swordsmanship, his skill on the lute and the viol, and in the making of songs, were hidden rather than displayed. He remained solitary therefore, and as it were lost in himself.

For my part I resented the fact that he should cut me off for no better reason than that I had dared to take another friend. So I declared to myself. But in truth I knew, as Robert knew also, that I had been guilty of a certain unspoken treachery towards him. For I had compared the accomplishment and graces of Guy de Passy with those of Robert of Kinwarton to the latter's disadvantage. In many matters I had preferred the Frenchman, and I had allowed my preference to be known. If love is at bottom nothing but a preference, then I had failed in love towards Robert of Kinwarton. It was this preference of mine, transitory though it was, which I believe cut Robert most unkindly. It must have appeared to him at this time as if all his world preferred de Passy, and had good reasons for doing so. Where Melisande was concerned I must have appeared to him both false and two-minded. I could not blame de Passy that the Lady seemed to prefer him, nor could I hold it against the Frenchman that he had come between Robert and Melisande, since after all nothing definite had been promised between them. Nevertheless I could not but feel certain that some other motive than love was at work in de Passy. Either a passion for conquest moved him, I thought, or a hatred of Robert and a desire above everything else to injure him. I remained torn, as I had feared, between these two men, both of whom were my friends. Though I was able to interpret much of what was in Robert's mind at this time, like a man infatuated I was unable to separate myself, as I should undoubtedly have done, from de Passy. I understand now what it is that men in the East call fate, that spider's web of destiny, made up of chance and circumstance, into which we are drawn by unseen spiral stairways until at last, in the heart of the web, the dead centre, we find there is no escape. I was in that mesh already, though I knew it not, and Robert was with me. De Passy, though he knew of the mesh, believed that he was free. In this, as events proved, he was more deceived even than I was.

For a variety of reasons, therefore, I was glad when towards the beginning of March a Captain John Harding, known as Harding the Englishman, master of one of the King's ships, having come from Southampton with Sir Hugh de Winton on board—the old knight having been sent to England some months back to report on matters there to the King—sought me out and gave me two letters from England for Robert, and one for myself, which old Sir Wisdom had entrusted to him.

I had some difficulty in finding Robert at first. I came upon him finally seated alone in a quiet spot outside the camp. Two trees, with grey-green bark, whose names I did not know, arched overhead ; a thin stream fell sluggishly over sand and lava stones. I gave Robert his two letters ; he thanked me politely and took some little time in breaking the seals. My own letter unread as yet in my hand, I looked at him. His face cleared and softened as he read ; when he spoke his voice turned eager and came alive. " It is from Father Andrew," he said. " Elfrida is lost without me ; Oscar grieves for me, silently ; both are well ; Elfrida has a gown with hanging sleeves ; the wheelwright has made Oscar a lance of apple wood." He folded this letter and put it away ; laughing, he took up the next. " Now," he said, " I shall hear : ' Spring has come. Oscar grows fat and forgets you. There are minnows and cresses. He goes fishing again.' "

He read and once more his face changed. I thought nothing of it for a moment. I turned to my own letter. " No, he is dead," I heard Robert say. " Oscar is dead."

I did not speak. I held my own letter—I had scanned it by this time— in my hand. It was not long.

The branches of the trees lifted overhead ; I could hear the stream moving sluggishly over the stones ; from a tiny hillock a small bird like a wren sang piercingly. I looked down at my own letter and was astonished to feel the smart of tears in my eyes.

Robert spoke strangely. " I wish Elfrida were with him. They might have been together in the dark."

To serve Oscar, to please Robert, Elfrida must die too, it seemed. My stomach turned queasy at the thought, my blood beat oddly in my ears. I leaned my head against the tree. As I did so I could feel how each movement of the wind was like a current flowing between trunk and bark.

" He was small and the fever took him," Robert said. " At the last he grieved for me."

I could not speak.

" And you ? " Robert asked. He waited. I believed he wished but did not dare to speak Eleanour's name.

" It is Raymond," I said. " It is he who has died. And I wished to make amends to him."

" They will not wait for us," Robert said. He left me strangely then. And the small bird, or one like it, returned and sang again as piercingly.

I never knew where Robert, neglectful of all duty to King Richard, went that day nor in the days that followed while Everard and I sought for him. I have thought since that only by being lost in body and in mind could he find sanity again and the will to return once more to himself. Everard and I had spoken of him until we had nothing more to say. Once or twice a day we had ridden out of the camp, on this errand or on that, always with Robert in mind, always looking for and hoping to find him.

We spoke of de Passy also and of the resentment the des Préaux brothers were said to feel at his wooing of the Lady.

"They have sworn to challenge him," Everard said.

The French would have sailed before any one of the des Préaux brothers could challenge de Passy, even if King Richard would allow a challenge, I said.

"He will not allow it," Everard returned. He broke off. "Holy St. Michael, look who comes! Gay as a June meadow!"

De Passy was indeed gay. His jerkin was embroidered in tiny flowers, his cap, which was embroidered also, had a cluster of cock's feathers falling over one ear. He waved impudently to us and came on. The child Beata rode behind him. She, too, was transformed. A hooded cloak of scarlet lined with green covered her, and the rough wool of the hood was overlaid with her dark hair.

We had no choice but to ride on together. To cover Everard's silence I spoke of the child.

This was their last ride together. Beata had become immensely inconvenient, de Passy declared. As if she understood at least the drift of what was being said the child began to weep despairingly. De Passy looked down at her. The child caught back her breath, hiccoughed once and was silent.

De Passy went on very smoothly to speak of Robert. "It is true, is it not, that he has gone without King Richard's leave? I have Robin de Herdecourt's word," he said, "that the King is angry." We were both dumb. He yawned. "I speak only to warn you," he said.

By the track leading to the villa we paused.

"Have they not barred the gate to you yet?" Everard asked and paused.

"If the gate were indeed barred we should leap over it, Sultan and I," de Passy said. With something too much of a gesture he laid his hand upon his horse. "And if we did not leap the gate," he added, "the Lady herself would leap the hedge."

I saw Everard flush. I felt my own cheeks burn. "You boast too much even for a Frenchman," Bogis said.

"I shall pay for it, I do not doubt," de Passy answered. "And you, messire Everard, shall pay, I promise you, for your modesty." He left us then. I remember how the child gazed after us with fixed wide eyes.

Everard looked at me. "And you are still bewitched!"

I said: "Every day I grow less in love with him."

We turned our horses and rode back. The French ships were busy in the harbour as we passed, the French and Genoese busy as ants about the quays.

That night through the agency of old Sir Wisdom I sought on Robert's behalf an audience of the King. The old knight—he had, I remember, a vast carbuncle on his nose glittering hard and round in the torch-light—had warned me beforehand—" The King's ague is upon him. If his anger burst on Robert of Kinwarton it will cover you also."

I considered the matter. My life was not in danger ; I had no favour left to lose. I must, I said, speak for Robert. Old Sir Wisdom gave way testily. I commiserated with him then over his carbuncle. He answered me with a great deal of tartness : " Better in sight than out o' sight. Better this end than t'other." And this time I agreed.

The old man's carbuncle still shining before my mind's eye, I entered the King's tent. The King sprang up when I entered. I remember how gaunt he seemed, how formidably he towered over me.

" By God's Body," he swore, " why do I lie here ? And why have you come ? " He dropped down on his couch bed ; he turned moody again.

I began my story ; I went on steadily. I could see how his ague held the King, and how stubbornly he resisted its humours, and I pitied him. As briefly as I could I told him of Robert's grief and its cause. When I had come to an end the King raised himself on his elbow and said : " I have hanged common men for the same offence."

" I know it, sire," I answered and was miserably silent.

" Then, Lord o' Life, why are you here ? " the King asked. From vexation or the ague he shot out both long feet upon the bed as he spoke.

I found strength to answer him straightly. " Because I would speak for Robert of Kinwarton now, sire," I said, " in order that he may not be condemned out of hand."

The King crossed his legs. " Even I," he said, " do not hang a good man unheard."

I went on. When I turn obstinate I no longer have the wit to be afraid. " Sire," I said, " when Robert of Kinwarton returns he will be so stricken he may refuse to speak in his own defence."

" How long have you known this Robert of Kinwarton ? " the King asked.

" Since we robbed the same orchard, sire, and before that," I said.

" Whose orchard ? " The King turned himself round towards me suddenly. I answered him in straightforward fashion once more. " Sir Hugh de Winton's orchard, sire."

The King's eyes, all the bluer for the small bloodshot veins that crossed them now, laughed for a moment, I thought. " Go ride out and find your Robert of Kinwarton and bring him to me," he said soberly.

I thanked him and kissed his hand and went out, a noose and a rope, for all that the King had laughed, before my eyes, and Robert dangling from the rope horridly.

On the morning of the next day Robert returned. He was like a man shipwrecked and brought in from the sea, I thought; there was that shadow of things scarcely to be borne about him still.

Everard and I asked him no questions; we were careful not to welcome him too warmly. We did no more than send word, as we were bound to do, of his return to old Sir Wisdom. On the morning of the second day Robert was sent for by the King. He went off declaring that, whatever came, he must return to Kinwarton. I said nothing. Once more I marvelled that in time of war any man should do as he had done and yet be blind to his offence.

He appeared dazed when he returned, one hand going up constantly as if to shield his eyes. When he spoke he astonished me once more. The King, he said, "had told him he might have the manor of Knighton and Inkberrow if he wished." I answered sharply out of a sudden envy that these were rewards indeed for absence without leave.

Both hands clasping his knees, his eyes looking past me, Robert said: "I told the King that Elfrida might have the manors, but I would not. I said I would remain in Outremer and serve him and see Jerusalem."

"And then?" I asked, amazed once more, but no longer envious, only glad and thankful, I think, that Robert was safe, that I should not be asked to finish our adventure alone.

"The King said," Robert continued, still with the same dazed gesture of one hand going up as if to shield his eyes, "that he knew my grief. But if I wandered again without leave and returned he would put me for a month in chains. I said that if I wandered again he should bury me up to the neck, alive, in my chains. And he agreed."

"That is the worst punishment decreed for a deserter from the host," I said. I felt a certain incredulous horror in my mind. "That is why I chose it," Robert simply said.

6

FAREWELL TO THE VILLA

FROM this time Robert appeared to withdraw deeper into himself. Sleepless and often fasting, he lived only, I believe, in the hope of our march upon Jerusalem. So much zeal astonished and alarmed me. I saw in it, I suppose, too much of the cloister and too little of the world. Increasingly, as the days passed, I wished to be moderate in all things and increasingly Robert seemed bent on becoming more fanatical. Nor was I altogether convinced that so much zeal would last; in my heart I felt certain, since singlemindedness had always been one of Robert's besetting virtues, that he had not forgotten and could not for some time to come forget the Lady Melisande.

Nevertheless by a concentration of all his energies upon the Cause he found, I can believe, some measure of ease and comfort. He had need of both. As one consequence of our attendance upon Queen Joan and the Damsel of Navarre at La Bagnara, whither King Richard had despatched Robert and Bogis and myself, we saw much of the Lady and not a little, in these final days before the departure of the French, of de Passy. The passion between them by this time had moved beyond rumour or conjecture : it was now fact and well known. I who was in personal attendance upon the Queen was able to observe how matters stood between them more closely than Robert or Everard, whose duties were those of captains of the Queen's guard. I marvelled at what I saw. She who had appeared as aloof from us as if she were indeed held in some kind of enchantment was transformed at the first touch of love. Her aloofness was translated now into terms of quick passionate giving. She demanded the same generosity of giving in return. In fact, always remembering that the Lady was as delicate in appearance as a flower, she showed herself as challenging and stiff-necked in tilting at love as her brother William was at a tourney. De Passy, as he had more than once declared, was one who took unkindly to chains. From being astonished, then overjoyed at the change in her, he was now, I suspected, in a fair way to being impatient and even a little bored. Pursuit and the excitement of pursuit were what he most enjoyed ; after them the pleasures of possession did indeed appear tame.

He and his Burgundians continued somewhat surprisingly to be frequent visitors to the Court of Queen Joan at La Bagnara. Even I who admired him was surprised that he should enjoy so much favour. There were some who declared that he had charmed even Queen Joan. I could not believe them. De Passy was no fortune-hunter ; he was too arrogant to dissemble ; he had never, to my knowledge, played at love. I think the truth lay here, that Queen Joan was widowed and childless. Her childlessness, I could believe, weighed more heavily upon her spirits than her widowhood ; she sought distraction, therefore, in music and dancing and in merry tales. In all these arts de Passy was proficient beyond the ordinary. It was Queen Joan, encouraged by de Passy's large talk of the child Beata, who had begged him to bring her to La Bagnara. The experiment was unfortunate, not least for the child. She clung to de Passy and would not be parted from him. In the end what had perhaps been intended as a pathetic show of love turned farcical. Gently at first, then not so gently, de Passy put her from him ; at once from a pretty poppet in a scarlet hood Beata was transformed into a small and fiery demon. From one paroxysm of rage she passed into another ; she cursed us in her own language, then in some bastard patois I did not know. From all that I could understand she cursed our bedchambers and the bed-chambers of our sons and daughters ; in small gross deliberate details she condemned us now and hereafter. She was indeed to be admired for her fluency in cursing. The Damsel of Navarre hurried away, her fingers to her ears, her long black hair bouncing over her stiff gold gown. Queen Joan, with a rueful gesture to de Passy, followed. The devil himself could not have stayed more motionless or looked more scowling than de Passy. Before I left the hall with the rest of the esquires I looked back. Beata lay exhausted and moaning, stretched out at de Passy's feet. She had apparently triumphed. It was certain that she would appear no more at La Bagnara ; it was not so certain that she would remain, as she had prayed to do, with de Passy.

The affair might have created more stir if about the same time other and larger matters had not filled our minds. It was known that the French would sail for Acre towards the end of March. A day or two before our own departure with Queen Joan from La Bagnara for Messina again, de Passy sought me out. King Philip, he informed me, would sail on the following Saturday, on the thirtieth of March. He was brief in his goodbyes ; I was brief also. I held out my hand. " Then at Acre," I said. " At Acre," he returned.

I came on with him for a moment towards the spot where his Burgun-dians waited. What had he done I enquired, with the child Beata ? He stared haughtily, then recovered himself and laughed. He had returned her to her own place, he answered. He went on speaking as if some shred of conscience did indeed trouble him. She was too worshipful, he said, and disobedient besides. Fleas bred on her : he suffered still. He had taken her to the villa ; he had brought her to Queen Joan ; twice he had arranged her life ; twice, provokingly, she had insisted upon returning to him.

I could measure his disturbance of mind by the length of his explana-tions. He continued to explain. His reputation, ridiculously enough, he declared, had suffered. The Duke of Burgundy himself had rebuked him. She was too young, his Grace had said. " Too young ! " de Passy ex-claimed. " If she had been older, nothing would have been made of the affair and nothing said."

I remained busy in my own thoughts. Would her own kind receive her again ? I asked at last.

De Passy shrugged. In doing so he dismissed Beata, he dismissed me also. " Acre, before long," he said.

" God grant it," I replied.

His Burgundians—they had been playing some quiet gambling game of their own—dropped their coins into their pockets once more and mounted their horses. I also dismissed Beata from my mind. Soberly I watched de Passy and his men ride away.

It was on the thirtieth of March that Robert sought me out. The French tents were empty. At any moment now their ships would sail. All day from the first hour of dawn—it was now noon—the camp had resounded like an immense fairground the day after the fair to the thud of mallets, the clatter of tent poles, the neighing of stallions and all the bustle and confusion of packing tents and gear and moving away. As if the occasion had given point and urgency to all that had been undecided in his mind Robert spoke to me. We must visit the villa, we must see the Lady Melisande ; he needed my company.

The confession, although stiffly made, meant a great deal since it came from him. And yet, as so often before a reconciliation, feeling hardened in me. I remembered my own causes for bitterness. " Take Everard," I said.

" Only," he answered, " if I must."

He waited, such a look of pleading on his face I turned away. Even while I reached for my cloak I could not help but ask why he must choose to-day ? " To-day," I said, " the Lady will be full of tears at the departure of de Passy and fuller still of remorse for all the little jealousies and disputes between them." In thinking so I found I did not altogether know the Lady Melisande.

On the slope of the steep path to the villa I observed Robert closely. Our stay in Messina had enlarged Everard ; it had broadened and thickened me. But Robert appeared leaner and finer, a delicacy of bone more apparent than ever about him now. Loving him as I did, I could not help but wish there were more flesh on his long frame, something more of common grossness about him. If life is a pure flame, if we do indeed live by an invisible fire within us, then Robert of Kinwarton was in danger of being consumed by his own fire. The thought came to me as coolly at first as if Robert were a stranger. But, suddenly, as I looked away, against all reason I became sharply alarmed. I leaned forward in a sudden small paroxysm of movement.

" What now ? " Robert spoke sharply.

" Could you not grow fatter, man ? " I asked. " Could you not at least appear more gross ? "

" Even you," Robert observed drily, " could scarcely expect a man rejected as I have been rejected, to put on weight over-night." He had begun by joking ; the joke tailed off towards the end.

"Even I ! " I exclaimed. " Whatever else comes to me," I said suddenly, " I would not be rejected by Elfrida."

" Elfrida ? " Robert appeared surprised.

I reminded him : " Did we not agree at Vézelay that I should ask for her in marriage ? " I went on, as I thought, to reassure him. " The waiting-maid was nothing," I said. He laughed at me. I blundered then. " Beside you and me, if the truth be told," I said, " de Passy is nothing either."

" You have no need to deny de Passy for Elfrida's sake," Robert said and turned away.

" I am not denying him," I answered. Yet was I not denying him ? I thought.

We rode on in silence. At the crest of the hill we paused. Sails set, the French ships were moving out towards the open sea. King Richard led them for a little way in his own galley, flying the leopard banner of Anjou ; King Philip's ship followed bearing the blood-red banner of St. Denis. We watched the ships move out, gather pace, grow small and move away ; we waited and saw the King's galley return.

" What lies," Robert asked, " beyond the farthest edge of the sea ? "

I caught his mood, remote though it was. I was forgiven, I thought. " Darkness and chaos," I answered, " or so they say."

" And beyond Jerusalem the great desert, and beyond that ? "

" Who knows ? " I said.

We turned and followed the track leading to the villa, skirting as we did so a small wood of fir trees. A smell of carrion reached us from the depths of the wood and a buzz of flies ; as we rode on, a snake, coloured bright blue and green, uncoiled itself from under our horses' feet and slid away. Without warning a stone struck my horse's flank, another grazed my chin. More stones followed. We rode into the wood. As we did so a pack of from twenty to thirty Griffon children started up, sudden as a covey of partridges, a few steps away. Bent almost double, they ran all but soundlessly on bare feet over the needles of the firs, then, squatting on their haunches, bayed at us like dogs. We rode on once more out of the wood. It was then that I remembered Beata. I spoke of her. I recounted all that de Passy had said. I had scarcely done so when a patch of scarlet on the hillside near the track caught my eye. I made my way there and presently held a fragment of scarlet cloth in my hand. It was lined with green.

Where the track turned finally towards the villa Beata lay. She was naked, so beaten and bruised she appeared to us at first sight to be dead. Robert raised her in his arms, wrapped his cloak about her. We put wine to her lips ; there was so much terror and wildness in her eyes when she opened them that my heart sank curiously for a moment and I was amazed. She turned her head. If she could she would have spat at us I felt. I looked away. In that second of time I think she died, for when I looked again there was nothing any longer to be read upon her face.

We rode back to the Convent of the Holy Anchorite. The Infirmière came out to meet us from the still-room, her sleeves rolled, a wooden spoon dripping syrupy juices in her hand. She greeted us breathlessly : "Another child. No, no, messieurs. We have six already, six devils from hell "—she pointed to an iron grille beside the convent door— "without light or mercy or grace." She came nearer. She rolled her eyes, green pale eyes in a smooth wax-coloured face. " Merciful God, she is dead."

We gave the child to her and came away. And the six little devils from hell confined behind the iron grille yapped at us and mocked us as we went. We looked at each other. There was blood upon Robert's cloak, blood on my hands. Out of so much violence only violence would come, I thought, and sickened at the thought. I did not speak. The sun beat hard upon us, the sky seemed of brass, and suddenly Sicily appeared not a fair island full of gaiety, but a brown lava spot smelling of carrion. Finally, by a kind of sympathy my stomach itself turned sick ; I swayed in my saddle and now I desired nothing unless it were to lie down and sleep.

By contrast with what we had seen, the villa when we reached it at last appeared as full as ever of order and a settled peace. The water splashed into the green bowl of the fountain, the Lent lilies ruffled and swayed below the terraces, the wind like a squirrel ran in and out of the cypress trees. One of Melisande's hounds waited for us on the other side of the bronze gates, then ran on ahead as if to show the way.

Melisande and Robert moved off together. My sickness heavy about me, I lay at Dame Isambeau's feet. The Dame brought me a herb cordial to drink ; she talked murmuringly of spring fevers and stroked my head. Before I slept I thought composedly of the padded paws and rhythmical tread of a cat's feet, and none of this, I reminded myself on waking, was kind to the Dame. While I dozed a second time Robert and Melisande returned. Said Melisande, bending over me, the Dame having gone off on some new errands : " Poor John ! I never saw so rough and round a head." And that was not kind either, I thought. The two of them moved away. They would talk all night when they should be making love ; there would always be endless talk between them, I thought.

Robert's voice came harshly to me : " De Passy boasts of his success with you."

I opened my eyes. I saw Robert in profile, I saw Melisande standing not more than a foot away from him and facing me.

"He would boast, oh, I know how he would boast." Melisande came forward, one hand to the folds of her dress. It was of some hard rose-coloured stuff, I remember, her neck and face tender and pale above. She sat on her swan chair not far from me, her feet crossed, her hands resting on the curved necks of the two swans. "Though I love him, you see," she said, "that I am not deceived."

"You love him?" Robert asked.

She looked up. "I think it will pass."

"What then?" He waited.

"I shall know love; I shall know true from false." I saw her touch one finger to her gown. "Truly he is not kind to me. He could never, I think, be kind."

"He is false," Robert said, "though it will not help me to say so."

I moved; I flung one leg over another. They glanced at me, but continued nevertheless.

"He loves only himself," Melisande said, "he trusts no one. I think he does not even trust himself."

"He is poorer than I am and worse placed. Then why must you choose him?" Robert asked.

She did not answer in so many words. She said:

"He has no heart. Therefore he will make conquests everywhere."

Robert turned away. "With me you would never be so bitter. With me your talk was never so high-strained."

"Do not reproach me," she said. "I would be different if I could. I seek something, I do not know what, to be safe, to be whole, to be content."

He grew impatient suddenly. "What will you do now?"

When she answered him her voice was light and afraid. "What can a woman do in this world except go from one love to the next? Or into a nunnery with four chaste walls about her and the damp smell of stones?"

"You are not for de Passy, it seems," he said, "nor even for Robert of Kinwarton, but for the most mighty, majestical Gavin Fitzgerold. And you will not, you have sworn, keep faith with him. Who are you, Melisande?"

She turned angry and quiet. "Who are you to reproach me?"

"I am nothing." He looked at her. "But I would have been your servant always, as I promised you."

"And now?" She spoke curiously.

"I will not think of you. I will pluck you out of my mind."

"Will you?" She was doubtful and thoughtful also. She spoke gently then. "Forgive me, Robert. Guy de Passy was my slave and I pitied him. Now that I am his subject it is only to be expected that he should not pity me. Though I do not think that I shall ever pardon him."

"I think you will pardon him." Robert bowed low to her. "I wish you the happiness I think you will not find with him."

"You are wrong, Robert," she answered. "Guy de Passy and I shall have some happiness at least of each other before we part."

I started up at this. These courteous bitter words were too much for me and I was tired of being ignored. I cried out to Robert who was moving away, to Melisande who gazed after him : "This bitterness cannot be love."

I went after Robert. As I did so I all but stumbled over the Lady Isambeau, seated—and this seemed comical to me, though I could not laugh—behind a rose tree planted in an urn. Her hands trembling, she asked : "Is she not spoiled ? Did I not tell you so ? "

I ran on. Melisande came flying after Robert and me. We halted. At the first of the stone steps she caught up with us. "Robert, tell me, where is Beata ? " She paused.

Robert looked at her, then looked away.

I spoke for him, bluntly. "De Passy abandoned her. The pack of children she had left behind envied her her cloak. Therefore they killed her."

"He treasures nothing that is his, nothing." Both hands over her face, Melisande ran from us then.

Angry at being moved and stirred to so little purpose, we came away. Once outside the garden we spoke for a moment unlike ourselves. "If I had had three manors the Lady might have decided differently. Though six would have been better," Robert said.

"You should not regret her. Let Fitzgerold have her," I answered. "A man can love fifty or a hundred women before he dies if he live long enough. Love does not take so long to flame and burn out."

"Six weeks from the first onset," Robert said. "No, I lie. Every word I have spoken since I left her has been a lie." He looked away. "She would have been safe with me."

I turned quiet. For some reason I felt ashamed.

Before we rode in to Messina we paused on the brow of the last hill. The wind was like wings beating about us ; we could feel darkness and mist coming in at us as it were bodily from the sea.

7

THE PERILOUS SEA

WITH the departure of the French, Messina and all our portion of the island appeared queerly desolate. To delay our own departure longer, even if King Richard had wished it, was impossible. The transports from England, for which King Richard had been waiting, had arrived; the Damsel of Navarre was willing to accompany him as he wished to Acre. Nothing, therefore, remained to be done, and on the Wednesday before Easter, which was April the tenth, eleven days after the departure of the French, we set sail. We did so to our own great joy and relief, and not least to the joy and relief also of the Greeks and Lombards of Sicily.

Robert and Everard and I had received our orders from King Richard on the evening of our return from the villa. Brand and Giles, from whom we had been absent since our stay at La Bagnara, were waiting for us with the King's commands. They were solemn and owlish with pride at the importance of the mission that had been entrusted to them by old Sir Wisdom on behalf of the King. Robert and I broke the seal of the long roll of parchment which Brand, awkwardly upon one knee, presented to us, and read the fine script within. "Richard, King of England, to his well-beloved and worthy of all trust John of Oversley, Robert of Kinwarton, Everard Mortebois, greeting. . . ." As we read our faces changed.

"What is it, master?" Brand was respectful enough, and yet he could not resist going on tiptoe and looking over my shoulder as if he were lettered and could read. I swallowed my annoyance, and went on to explain with as great a show of modesty as I could muster that the three of us were made members of Queen Joan's escort and would sail in one of the three ships of the King's fleet that had been apportioned to her and to the Damsel of Navarre.

"Ah, then she whom they call the Queen is still Queen Joanna," Brand exclaimed. "For the other, I know, is not yet Queen. They say she of Navarre is but a little thing, master, and will be lost in the King's great bed."

"What can beds or the size of beds have to do with us?" I asked.

"Well, master," Brand was beginning, but I interrupted him. "We shall sail ahead of the main fleet; our ship will be commanded by Captain Jones of Bristol; the Queen's ship, and the one accompanying it, will be in charge of Stephen of Turnham."

" Why is this port of Bristol so full of Welshmen, master ? " Giles enquired suddenly. " In all of Pershore, master, there is not one called Jones."

On the next day we set sail. Our arrival had been sight enough for the people of Messina ; the departure of our two hundred ships was an even greater spectacle. King Richard himself stood at the prow of the leading galley, Alan Trenchemer once more at the helm. The King was armoured but bareheaded ; he wore his surcoat of azure embroidered with the dancing leopards in gold ; in his hand he carried neither sword nor battleaxe but a silver trumpet with which to muster his ships should they be scattered by storm or ride out of their course. A vast silver-gilt lantern, specially fashioned for our voyage by one Lukas, a goldsmith of London, swung at the masthead. When its vast wax candle was lit the lantern light would serve as comfort and guide, and as rallying point also, to all the ships and men in the King's fleet. Every man of us knew the order of our going, for the King's criers had cried it before us twice throughout the host. Our orders were these : that we should not separate, that we should set a course direct to the east, that no ship should sail further from another than a man's voice could carry, no squadron of galleys or transports move further from the next squadron than the note of a trumpet could be heard. So, with the King's lantern and the trumpets and God's grace, we set out hopefully over the Great Sea.

At first all heaven seemed with us. The waves, like the Griffons and Lombards, appeared to dance to our going, the sea was an azure floor, the wind drove us gently on. The pilgrims sang, and the fervour and passion of their singing came to us where we were in Queen Joan's ship, though their words, like foam, were blown away. Robert leaned against the ship's side at first and played his lute ; then, when the sound of music came to us from Queen Joan's ship, laid it quietly away. I walked the deck in studied carelessness in my new short cloak, until the wind, taking it suddenly, almost strangled me with the silken cord with which, most elegantly and perilously also, it was fastened at the throat. Afterwards I cast off my cloak, I played draughts with Bogis, until from boredom and the irresistible inclination he had for sleep he gave every game away.

It was not until we were between Calabria and Mount Gibell that the wind dropped and we were becalmed. It was at this point, when orders had reached us by trumpet and the herald's voice that we must cast anchor for the night, that Captain Jones, the master of our ship, sought me out with some request that the cargo should be more securely stowed away and the hatches battened down. For a great storm, he declared, threatened us. I never saw, I thought, a fairer sky or smoother sea, yet I did as he wished.

I stood by, while our cargo, a large portion of which consisted of the household gear of the Damsel of Navarre and another portion of the treasure of King Richard, was stowed away more to the satisfaction of Captain Jones. We carried other cargo besides, though none so valuable : forty men-at-arms ; a few waiting-women (though I had done with waiting-women) ; a number of goats in kid (for the comfort of any of the women in the Queen's train who should become pregnant, as one or two of them were certain to do, it was thought) ; a few ewes about to lamb and bleating piteously ; two French beds for the two Queens with fine hangings of Arras ; Captain Jones' dog, a mangy cur for ever hunting fleas ; Everard's pet lizard, Jeroboam, which he had tamed upon the island and which he kept normally about his person ; and the ship's cat, which was black and white in almost equal halves and which was called, most suitably, after the Sultan's brother, Saphadin.

The weather continued calm and the captain, like all prophets who wait for their prophecies to be fulfilled, remained glum. On the morrow of Good Friday, however, contrary winds blew upon us ; a cloud no bigger than the King's cap of Poitou appeared above us suddenly as though shot from the sun. Sooner than a clerk can chant his *Nunc Dimittis*, the storm was upon us, and the King's ships caught, as it were, in a great hollow of the sea. Every moment the violence of the wind increased, great waves with monstrous tops and rounded sides hove us up and bore us down ceaselessly. We were driven here, driven there, no longer a fleet but a rabble of ships. Now lightning in darts and bolts of fire came at us, it seemed, over the heaving surface of the sea, and the noise of the thunder reached us through the sound of the waves. Rain came with the storm. We scarcely felt it for the crash of the waves, the cries of the pilgrims, and the fearful groans, as though uttered by souls other than human, of our own ships. Our masts were broken, our sails rent, our decks constantly awash. In the midst of the tumult ever and again we saw the faint light burning in the lantern of the King's ship. For whole moments it would disappear, only to emerge and give us some faint comfort again. From sickness and vomiting, and so much drenching, we died, I think, a score of times. All day we endured, all day the storm ruled and we, who had appeared like gods a short while before, were now no finer than separate mice sailing on driftwood rafts. It grew dusk, then dark ; the night, lit by watery flashes from the sky and by the evil shine of the sea, was greenish-dark. Presently we saw the light from the lantern on the King's ship no more ; we saw only the dark shapes of floating spars from our wrecked ships ; we heard no trumpet note, only the small thin cries, like birds calling in the night, of drowning men. So we drifted on, no bigger than an acorn in the vast sea, as much noise and babel between our decks as the great seas broke in on us as ever came from Noah's ark. For there were no waves, I think, nor storms in Noah's earthly flood.

Towards morning the wind dropped, the waves abated a little. Gradually it grew calm, and another day broke as though unwillingly upon us with the first yellowish wash of dawn. In the light of morning we saw a sea rimmed with mist but empty to all appearances of ships; we saw our decks swept and bare and all our gear plundered and broken by the sea. We looked at each other and scarcely knew our friends, so changed were we, so stripped of everything but fear. Gradually again the sun rose, the mists shone rainbow-coloured, the sea showed green-blue. Once more, shading our eyes, we sought its surface for more of the King's ships, or for the two vessels that until the moment of the storm had kept company with us. Once more no shape of any vessel could be seen. We comforted each other: when the mists lifted, we assured ourselves, we should see others of the King's ships. It was not credible, we repeated, that all the King's vessels should have perished since we ourselves had survived. Nor was the wreckage which had passed us considerable enough for so great a shipwreck. The galleys, Captain Jones thought, would ride out the storm, and the dromon or transport vessel upon which Queen Joan and the Damsel of Navarre had embarked was the stoutest in the King's fleet. Surely, we said, this vessel at least would have survived. We set ourselves, therefore, to make good the destruction of the gale. Here King Richard's foresight in providing us with spare parts of every kind served us well. The decks were scrubbed; we were fed and warmed; before long our thoughts, that had seemed sodden with sea water, for all our anxiety turned fresh and quick again.

I sought out Brand and Giles. I found Brand with the sheep in the hold smelling now most filthily of the byre. There was nothing of the storm or the sea in Brand's face. He eyed me as calmly indeed as if he were in our great outer kitchen at lambing time in Oversley. "All safe, master," he said, as he had said many a time to me before this in bad weather beside a ewe. And Giles, looking at me reproachfully from not far off out of one eye only—the other was nicely closed and his forehead gashed open—remarked: "That was a pretty good buffeting those shrews of sea serpents gave us last night, master, whether or no."

I looked for Everard. I found him in his shirt, his jerkin and breeches fluttering in a housewifely manner from a portion of rigging overhead. He appeared to be searching minutely for some small lost thing. From peering under one more piece of sailcloth he paused, and looked up, and spoke testily: "Where is he? Where in the devil's name?"

I spoke absently, my mind still with Giles and Brand. "What devil?"

Everard straightened. "Jeroboam. I held on to him all through the storm and now I must lose him in the calm." He peered under a loose board again and once more, engagingly, the wind lifted his shirt. " I took off my jerkin. It was then that I lost him," he said, still distracted and upon his knees. Clearly there was nothing sensible to be had from him.

I went on, and met Robert. He was as pale and haggard as he had appeared at the first light of dawn. I looked at him, and suddenly his face twitched uncontrollably as if he could have wept. He turned from me and once more shaded his eyes and looked out towards the east where the Queen's ships might be. I stood beside him ; I, too, kept watch. The mists were lifting, and still the eastern horizon showed empty of everything but sky and sea. We parted and came together again, and waited. Gradually two faint shapes of ships showed apparently motionless on the far horizon. We looked and did not speak and scarcely dared to hope. Ghostly at first, they gained in substance and in shape as we drew near. There were no more than two of them, anchored, we believed, and waiting for us, we hoped, between that immensity of sea and sky. Still uncertain, every sail set, we drove on towards them over a freshening sea.

I left Robert and returned by the way I had come. Bogis was in much the same spot, but dressed by this time in jerkin and breeches. He was looking both foolish and proud, it seemed to me, and I stared at him, the starkness of the moment, which had scarcely touched him, clouding my mind. He opened his hand speechlessly. The lizard, Jeroboam, was enthroned there like some small heathen image come alive, darting out a liquid tongue of black, winking its triangular-shaped black eyes. " A flicker on that board "—Everard pointed proudly—" and there he was."

Together with half the company on board we crowded the deck, shading our eyes and looking out to the horizon and the waiting ships. As we drew near the three standards of England, of Navarre and of Sicily crept falteringly up the mast of the larger of the two vessels. For an answering signal we hoisted the dragon of England at our masthead and came on. When we were within earshot Stephen of Turnham, who, as I have said, was in command of the Queen's ship, caused the trumpets to sound ; our own answered them. And at this moment, as if the trumpets were sounding for him, the ship's cat, Saphadin, whom everyone had believed drowned, appeared from under our third spare sail where he had sheltered all night, stepping, like Agag, delicately.

" Truly, we are all united," I said. I found I spoke from my heart, thankfully.

Driven southward still and somewhat out of our course, which was direct to the east, our three ships voyaged on in hope of finding the rest of the King's fleet. We met only fair weather. Time passed so smoothly indeed and so emptily, our minds grew empty also of fear and almost of desire. Those of us who had little work to do lay about the decks and dreamed for days, almost for weeks, for what seemed to us a long silken skein of endless time.

I know now why sailors love and fear the sea ; I know why they compare it to a woman and call it fair and treacherous, and would please it with gifts if they could as the Venetians do. The sea is no man's friend. As a man's own self strikes at him from unexpected depths, so the sea from unmeasured soundings, out of sight or journeying, turns perilous and stormy. At one time smooth and crystal-clear, its surface broken by wavelets no angrier than those in which swallows dip their wings, in half a night or less it turns unquiet and mountainous and dark. I know this now, but at that time I was as unsuspecting as if I were asleep. I knew little and had forgotten even the little that I knew of the terror and the fearful dwindling of a man's own self that can come to him from too much sea.

We were to live through a repetition of Good Friday's storm. I say live—it is true that a handful of us lived, but of the many scores of men that were on board our three ships the greater part died. During all this time, while King Richard and his fleet, as we learned afterwards, were sailing by the north coast of Crete to the island of Rhodes, our small squadron had been making its way through the open sea between the south coast of Crete and the shore of the Great Desert. We had almost suffered drowning on Good Friday. Now, on the evening of April the twenty-fourth, the day of St. Mark the Evangelist, when our ships were trying to put into the harbour of Limasol on the south coast of the island of Cyprus, a fresh storm fell upon us. In an instant, it seemed, we were driven helplessly towards the rocks. We had scarcely known their whereabouts until this moment ; now, suddenly, we were among them. The waves lifted us, the wind bore us on, the clouds floated mast-high like birds. Good Friday's storm had been like a slow dying ; this was the sudden snatching-off of a man's life. We had no time for safety, or thought, or prayer.

We were first ground, then caught upon the rocks. I remember how our deck slanted up steep as a hillside, how a wave greener than all things green broke over her, how afterwards our ship did not break so much as melt before our eyes. Taking off like swimmers we left her ; we took to the waves. They were full of casks and bales and dead sheep and goats and the tumbling bodies of drowned and drowning men. I held on to a ship's timber and rode with it. Among all the bobbing heads and floating spars about me I could almost have laughed to see Brand and Giles closely clasped, astride, as if it were a dolphin at a fair, the ship's prow, which was a dragon painted and gilded marvellously. Robert and Everard I did not see. In the next breath all thought, all feeling except fear left me as our second ship heeled over and was, as it were, smoothed out upon the broad flank of a wave. I shut my eyes. Before I did so I caught sight of the ship's captain mounted high in the rigging, praying or cursing, I do not know which, for he held a short sword in his hand. When I looked again no trace of ship or captain could be seen. Half-drowned as I was, I was lifted again and carried forward, perhaps by the last wash of the same wave, into a smaller inlet of the sea, boiling and flecked with foam, and thick with rocks, yet quieter a little and out of reach of the worst waves. Presently, how I do not know, and by that time I was past caring, I felt sand under me ; I was thrown forward bodily ; the sea withdrew from me again. Like a piece of driftwood I had come to Cyprus to the shore.

8

THE HARBOUR OF LIMASOL

I LAY all night upon the shore. When I awoke I thought that I had died ; but then a ray of sun warmed me, a bird perched upon my chest and pecked at me, and I knew that I was alive, that it was cold morning now. I rolled over, and as the sea had vomited me up, so now I vomited up my portion of the sea. Next a voice hailed me from not far off and a tall figure in skin-tight breeches and tattered jerkin hung with seaweed, whose hair and beard were stuck about with sand and tiny shells, came towards me, dripping salt water upon the sand. I stared at him. He was daubed most savagely with blue.

He said, picking the seaweed from his arms : "A pest upon the sea, and a plague on that Genoese tailor who has been the means of dyeing me blue."

At that I rolled over, I laughed outright, and vomited a second time. Sitting up and wiping my eyes and mouth, I said : "You look like old Neptune, man."

"I have nothing of the paunch and scarcely anything of the beard," Robin de Herdecourt said. For it was he, a noted horseman and the most dandified esquire in Queen Joan's Court, whom the sea and the tailor of Genoa between them had so glorified.

"I have scarcely a pair of breeches left and you are pleased to be merry," he said, and he stooped and untied a piece of seaweed as carefully as if it were a fine ribbon from between his toes.

"We are all that are left. Why should I not laugh ?" I asked.

For answer de Herdecourt pointed towards a welter of rocks about fifty yards away. "There are two fellows there who have kept even their breeches whom the sea has not dissolved."

We made our way towards the spot. As we did so I saw that indeed we were not alone. Other figures, grotesque as we were, could be seen moving in a half-dazed fashion along the shore. A little way from my feet, still washed by the sea, lay the splintered dragon prow of our ship, the gold paint glittering and new upon it even now. I touched it with my foot; I thought of Giles and Brand and could have wept, though I had laughed a moment before, for I was weak and empty still and light-headed from the sea.

De Herdecourt turned impatient. "Why grow maudlin over a ship's prow?"

"Not over a ship's prow," I began. I stopped short, for in that moment of my grief for them we came suddenly upon Brand and Giles. They were a few feet away, squatting in a hollow between two rocks. A small fire made a smother of smoke which half hid them; Giles was shivering and grey-faced, Brand, almost as stout and leather-coloured as if he had come ashore in a dead calm, was weighing a large flat fish thoughtfully between his hands.

I held up a finger. I had a fancy to hear what these worthies of mine fresh from drowning would say. De Herdecourt looked astonished, but waited nevertheless.

Giles said fretfully: "I tell you, brother Brand, he was a sea-devil. He was stuck with shells and weed and smelled most evilly of monsters."

"He was a poor shipwrecked creature as we are; he was no sea-devil," Brand said, still weighing the fish.

"He was tailed in his hinder parts. I observed them," Giles said, sweating and shivering now.

"Was I so?" de Herdecourt muttered. "Holy St. Denis! And I smell evilly also. I will fetch both these fishers a sea-clap on their ears."

I held him back.

"If he were a sea-devil he would be in company with other sea-devils," Brand declared. "For devils, like holy nuns, do not go about their errands singly. As for this fish," Brand went on, "vile though it is, and a foreign fish also, we will yet eat it. Men were not made to eat sand." Very cleverly, with a sharp stone, he began to gut the fish. "And I do not believe," he said, scraping vigorously with the stone, "what you swear as to this sea-devil's hinder parts."

De Herdecourt presented himself. "Judge for yourself then."

Brand and Giles were on their feet, gaping like fishes indeed and pale as ghosts.

Brand saw me and said, gaping still : "We thought you drowned, master."

"I found a good plank," I said. I spoke carelessly, though I was not far from trembling even yet.

"Judge then. Am I tailed or no?" De Herdecourt turned himself roundabout.

"How could you make a fire?" I asked Brand. I sat down and stared at the little yellow leaves of flame that curled out of the grey smother of smoke about the damp sticks.

Brand answered me lengthily out of relief. "My wallet is of good hogskin, master, and of sheepskin under that, and my flint and tinder are tied up in a piece of red Spanish leather, and bless my wife, Constance, whom I do not always bless, for she is not constant, who provided all this."

I was scarcely listening. For now Giles cried out louder than usual : "William Brand, cut off the head of that fish," and shuddered, and turned his eyes away.

"Ah, do so. The thing has drowned eyes," de Herdecourt said.

I stumbled to my feet. I turned away, for suddenly I had Robert, and Robert only, in my mind. I think I had the good sense of a dog that day, for only sense guided me. I came on Everard about a quarter of a mile distant. Stark naked, he was seated like a god among the rocks, his clothes spread out and drying around him.

He greeted me : "I am monstrously hungry." When I did not answer him at once he said : "Are there conies here?"

I threw myself down beside him. Where, I asked, was Robert?

At first Everard shook his head. "He had his crossbow," he said, "and would shoot nothing. And I had never much stomach for shells and snails."

"Put your breeches on," I said. "This is the way a man talks in a dream."

While Bogis dressed he went on talking. "A man full of nothing but sea water cannot be comfortable." He sat down abruptly, and I asked him again : "Where is Robert?"

This time Bogis answered me intelligently. "First he must go looking for Stephen of Turnham's ship on which Queen Joan was and the Damsel of Navarre. And not only them. Now he is off to Limasol to bring help and has taken two men with him."

I looked at him. "No one has seen anything of the Queen's ship?"

"I believe they are all drowned ; I am half out of my wits from thinking so."

Once more I looked away. Wherever I looked there was only the sea and the sky low over it.

In desperation I suggested that we collect all those men who were fit and make for the port of Limasol ourselves.

We had not gone far on our way when we encountered Robert and the two men who had set out with him. They were not alone, but were surrounded by a band of from twenty to thirty Cypriots in cut-away jackets and stiff short pleated petticoats, villainous yellow-faced men with black eyes and curved knives and noses. On seeing us, Robert spoke quickly : " These Cypriots are no friends to us or to King Richard."

So indeed it proved. It was as prisoners of the Cypriots, rather than as shipwrecked men in need of succour, that we first came in to Limasol. That night we were lodged in a small round fort of stone not far from the shore, so small we had scarcely room to stand and could never, all of us together, sit or lie. The air, foul enough at our entrance—four dead falcons lay rotting upon the floor—grew more foul with every breath we drew. As we took our turn to sit or lie, so we took turns to breathe the outer air from the half-dozen arrow slits that ran around the walls. We had no food or water within the fort, but once a day our guards would unbar the door a hand's breath and throw us a few loaves, a few skins of water.

We endured treatment of this sort for close on a week in hope of something better, and in some fear that worse might follow if we offended, not only for ourselves but possibly for Queen Joan and her people also should her ship by chance have been cast away at some other point upon the Limasol shore. But about the sixth day Robert and Everard and Robin de Herdecourt and William du Bois, one of the two men who had gone off to Limasol first with Robert, and Hugh the Brown and myself discussed what we should do. We were almost without arms. I say almost, for a few of us had kept our knives ; Robert and William du Bois had preserved, by some miracle, their crossbows, and Brand had discovered a rusty axe in a dark corner of our round fort. It was not a great deal with which to help overcome an Emperor and conquer an island.

We posted look-outs at each of the arrow-slits and busied ourselves meanwhile chipping away with knives at the masonry, at digging, like moles, at the earth in the hope of tunnelling a way out. We grew faint with want of food and parched with thirst, and breathless and faint for lack of air. I have always loved a wind and clean air about me—it would be worth dying, I thought now, to breathe sweet air again. I said as much. No one answered me. But Giles, who had his nose stuck happily in one of the arrow-slits, spoke : " A sail, master, coming this way. A sail."

One by one, silent and disbelieving, we took Giles' place. We, too, looked out to sea. A solitary ship did indeed appear to be coming in to

Limasol. Our guards were aware of our excitement and its cause ; they mocked us first, then blocked our arrow-slits. From our last glimpse of her we could see the ship coming slowly on. It was the Queen's ship, he would swear to it, Robert said. But I, who did not enjoy such eyesight, or suffer from so dreadful a fear as his, dared not be certain.

I do not know what bitter stifling death we might have died if our guards, made over-confident with Cyprus wine, had not themselves thrown open the door of our prison-house, impatient, I can only suppose, to complete the work foul air and starving had begun. In the next moment we were out and upon them and racing towards the quay. Our ship— it was undoubtedly the Queen's ship—had come near the shore. Already a boat was putting out from her loaded with armed men. They landed and at once the hospitable Cypriots set about them. Yelling like demons for all that we had almost died from lack of air, we arrived and took the Cypriots in the rear. I think they scarcely knew what men we were, or whence we came : terror and surprise did more for us here, it is certain, than our odd muster of weapons or our fierce cries. In the mêlée that followed it was difficult at first to tell friend from foe among so many heaps of cursing and struggling men. " Save us, Holy Sepulchre," we heard, and many other not so pleasant cries. We fought with what weapons we had, with our hands and our feet also ; there were no horses and little armour and less chivalry in this fight. We might, so great were the odds against us, have been exhausted or even overwhelmed, but suddenly—all was sudden with them—the Cypriots withdrew. Leaving our dead behind, we crowded into the boat once more and rowed towards the Queen's ship. Never in my life have I been so full of fear. Our boat was so heavily burdened and rode so dangerously low in the water I expected every moment that we should be capsized ; and the Cypriots, sudden again, had returned. They waded after us, hurling knives and discharging darts and arrows thickly around us. I looked down and the clear sea seemed monstrously shining and greedily deep and waiting. Looking at it I found again the horror of drowning I had begun to forget. To comfort myself I looked ahead. No comfort was there. The Queen's ship appeared an eternity of darts and arrows and drowning sea away.

That same night, safely on board, I was visited by an ague sharper than I had ever before known. I burned with fever and yet I shook with cold, and always I dreamed of deep water in which I struggled and sank endlessly. I would cry out and wake and find Robert or Brand sitting beside me, and be reassured, and sleep again only to dream differently. On Sunday, the fifth day of May, two days after our arrival on board the Queen's ship, I woke early. Immediately I was aware of myself, of my mind that felt curiously light and clear, of my limbs weighted as though with lead. Robert, his chin on his hand, dozed beside me; no breeze stirred; I felt the movement of the waves under me, saw the standard wrapped about the mast.

I stirred, and Robert spoke to me. He told me nothing of what was in his mind, nothing of Melisande whom I remembered now but of whom I did not dare to speak. He appeared to guess my thought, and very courteously made shift to answer. "They tell me the Lady is sick."

"Of an ague?" I struggled to sit up.

"No, of a plate of salt beef." Robert began to laugh silently.

I closed my eyes. "What now?"

Robert answered, no longer smiling: "If the King's fleet does not come soon we shall be the guests, or rather the prisoners, of the Emperor Isaac."

I asked how long the Emperor would allow us to wait for the King's ships?

"Until one hour after to-day's sunset," Robert said.

We waited all day, whiling away the hours, as best we might, with games of chess or backgammon or tournaments of quoits and darts. The Queen's chaplain, Ferdinand, prayed for us, squinting at us as he did so out of half-shut eyes, for our souls, our sickness and wounds, for our little faith and our happy deliverance. Down upon their knees on the ship's deck were all the ship's company together with Queen Joan and her ladies, her esquires and men-at-arms and waiting-women. I had no liking for Ferdinand and would not listen to his petition: I disliked his eyes, which were popping and a vile sea-green, and his slobbering lips and raw red hands. The sun burned on his shaven crown, a sudden wind lifted his fringe of hair, ragged and coarse as the end of a cow's tail and red also. It was not for his beauty that Queen Joan had chosen him.

The prayers continued and presently, my eyes closed as though in reverence, I slept. I woke and it was pleasantly silent and late afternoon and there was no more Ferdinand. Instead Robert brought his lute and sang to me. I listened with half my mind, the other half, as if it were free of my body, ranging indifferently away. There is no peace, I thought, no permanence; all the tides are in us, the busy seeking, the continual change. It was the sea and the movement of the ship, I think, that drove my thoughts. The afternoon wore on; the shadows grew large and squat upon the deck; a tenderness spread and deepened in the western sky. Robert laid aside his lute and got to his feet and began looking out to sea, something he had done so often there seemed nothing to be gained by looking again.

But presently the look-out man blew a long blast upon his trumpet; at once everyone on deck stood up and shaded his eyes.

Presently again, while the Cypriots could be seen running to and fro as though in panic upon the shore, Queen Joan and her ladies, their veils streaming, their kirtles held before them, came tumbling on deck like so many gay pouter pigeons. The rest of the Court followed. It was then at last that I spied two ships, looking dark and small like crows against the light, lying out where the line of the horizon seems to end and the first mists of night begin. While we were still in doubt as to what ships these might be two more appeared, and more after them, and still more, until the sea seemed full of ships, every one of them making for Limasol. We laughed and shouted, almost beside ourselves with sudden confidence and gratefulness. Here, at last, despaired of for so long, like another deliverance, was King Richard's fleet. The King was safe ; together we might yet turn our backs upon Cyprus, together we might see Jerusalem. Joy made us drunk for a moment like wine ; men embraced each other ; a sailor danced a hornpipe solemnly and Ferdinand appeared and demanded that we give thanks upon our knees. Many of our people did so, choosing some quiet corner of the deck in which to pray. Everard crossed over and clapped Robert upon the back and said : " Laugh, man, and be glad." Robert stood off from him. " I will not laugh, though I am glad." He laughed then in spite of himself, while I discovered that I was tearful and joyful in the same breath like a girl.

Trumpeters drawn up on deck, every pennon flying, we waited for the King's fleet. When the foremost galley drew near we hoisted sail. Not humbly like petitioners and captives, but as part of King Richard's fleet we moved for the second time into the harbour of Limasol.

9

ROBERT AND MELISANDE

On the night of our entry with the King's fleet into Limasol my fever returned. While my sickness continued another chapter was added to the tale, already long enough, of our journeyings ; another stage of our progress to Acre all but passed. It was only afterwards from talk with Robert and Everard, from news given me in clearer terms by Ambrose and the Chronicler, both of whom visited me, that I learned of the Emperor Isaac's warlike reception of our ships, and of the subsequent storming and capture of Limasol by King Richard and the flight of the Emperor to Famagusta on his yellow horse, Fauvel. I learned also how King Guy of Jerusalem had set out from Acre to bring King Richard news of the siege of that city. Finally I was told how King

Richard, on May the twelfth, on the day following the arrival of King Guy, had both married the Damsel Berengaria of Navarre at Limasol and crowned her Queen. When he moved, the Chronicler said, the King moved quickly. All this I had missed.

Meanwhile, neither sick nor well, I lay in Queen Joan's lodging, a white house set in a garden of fig trees between the shore and the Limasol road. Here, where I lay between the fountain and the cypress trees in the paved courtyard, Melisande would visit me. She came as frequently when I was recovering as when I was ill. Sometimes we played at chess, and sometimes, not always by my arrangement, she won. Now and then she read to me high-flown passages from some French romance lent her by Queen Joan. While she read I would look at her and marvel at all the fair colours in her face, and wonder also how much she came to see me for my own sake, how much that she might have news of Robert. I even played a sour sort of game with myself : how soon, I asked, would she bring in Robert's name ?

In the end it was I who spoke of him first. I found myself talking suddenly of his reserve of manner, of his pride that was so secret, of his strength of will and spirit. Robert was torn, I said, between this world and the next ; eternity drew him like a star ; he was not now, I said— nor had he ever been since I knew him first—like other men. Melisande, I remember, stirred abruptly all at once, as if she wished to speak. I waited, but she stayed silent. Driven by some sick-bed demon of loquaciousness, I continued. I painted a picture rosier than truth of Kinwarton, and the moat and the swans ; I spoke of the bower of leaves and birdsong and blossom our valley of Evesham was in spring. " About this time," I said, and saw it all. " If there is no cold spell," I added hastily.

Melisande sat, her chin upon one hand, as if she were listening with no more than a quarter of her mind. " Poor John ! You are homesick," at last she said.

I denied the charge angrily. I accused her in turn. I said : " I think you come to me chiefly for Robert's sake." I added, which I need not have done, " I cannot think you will ever be reconciled with him. A man is not an apple to be picked up and thrown away."

She rose and curtsied to me, polite and strange. " I have not deserved this of you, messire John." She left me then.

Later Dame Isambeau appeared. We talked yet once more at cross-purposes. I spoke of Queen Joan, for the widowed Queen of Sicily was always a fruitful topic with the Lady Isambeau. The Queen, I said, went riding every day for the sake of her figure.

The Dame tossed up her hands. " Five children ! I had thought the Queen of Sicily was childless."

"She has gone riding," I said. "She has no children."

"Why should she not have children?" queried the Dame. What were women for, she asked, if not for the comfort and consolation of men and the blessings and sacrifices of matrimony?

"Oh, I am weary," I cried. I had no thought that she would hear. She heard, and clucked her contrition, and rose and went away.

It was then that Robert came. He eyed the Dame's knitting, which she had left behind, warily. I groaned. "I am destined," I declared, "to receive yet another cordial."

The cordial (of wormwood) did, in truth, arrive. It washed, perhaps unkindly, the roots of a cypress tree and smelled vilely there, and Robert, with whom by this time I was alone once more, said: "The King is to have the Emperor's yellow horse, Fauvel, and the Imperial treasure, and all Cyprus also and the Emperor's daughter if he wishes."

"He will not want the Emperor's daughter. The Emperor's horse is another matter," I said.

Robert laughed. The Damsel of Cyprus had been placed in Queen Joan's care, he said.

I interrupted him to speak of the Lady Melisande. I pleaded for her: "She has visited me daily chiefly in order to speak of you."

He answered me quietly. "I will not be trifled with a second time."

"Are you God," I asked, "that you can bear to speak so haughtily?"

He looked at me. "Can you not see that I, too, have changed?"

I attempted to argue with him. "I think your pride consumes you."

"Not my pride," Robert said. "God help me, I love her still, though I think she has become too small for me."

I was startled as much by the truth as by the arrogance of his answer. "You are abandoning her," I said. "You are leaving her most unsafe as de Passy left the child Beata." He did not answer me.

I went on angrily: "Go your own way. I cannot go with you since I am neither saint nor monk nor Pharisee. For my part I would know all life; I would not deny the beauty of the world."

Robert got to his feet. When he spoke the colour darkened in his face. "Behind so much beauty I see always darkness and pain. Behind the beauty of the world is a Cross," Robert said, "and Christ and man crucified."

"I cannot follow you," I answered. I said: "Oscar's death and de Passy's malice towards you have unseated a part of your reason." He turned away. I called after him. "Will you not at least see the Lady?"

He looked at me. "If I saw her," he said, "I should forget everything."

The sultriness between us held for days. Then, at a wind from a different quarter, our minds changed. The occasion—that of the formal surrender of the Emperor Isaac to King Richard—was one of rejoicing for the army and the fleet. We could not help but rejoice with them. Now that he was defeated, the Greeks of Cyprus reviled as a tyrant the Emperor whom formerly they had worshipped. On our victory every Cypriot appeared to rejoice with us ; throughout our triumphal progress through Limasol no one wept.

I said that no one wept. Robert and Everard and I rode in Queen Joan's train, and the Damsel of Cyprus, the captive daughter of the Emperor Isaac, together with her waiting-woman, travelled not a yard from our horses' heads in a litter of Imperial purple and gold. All the way through the streets of Limasol she wept so softly as scarcely to be heard. Imperceptibly the sound of her soft weeping—she was no more, it was said, than a child—wore on all our minds. That soft weeping in my ears, I pitied her and wished there was no need of ruthlessness in war. Robert did more than pity. Catching at a garland that was thrown to him, he rode nearer the litter, and, parting the curtains, laid his wreath of flowers like an offering within. Presently, to a murmur of Greek from the waiting-woman, the curtains parted once more, a child's hand weighted with a great ring of gold came out and proffered, somewhat tremblingly, a rose. Robert took it and pinned it in his cap. And presently again the soft sounds of weeping and the murmur of Greek also from within the litter ceased.

We moved on. The heralds and the trumpeters met us upon the outskirts. Our men—they had been forbidden the streets of Limasol—lined the way. As the procession paused before entering the courtyard of the King's house, where still another feast was to be held, I looked back. It might be true, as Ambrose, with a touch of ague in the soul had remarked miserably enough only the previous night, that though we rejoiced to-day we should weep to-morrow. What of it ? I asked. To-day our men's cheers were heartening. A burden had been lifted from all our minds and the cheering we heard now was surely a measure of our relief. We were glad, for at last we were for action and movement again ; our long delays were past ; to-morrow or the day after to-morrow we were for Acre. Beyond Acre Jerusalem waited and the end of all our journeying. So at least we believed. To the sound of more trumpets we moved on to the banqueting house ; we dismounted and passed in.

Our feast over, Bogis and I rested in the orchard of fig trees that lay next Queen Joan's lodging. Either the air was sultry or we had feasted too well. Whatever the cause we had no wish to move or speak. While Everard dozed, his mouth open, small beads of sweat on his froth of new yellow beard, Melisande came running towards us between the lines of fig trees, over the crooked shadows their long branches made. There were wine stains on her white gown ; her eyes were large. She paused uncertainly at sight of us.

I greeted her. " I am to hear more of Robert, I know it," I said. " Well, it is true," I added, " monk though he is, that I love him." I rose, somewhat late, and bowed to her.

" I will not tell you then." Melisande appeared vexed ; she appeared full of longing also.

I encouraged her. " You spoke to Robert at the feast. He answered you coldly."

" So coldly." She caught back her words, then rushed on. " He would punish me, I know. It is all punishment with him and the taking away of his love if we offend. That I should woo him," she said, and drew a deep breath, " and be rebuffed ! I spoke to him ; I laid a hand on his sleeve. He stayed as distant as if I were Queen Joan. If he had been his own effigy in stone he could not have been more marble-cold. I would not torment myself if I did not feel nobility in him, if he had not always been courteous and gentle with me, gentler than anyone," Melisande said, and clasped her hands. " I would not think of him, I say, if it were not for all this. I think I love him," she said, childish tears of anger and despair upon her face. " Or "—she corrected herself—" I would love him, if he would allow me, if he would be patient with me for a little while. Oh, what am I but a fool ? " she asked swiftly, her tears drying in a hot gust of anger, her mind swerving again, " a fool to woo a man whose mind is set on higher matters than love."

I felt myself not for the first time somewhat daunted by so much talk of love. I said so.

Melisande stood still, then spoke furiously. " Why will not some man marry me as I am and bear with me, and change me from the light fanciful thing I am ? " She paused, and Bogis, whom I had supposed to be much more than half-asleep, shot up suddenly. Both hands smoothing his hair, he began : " Are you serious ? If you are "—round-eyed he stared at her. " No, clearly you are not." He left off smoothing his hair ; abruptly he lay down again.

Melisande spoke wonderingly. " Why does he ask ? "

" Because he also is a fool," I said, " and thinks himself in love. As for me, I feel tenderly towards none unless towards the Damsel of Cyprus."

The Lady was scornful. " Why ? "

" She wept so softly," I said.

Melisande wasted no pity. " Quite soon," she declared, " this Damsel of Cyprus will be older and then her grief will be nothing." She appealed to me afresh. " John ! "

I turned to one side. "Make no offer to me, I beg you. I would preserve myself."

Melisande said slowly : "So you also, even you, scorn me."

I was not flattered. "You are too vain," I said. "All the world of men is not for you to choose from." I mimicked her. "Even I say so, even I."

I did not triumph for long. The Lady—for she was often merciless— turned all her weapons upon me. "You are very little sometimes, John of Oversley," she said. "Very pert, and very little, and inclined to be pompous as well. And very vain also. I think you are nothing very long, I think that you cannot help but change colour like a chameleon."

The shrewdness, and the ungratefulness, of this speech almost silenced me. I turned sullen. "Why come to me ? Why ask my help ? "

She curtsied low to me. "Did you dream I was so meek as not to answer you ? Indeed, you see how wrong you were." Small, defiant and, like all outraged women, however small, a shade viperish also, she left me.

While I stared after her Bogis sat up and yawned, I thought falsely, one hand over his mouth. "All that I have heard—and I missed nothing— was pure fantastical. As if a man talked of treasonable weather."

"Who talks of treasonable weather ? " I asked, and stared.

"Some fops o' the Court. May the Saracens silence them, or worse."

I went off with him. We found Robert, as if he were any crossbowman re-assembling his crossbow. He looked at us apologetically. " I am sick of feasting."

That night, our last upon the island, we danced in the hall of Queen Joan's lodging until the stars were dimming in the sky ; we even danced in the orchard of fig trees to the light of lanterns swung high on the twisted branches. The sky seemed vast and deep, the night magical ; a south wind blew. In the harbour the horns sounded now and then ; trumpets from our outgoing ships answered them ; seamen called to each other about the quays. Sails were hoisted, anchors weighed, the last prayers sung and the King's ships, forerunners of those in which in a few hours we, too, should set sail, moved out silently into deep water. Our turn was near ; we were content to let them go.

I had mislaid my lady of the evening ; I sought her half anxiously, though she was heavyish and dark and not altogether to my taste. I came upon Robert and Melisande instead, facing each other in an ante-room lit by guttering wax tapers in sconces of bronze. Melisande's hands were on Robert's shoulders ; her face was lifted to his. I would have left them to each other, but the Lady called to me. There was never any malice in her ; she forgot a grievance as soon as it was past ; she would share everything down to her most private moments with a friend. Not altogether willingly I returned.

It was then that Dame Isambeau, where these two were concerned, played Providence or Fate. She came, headlong as a May bug out of a lime tree, into the room. At sight of her Melisande and Robert shot apart, then stood side by side. The Dame, I believe, was scarcely aware of them at first. She had her tasselled nightcap on ; her gown, displaying her bosom and an even odder figured kirtle of red dragons on a yellow embroidered ground, was open and flowing wide. She had mislaid her knitting, it seemed, and had awakened in a horrid flutter from her first sleep. She sought it now and we must seek it with her. So, with moving of chests and stools, with the knocking of our backsides together in the small room, with begging pardons and looking and bending in the taper-lit dark, true love for Melisande and Robert was lost a second time. As suddenly as she had come, and still without her knitting, the Dame made off, her head and body bent forward, her hands to her gown.

The horns sounded once more from the harbour ; our own trumpeters answered them from the Queen's courtyard. This time the trumpets sounded for us, for the King's men and the King's ship. Bitter and yearning, Robert and Melisande looked at each other. With a strange lift of his hand—strange because it was that of a man giving something that he held to its owner again—Robert, too, was off and away. Through the orchard of fig trees, down the Limasol road, in the grey edge of day I followed him. And the Lady Melisande ran, too, in an opposite direction, for her maid, for her cloak, for all that she wished to take with her that she had left behind and for the rest of Queen Joan's company.

PART THREE

LAND OF OUTREMER

1

THE WALLS OF ACRE

ONLY a few weeks before the trumpets had sounded for us to come in to the port of Acre. For a brief moment, as if the rain fell blessedly after drought, there had been agreement once more between French and English, between the Marquis Conrad of Montserrat and King Guy of Jerusalem, between all the rest of the many minds of which our army was composed. But already tempers and minds alike had changed. Once more Conrad of Montserrat laid claim to the Kingdom of Jerusalem ; once more King Philip of France supported Conrad, and once again King Richard and King Guy of Jerusalem, the latter of whom already held the title, were opposed to the French and to the Marquis Conrad. Again the Christian army was in bitter disagreement over the dominion of a city still in Turkish hands whose only rightful ruler was the Prince of Peace. In June the trumpets had sounded for us to come in. Now, on the fourth day of July, I could hear the horns sounding for the French retreat. From the little hill on the left of our lines where I sat under the sparse shade of a thorn tree I had seen the French set out in all their glitter and array ; I had seen the French king's stone-throwers hurl their missiles upon the Turks, I had seen the scaling ladders set against the walls and the French swarming up them, only, more easily than lizards, to be swept down. Most horrible of all, I had seen the jets of Greek fire directed upon the French from the Turkish battlements, descending straightly as rain upon the besiegers' heads. I had watched all this and observed the wave of men falter, then rally and come again. I had marked how hope and discouragement swayed the mass of them as fitful gusts of wind sway the barley ears. I had pitied them then ; I pitied them now while the horns sounded for the retreat and the Saracen drummers came out, beating a tattoo of triumph upon their drums.

Like every other member of King Richard's army I was a spectator only, for to-day, so King Philip had decided, the French alone must be in command, the French alone must be allowed to possess the praise and the glory. There was no glory and little praise, only the huddle of bodies in the deep ditch, only the Christian prisoners for the scimitar or the galleys, only a scurrying host of disappointed men. And on my right the tents of the English camp, and our men standing and watching ; on my left the half circle of the great ditch, and beyond the ditch the walls of Acre, battered for two years and almost unbroken still. Beyond the walls lay the plain and the hills crowded with the tents of Saladin.

As I watched, despondency which I had already resisted so often gained the upper hand. I looked down at the stones at my feet : they were of flint, most curiously shaped, so that they looked like bones. A man should blame none but himself for his discouragement. And yet in this moment I blamed the land of Outremer. The enemy, though they were brave and skilful, were nothing. We fought, it seemed to me, monstrous shadows. Intangible presences, unseen Titans blocked our way, and the land of Outremer appeared to be mother of them all. The land mocked us, I thought, as it had mocked our Lord ; it filled all our minds with strangeness. Though we resisted it, and even made merry against it, strangeness remained in the sky over our heads, in the air we breathed, in the sun that bore down so mercilessly upon us, in the earth that blistered and scorched our feet. Under so fierce a sun, our food—bacon and beans and half-cooked salted meat—bred depressing humours in our blood. We cooked in our armour like hedgehogs baked in mud, and many a knight, buckled up so doughtily by his esquires and cased from top to toe in plates of steel, stifled as though in a dungeon made to his own shape and never came forth from it alive. What wings are to an eagle our horses were to us, and yet in all the land round Acre little or no forage was to be found. Wherever rain fell or green grass grew the Turks, or the sun, came out and burned it up again.

When our minds were as black as mine was this day it seemed to us that everything killed : the scorpions, the food we ate, the fruit we plucked, the flies. Queer tales were told, every one of them ending in sudden and dreadful death. You laughed at them ; you forgot them like a song once heard ; like a song once heard they returned in snatches to the mind again. Or else you dreamed at night that you were greeted by two strangers robed in white with scarlet girdles to their robes. " Hail, master ! " you heard. Having stabbed at you they were gone like spectres.

We were right to dismiss a half of what we heard, and yet it was true that here in the East more than one man was King. From his fortress town of Massiat under Mount Lebanon, Sheikh Sinan Rashideddin, Chief of the Syrian sect of the Assassins and Lord of Massiat, wielded a power greater and more absolute than that of the great Sultan of Egypt, Saladin. In my mind's eye I saw him, like some devil in white saint's clothing, seated, for this was a symbol of his pride, in a plain chair. One small hand, I thought, with pale long nails, combed his white forked beard.

I looked up ; I waited expectantly. A stout fellow in dabbled scarlet was picking his way towards me. He had a too earnest look ; there was spittle and foam about his mouth ; his head was smooth and shining as an egg, and his chin carried a sparse tangle of black beard. A finger to his lips, he said : " I am the King's spy. You must be careful, young man. You must hold your tongue. You must seek other friends."

Strange characters, the mad, the maimed, the blind and the abominable, like half-starved dogs, roamed the camp. This man, I thought, was merely mad. " If you are the King's spy, who am I ? " I asked.

He gave me my name, surprisingly.

" Why warn me ? " I asked again.

He looked cunning. " Because, brother," he said, " in these days when fortune has turned so unhappily against us, any man may turn traitor."

I turned angry. " Be off," I threatened. " Leave me. Leave me in peace."

The fellow simpered. " Were you so much at peace when I came, young master ? " For a moment his look was that of a sane man. A second afterwards he was mad again. With a cackle of mirth he went off.

I got up from my seat ; I went on to meet de Passy, for the Duke of Burgundy's men also had taken no part in the day's assault. I had encountered de Passy on the day of King Richard's arrival in Acre. The French King and his knights, followed by the Duke of Burgundy and his train, had come out in pomp and ceremony to greet us, burning so many torches that the Turks, we learned afterwards, had believed all the Christian camp to be on fire. I thought de Passy bolder and more assured in manner than when we met last, wilder and more reckless also in his talk. As before, his beauty held me ; something different in him drew me on unwillingly. Of one thing I was certain : his mind was set more singly than ever upon himself and his own purposes.

I came upon him in a pleasant enough spot, a quarter of a mile away and within sight of the sea. He was stretched out and intent, drawing with his dagger point some complex pattern in the sand. I came nearer and saw a castle ringed by an outer and an inner wall, set high among mountains, and approached only by what appeared to be steep steps cut out of the mountainside. I peered closer. " You chart well," I said.

" One of my many arts." He looked up at me for a moment, then went on drawing. I watched while he sketched a garden on the far side of the fortress walls, a garden full, it appeared, of small apple trees and roses set on tall upright stems. " Here is a pool full of lilies "—he sketched it roughly—" and nymphs bathing "—he drew one shamelessly, then paused and looked at me. " What a simpleton you are to be so shocked," he said, " a debauched simpleton ! "

From astonishment I could not immediately feel annoyed. I said : " Your castle is not so different from the descriptions travellers give of the castle of the Old Man of the Mountains at Massiat. The gardens might be his famous gardens of Paradise also."

"The castle is any castle," Guy declared, "and the gardens are what you please." Deliberately—how deliberately I did not remember until afterwards—he wiped both castle and garden away.

Only then did I recover from my astonishment. "I do not like your manner, though I am late in saying so," I said. I got to my feet.

"Do not go." He faced me. "I am out of humour to-day."

"When are you not out of humour?" I lay down again.

He began to draw in the sandy soil at his feet once more. This time he sketched a mountain stream ; above it, small on its mountain top, the same castle, or what appeared to be the same castle whose outline he had sketched before. Falling rapidly, the stream broadened under his hand into a large pool almost enclosed among the rocks ; from the pool, widening still, it fell steeply again.

Later I was to know that river and that pool. But I watched idly that day, only curious to see what might be added next and waiting in an odd sort of excitement for de Passy to wipe river and pool away.

He paused without looking up. "Why should I not be out of humour? What do I owe you or the world? I have no country." Here he looked at me, something humbled I had never seen before in his eyes.

I said : "You travel light. Those who travel light, they say, go far."

"I want no comfort," he said. "I have built my life round this lack of belonging. Now it is too late to change."

I said : "Has a man then no power over his own life?"

He said : "We draw on us, I think, our own fate. Even our sorrows are those that suit us best." He looked up. "See if it is not so with King Philip and with King Richard. And, if you like, with yourself."

I spoke gloomily. "I already see it. I think I was blind before that I could not foresee the consequences of the disputes between the two kings."

He said : "I care nothing for them. I do not, as you know, share your mountain-moving faith. For Saladin has it also. Jerusalem is as much to a follower of Mahommed as it can ever be to a Christian. It is the place from which Mahommed made his night ascent into Heaven, just as it will be the gathering place of all the Sultan's people on the Day of Judgment. I am no fanatic. I am unable to shut my mind to the other side of truth."

All this seemed reasonable. And yet I did not care for what I heard. While I struggled uncomfortably with my thoughts my madman of an hour ago reappeared. He addressed de Passy. "Sir, did I not pass you in Saracen robes by the thornbrake yesterday?"

Guy answered smoothly and at once : " Speak humbly, fellow. Do you not see I am the King of France ? "

The fellow persisted. " There were two of you and one had a hump upon his back."

" Leave us, good soul," I said, for I have never cared to mock at naturals. The man began to move away, muttering as he did so : " I will tell my master. I will tell him."

" Who is your master ? " de Passy called after him.

The fellow started and crossed himself. " The Prince of Peace."

" Mine is Lucifer," Guy laughed at him.

" I knew it. I recognised you," the man said. More quickly than I would have thought possible in one of so shambling a gait, he hurried off.

Guy looked after him. " Another zealot," he declared, " whom too much faith has made mad."

" I think he acts a part." I looked at de Passy. " Robert says the same of you."

" There is more in your Robert than appears. Though I hate your Robert," de Passy very pleasantly said.

" I am sick of your hates. I could wish we were all like Everard who hates no one," I returned. I got to my feet. De Passy came on with me.

It was then that we encountered Everard riding out of the camp, a company of crossbowmen, Gomorrah at their head, following him. Everard was singing in his tuneless voice a song I had often heard from Robert's lips.

I hailed him. " Whose song is that ? "

" Why, Robert's," he answered.

" He no longer sings it," I said.

" Then I have all the more right to it." Everard went on singing :

> " *Gentle heart, could you love true ?*
> *Heart to whom my love I've tendered.*
> *Night and day I think of you.*
> *Gentle heart, could you love true ? . . .*"

I greeted Gomorrah. " Whither away, Gomorrah ? "

He looked at me warily over the great curve of his nose. " To the wall, sir, to the wall."

Bogis gave up singing. He said cheerfully : " That is where we shall all be to-morrow."

" To-morrow ? " I looked at them. That King Richard's assault would be made soon I knew, but to-morrow was soon indeed.

"And the tortoise must be ready," Bogis went on, "the largest, and strongest, the most magnificent tortoise in a world of warlike tortoises."

Gomorrah swore stoutly that he disliked sieges, that he cursed all tortoises, that he preferred to fight in the open.

I parted from de Passy ; I went on with Everard and Gomorrah and his men to help in the building of the tortoise. Numbers of our people had been busy upon it for days, laughing and joking as they plaited and wove wattle and withy and reeds into the form of a giant shell, as they sewed thick hides together and covered the dome of the shell. Men from Sussex and Norfolk, from Worcester, from the Welsh border and the Western shires, together with tanners from London and carpenters from Aylesbury, plied their trade about the tortoise. I found Giles shaking a man of Pershore by the hand. Wolf Honeybun was his wife's third cousin, he told me with a beaming face. I attached myself to Giles and to the man of Pershore. Meekly, since I knew nothing of wattle-weaving and basket-making, I did as I was told. I went on to stretch hides and assist in stitching them into place on the light woven frame with leathern thongs. The tanners worked silently, long laces of leather hanging like moustaches from their lips, rough steel needles from Alyncestre occasionally in their mouths. We laboured side by side as King Richard would have every man do when need arose for the Cause, esquire by tradesman, crossbowman by esquire. We worked on, silent at last, against the dark. When the light failed, we stitched and plaited by torchlight until the work was done. Mounted on long stilts like legs, the tortoise of our own making appeared ready to go on tiptoe, elated as any ordinary tortoise is at the coming of spring. The last hide stitched in place, the last cord tied, our men seized hold of the stilts, the creature moved forward, with slow, uneven yet remorseless motion, a tortoise indeed.

"How if the Turks use Greek fire against us, master, and against our machine ? " Giles, who was standing beside me, asked. He had always an inconveniently inquisitive turn of mind.

I did not know. I, too, had a dread of Greek or any other fire. The master carpenter from Aylesbury answered us stoutly : "Sirs, these hides are soaked in vinegar. For twelve days we have soaked them and dried them in the sun. The fire of the Turks is nothing but nitre and bitumen and sulphur." Nothing but that ! I thought. "Vinegar and good hard ox hide will master it, see if they do not, sirs," the man said. He spoke proudly and confidently. I watched the monster as it moved off unsteadily into the dark, the torches casting their sooty shadows over its vast domed sides, our men, half-naked and red like demons in the light of the flares, thrusting it slowly on.

"Master," Giles persisted like a child, " my grandame, God rest her soul, for she was a great liar, was burned in her own thatch. I like not the sound of that Greek fire."

The tortoise, sadly rent and torn, had served its purpose. The assault, only half-successful again, was over. Our men rested still, sprawled everywhere in attitudes of sleep. A few cried out ; most were silent ; the wounded died quietly. In all the camp only the harlots and the Turkish women who had sold themselves for bread, moved abroad. It was almost night : the waves of heat shimmered to a blue rim ; upon my right a black cone of flies clung quivering from some gobbet of flesh hung on a skeleton tree. After the din and the tumult, everything, except for Everard muttering in his sleep inside my tent, was still. But from the near distance we could hear the reverberating thud of the stones hurled without pause by our stone-casters against Acre's walls.

I turned. I wished to say to Everard that I loved his talk better awake than asleep. I said nothing ; I laid my head upon my knees. I felt a fever in my bones ; my skull ached still from the crack my helm had taken from a Turkish mace during our assault upon the Accursed Tower. We had fought all day from the first coolness of morning to the last heat of the sun ; our miners, tunnelling all day and half the previous night in the shelter of the tortoise, had broken down part of the curtain wall of the Accursed Tower, the Tour Maudite, only to be surprised and conclude a singularly friendly truce with the Turks, who, tunnelling under them, suddenly, like so many rival moles, appeared. At the last moment all the esquires in one body had stormed the walls, each man intent upon bearing away one of Acre's stones. From the shelter of the tortoise King Richard himself, wrapped in a silk counterpane, had directed our attack, and had shot many an arbalest into the ranks of the Turks crowding upon the battlements. It was a war, I think now, of ants and moles. Against the walls, so dense, so thick with towers, and so impregnable, a man was nothing, a thing that clung, that scarcely cried, that fell and was crushed and died, his fellows, like other ants, swarming over him. In our assault Everard climbed the scaling ladder behind me. It was well for me that he did so, for when I was almost felled from the Turkish mace blow he held me up and guided me down to safety. In this manner, like the hero I was not, I spoiled the encounter for him and for myself.

Fighting, as ever, was fiercest around the Accursed Tower, the cornerstone of Acre's walls. That fallen, the great right angle of the outer wall might be pierced and the way lie open to the heart of the city. The Accursed Tower overcome, the eleven remaining towers might be surprised. It was to the defence of the Tower, therefore, that the Emirs Mashtoub and Karakush, who were in command of the Turkish garrison, directed their best men and the greater part of their strength ; it was here also that King Richard's stone-caster, the Bad Cousin (called, some men said, after the French King), was placed. All day long, and all night also, the Bad Cousin hurled vast stones of Sicily, which King Richard had brought specially for this purpose from Messina, against the breach our miners had made at the base of the Accursed Tower. But the walls were stout and half our missiles fell away like hail, bruising only our own men and the ground. As fast as one set of stones were dislodged the Turks from within the walls replaced them with others again. So the wall held, and the Accursed Tower stood, as firm as though the Evil One had indeed spread his black wings above and shielded it from all calamity. At one moment we did in truth appear to be within sight of victory. Our last desperate assault, led by the Lord Bishop of Salisbury himself, reached the battlements. Our men fought upon them sword to sword against the Turks, only once more to be forced back by the multitude of Turkish defenders to the scaling ladders. The enemy upon the Tower resisted this last assault—last, since none was to follow—upon their city like men who no longer have their lives but only Paradise to lose. We might well have returned to the attack had it not been for the Greek fire that the enemy directed upon us, that burned our men and blinded them, that destroyed the scaling ladders, that was like a curtain of flame set between them and safety. The fire seared our flesh and scorched our eyeballs ; the horror that it bred lived on behind our eyes. I rested, the assault over, my head upon my knees, but still the jets of fire sped towards me with strange hissing serpent sounds. And every jet of flame, I felt, my body shrinking, my soul dumb and waiting, was for me.

When part of the wall fell earlier in the assault, Gomorrah and many of his men, who had left the shelter of the tortoise the better to discharge their arrows upon the Turks, fell also. In my mind's eye, I saw again the wall doubling outwards, like a slow fist clenching, as the supporting beams many feet beneath the soil's surface were first undermined, then burned away. I saw the bulge of the wall open like a vast clenched hand, and the men in the deep ditch beneath looking up, silent and unmoving, as if the wall were indeed the hand of God turned against them. I could hear the rush of the masonry still, and the fall of the stones, see the vast uprising cloud of dust, hear the cries that were so weak by contrast, that presently trailed off into silence. " Master," Brand said, coming to me after the battle, " God has smoothed Gomorrah away with his clenched hand." As he spoke the tears made clear channels down his blackened cheeks.

Everard woke and stretched, and rubbed his eyes, and Ambrose and Richard the Chronicler came in.

The Chronicler sat down and, spreading a roll of parchment upon his knees, began to grumble. There was not, he swore, a good quill pen to be had in all the camp.

Robert arrived next, a fever of excitement, for all that he tried to be calm, plainly to be read upon his face.

" In four days from now," he announced, " Acre will be ours with no more shedding of Christian blood, without one more assault upon the Tower."

We stared at him.

The Chronicler shook his head slowly and incredulously.

" Holy angels," Robert declared, " have appeared to our men and foretold this. Even yet a radiance, which is surely sent by God, lights the place."

The Chronicler asked very soberly and carefully to whom this vision of angels had appeared.

" To John Jenkyns and Taliessin Edwards of Hereford," Robert replied, " during their watch not an hour ago at sundown on the Saracen side."

When no one spoke he challenged us quietly. " Do none of you credit the vision ? "

I kept silent. Ambrose was judicial. " I do not believe or disbelieve," Ambrose said. " After battle, with a great desire in his heart and the sun in his eyes a man from Hereford may see a great deal."

" We may not always believe what we see," the Chronicler said.

Robert appealed to us a second time. " Will you not judge for yourselves how miraculously the light still lingers ? "

We left the tent. We looked, as he directed us, across to the Saracen side of Acre's walls. The moon was rising and sharply bright and every stone cast its separate shadow. In the west the sky had indeed stayed strangely light, and in the hollow where the sentries had stood a faint radiance did in truth tremble and burn. While belief strove with a faint incredulity in our minds the sound of drum-beats came to us from Acre's walls. They were not loud, but steady and insistent, a disturbing undercurrent of sound we both feared and knew. While we watched two figures, grotesque as vultures and straddling like them, appeared. First one, then the other, then both together began to leap and posture upon the Accursed Tower. It was not a dance we witnessed so much as an incantation with gestures, a prostration to evil and all evil powers. The drum-beats quickened and the two figures leapt in frenzy then like the priests of Baal. We shivered, we left the Saracen witches, two dark shapes prancing against the bright moon, and came in. A low keening rising to a sharp pitch reached us from the Tower. Though we shut our ears against it, it continued. But so, reassuringly once more, did the repeated thud of our stone-casters, silent this half-hour past, against the walls.

2

STRANGE ENCOUNTERS

THE weather did indeed change with us after our assault upon the Accursed Tower. Christian prayers prevailed against Saracen incantations : Acre was ours and the witches also, and prophecy and promise alike were most wonderfully fulfilled.

The morning of which I write was cool yet ; rain, almost as blessed as the surrender, had fallen. The plain before us was thickly patterned with flowers ; the sun, like the women of the country, showed all the fairer for being veiled. Captain for the first time of our foraging expedition, I was well pleased with myself and with all that I could see of what lay ahead. Brand and Giles rode one on each side of me ; half a dozen mounted men-at-arms followed. The world, I felt, was good to me ; I resolved, ridiculously, to be good to the world.

I turned my horse, therefore ; I avoided the hollow of the plain and the tents of the Saracen prisoners. I had no wish to appear to gloat upon their captivity, or to disturb their prayers or the many ablutions enjoined upon them by their prophet Mahommed. I saw numbers of them moving, as men in captivity must surely always move, without purpose or haste, about their encampment, the wind fluttering their shirts (all other garments in the interest of safety having been taken from them) as it had fluttered them on the day of their surrender.

I turned, therefore, from the rough track that skirted their encampment and headed my small party towards the north. The surrender of Acre was indeed over and my bout of fever with it. From the sick solitariness of my tent I had seen little of the events of that day and all that had preceded them. But the little I had seen was memorable enough.

Once more all that I had witnessed that day returned to my mind. I heard again the shrilling of the trumpets and the many sharper cries, the deep voice of the host, like hounds baying, and the mad rush past the half-open flap of my tent of many hundreds of pairs of feet as our men went in.

All day until afternoon the clangour and the sounds had gone on until the air about me seemed as full of noise as hell, men say, is full of pain. The hysteria that flourished in Acre that noonday had gripped me at last : the trumpet sounds were lightning flashes across my sky ; the confusion I could see and feel was like the storm. I sat up in my bed ; from a new height of fever I cried out, though why I cried out, since I was in no danger, I do not know : " Deliver me. Lord God, deliver me."

Presently Robert came in. He sat down and leaned his head upon his hands, his sword-point upon the ground. " So much killing is not Christ," he said, " nor Christ crucified." Taking up his sword, like a man dazed and almost blind, he had gone out into Acre again.

On the next day, or perhaps on the day after that—precisely when I am not certain since time during those forty-eight hours was stretched to an unconscionable length for me—the truce between King Richard and the Sultan Saladin was formally agreed. For the first time the clangour and the fighting ceased within the city ; against a background of silence the Christian host moved in. I heard different sounds then—in imagination, as I rode on, I heard them again—the creak of harness, the rustle of cloaks, the sound of heavy bodies swaying in steel saddles. Until my sight blurred I had watched from my bed the passage once more of innumerable pairs of feet. All day it seemed to me they passed. As our men moved in to Acre so the two Emirs, Mashtoub and Karakush, and their garrison of six thousand Saracens came out.

I rode on between Brand and Giles and, as I did so, in imagination I could hear again the thwack upon the ground that day of the ends of the ropes which bound the Saracen prisoners lightly, man to man, and the shuffle and pad in the sandy track of their naked feet ; I saw again the fluttering of their shirt tails. They were of linen, I remembered, of fine woollen cloth also and of coarse hemp ; they were both foul and clean. I should never, I thought, glimpse again so many legs : the thin, the stout, the crooked and the straight. All that day, until my eyes grew tired of seeing them, they had passed. Afterwards the choirs of the host sang their *Te Deums* : never had I heard sweeter singing. Almost it was as if by praising God men thought to wash their hands, and their minds also, of the blood that had been shed. Afterwards quietness and peace seemed to take hold of all the camp ; and presently, through the quietness, I heard a small wind blowing. It was then that Robert came to me a second time, and once more looked out of my tent. " This wind is like the breath of God," I heard him say. Then he also had grown silent.

I came out of my thoughts and was brought sharply back to the matter in hand and to myself. Brand's voice spoke in my ear : " Master, we are moving directly out of our way."

I turned to him. " What of it, if there is forage ahead ? "

" It is not safe, master. We move towards enemy country." He spoke obstinately.

" Well, have your arms ready. We will not be ambushed," I replied good-humouredly. I looked at the men. They were ready ; they had not waited for any word of command from me. Surprised and vexed, I rode on.

Giles, who was often no better than an echo, must support Brand with a near-tragical story of a forager called Nicholas of Colchester who looked up and spied a band of heathen horsemen waiting for him and his party— they were as motionless, Giles declared, under their grove of olive trees as if each one of them carried a bird upon his head.

I cut Giles short. This was plain country, I said, and unsuitable for an ambush.

Plain country it was when I spoke. It soon ceased to be so. Our track led presently between low dusty hillsides pitted with white stones. Greener country appeared to lie beyond. We pressed on towards it, therefore, for our forage bags were still no more than a quarter filled. Suddenly we were brought up short. Three horsemen faced us in the narrow track. The hills came sharply down on either side at this point ; the track doubled as sharply out of sight. Certainly it was no place for an encounter.

We took stock, I suppose, of each other. To my eyes the strangers appeared peaceable enough. Their leader, a slight figure in a white robe, from the black hooded cloak that he wore and the black caftan appeared to me like a learned doctor or teacher in the Arab schools. One of his attendants I took to be a Syrian. The other was a monster to dream of. His skin, black as sea-coal, was dusted over with a soft bloom. One round eye stared threateningly ; his other he had parted with, I judged, long since, for now only a loose flap of lighter skin hid the empty socket from the world. The white-robed doctor, if indeed he were a doctor, carried nothing more deadly than a scroll ; the other two were well armed with sword and dagger, and each, which surprised me for a moment, carried a small but useful axe at his saddle bow.

Their leader bent his head courteously to me as if in greeting. He was not young for all that his skin showed so smooth. Both beard and hair were white. I asked him as courteously as I could his name and errand.

He answered me in Arabic ; the Syrian gave me his words again in smooth Norman-French. Gamel el Din, I understood, a learned doctor from Damascus returning to that city, together with his secretary Hakim and his black slave, Abdul. " Sir," the Syrian asked, " do we go in peace ? "

The old man's eyes, watchful, far-looking and bright, held mine for a moment. I hesitated, then spoke quickly, for I did not wish to be thought lacking in courtesy. " In peace," I said.

I would have made way for them, but Brand said in a loud whisper : " Master, you should question them now if you will not hold them for questioning."

The sergeant of my party differed stoutly from Brand. " Best press on, sir," he said, " so that we may be back before sundown. Our Lord King Richard needs forage for the horses more than three peaceful travellers."

While I hesitated, and still did not make way, the stranger's two attendants moved forward almost imperceptibly so that they stood a little in advance of the learned Gamel el Din. They were three to our six, but we were lightly armed and cumbered with forage bags, and the advantage of the ground lay, I thought, with them. Their leader spoke again, and once more the Syrian translated his words. " Do we in truth go in peace, Sir Knight ? "

" I am no knight, as you can doubtless see," I answered, " but an esquire. And I think you carry a good store of weapons for peaceful travellers."

The learned doctor answered me meekly, with lowered eyes. His Syrian translated quickly : " My master says, ' Sir, there are brigands, as you must know, by the way.' "

Brand interrupted unwisely again : " Master, I think that you should question him."

I drew to one side. " In peace, since I have promised it," I said.

" Then peace be with you." Master Gamel el Din bowed courteously. The three of them passed me close and in silence. The Nubian left behind a reek of musk, the learned doctor a faint whiff of sandalwood. Sedately, in single file, they rode on.

I thought they swayed stiffly in their saddles as they went. " They wear armour," I said.

Brand reproached me. " Then they cannot be peaceful travellers, master."

Full of doubts of myself, I rode on. King Richard gave right of passage to peaceful Moslem travellers, I knew. And my mission, I told myself again, was to bring in forage, not prisoners.

In order to resolve my doubts I sought out Sir Hugh de Winton on our return. The old knight's judgment was a model of pith and clarity. He said, puffing out his mouth and his moustaches as he spoke : " You have yourself borne witness that this stranger was no ordinary traveller. For that reason and because you were impressed by his bearing you allowed him to pass. For that reason you should have detained him."

I said : " Had I done so, I should have left half my men behind."

" We are here," Sir Hugh answered, " if need be, to be left behind." From chagrin I could not speak.

Old Sir Wisdom said : " Do not a second time be so overcome by chivalry. Is it not enough to have one Lord Richard in the host and one Sultan Saladin among the enemy, the two of them for ever exchanging gifts and courtesies ? "

I left Sir Hugh, my new-found pride in myself thin as an Easter wafer again. When I related what had passed to de Passy, whom I met on my way to my tent, he shook with laughter. " You act the part of a simpleton and publish the fact. What an honest simpleton you are ! "

While he still mocked me and I defended myself, Melisande's Syrian-born maid sought us out. She was as soft and purring as a cat, and almost, I felt, as kind. She looked from Guy to me, then to Guy again. She addressed him at last, mincingly : " Master John of Oversley, my mistress sends word : ' Will her friend speak with her ? ' "

I corrected her ; I took her message and answered it again. I turned to de Passy. " The Lady is in need of comfort and so am I."

There was an edge to his voice when he answered. " You will not find it together, I think."

He and I agreed to meet that evening outside the royal palace of the Sultan in Acre, where Queen Joan and her ladies and Queen Berengaria also were lodged. From the palace we would go on to see what we could of the city and the harbour and the Tower of Flies.

I rode out to the palace at sunset that same evening. Brand insisted on riding out with me and afterwards upon returning alone.

" Those white daisies are abroad, master," he informed me. I looked at him. He had grown lean in Acre ; the leanness suited him.

" White daisies ? " I said.

" Those men in white, servants of the Old Man of the Mountains," Brand explained.

" I do not believe it," I told him.

Brand persisted : " Master, it is true for all that it was Giles that said it."

" What other tales are current in the camp ? " I enquired.

" Many tales, master. That the King of France will leave King Richard and the Cause and will take half his men with him and leave the smaller and better half behind with the Duke of Burgundy. It is armourers' talk, master, and cannot be denied."

" I do not deny it," I said.

" Well, the French were never our brothers though they called themselves so," Brand declared. " Master, these French are like children who play ball together : they must always be first or they will be nothing."

" Messire Ambrose has penned a few lines on the matter. Do you ever speak verse, Brand ? " I asked.

Brand, as well he might, looked astonished. " Only on feast days and holy days, master, or when I have mead taken and there are catches and ballads sung at The Bright Star, at Alyncestre."

We were waiting our turn to cross the foot-bridge into Acre over the deep ditch which we ourselves had dug under Acre's walls. I had time, therefore, to recite Ambrose's lines on the departure of the French. They made a poor jingling sort of rhyme and are not worth the quoting here.

Brand was certainly not impressed. "If I were at The Bright Star now I would not leave it till morning light," he said.

Once over the foot-bridge we could scarcely speak for the renewed din of mallets and hammers, and the thud of gravel and stones, and the shouts of the masons busy re-building Acre's walls, those walls which we had spent so many men and so much labour upon breaking down. We rode on, and presently Brand said again: "After Acre, master, what then?"

"Why, Ascalon," I answered confidently. "But, first," I added, "the Sultan Saladin must keep the terms of his truce with King Richard. He must deliver up the true Cross, and the seventeen hundred Christian men whom he holds prisoner, and he must pay the two hundred thousand gold besants he has agreed to pay."

"Ah, and if this Sultan does not?" Brand wagged his head. "Then I reckon it will be for King Richard to say what he will do."

"It is certain we dare not wait long in Acre if we are to press on to Jerusalem before winter," I replied. "All the host knows this, and Saladin knows it also. It is possible he may fail to keep the terms of his treaty and hope by doing so to delay our march upon Jerusalem. But Saladin cannot forget, I think, that we hold three thousand of his men as hostages. Whether he will put the lives of the hostages first, or the delaying of our armies first, I do not know."

"There is comfort in not knowing, master," Brand declared. "And in being nothing, as Brand and Giles are, for no man will ask Brand and Giles to decide anything."

"You would find comfort everywhere," I said.

The Royal Palace stood in the centre of the city and all roads led to it. We turned in to the city by the ruins of the Accursed Tower. Here, remembering Gomorrah, Brand crossed himself and fell silent. Among the ruins the flies and carrion birds were busy; great purple butterflies gorged with rottenness sunned themselves upon the stones; here and there a broken fragment of armour thrusting up out of the dust and rubble glittered in the light. Already many plants—among them the deadly nightshade, small sun-baked roses, henbane—were beginning to flourish among the waste of stones. There was an odd silence, I thought, about the tower as of a dead and finished peace.

We rode on into Acre itself between blind and shuttered houses, down narrow twisting streets, past defaced Christian churches not yet consecrated anew, past Moslem mosques recently and horribly defiled. The sunlight was hard white on the cobbles; the shadows were folded and black like bats' wings over the hot stones. We passed a cool alleyway; at one end we glimpsed a courtyard, saw a fountain playing and the faint sway of flowers; outside a slit window, as if it sang in Christian fields, a caged lark sang in a dusty shaft of light. We paused and looked up: from somewhere within the house a woman laughed, a small tinkle of sound; as we moved on we heard the different tinkling of a lute. We passed the fine houses of Pisan and Genoese merchants, at their back a huddle of foul streets. There the buildings jostled together; the alley-ways were dagger-thin and dark. In the gutters all the filth and ordure of four years of siege lay piled, all the wastage of four years of war. Herds of fierce and fattened swine grunted and rolled among the stinking heaps, and mongrel dogs hunted in packs or, from a safe distance, bayed like wolves at all those who passed by, or themselves made war upon the packs of jackals that, numerous as the swine, thronged the streets and fed on refuse too. We fled these streets, full as they were of plague and every kind of death. We went on. From the shuttered houses unseen eyes looked down on us; from shadowed doorways men watched as we rode by: the city brooded and sulked, I thought, unsubdued still, and swelter-ing in its own reek and blood. The sun was falling; the wind that had blown freshly from the sea dropped suddenly, and now the unmoving air seemed so packed with evil as scarcely to be breathed or borne.

With the onset of the dark all Acre, like a wood at night, became stealthily alive. Men appeared in doorways; shutters were opened covertly; from the battered Christian churches came a clang of broken bells; from the Saracen camp, faint but unmistakable in the stillness, came most impres-sively the Moslem call to prayer.

The King's Standard floated from the palace roof; Hugh the Brown, who had been with us in Cyprus, was the captain of those that kept guard. I spoke to him; I told him my errand. He was pleased, for this was an off-duty moment, to make a number of jokes. I bore with them stiffly. Hers, he informed me finally, was the garden room by the inner courtyard. I sent Brand on his way and thanked Hugh the Brown—though he deserved no thanks—and went in search of the Lady Melisande.

I had no great relish for my role of comforter; I was in need of comfort myself and the Lady—I suspected it already—was no easy one to console. Amaury de Montfort—the same pretty youth who had acted as old Sir Wisdom's messenger to us from the King at Vézelay—danced forward on his toes to greet me. " Another gallant ? " He paused in astonishment. " I swear the Lady has more callers than any in the Court."

" I do not care for your oaths, child," I said.

" Child ! " he repeated. He halted his dancing steps once more and stared at me. " Why, you have no beard either. And from all that I can see, no quarterings of a knight for all that you are pleased to be so very formal to-day." He danced on ahead of me once more.

"How many callers has the Lady?" I asked when once more he paused and pointed the way.

He bowed, he flourished the corners of a short square-cut cape as he did so. "One every half-hour, may it please you, sir Hairy-One, and two for the quarters." Before he could be cuffed or caught he ran off.

I called after him : "There are not so many gallants in Acre."

He halted. "They are not all gallants, Sir John. There is one "—with his two hands he described in the air what I took to be the girth of Fitzgerold—" and one "—here he made a pretence of pulling at a short beard—" who is even greater." With that he turned a handspring on the tiled floor and was gone.

I passed, as I had been directed to do, under an arched doorway screened by a Persian hanging to Melisande's garden room. She sat in her swan chair, a Book of Hours held slackly upon her knees. Her kirtle was of green, her gown of yellow, embroidered darkly with small fleur de lys and quaint strutting birds. Her hair was held in a gold snood ; her shoulders and half her bosom showed rosy-white and bare. Her hands out, she came towards me and the Book of Hours, as if it had been no more than an apple, fell forgotten to the floor.

"I came because you sent for me," I said, "but I am in no mood to be so very comforting."

She scanned my face. "Why?"

I said : "If you must know I do not love myself or this land of Outremer. And I am beset by perplexities. Besides that, I am out of love with a lady who treats me as if I were a eunuch or her uncle."

She clapped her hands and appeared delighted with my wit, and straightway poured out red wine of Banias for us both, and gave me Turkish sweetmeats of sugared almonds and frosted rose petals to eat.

My mouth full, I continued violently : "Here I can do nothing creditable ; in this place it is as though any judgment I might once have possessed has left me." I went on to tell her of my bouts of fever, of my failure at the Accursed Tower, of my error of the morning and of Sir Hugh de Winton's rebuke.

She held her cup of wine in her hands and looked down at it. "Only Aziz has remained the same, and to-day even he began to mope and change. Isambeau sees visions as long as her grey stockings ; William is angered with me and with the French. ' Let us go on to Jerusalem alone,' he says, as if Jerusalem were a boar in a not very far-off thicket. The King has changed also. His temper grows altogether too short." She looked at me. "He has torn down the Austrian standard that the Duke

Leopold set up on Acre's walls—it is true the Duke had not earned the right to plant his standard there—and he has kicked the Austrian standard-bearer, which he owns himself now he should not have done, into the deep ditch."

" Then the Austrians will leave us also," after a moment I said.

Melisande nodded. " William the Marshal says so."

" You have seen William the Marshal?" I stopped short. I remembered Amaury's miming of a tall man with a great girth and a short beard.

" What Abigail the Shulamite was to King David I might be to the Marshal, if I wished," the Lady said.

I spoke bluntly. " Why have you sent for me?"

Melisande set down her cup of wine. " Because I will not marry him."

" Which of these two great ones will you not marry?" I asked patiently.

" Gavin Fitzgerold. Whom else?" she said, wide-eyed.

I was brief. " Then do not marry him."

She pressed on swiftly. " Already he commands me. I must cover my bosom and live in Essex. What is Essex?"

I looked at her gown. " It *is* flaunting," I said.

She gave me a quick sidelong glance of wickedness. " I would have it more so, if I could, in order to anger or perhaps to dissuade him."

" It would not dissuade him," I said.

She went on. " He would have me leave the Court and live quietly with his lady mother in a house outside the town. And when I am with child—already he has arranged so much—his lady mother will conduct me by slow stages to that slow sluggish spot Essex." The lady paused once more and flourished a hand. " Pleasure is destroying me, my brothers say. Therefore I must be preserved from destruction by a long servitude and frequent doses of a little sharp pain."

" Your tongue runs away with you," I observed.

" Because I am not modest?" she asked quickly. " I think modesty in women," she said, " is something invented by men to balance their own shamelessness."

I moved away.

" What shall I do?" She took a step towards me. " Even William has turned against me."

" All the Court envies you," I said. " Why should anyone help you?" Almost at once I relented. " You must speak to Queen Joan," I said, " or to King Richard. Or you must fall sick, or go into a nunnery."

" I was never sick in my life," she answered, " except at the thought of Fitzgerold. And Queen Joan listens only to Isambeau, who listens only to her visions. And they have told her that I need correction and morti-fication." She waited. I said nothing. She turned plaintive then.

" Isambeau has never loved, me, John." She paused. " The deaf," she said, " are jealous of all the world and love no one."

" Do not flit about so in your mind," I said. " Could you not speak to King Richard ? " I asked.

" He is sick," she replied, " and thinks only of William. Yes, that is true." She put a hand to her cheeks and flushed suddenly. " And Queen Berengaria, poor lady," she hurried on, " weeps and prays all day, ' Holy Mary, sweet Virgin, give me a son. Let me give my Lord Richard a son.' Poor soul ! I pity her."

She stopped short. Her body held in a sudden stiffness, she looked past me.

I turned. Even before I did so I knew that Robert faced us there. I heard Amaury's feet running away and spoke jealously. " You sent for Robert also ? "

" Robert ! " She moved a step towards him, her hands fluttering, her face aflame. Clearly once more she had no eyes, no ears either, for me.

Robert looked from the Lady to me, then back again. He spoke slowly. " Why have you sent for us ? That you might be assured of our love and comforted because of it ? What can we do ? Do you not grow more important daily as your brother grows nearer the King ? What torment would your vanity deal out to us who love you ? " He came nearer her. " Leave me, I say. I am not for you, nor even for myself. Already I have put you one remove from me. In time the rest may follow. I think you are part of all the beauty of the world, and I have loved you. But now I have finished with the world. So leave me, I beg of you. It is I who beg, Melisande, it is I who am still your suppliant. Leave me. For a little while we deceived ourselves. Then it was as if after desert country a man comes suddenly upon a flowery place." He paused.

Wide-eyed she looked at him.

He said : " Forgive me if I speak harshly."

" You are dedicated," she said, her voice quiet.

" I am tormented," he returned.

I saw hope struggling for a moment in her face.

He spoke gently again. " I left all that I had ; I lost the greater part of what I loved ; I forsook all that I knew of duty to follow the Cause. I cannot change now."

She shook back her head in sudden pride. " When did I ask you or any man to desert the Cause ? "

He said : " A man cannot love Christ and possess the world."

Melisande pleaded with him. " Why must we deny life in order to love God ? There is only the one love, only the one life."

" Once I thought so also," Robert said, his voice quieter by far than his words. " Now I see only the soul's life. To each one his own life, his own light," Robert said. " But the soul must live." She turned from him. He spoke gently a second time. " I do not speak arrogantly as one who knows. I do not know. I am tormented even yet. The world does not go suddenly from one's sight like a stag over a hill."

He waited. Her shoulders—she had turned from us both—moved as if she wept.

Robert came nearer her. " If I had my arms about you," he said— and now he seemed to me like a man thinking desperate thoughts aloud— " I might change again."

She came close to him ; she laid her arms about his shoulders. " Then change," she said. " I will be everything to you, or I will be nothing for your sake."

He stayed stiff, not speaking but looking down at her, then slowly, with an air of finality, he disengaged himself. His voice queerly aloof, he said : " If you had loved me you would not have tempted me, you would have done as I wished."

He left her then.

Bitter and unbelieving, she looked after him.

" Could you not have left well alone ? " I asked. " He is half yours still."

" He thinks only of his soul," she said, " and not of me."

I began scolding her. " There is a streak of no feeling in you."

She looked at me coldly. " If you knew more of women you might be glad, messire John, to find a woman capable of coldness. It is, after all, only a spice of reason in an otherwise unreasonable creature."

I retorted : " You have learned altogether too much."

She turned quiet, and while I wondered how I should take my leave she spoke again, a hint of desperation in her voice : " I, too, have no choice : this way is not possible for me ; that is closed. What if there is only one way open ? "

I shrugged. I had grown tired of the conversation. " I do not know what you mean," I declared.

" I must submit or turn wild," she answered. " That is what I mean."

She was wild enough already, I protested. " I am sorry for Fitz- gerold," I said.

She gazed indignantly at me. " He can beat me and drag me by the hair to his bed as the first King William of England dragged his Queen, Matilda. He can ravish me lawfully and shut me up in an iron girdle, and imprison me and take my life away. And you pity him ! "

I remarked impatiently that it was far from certain that Fitzgerold would do any of these things.

She stared again. Then, very deliberately, she sat down and hurled first her slippers, then the cup of wine, then the dish of sweetmeats and, lastly, looking quickly around her, the Book of Hours, about the room.

I stood still under it all. When she had finished I said again : ".I am indeed sorry for Fitzgerold."

She grew thoughtful. " I think," she said, " I am a little sorry for him too. Pray, hand me my slippers," she requested, " dear John. I did not mean to throw them."

I was stooping like a fool and picking up her slippers when Fitzgerold himself came in, and once more Amaury slipped away.

Melisande straightened. She held one slipper in her hand ; her hair was loose, her gown had slipped from one shoulder. The two of them faced each other.

I said stupidly : " My lord, we were tormented by a bee."

" Yes, a bee, my lord, a bee." Melisande curtsied, snatched her second slipper from me and fled. I thought she shook with laughter as she fled·

I looked at Fitzgerold. He returned my look as pleasantly as if he would vomit Greek fire at me. I bowed ; I excused myself. I left him also.

To my astonishment Everard was waiting with de Passy at our trysting place at the corner of the Rue de la Boucherie.

He was airy and brief. " I called at the Palace but the Lady could not see me ; I did not mind that greatly. Afterwards by chance I met de Passy. Now I would come exploring with you if I may. I hope I am welcome."

" Most welcome," Guy said, somewhat dry.

Bogis' cap was tasselled and on one side ; his hair was brushed and shining ; he looked, I thought, as he always looked, too big for his clothes and too young for the world.

We rode off. I laughed at Bogis. " Why call on the Lady if you were so indifferent ? "

" I called," Everard said, one hand to the tassel of his cap, " about a palfrey the Lady wished to buy, a grey palfrey called Amour."

" Sir Ralph d'Issembourne's palfrey," Guy put in. " Sir Ralph," he explained, " who lost all his possessions at backgammon and fled to Saladin."

" And returned," Bogis laughed. " And was forgiven by King Richard and fought at Acre. And played backgammon again ! "

" The camp is full of madmen," I declared. What answer Everard or de Passy made I do not know, for in the next moment we had entered the Rue de la Boucherie. Here I could not help but clap a hand to my mouth and keep it there. I have always been blessed with an acute sense of hearing and cursed by as keen a sense of smell. The two exist together and depend upon one another, the physicians say. However that may be, the stench of the Rue de la Boucherie, a thick, foul stench of offal, of rotting lumps of dead carcases, hung heavier than a November fog in the air. The odours of the mean streets behind mingled with the reek of the slaughter-yards. Evil matter oozed from the stones of the houses, thrust up in place of plants between the rough cobble stones. All the scum of the west had gathered in this quarter of Acre : brothel keepers and pandars, harlots and murderers and thieves, and the traitorous of all nations, men and women who had changed the skies over their heads but not their skins. I had smelled and tasted odours innumerable in Dover and London, in Messina and in Cyprus, and not a few in Oversley ; I had tasted none so rich as these. With a sick head and a heaving stomach I began to think I would prefer to be anywhere rather than on my way to the harbour and the Tower of Flies. Even Bogis by this time had his cloak over his mouth. Only de Passy rode loftily erect as if the foulest of all foul smells were only something more to be despised.

The Tower of Flies stands apart from Acre upon a narrow spit of sand partly enclosing the harbour and running out to sea. In front are the tides of the Great Sea ; behind the Tower a stone causeway links the spit of sand with the city walls ; on the other side the waters of the harbour lie, shark-infested, and thick with a slowly-coiling, evil-smelling slime. Below the Tower is the rock where in ancient times bloody sacrifices of bulls and oxen were made to the old gods, and the entrails of the slaughtered beasts cast as offerings upon the stones. Although sacrifices are no longer offered upon the rock, the Tower and the spit of sand around are still a rendezvous of evil and a place of blood. And all about them still can be heard the buzzing of innumerable great flies.

The buzzing reached us before we arrived at the causeway ; it swelled as we drew near. If the Tower was a place of evil, here was the voice of evil itself, I thought, menacing and dull, a ceaseless drone. Though the moon shone fitfully elsewhere, here by the Tower the sky was all but dark from the vast multitude of flies. I looked down into the waters of the harbour. In the scant light they moved like writhing water snakes, and as they moved the dark shapes of dead bodies, thrown there for secrecy, tumbled and rose, and sank and rose again. As I watched an arm tossed up as though it lived still, a whiteness showed that might have been a face. And after these tumbling bodies came the still gluttonous sharks, invisible except for the dark ripple of their fins. Under the shadow of the Tower a hyaena yawned, an almost human sound.

We dismounted and crossed the causeway in silence. Shadows of pillars, shadows of clouds lay across our way ; shadows of unseen things lay upon other shadows between the upright stones. Though we walked three abreast I confess the blood beat in my ears, my hand sought my dagger's hilt. Where the causeway joined the harbour wall the attack, which I had been half expecting, came. I saw the white robes, the red girdle of which I had dreamed, heard the greeting, " Hail, master ! " saw the uplifted arm. The fellow looked at us, then turned instantly ; before he did so I was aware of the sudden downward movement of de Passy's hand.

The scuffle, heard rather than seen, that followed among the shadows under the wall bewildered me for a moment. Two figures, the stranger and another, the latter round as a tun and heavier, in a robe of dabbled scarlet, were at grips and rolling over in the foul slime that at this spot hid the sand.

The affair, of momentary duration only, was so like all that I had heard and imagined of the sect of the Assassins as to appear unreal ; the issue, after the first second of the Assassin's failure, was never once in doubt. Already the stout fellow had the white-robed stranger by the throat, and, kneeling upon his chest, was shaking him to and fro and bellowing in a voice I vaguely knew : " Know, fellow, you are mistaken. I am no other than myself."

Bogis caught him by the shoulder. " Can you not see your man is dead ? "

" Ah, is he so, master ? " The stout fellow looked up stupidly, though without relinquishing his hold.

Once more I saw the bald egg-like pate and dark fringe of beard of my madman who, at our first meeting, had declared himself to be the King's spy. " Hail, friend ! " I greeted him.

" Well met, sirs," he said. Looking down at the limp figure between his hands he remarked with a foolish kind of cheerfulness : " These fly-by-nights, like cats, are hard to kill." As though unwillingly he loosed his hold and scrambled to his feet. " He's dead now, sirs, as you say. He has finished his hail-mastering and will wear no more red slippers. If it had not been for the fear o' the moment I had kept the life in him, for I could have preached Christ to him then. But it is all one to him now. He will burn in hell and salaam to the prophet Mahommed at the third gate of Hell and never know better." He turned and blinked small cunning eyes at us. " This fellow believed I was Ferdinand of Lisbon and first cousin to the man that wronged him."

" You are fooling," I said, " and we cannot stay here."

" Can we not, lordling ? " He looked impish for a moment.

I halted him sharply. " If you value your life you will come with us now."

"If I value my life!" The fellow roared with laughter. "I am to come with you if I value my life!" He roared again.

"Quiet," I said roughly, for other figures were stepping out from the shadows, coming a pace or two forward from the side streets, and halting, then advancing again.

"These Assassins are reported to hunt in couples." Everard spoke calmly. "I cannot think," he said, "why one of the Old Man of the Mountain's followers should attempt the life of so insignificant a man."

Ferdinand of Lisbon, if that indeed was his name, answered eagerly: "When I was well and truly mad I declared I was Bernard, the King's spy."

"Are you not mad now?" Guy asked.

"Why, no, sir. But this lordling"—here the fellow touched the dead body with one foot—"while he lived was, I am certain, most truly mad. And so, I take leave to say, young sir"—here he addressed de Passy—"are you."

"Why are you here?" Guy asked again.

"Truly, I do not know, lord," the man said. "Except that I do love to see the big fish come up and eat their prey."

"We waste our time." Everard moved on impatiently and de Passy and I followed.

"Food for fishes," we heard our fat friend shout. "More food for fishes." While we watched he caught up the body and ran with it a little way and hurled it into the waters of the harbour. He made as if he would come with us, then suddenly sped on ahead. As he did so a second figure in white came out of the shadows and fled before him.

We mounted our horses and rode on by the same way we had come up the Rue de la Boucherie again. Drabs enticed us from doorways; lights and music beckoned to us from flung-back shutters; a small night wind blew, stirring the smells as thickly as the current of a stream stirs the water weed, drawing off some part at least of the swarm of flies that had followed us.

I did not speak. Everard also kept an odd silence. Our thoughts, I knew, were busy on to-night's affair. Look at it how we might, it could not be interpreted as yet. Too much lay in the identity of our fat friend, and that, I told myself, might for ever be in doubt. Faithful to my rule, I did my best to dismiss the matter from my thoughts. And yet, like the affair of the pigeons, it returned unreasonably to my mind.

We were back at the Accursed Tower. Everard, who had begun to whistle softly to himself, broke off and asked: "Where is our fat madman now?"

"Food for fishes, it is likely," Guy said, an uncontrollable impatience in his voice.

Once on the plank bridge that spanned the ditch we parted, de Passy riding towards the Burgundian lines, Bogis and I to the English camp.

Everard spoke simply. " I would not swear it, but I think the first Assassin took the movement of the Frenchman's hand for a sign."

" Did not his hand move to his dagger ? " I asked.

" He moved his other hand," Everard said.

All the uneasiness I felt showed, I think, in my voice. I said hastily : " Once more it can be nothing."

" Once more ? " Everard questioned.

I stayed silent. From loyalty to de Passy I had not yet spoken of the affair of the pigeons. From obstinacy, more than for any other reason, I kept silent once more.

3

THE MANY VOICES

IT was quiet beyond the eastern ditch and from the flat roof-top of the King's palace at Acre little or nothing of the morning's work remained to be seen. Spent with fatigue the last horsemen passed ; the Saracen cavalry had retired once more into the hills. Of all that we saw of King Richard's slaughter of the Saracen prisoners on that August evening I remember only fragments now. The sun had set, not appropriately, as one would have thought, in flames and fire, but coolly, in pale colours of rose and grey. Beyond the green of the plain the desert was washed in shadow ; where all the fury and stir of the afternoon had been two clouds of red dust hung motionless like fiery witnesses ; the wind had left no more than faint marks of all the footsteps and the trampling in the plain.

What happened earlier that day was behind us, part of the evil which even the holiest war must leave behind. We talked little upon the roof-top of the palace, we rested our bodies and, even more, our minds from the many voices that had clamoured a little while ago. They were not yet silent : many of them, I felt then, might never be silent. I was wrong. Time, like shoes of felt, deadens even an echo in men's minds. I lay on my stomach looking out over the huddle of Acre's roof-tops to the arena and the hills and the bare mountains of burning red beyond. Beside me Melisande and de Passy played a game of draughts ; well removed from them, as if Robert had arranged it so, Ambrose and Robert, with what appeared to be a more than ordinary absorption, played at chess, while

Everard and Richard the Chronicler, their heads together, conned the latter's manuscript line by line. Said Everard : " I do not know what this record of yours would be like for accuracy without me, Chronicler." I heard the Chronicler reply humbly, and Everard, even more grandly, say again : " I am no scribe, but I believe I can catch the drift of things plain enough. If I met the devil I should recognise him even without his tail."

At any other time I should have laughed ; that day I had not a gibe left in me even for Everard ; I remembered too much of what had gone before ; I remembered it too vividly. Though Robert might say, " It is Mahommedan truth against Christian truth, their Cause against ours," I was unconvinced. Robert and I had argued the case back and forth on our way to the arena and before that. I went over our argument again in a sick fashion in my mind. " Three thousand prisoners at least for the sword," I heard myself say. I heard Robert answer me : " Already we have waited three weeks beyond the appointed time. This Saracen delay is a trap Saladin has set for us and pity is the bait. Would you sacrifice all we have won so far to pity ? "

It was most true. But still I had not been able to put pity out of my mind. It was, I agreed, all the more difficult for King Richard to be merciful since matters were moving not too fortunately for the Cause, since King Philip of France, as rumour had declared he would, had sailed for home, leaving behind him a fistful of pie-crust promises and half his men under the command of the Duke of Burgundy, since moreover the Marquis Conrad of Montserrat was back once more, playing now the fox and now the wolf in Tyre. For all these reasons it was most true that we could not burden ourselves on the march to Jerusalem with a host of prisoners whose ransom should have been paid three weeks past. I was aware of all this, and yet my mind continued to echo de Passy's mind : the killing of the Turkish hostages, I told myself, would be held against King Richard for ever.

Throughout the morning the King had consulted with the captains of the host. We had been told nothing of their deliberations ; yet as the hours passed we knew, as surely as a hill shepherd knows of rain, that Saladin would delay us no longer. The morning advanced and we remained uncertain still of what was to come. Whispers, like small desert winds, blew hotly here and there. We discounted them. When the King sent his tents to the pits at the foot of the hill Ayadiyeh, from which the Saracens had withdrawn only a few weeks before, expectation of the slaughter that was to come, sultry enough until then, reached thunder heat. All the host that were free to do so, most of the pilgrims and many of the priests flocked above the pits and stayed motionless there, like crows·

Between them and Ayadiyeh the prisoners' encampment lay. From them there came as yet no sign. They stayed within their tents, or moved slowly under the sun like half-dead flies. Two miles from Ayadiyeh, to the south, on the hill Keisan, the watchers in the Saracen army waited also. From Ayadiyeh it was possible to glimpse their movements, catch the glitter of their round shields. Between the tents of the King and the distant Saracens an empty stony plain, the arena, lay.

Robert and Everard and I, Brand and Giles following, were the last of the esquires to ride out to the hill. Ambrose strode before us in his brown gown; the Chronicler, a roll of parchment inevitably under his arm, scurried beside him like an old woman or an eager mouse. In the general atmosphere of excitement the camp dogs, wolf-like, ran here and there, tongues out, panting; the camp idiots, of which there were not a few, ran beside the dogs and slavered also. Only the camp washer-women, bending over their wooden wash-tubs, and the old dames busily picking out lice from the heads of the pilgrims, appeared unmoved. In all the camp the fires smouldered untended, the spits did not turn; only the teams of water-carriers bringing water from the River Belus, like burdened ants, laboured heedlessly to and fro. Small moving figures could be seen on the flat roof of the palace from our post on the hill Ayadiyeh, and the King's Standard flew mast-high.

Screened by our horses we waited on the hill top. Just after noon the King and all his knights rode out from the tents and ranged themselves in a deep circle of armed and mounted men around the plain. It was all done silently, without heralds or trumpeters, and the crowd that waited stayed silent from expectation also. A movement among the Saracen prisoners in the encampment could presently be seen. I remember once more the flutter of their shirts as they moved, and how, their ankles bound, they shuffled awkwardly in the sandy dust like ungainly birds. No one hurried them. Their guards walking beside them, they came on at their own pace into the plain. And the knights waited patiently for them also.

The work of slaughter, begun just after noon, was finished just before sunset. It was too much for rejoicing or triumph; even horror, I think, was dulled. I know my mouth grew parched, my vision blurred. Every one of us who watched from Ayadiyeh was moved differently. Guy turned peevish. The King was not wise to show so little pity, he declared. Later, a silver scented pomander to his nose when the wind turned, he complained that the arena was too small and inconvenient for the task. Everard, his face heavy and flushed as if he had overeaten, watched sulkily for a while. Then, flinging himself down, he turned obstinately away from the spectacle. Once in momentary dizziness I trod upon him. Not cursing me at all, he said: "How cunning is Saladin! Either way

159

he injures us and the Cause." As if the King's eyes were on him, Robert stayed motionless. What ecstasy of faith or horror held him I do not know, nor, since he spared himself nothing, what conscious hardening went on in him of mind and will. His face, white at first, grew patched with scarlet, his lips tightened and grew thin. Brand, good Christian soul, prayed Christianly, his hands over his face : " Lord, ha' mercy upon them, poor miserable sinners."

It was all done at first as silently, I say, as if it had been night, for the Moslems, seeing death so close, died quietly.

Only at the last a great flurry and stir was to be seen among the Sultan's men on the hill Keisan. Presently, to a hammer thud of hooves and sharp clanging cries, we saw the Turkish horsemen wheel out of their olive groves and ride breakneck into the plain. Part of our men turned to meet them. Since, by King Richard's orders, no one of less than knightly rank might take part in the day's work, we mounted and almost indifferently came away.

I stirred. Only half returned to myself, I looked at Melisande and de Passy.

Melisande's voice broke in upon my mood. " Take all my kings. Take everything." Flushed and as though overwrought, she faced de Passy. Their game was finished, it seemed. " I cannot win," she said. " Are you content ? "

" Not yet," he said, his hands busy about the draughtsmen, a gleam lighting his face.

Melisande turned to Robert. " Could we not have music now ? To-night for the first time in my life I do not love the dark."

Robert refused her courteously. " Forgive me."

Servants brought flares in bronze sconces and lit them about the walls.

Everard leaned earnestly upon his elbow. " Lady, what is it you would have us do ? What is it that you desire ? "

She moved her hands restlessly, then held them still. " Indeed I do not know. I am restless and you think me strange. I think that I could weep. No doubt the pagan wives weep too, they have a better cause and love as much. To-night I grieve as when the deer were slain in our great park. They died as these men died without a sound." She looked at us. " Until I came to Outremer I did not know what courage was. I did not think there was so much valour in the world." We looked at her ; we did not speak. She said : " It is as if in suffering men knew themselves and felt their strength. Men grow tired, I have heard, of little things, and love, I think, is a little thing."

De Passy leaned towards her and spoke softly : " No. Love is a very great thing."

Everard said obstinately : " Even yet I have not heard what it is, Lady Melisande, that you desire."

" Why, I desire happiness." Somewhat tremulously she laughed at him. " And you, messire Everard, what is it that you desire ? "

" The same," he answered, " though normally I do not deal in words." He turned abruptly towards the Chronicler again.

The Chronicler enquired : " What choice would you say King Richard had, except to do this evil ? "

" What is it that you call evil ? " de Passy asked. He leaned on one elbow. " I am always asking the same question, and no one answers me."

" Evil," Ambrose said, " is one of the great tides of the world."

" There are two words of which I scarcely know the meaning," Everard said. " No, stay, there are three. There is this word happiness, and there is this evil and this good of which you speak. I would take all things squarely, happiness and unhappiness, good and evil, as they come."

" Except that they come not squarely." De Passy spoke softly again.

Melisande turned to me. " What were you thinking, messire John ? "

" If you must know," I answered, " of primroses."

" And I of lilies." Robert looked at her. " I saw them in a sanctuary cut off from me, in a window of bright painted glass." He moved one of his chessmen. " Why do we speak of flowers ? I was thinking also of a music that I used to hear on mornings before the birds stirred, as if each morning were the first morning of the world. Though I listen and wait, I do not hear it now."

" I also have heard it," Ambrose said.

Guy observed softly once more : " Messire Robert of Kinwarton is a true poet, I see."

" I had forgotten you," Robert said.

He got to his feet. I followed him. He bowed low to de Passy, very low to Melisande. She gave us each a hand ; she did not speak. I think she went that day upon the razor edge of love : a word, a touch would have swayed her mind. None came. And she must be in love always ; she must turn from one man to another ; she was one of those who could never wait.

Robert and I had gone only a little way towards the camp when I remembered I had not my cloak with me. On returning for it I found Melisande and de Passy alone. Her hands were on his shoulders, her face was raised to his. " Do not ask me. I will not. I cannot," I heard her say. When they saw me they stood apart from each other quietly. Not one of us spoke. I could not see my cloak nor the Syrian waiting-maid either, though she had not left us once before that night. Cursing silently, though my cloak was of good Norwich camlet and proof against even the rains of Outremer, and sent me by my mother out of her egg-money through John Pilgrim of Oversley, I left without it. I was to lose more that night of commodities I had no wish to lose : a little of my new-found peace, a part of my good name and half at least of my attachment to de Passy.

Together again, the night cool about us, Robert and I rode back into the camp. On the outskirts we paused. Once more we could hear the heralds and the trumpeters crying to-morrow's orders throughout the host. We listened. " Know ye all," we heard, " know ye all, lords and knights and esquires, and all ye, King Richard's faithful fellows, to-morrow the Lord Richard will set out to march by the Forest of Arsur, to Joppa, to Ascalon, and, by God's providence, to Jerusalem. Make ready, therefore, with burnishing of weapons and all gear, with ten days' provender for the journey, and with cleansing of your body's sins and with fervent prayers. . . . Amen. Amen. God give us all good ending."

The host, every man bareheaded and upon his knees as we were also, took up the cry : " Amen. Amen. God give us all good ending."

Though the trumpets had sounded for to-morrow's march another and very different summons awaited me. When I was in nothing more than my shirt and struggling with it, Amaury de Montfort appeared again. He stopped short in the midst of a yawn and, gazing at me in amazement, said : " Holy Virgin ! Never have I set eyes upon a more ape-like man." Having ducked to avoid the shirt I threw at him, he delivered himself further. Old Sir Wisdom demanded my presence and I was not to be surprised if the *Melek* himself (*Melek*, it must be understood, was the Turkish word for King, which was much in vogue at this time among the fashionables of the camp) were there also. " If I were asked," Master Amaury de Montfort added—he was, I had discovered, some poor cousin to the great Earl of Leicester and protected by him—" if I were to be asked, Hairy-One, I would say you were certain to meet trouble, though since you have so simple a look and no doubt a simple and an honest heart also "—here he removed himself nimbly out of my reach—" you will probably receive no more than a trouncing."

I found old Sir Wisdom much changed since his stay in Outremer. Before he had been like a bull in his bellowing prime ; now his curly front locks were grizzled, his large frame fallen in. But his eyes, even if they were more bloodshot than I had known them, were still as watchful and intent.

He was not alone. The King was there in a blue and scarlet robe, his bare feet thrust into curled Turkish slippers. Beside him, in small body armour, stood William des Préaux. He appeared as stiff as an effigy and more uncomfortable. Another figure whom as yet I had no time to observe waited, withdrawn a little into the shadow on the other side of Sir Hugh.

The old knight himself questioned me. He did so in an odd snorting fashion, for the dust of to-day's work had given him a thick November rheum in his head. "You have been much in the company of an esquire to the Duke of Burgundy, de Passy by name. What do you know of him?"

"He is my friend," I said.

I resolved at once to speak the truth in every way I could. At the same time I decided, since I had kept silence so far, to say nothing of the affair of the carrier pigeons. I told a great part of all that I knew of de Passy; among other things, that he was landless, that he described himself as of no country.

Sir Hugh cut me short. "What else?" And the lean fellow whom I had not observed closely yet and whom I took to be one of King Richard's spies, came forward a little way into the light.

I said: "De Passy's words are always stronger than his actions. I have never known him less than dutiful." I was pressed to relate what de Passy had spoken of the killing of the hostages. I told them flatly what he had said. I added boldly: "He said the King was not wise in what he did since posterity would blame him."

King Richard nodded moodily. "That is truth, not treason." He leaned towards me. "Would you vouch for him?"

I hesitated. "Sire, he is my friend, though we have come near parting more than once. His ways are different from mine; often I think he is no better than a stranger to me."

The King looked at me. "You would shield him even if you knew him to be disloyal?"

"No, sire," I said.

Sir Hugh said curtly: "Then tell all you know."

I remember that I felt a coldness and a separateness about me as if indeed I were suspect. I remember that my cheeks, for all that I was cold, burned. I told of the incident by the Tower of Flies. "No man could swear to anything," I said, "in so deceiving a light."

The lean fellow stooped and whispered in the King's ear. I burst out then, for suddenly I was afraid: "Sire, de Passy is unknown and penniless. I cannot believe any man has bought him for favours or for gold."

"Will you keep watch on him?" the King asked, his face grave.

"If you have proof, sire," I said. I sweated now.

"We have no proof; we have suspicion only," the King answered. "If we had proof we would not question you."

Old Sir Wisdom stood up at a sign from the King. He addressed me. "You will keep all this secret?"

I promised him. I was stricken and confused; I scarcely knew what was demanded of me or what I said. I made my obeisances; I thought there was silence as I left, broken by a sudden buzz of words.

Old Sir Wisdom followed me out and spoke to me like a brother. "You are simple. You have the makings of a fool in you, as I, Hugh de Winton, had at your age. But I was schooled. King Henry and Arch-bishop Thomas à Becket o' Canterbury schooled me. There you might see two minds," the old Knight said, "two lions, two serpents. They matched each other though they were without their match in Christendom. Now you, John of Oversley "—he halted a foot away from me—" have you told all that you know?"

"All that resembles fact," I answered. I remembered the affair of the pigeons. I had not spoken of it, and yet it might appear larger to the King than the incident by the Tower of Flies. But still, from obstinacy once more and from fear also, I did not speak of the suspicion I had had of de Passy then, that I had still; I related only our talk of Jerusalem and of Saladin.

"He is a cockatrice, that one. And so," Sir Hugh added, " is the Duke of Burgundy." He came on with me another step or two. " We have word of this Frenchman or of one like him. This one will be watched. And you also, John Simpleton. Take care, therefore, that you watch yourself. The King has more eyes and ears than God gave him and so has Saladin." He came nearer me. " What said this Frenchman of no country and no faith of the Marquis Conrad?"

I was able to answer truthfully that de Passy had said nothing of the Marquis. The old knight appeared reassured. He clapped too heavy a hand on my shoulder. " If you are ever a fool, run from your folly, boy, like a ship before a storm. For though the King is merciful he will often have no mercy." Shaking his head a little, Sir Hugh left me.

How I ran from my folly and paid for it too I have still to tell. My folly would have been less had I been content to ponder all that I had heard. Instead, in order to straighten out, as I thought, the confusion in my own mind I must seek de Passy. I had no intention when I sought him of speaking of my interview with old Sir Hugh and the King; I wished only to see and talk to him again. In the light of all that had been suggested to me, something, I felt, must show of the kind of man he was.

I made my way in hot haste to the Burgundian lines. I know I blundered and stumbled as I went; I know the moon was harvest-full and red, that a mist crept along the track, that the camp before me was lit by flares and as busy as if it were day. I passed long lines of men waiting patiently by the camp ovens for bread for the journey ; further on, the camp washer-women were stringing out the last shirts, the last leg wrappings ; not far off a priest, a hedge priest he seemed to me, sat cross-legged upon a stone, busily writing upon his tablets messages for wives and mothers and sweet-hearts of our men. He did this for something colder than charity, for a pewter dish heaped with coins waited beside him. Further on, within the French lines, a cock crowed lustily—no Frenchman, I told myself, would be without his fowl in a pot. As I went on I could smell garlic and cloves and hot frying oil and the sour lees of wine. If I had been blind I think I should have known I was in Burgundy.

Without warning I thrust my way into de Passy's tent. What I saw drove all good sense and all remembrance from my mind. He was stand-ing sideways to me, a carrier pigeon between his hands. Quick as an adder he turned about and confronted me. As he did so the bird let out a soft, confiding, domestic " Cu-curr-u." De Passy laid a hand over its beak.

My throat was once more dry, my anger so hot suddenly I could scarcely speak. I forgot caution and secrecy. I said, and took a step towards him : " And I have just been asked to vouch for you ! "

As I spoke his face changed ; I think his whole body stiffened and changed. " By whom ? Do not answer. I know."

I came nearer him. " I believed you before. I cannot believe you now."

He spoke carefully. He lied, I was certain. " This fellow," he said, and began to fondle the bird, " came to me from Tyre."

" That nest of treasons ! " I said.

" The same." He looked steadily at me. " From Ralph Pierrepont, my friend, a good Frenchman, but one who is sick for France and waits at Tyre until he may return."

" Why should he send to you ? "

" Why ? To test a good bird. For what other reason ? " De Passy kept his eyes coolly on mine.

" You swear it ? " I could hear the obstinate pleading in my voice. " Will you swear by the True Cross ? "

He did not answer me. He said : " I shall not die by hanging, do not think it."

I had pleaded with him, I realised, when all my better sense told me to stay masterful. I turned masterful again. I said : " You must kill this bird also."

We stared each other out. I made myself remember the Cause, my promise, my own folly and my own safety. By a small margin I won.

He moved away from me and the bird. " Never vouch for me again."

"I did not vouch for you," I said.

Incredulously he stared at me. I think we hated each other then; I think that the attraction we had once felt towards each other served now only to sharpen our hate.

Having killed the bird, I dropped it on the floor of the tent. "How these birds beset me!" I said.

De Passy burst out then. "You meddling fool! You fools, you utter meddling fools!" He was so beside himself he appeared incapable of more than the one or two reiterated words.

I could not prevent myself from triumphing over him a little again when I left. "Bury your bird," I said. "Bury it deep."

Not until the night air was cool around me did my fears return. I had, I realised too late, been several times a fool. I had broken my word to old Sir Wisdom; I had conveyed only too ample a warning to de Passy. I had done all this without wishing to do so, out of unpreparedness and weakness. I had no feeling of triumph, nor of pride in myself left when I reached my tent; I was conscious only of doubt and misery. A problem worse than any I had encountered so far lay unresolved yet in my mind. Though with all my heart I feared what he might do, I could not bring myself to move against Guy de Passy. I did, I think, what most men in a similar case would have done, I postponed decision, I took refuge in to-morrow.

From to-morrow, though I did not know it, chance or my own secret self led me gently on. I slept soundly. To-morrow I was for Arsur, I believed, and afterwards, if I lived, for Joppa and for Ascalon.

PART FOUR

THE FOREST OF ARSUR

1

THE RIVER OF CROCODILES

JOPPA, whither the army was bound, lay eighty miles away, under the hot August to September sun. Between lay all the armies of the East, all the pride of Syria, Mesopotamia and Egypt under the command of the great Sultan of Egypt, Saladin. Perhaps it was as well that we in King Richard's army thought little of the immense forces arrayed against us, little of the difficulties ahead. We thought scarcely at all, I believe, in that first excitement of our march, unless it were of Joppa which was reported to be very pleasant, and of our goal which was Jerusalem. For all that our time was short we took, not the inland road which led more directly to the Holy City, but the coast road the Romans had made along Acre's white sands. As we came by sea so we were fed by sea, and wished to return that way. In order that our armies might continue to be supplied without danger, King Richard, I think wisely, judged that the coast and the ports must be in Christian hands before we could safely turn inland towards Jerusalem. We who rode or marched with the armies understood the reasons for the King's decision, but the pilgrims, like children, like the Children of Israel, murmured and complained : " Why Joppa ? " " Why Ascalon ? " " Have we not come over the Great Sea to march to Jerusalem ? "

I heard a band of pilgrims complaining in this fashion. Their leader, a stout fellow, had a butcher's knife at his girdle and was gnawing in a practised manner at a beef bone. " Mark my words, fellows," he said, " the captains and the King go to Joppa to win riches and ease for themselves. And for why ? The merchants of the City o' London sent them. For the merchants are as greedy as maggots in offal for the riches o' the East. I hate 'em," he declared. " I know them. They learned me my trade, or a part of it. Oh, the May bugs in velvet, the furred black beetles, the weevils ! " He might have gone on through all the catalogue of creeping things if I had not fetched him a buffet on the side of his head. " Weevil yourself," I declared, " that you eat away the trust and faith of other men." And picking up his beef bone which was sweeter by a hair than I had feared, I whacked him soundly across his leathery buttocks. " Know," I said, " that if we take Ascalon we cut off the road to Egypt and all the source of his power from the Sultan Saladin." Before the fellow had time to recover his wits and pounce upon me, in which case I might not have fared so well, I was mounted and gone.

We moved out from Acre towards the river Belus on the first stage of our journey before the sun was up or the mists cleared. We were three hundred thousand men, all told. I waited beside Sir Hugh de Winton where the road curved out towards the Belus river from the camp : together we watched the army pass by. When the esquires, riding in a body, rode past, Sir Hugh cried out in an odd cracked voice, startling me : "This is the very flower o' the world's spring."

I did not answer him : my conscience and not the spectacle of the flower of the world's youth, of which I was one, troubled me. I had supposed I would keep company with Everard and with Robert. But this morning Sir Hugh had sent for me again. My place, he said, was to be by his side. By his side, therefore, I was, chafing and miserable, but keeping, I hoped, a wooden face. While I waited de Passy himself rode past beside his Burgundians. He went by with an unseeing air. I watched still while the King's Dragon Standard, flying from its tall central staff, passed on its wheeled carriage (which the King had ordered to be made specially for the march) drawn by four grey horses. I had looked for Robert and Everard in vain among the esquires : I saw them now. They rode with the Normans and Englishmen beside the Standard in the most cherished place. Where I, John of Oversley, might have been, Brand and Giles rode without me.

The foot soldiers followed. There were many miles, it seemed to me, of plodding men. Those that came first carried no burdens except their arms and provender ; for armour they wore round or pointed steel caps and shirts of mail, and over their shirts of mail thick jerkins of grey woollen felt of Gloucestershire or Ghent. They passed, and after them, rumbling endlessly, came the baggage trains and between each baggage train companies of loaded infantry. I pitied these. Loaded higher than pack-horses with tents and gear, with sacks of flour and salted pork and bags of beans, with spare weapons and fuel for the camp stoves, theirs was indeed, I thought, the greater burden and under this sun the greater suffering.

I spoke to Sir Hugh. Sucking his two front teeth, he said : "On King Richard's orders one half is to fight, one half to carry. The foot soldiers will take turn and turn about with the baggage-bearers. To-day it is the turn of these men whom you see ; to-morrow of those who have passed." The arrangement seemed fair enough. King Richard—for the moment I had little love for him—was, I confessed, almost always fair. I prayed that if need arose he might be fair to me.

Sir Hugh and I continued to wait, for what I did not know and did not care to ask. Two figures approached us, cavorting on their steeds like yokels on a fairground or mummers performing their play at some feast.

At sight of them Sir Hugh muttered, and I stared. Ambrose and the Chronicler drew near. Their mounts, two mules called by the camp muleteers Jacob and Esau, were well-known. Together, like many married couples, they kept each other sweet ; apart, or when the fit took them, no twin devils could equal them for rages.

I greeted Ambrose gaily ; he bowed to me in as stately a fashion as if he were the late Baldwin, Archbishop of Canterbury. The Chronicler, all hung about and rattling with parchments, was too shaken to offer any greeting.

Last of all, shabby as Christmas geese that have been too long upon the roads, the camp washerwomen passed. One less solid than the rest gazed at me. I glimpsed goose-grey eyes in a pale squarish face under a wide flopping hat such as pardoners wear, and a bunch of many-coloured petticoats. I waited while Brand, who had returned, I did not doubt, to speak to me, addressed her : " Good Agnes, are you not from Alyncestre, from the Tavern of the Needlemakers in the Malt Mill Lane ? " I heard Agnes answer him slurringly between her teeth, as good Alyncestre folk do, something about her grateful remembrance of gifts from good Master Brand of fat lamb's tails and sweet pig's chitterlings—all of which, I reflected, should have been mine. Somewhat guiltily after that, I thought, Brand turned and spoke to me : " Master, if you are to be elsewhere than with the Standard, I would be with you." To-morrow or the day after, he should be with me, I told him, if Sir Hugh de Winton would allow. Sir Hugh did not answer. " To-morrow, then, master," Brand said very steadily.

Somewhat comforted, I watched him go. I might pretend that to be with Sir Hugh was a distinction : Brand, with that keen sense he had, had guessed differently. Presently the King and William des Préaux and a number of knights and notables appeared. It was plain that I was out of favour, for though every one of them greeted Sir Hugh, not one, excepting William des Préaux—he was as loyal to his friends as he was brave and pitiful—tossed a look towards me. It was a far cry indeed, I thought, to the boar hunt in the woods of Vézelay. I held my face impassive ; I kept back my tears. Together with Sir Hugh I rode, though at a great distance, behind the King.

That night we camped beside the river Belus ; after a halt of two days, we moved on in the cool of the morning again towards Caiaphas. It was late August, the country ahead of us arid and burned. The flowers that had made wide tracts of colour on every side when we came to the country were fled, but the larks, small tame creatures with crested heads, still sang as high. The fleet sailed beside us all the way : we could see the tall masts, the pennons, the crimson sails, hear the oarsmen singing to the beat

of their oars, catch the sound of their voices through the wash of the waves.
No army marched in better order, no march was ever more carefully
planned. We filled all the narrow coastal plain from the white sandy shore
to the bare foothills of the mountains, where Saladin's army waited motionless as vast drifts of darker earth, to the olive groves where his mounted
skirmishers wheeled and darted on their long-tailed Arab horses, swift as
sticklebacks among the shallows. Our army moved in three great columns,
the ranks of men so closely set scarcely an apple could be thrown between.
Next to the sea, for ease and safety, went the baggage trains and with them,
as porters, went one half of the infantry. Next came the mass of mounted
knights and men. In their centre the King's Standard rode. As the
lantern on the King's ship had been our signal by sea, so now the Standard,
held aloft by timber baulks in its carriage of wood, was our rallying-point
by land. Around it, as I have said, were grouped the Normans and
Englishmen. Of the mounted knights, the Templars rode first in the van ;
the Hospitallers held the rear. On the side nearest the enemy, next to
the mounted knights, the rest of the infantry marched like a protecting
wall, while the King and a chosen company of knights rode up and down
the ranks, watchful alike of the order that we kept and of the movements
of the enemy.

I rode with Sir Hugh de Winton on the coastal side with the baggage
trains. At first all went smoothly : the clouds were high and piled, the
Saracens, while they watched us from the hills, still kept their distance ;
a cooling wind blew. Our men had set out warily ; they turned merry
now and marched to their own singing. They sang, not hymns nor chants
nor even snatches from the Lays of Antioch or of Bohemund, but tavern
rhymes and catches, senseless but encouraging somehow for the men's
minds and feet. I marvelled they should be so gay. Until a little while
ago the world to them had been no more than a field of strips they knew,
a haystack or a cluster of hovels by a stream. For them strangeness, as
if they were children in the dark, had been their greatest fear. Strangeness
seemed banished now that the enemy and the occasion also waited for
them. It is true that the mounted knights were the spearhead, the battering ram—a man may choose what metaphor he will—of the army ; but
all our fortunes hung upon the steadiness of the foot soldiers. Every man
in the host knew, and Saladin and his emirs knew it also, that if our ranks
could be divided, our order of march broken, then indeed the army and
the Cause with it were lost. So I told myself, riding like a page-boy on
horseback up and down our lines in Sir Hugh de Winton's wake.

Presently the road narrowed, and for some distance became almost
impassable on account of the dense hedges of prickly thorn that here grew
some twelve feet high. Unavoidably at this point the line of our march

thinned and lengthened and spread out over the plain. In order not to be jammed helplessly in the narrow way the knights waited for the foot-soldiers to pass. They passed in safety ; the baggage trains followed while old Sir Wisdom and I beside him waited anxiously on the far side. Before our men had time to re-form, the Saracen skirmishers were upon them like a cloud of stinging flies. The men of the baggage trains, who had no weapons with which to fight except their fists and the burdens that they carried, were overwhelmed, their baggage scattered. It was difficult in so narrow a way to give help to them or warning to the rest : in less time than it takes to write, half our men were fighting, manfully indeed, but without order or discipline. Once more a stir could be seen among the Saracens upon the hills as Saladin prepared to pour in upon us an even vaster body of his mounted men.

It was at this juncture, so perilous to us all, that I was bidden with Robert Fitz-Luke to warn the King. I read Sir Hugh de Winton's thought : I was to be trusted, or partly trusted, since Robert Fitz-Luke rode with me ; I was to be tested also. It was I, on old Sir Hugh's horse, not Fitz-Luke, who warned the King. I came upon him riding slowly in the rear of the mounted knights, out of sight, out of hearing also of the danger we had encountered ahead. Without ceremony I gave him my message : " We are caught in the narrow way and the enemy are coming down upon us from the hills."

I have become a man of peace since then : in quiet I have had time to see what Robert saw first and forgot and saw again before the end, that there is something contrary to Christ in this slaughter of one side by another in war. But since wars must be fought I would have all men fight as King Richard and the men behind him fought that day, with irresistible might. For the Turks were scattered by the King's charge, our line re-formed, and our march went on. I followed ingloriously on foot, for old Sir Hugh's horse had dropped under me. He had suffered much, poor beast, from the scant fodder of the Holy Land. No doubt, I thought, before he died he dreamed, if horses dream, of greener fields.

At Caiaphas, where we camped for two days by the cisterns, I sought Everard and Robert. If I was not yet in favour I was no longer in disgrace, but free to come and go as I pleased. As I approached I heard Bogis speaking softly to his lizard, Jeroboam, under a grove of date palms. The leaves made gentle shadows ; the lizard winked its triangular black eyes upon a round stone. " Would you leave me, mommet ? " Everard asked and touched the creature with a grass blade. " What is it that draws you ? A fine cranny in a wall, or the fat fleas of the Saracens ?— even our fleas are lean. It is not for fair red and white," Everard continued, " no, nor for a flower-tinted face——" He stopped short ; he looked owlishly at me. " Whose face ? " I teased him.

When Robert came up he asked me over-carefully if I were still with old Sir Wisdom ?

" By my own choice, now," I said, and felt my confidence dwindle as I answered, my spirits turn leaden again.

Bogis walked back to my tent with me. " Why did you shield de Passy? All the spies in the camp are watching him."

" I care not," I answered. Though I was on the way to being pardoned I remember now how I stood there between the sand dunes and the sea and felt a sick loathing of everything within sight ; I remember how I turned away and with what bewilderment Bogis looked after me.

From Caiaphas we moved on round Mount Carmel to the House of the Narrow Ways. We passed through mountainous country, over roads winding steeply round the rough faces of the hills. The Saracens retreated as we advanced, yet always, when we camped at night or paused by day to rest, we could see them posted between the river gulleys or about the hillsides. A man had need of the stoutest courage to remain unruffled under the watching eyes of so vast a throng. They retreated as we advanced, and yet with every day's march it seemed to us that while still keeping aloof they drew more near : every day now we could catch more easily the glitter of their armour and the glint of lance heads, hear their trumpets blare with a shriller note than ours, and the quick impatient roll of their small drums.

By this time the sun even more than the Turks was our enemy. We marched only in short stages of from eight to ten miles ; we began early before the birds were up or the grasshoppers chirping in the thickets. Even so the sun outpaced us. Our men, the half of them cruelly burdened, walked in a still furnace of heat between the hot sandy paths and the unkind sky. Tormented by flies, parched by thirst, visited by strange fevers, beset by constant dangers, I think their minds were no longer filled with thoughts of Jerusalem but of the rest ahead. For Jerusalem lay hidden behind the vast cloud of dust through which we moved, beyond the still distant mountains of Judaea.

The road narrowed, as we expected, towards the House of the Narrow Ways. Once wide enough for the legions of Rome to pass to their conquest of Judaea, it was now no more than a winding track between coarse jungle grasses reaching up on either side to more than a man's height, stiffened with tamarisk groves and pomegranate trees grown wild and dense thickets of acacia and prickly thorn. Our men appeared to dislike the jungle that these plants made almost more than they disliked the heat or the sharp stones. To minds disordered by hardship a dread of what was unknown and strange had returned. They feared, among other things, that small legions of devils, summoned by the Saracen witches, waited for them in every thicket along the way. When the acacia trees, smitten by a sudden wind, leaned over and struck them with their thorns they could not but believe that evil spirits inhabited the acacia trees. It is true that wild beasts, leopards and lions moving quieter than the grasses, and small venomous scurrying snakes, inhabited the thickets and molested our men when they could, true that numbers of our men had died from their attacks, or vanished mysteriously.

It did not altogether surprise me, therefore, that at this point in our march Giles should fall sick. For some days he had been haunted by spectres : a lion had leapt out at him from a thorn thicket and roared. " It was," Giles had declared, " as if I, Giles, had roared." He had seen yellow eyes like lamps in the dark ; he had smelled the stench of animals, as indeed had I, more noisome than foxes ; he had even beheld a small brown devil in pointed cap seated on a cushion of dock leaves upon a white stone. " Why dock leaves ? " I had asked impatiently. " Why, to cool him, master," Giles had said. In the end he fell sick of a fever, and raved of the real leopard that had sprung at him that morning from behind an acacia tree, and of all the other spectres that were present in his mind. We carried him with difficulty to the House of the Narrow Ways. Brand wept to me. " I would not lose him, master, for the half of my body." That night Giles raved of leaves and flowers out of which, he said, devils' faces peeped. Robert, whom fasting had made fanciful, brought him Turk's Cap lilies. " Here you may see angels' faces," he said. Giles, who was not far from his right mind at that moment, asked : " Why, then, am I in heaven ? " Robert had lost patience. " No, fool," he had answered and had come away. He was unreasonable, I thought. Giles had small use for lilies or for poesy. He liked his feet on earth, his victuals plain. I followed Robert and said as much.

He showed me the face of a man consumed by his own fires. " Neither devils' nor angels' faces come before my mind. I see only de Passy's face and hers, set lip to lip, like lovers in the moon."

I thought him distracted. I had no comfort for him and no news of de Passy or of Melisande. And I was concerned for Giles. Therefore I turned away. Jerusalem was too far off, I felt ; all that I knew was too distant from me in mind. On an impulse I passed through the jungle of thorns by a narrow track to the other side. The sands here were warmer in colour than Acre's sands and bare. There was not a cloud in the evening sky, not a sail on the sea, for the fleet had fallen behind. I sat down where a trickle of water no wider than my thumb welled up out of the sand. If I had any conscious thoughts I do not remember them :

everything appeared alike to me, and this—I remember thinking so—seemed strange. I waited, then turned my back on a sky that was fading fast and made my way once more towards my tent.

Hardly had I reached the outskirts of the camp than a most fearful din, of trumpets, of horns, of shouts and cries, assailed me, together with dreadful clashing sounds of helms and shields and platters and cooking pots. That the enemy could be the cause of so much noise I could not believe. Nevertheless, from uncertainty more than fear I ran towards the centre of the din. Before I reached the first avenue of tents I was aware of small writhing creatures like tiny serpents shivering away from under my feet. The din increased as I advanced. I passed a knot of men beating wooden poles upon casks. I fell on them breathlessly. " What was all this ? " I asked. They were Genoese. The tarrentes had come, I understood them to say.

I ran on to our own lines, the ground under my feet quick with little leaping things. I collided with Brand. He was most patient under my questionings. " The tarrentes, master. I know not what they are. Small elvers, or little scorpions, it may be. Demons, some say, for they torment us o' nights and come in legions and sting us in the dark."

" But the noise, man," I said, " the noise ? "

" To astonish the demons, master," Brand replied. " Did you not see them go shivering away ? "

I sat down to recover my breath and consider the matter, only to be stung most vehemently. I started up and asked after Giles.

Brand beamed at me. " He is happy, master. Dame Agnes, from the Tavern o' the Needlemakers, has dosed him with a draught of feverfew. He is recovered, master. He is now, he thinks, in Alyncestre, on October Mop night." Brand went on clapping his great hands. " These tarrentes are most crafty demons," he declared, " to know a noise when they hear it."

" This is a land of demons," someone said. It was Richard the Chronicler. His gown tucked up, taper in hand, he trod cautiously about the camp, observing all that any one man could, and perhaps more, of the tarrentes.

The shivering and the creeping over the earth went on until dawn and the din with it. Before dawn I agreed most heartily with the Chronicler.

I think our men never endured more from heat or fatigue than on the next stage of our journey from the House of the Narrow Ways to the River of Crocodiles. The sun rode high in the sky ; the road was strewn with boulders and sharp stones ; a hot dry wind full of white dust blew down upon us from the hills. Worn by sleepless nights and days of marching, their blood full of poisons from the bites of the tarrentes, our men died as they marched and were buried where they lay. Others turned raving and were dragged unwillingly along by their comrades ; others still fell sick and wandered away into the hills, while not a few rested quietly by the wayside, saying they would come later and did not come. The rest went on.

That night we pitched our tent by the River of Crocodiles. On our left the mountains protected us from the enemy ; all around us were monsters and the river. The Chronicler and I stood off and looked at these crocodiles, or, as some have called them, cockodrills.

The Chronicler said : " They spawn once in twenty years."

" Then they spawn well," I answered, for the river abounded in them. Having spoken, I remembered Giles and his fears of cockodrills and went to enquire after him.

I found him more scarlet of face than before and breathing stertorously. But Brand was overjoyed. " He is recovered, master," he said. " A' dreams of pork and steaks. All that you see in him is wine of Banias only."

I looked at Brand. " And you had none ? "

" Two skinfuls, master," Brand replied.

We remained by the River of Crocodiles two nights. On the second night all the army was bathing and washing by the river, foul though it was and full of creatures. Never could the Saracens upon the heights have seen so many infidel white backs and bellies ; never could there have been since Noah and his ark so many astonished cockodrills. The camp washerwomen were present also, looking on admiringly or busily scrubbing the men's bent backs. Robert and Everard and I stood upon the bank and watched, and applauded also, and envied the men.

Sir Hugh de Winton came upon us there. He waved a short dagger and a roll of parchment in our faces. " He has gone," he declared. " God's vengeance upon him ! " The knight overflowed with rage.

Everard took the parchment and read it coolly. " Know by this," the message ran, " you owe me your life."

" Pinned to my cloak while I slept "—old Sir Wisdom flourished the parchment. " Pinned moreover with this ! "—he flourished the dagger. " The Frenchman's dagger," he declared. " Whose could it be if not his ? "

" I know not and I care not," I said loudly.

Now I was to be taken, I thought, and hanged, or put in the ship's hold when we reached Caesarea. With an effort I looked from one to the other of them. " You should all know I have not seen de Passy since Acre nor had any word with him." Since no one answered me, I spoke again wildly. " He had a pigeon he was sending, or so he said, to Tyre. I killed it."

"And did not speak of it," Sir Hugh said grimly. "Though afterwards, ay, afterwards, we learned of it." He left us then.

"I think the Frenchman is on his way to Tyre," Robert said. "I think the Lady Melisande des Préaux will have fled with him."

I, too, thought so. I waited and did not speak. As if from the bottom of the sea I heard old Agnes' voice : "Master Brand, you have the fairest white back in all Christendom, master Brand."

I spoke slowly : "There will be no end, I say, to all this."

2

THE RIVER OF SALT

I HAD seen myself hanged or put into chains. To my astonishment I was not accused nor held ; nothing new came to me as the result of de Passy's desertion. I could only tell myself in explanation that I had all this time been well spied upon and that nothing suspicious had been even so much as reported of me. As if I had never been the Frenchman's friend, had never been questioned and held suspect, I rode with Everard and Robert beside the Standard. Brand, together with Giles, who had flatly refused to go off with the other sick and wounded by ship at Caesarea, were with us ; Ambrose and the Chronicler kept us company also.

Ambrose beguiled the way, which at this early stage was uneventful, with solemn stories of travellers' wonders. He had arrived at his second wonder. I half-listened, half-thought my own thoughts while the host, almost concealed in its own cloud of dust, wound out of Caesarea into the country which Christians call the Level, and Jews the Vale of Sharon. There was a well, Ambrose related, not far off that same country of which he had spoken, where in rainy weather men sheltered under cover of their own vast feet, called the Well of Youth. At every hour of the day it gave out a different sweet odour, and whoever drank of it remained young for ever.

"Who would wish to be young for ever ?" Brand joked. "Sirs, I am one of those who wish to grow old and die wise."

Lastly, Ambrose continued, there was on the other side of the earth the land of Antarctica, where, if the earth were round as many notable sea captains had declared it to be, other men and women lived and laboured, walking step by step with us, foot to foot, yet for ever out of our sight.

"I do not believe these mariners, messire Ambrose," Giles said craftily.

" For if I did walk upon a round great ball like this earth is said to be I should of a certainty fall off. Now why do these Antarcticans also not fall off? And wherefore do we not fall upon each other?"

At this the Chronicler laughed loudly, neighing like a horse as he did so, and Amaury de Montfort, who had paused beside us for a moment, burst in eagerly : " Hairy Sir John, is this tale new to you? I have heard that in the Moslem Paradise a man may have three score wives, and however many times he may embrace them he will always find them virgin!"

" Well now, think o' that," said Giles, open-mouthed.

The Chronicler proceeded contentedly upon a loftier note. " The greatest wonder I, Richard the Chronicler, have heard or am likely to hear is of that land among the far-off stars where there is always peace."

" Well, I have killed no infidel yet," Amaury boasted, " but to-morrow, or to-day, or the day after to-morrow, see if I do not, messire John." Impudent as ever, he sped off, for by that time we were approaching open country where it was likely the Turks would allow us no more respite. So, indeed, it proved.

That evening, spent from the march and the long running fight that we had had with the enemy, we camped beside the Dead River. It was most aptly named, for not only had its waters withered near their source but what remained of them gave out most foul odours. All around were boulders and crumbling stones. Lizards abounded here. Black as the shadows of this bare spot, they peered at us over every large stone or stared unblinkingly with eyes of jet into the full face of the sun. One of them by some subtle message of lizard love had lured away Jeroboam. Everard mourned his loss to the exclusion of all else. " He was here," he pronounced in all the accents of grief, " now he is gone."

On the next day we journeyed towards the Salt River. All that had happened to us so far was nothing to what we endured now ; and worse, we knew, was to come before Joppa was reached. All that day the Turks came at us as we marched in small stinging swarms ; they attacked us in flank and rear unceasingly, keeping step with us all the way. Since we could neither avoid them nor as yet stand and fight them, we were forced to bear patiently the worst they might do. Their mounted archers poured so dense a cloud of arrows into our ranks scarcely five feet of clear ground remained. Attacked from the rear, our own archers turned and walked backwards, discharging their arrows as they walked. I marvel even now at the steadiness with which they fought and their unhurrying pace. For this terrible war of arrows continued from sunrise until nightfall ; it was accompanied by mace blows and sword thrusts and by a dreadful din of tabors and trumpets and drums. The fight was waged on our part by men without food, without water, moving at a snail's pace over uneven sands, in a dense mass of horses and vehicles, under an unvarying sun. There were men—I myself saw them—who had from one to ten shafts in their felt jerkins, and who yet moved on at their ordinary pace. Great numbers of our mounted knights had their horses killed under them and were obliged to march and fight on foot. King Richard himself was wounded by a dart. The pain served only to enrage him the more. Not once withdrawing from the fight, he rode without pause up and down our flanks, cutting into the ranks of mounted Turks and out of them again, his own company following him. We could hear his cry, " To me," " To me," and the knights' answering cries, " Out," " Out."

I rode that day with Robert and Everard next to the Standard. It was strange and somehow quietening to see the black cloud of arrows come before us and the bright sky, and the great banner of blue and gold overhead ; strange to hear the thunder of horses' hooves, and the shrill neighs and those other pitiful sharp cries ; strange and terrible also to see the flight of our own arrows winging back again. There were other more comical sights I can remember now : of Gavin Fitzgerold unhorsed and stumbling and cursing beside the foot soldiers. I remember Brand and Giles astride Brand's scarecrow steed ; Giles rolled wild eyes, Brand had the look of a playful hare.

We camped by the banks of the Salt River that night between the salt marshes and the sea, and once more the enemy withdrew into the hills. We were no more than two or three days' march from Joppa by this time. But as the last ascent is often the steepest so the most perilous miles of all the many we had traversed lay ahead. For between us and Joppa lay the Forest of Arsur, covering the lower slopes of the hills, running out here and there to within two hundred yards of the shore, and stretching for twelve miles, no dense impenetrable forest but pleasant woodland country that afforded perfect cover from arrows for man and beast. Half-way to Joppa lay the River of the Cleft Rock, or Rochetaillie, set in salt marshes again. To the River of the Cleft Rock would be our next day's journeying.

While we ate and rested, we talked a little of the chances of the next day. In places we must pass through the forest. Already rumours, like another kind of tarrentes, nipped at us and disturbed our minds : Saladin would fall on us in overwhelming strength out of the forest ; Saladin would set fire to the trees and burn us as though upon three hundred thousand stakes. We listened in silence where we sat round a smoking fire—kindled not for warmth so much as to annoy the clouds of midges, good infidels, bent upon annoying us. Then Robert, smilingly scornful alike of the Sultan and our own momentary fears, declared : " Let Saladin light his fires, the wind from the sea may well blow them back upon him."

He got up and went away. He was abrupt in manner in these days and grew ever more solitary. No news came to us from Acre or from Tyre of the Lady and de Passy. Though Robert fretted in secret and longed, I believe, to set out for both places in order to discover the truth for himself, with each day's march the two lovers, for so I must call them, seemed to me a hundred years away.

I wrapped my cloak more closely about me. Everard said—he had an odd gift for speaking outside the current of other men's thoughts—" The god of Outremer is certainly the God of Flies."

The Chronicler said, half-laughing at him : " Do not let Anselm hear you."

Anselm, the King's chaplain, was known to be something of a bigot. He hated Saracens and heretics as much as he loved King Richard and would often deliver long homilies to the King, which the latter received penitently, and afterwards forgot, upon his sins.

Bogis asked absently again : " Did they burn the long priest we met at Vézelay ? "

" Joachim ? " Ambrose said. " I cannot think of him except to remember that he stood on his head better than any man in Siena. Yes, they burned him."

" One day," said Everard, " men will grow tired of so many burnings."

" One day," said the Chronicler, " men will grow tired of everything. One day the earth will be very old."

Ambrose spoke broodingly as if a finger of the dead Joachim had touched him. " How old is the earth ? Thinking of Time and Eternity, I myself have grown old."

The Chronicler held up a finger for silence and bent his long head as if he were listening. He heard everything before we did : a trickle of water, the cry of a bird, the feet of a messenger running to us in shoes of felt, the crying of the heralds and the clink of panikins for our mid-day meal of pork and beans.

We listened, and presently we could hear trumpets and the voice of Philip, the King's crier. On our feet, we waited and listened again. King Richard greeted every man and sent us word : To-morrow we must do battle with the enemy for the road to Joppa and Jerusalem. " God be with us," Philip and the heralds who came after him cried. " Let Christendom triumph ! Let Christ be justified ! " In the same words, speaking all together, the host answered them : " Let Christendom triumph ! Let Christ be justified ! "

Made suddenly restless we parted. Everard went off, murmuring that the message was only what we had expected ; Ambrose and the Chronicler drew together near a boulder and prepared nervously to write, while I, with no particular purpose in mind, found myself at last where, in a space shaded by a fringe of willow trees beside the river, the wounded lay. They lay in rows on sailcloths, on cloaks, on whatever served to protect them from the marshy ground, a rough awning stretched over them. Under cover of this the priests laboured to bring comfort to the dying ; the Knights Hospitallers and their Serjeants busied themselves in bandaging and dressing, as best they could, the men's wounds. A few of the camp washerwomen, old Agnes among them, trafficked between the rows, bringing water from the river and clean linen cloths for the wounded, and taking other cloths, other panikins away. Robert was there already ; I stayed and worked with him. Together we fetched and carried ; together we did everything that was asked of us, though there was little enough that we could do.

I wondered at the Knights Hospitallers. I was to wonder more before my journey was done. With the Knights Templars they had borne much of the burden of the day's encounters. Now, neither rested nor refreshed, their armour scarcely laid aside, they served the wounded and the sick. They did so with no thought for themselves, no misgiving as to the usefulness of their labours. My own mind was neither so Christian nor so unclouded. What could be done, I asked, with all these helpless men when we came into the Forest of Arsur ? If the battle were only half as severe as we feared, we could neither carry them with us nor protect them for long. While I thrust my misgivings aside someone from the ranks of the wounded called my name. I looked among the lines of wounded men.

Amaury de Montfort, white as the Templar's horse-cloth upon which he lay, beckoned to me. I bent over him. He turned drowsy. " Greeting, messire John," he said. " Likewise farewell. My pagan, whom I slew, waits for me."

I crossed his hands ; I crossed his legs also. For a moment I grieved for him.

When we could do no more, Robert and I came away. More than ever in these days he and I lived in two worlds whose shores did not meet. Since I was unwilling to speak of what was in both our minds, only trivialities remained, and of these neither of us had the heart to speak. I kept silent therefore, and was unwillingly reminded of my dream in which I had sought for Robert over sands and deserts and had not found him. Nothing, I reflected with a weightiness which comes back to me now, cuts a man off more surely from his friends than his own misery.

I had resolved never to reproach Robert. In stumbling over a stone, I broke both the current of my thought and my resolve. I tried to disguise my hurt. As if I were joking, I said : " I can no more come near you than if you sat on the peak of Mount Carmel."

Robert said : " Like a woman you always wish to come close, to come near."

The shadows of the rushes lay like crossed swords, like minds out of tune across our path ; the reeds by the salt marshes rustled with small stiff sounds. Robert stood still for a moment. " Since you know my mind why reproach me now ? "

" It is true. No one can come near you," I said again, and spoke bitterly.

Robert walked on faster as though to increase the distance between us. To-morrow the battle would be fought ; I determined, therefore, not to part from him in this manner and kept doggedly behind. We reached the outskirts of the camp. Perhaps I was indeed, I thought, like a woman pursuing her lover. I kept on. Men stared at us, at Robert striding angrily ahead, at myself—he was taller than I—dogging sweatily behind. I might have ceased to follow, but suddenly the light faded from the Forest of Arsur, the sun splashed out from behind the hills and was gone.

In that moment—I had been expecting it—the cry of the heralds, made every evening at nightfall, reached us from the midst of the camp. " Aid us, Holy Sepulchre. Aid us," the cry came. At once the army took up the words. On his knees—by this time Robert and I were on our knees also—every man answered : " Aid us, Holy Sepulchre. Aid us." The sound, caught up at first by a few, then by many thousands of voices, moved through the vast numbers of kneeling men like a wind over the meadow grasses. The heralds repeated the cry twice ; from their knees, hands uplifted, twice our men answered. Repeated for the third time, the words seemed to linger in the air. Many men wept ; Robert, as he knelt beside me, trembled and was strangely moved. I remained dry-eyed, my mind watchful and apart. The army, I told myself, was much refreshed by weeping and crying out in this manner.

Robert and I went on, side by side. I believed I caught the glisten of tears upon his face. Though I sought remorsefully in my own mind once more I found nothing to comfort him. Already he had moved, I thought, beyond comfort. We walked on. To the stiff rustle of reeds by the salt marshes night came down.

It was then that Robert, speaking out of the darkness, said : " Do not hinder me, John. Nor misjudge me. I know now which way I must take."

3

THE SEVENTH OF SEPTEMBER

IN the early hours of the next day a small smack put in in great haste from Acre with news for William des Préaux. Before we had set out half the camp and all the esquires knew that the Lady Melisande had indeed fled to Tyre. Rumours sped screaming everywhere : the Lady had turned traitor and was gone to join the Marquis Conrad ; the Lady was loyal but burned so hot with love for the Frenchman, de Passy, that she had followed him ; the Lady had no particular love for de Passy, but so great a detestation of Fitzgerold that even the Frenchman, landless though he was, appeared preferable.

Everard and I rode out side by side. He had, I knew, seen William des Préaux only a few moments since. I questioned him therefore : how, I asked, had the Lady made her flight to Tyre ? I had a shrewd notion how she would go : in the best fashion, I thought, of every French romance.

"As you would expect," Bogis replied gloomily. "By a great bell rope paid out from her window by her waiting-maid."

"And the Lady Isambeau ? " I enquired. "Too deaf to hear, no doubt," I said, "or too rapt to understand."

"Neither," Bogis answered. "She was tied to her bedpost, and her mouth was tied also, and a note was left : ' Forgive me that I must pull the skein so tight ! ' "

I struggled for composure.

"It was not well done," Bogis said, his face dark.

I said : "Even de Passy will not hold her long."

"She will come to great harm," Bogis declared. "I cannot laugh." He spoke so simply I became ashamed.

"And Robert ? " I asked, sobering.

"As gaunt as if he were in his shroud," Bogis answered. He added, red-faced : "We should have killed the Frenchman by the Tower of Flies. But we do nothing. In the Lady's eyes we do not add up to one man worth her considering."

We rode on. "Surely the affair is finished," I said at last. "Surely it cannot concern us longer."

Everard muttered. He went on muttering. "Finished ? It is not finished. You would surprise me if this were finished."

The rest of the day remained uneventful for us and for the army. The Turks held off ; by nightfall we had completed the first six miles of our march from the Salt River to Arsur—a half of the length of the forest—

in safety. That night we pitched our tents by the River of the Cleft Rock. Though we rested sleep came to us late, or came scarcely at all. We were thankful that the Sultan had not burned the forest behind us as we marched ; we rejoiced that we had come so far—close on eighty miles— without mortal hindrance. We knew, for our scouts had reported it to us, that to-morrow the army of the Sultan would be drawn up and waiting for us on the hill of Arsur and on the hills around. There were, our scouts estimated, three hundred thousand of the enemy, while we, from wounds and sickness and desertions and death, could muster by this time scarcely more than a third of that number. Even while we slept, or sought for sleep, the Sultan's horsemen were making their way, fast as mountain streams, down the dry watercourses of the hills into the plain. If we trembled—I know that my own hands were forced to clasp my knees— it was not so much from fear as from suspense and waiting. The enemy were more numerous than we were, yet we believed in ourselves ; we had faith in King Richard and in each other ; and now that the moment was upon us, the greater faith that had brought so many of us upon this journey returned. I was conscious of no deep thoughts, nor was I tranquil : I wished only that to-morrow were come and gone, and the next morning here. I slept at last, only to be awakened by Everard crying out repeatedly in his sleep that he would not eat fat bacon. I turned over on my stomach ; I split my shirt from relief and laughing. He sat up rosy as an infant, and as ruffled. "You will not eat fat bacon," I said. "You will be lucky, and so shall I, if after to-day we eat anything."

While I slept, Sunday, the 7th of September, the day of the Battle of Arsur dawned.

The attack of the Sultan's army began at dawn when we set out ; it ended in the outskirts of Arsur just before night. From the beginning it was endurance for us ; only in the end, and just before the end, was it victory. When I look back upon the events of that day, I remember not the confusion nor the terror, but the vastness of the spectacle. I marvel again at the fierce shout of colour until all was drowned in dust, the irresistible clash and movement, the strange wildness of it all. I was glad to be stationed near the Standard : from this almost sheltered place it was possible to watch the battle and, as it were, remain outside. Though I had cause to be glad on my own account, I grieved that Robert at the last moment should have chosen to ride with the mounted knights on the flank of the army and nearest, therefore, to the enemy.

We marched in much the same order we had kept so far : the foot soldiers and the archers like a protecting wall between the enemy and the knights ; the Templars in the van, the Hospitallers in the rear, and the Standard almost in the centre with the Normans and Englishmen.

Next to the sea the loaded infantry and the baggage trains moved as before.

I remember how our men joked and laughed as we set out, how one man swore he would give the Sultan's suit of golden armour if it were his for one sweet shower of rain ; how another swore this was hard heathen country we were in where even the soil came up looking white and spiteful at a man. We marched undisturbed again for a little while. Then, suddenly, without warning, the Turkish horse-bowmen came at us ten thousand strong from the hill slopes, hurling their darts and discharging their arrows upon us, and yelling, perhaps to frighten us, like demons let loose on holiday from hell. After them came the black Sudanese archers, terrible to see, and the fierce men of the desert called Beduins. These last fought on foot with daggers and long bows and arrows and a round shield. Behind them, like those vast flights of birds that in autumn darken the evening sky, the rest of the Turkish horsemen appeared. Pennons fluttering from every lance-head, they came on irresistibly, it seemed, on their light-footed Arab horses. So great was the cloud of dust stirred up by so many feet the air grew dark, sounds were muffled, the fierce colours were obscured. The Turkish admirals, as it was their duty to do, rode first in the attack, preceded by a hellish band sounding upon clarions and trumpets and loud brass gongs. Presently all the plain seemed filled with the enemy ; like a river in flood they came at us from every side and even, for the road curved inward at this point, from the shore. Hemmed in by so vast a horde, our men nevertheless kept their stations and marched steadily on.

For hours we endured, our crossbowmen giving the Turks bolt for bolt ; our archers, stepping backward once more, discharging their arrows into the ranks of the enemy. The Knights Hospitallers in the rear and the infantry in the extremes of our long line of march suffered most. The Sultan's mamelukes themselves engaged our foot soldiers, thundering at them with spiked maces, hewing at their limbs with bright curving scimitars, their blows resounding from our men's body armour like hammer blows upon anvils. Most terrible of all was the rain of arrows, so many that even the air we breathed seemed full of death and the enemy. Yet our lines held ; there was no point at which our men gave way. I heard a Turk cry out in good Norman-French that our men were of iron and would yield to no blow. About noon, the Sultan himself, as if in desperation, took command. Attended only by two pages leading fresh horses, like King Richard he was everywhere, urging on his men where any sign of wavering appeared. Yet our men stayed patient.

For the Knights Hospitallers patience was perhaps something beyond the capacity of mortal men. They numbered some of the most renowned knights in Christendom, and yet for hour after hour they were obliged to receive every attack of the enemy and give no blow back again. It was for them to remain as rearguard for the whole army, never on pain of death to break ranks, never to swerve from their place until King Richard should give the signal—six trumpets sounding at once—for attack. Repeatedly the Hospitallers sought permission to turn upon their attackers ; to every request the King would answer only, " It must be borne." Though, as I have said, it was past bearing.

Towards evening when the advance guard of our men was approaching the walls of Arsur, the Turks, as if to decide the matter, launched a fresh wave of men, twenty thousand in number, against our tired ranks. It was then that the patience of the Knights Hospitallers broke. The Grand Master himself, Garnier de Naplous, cried out like a man upon the cross : " Blessed St. George, how long must we endure ? " Then the Marshal of the Hospitallers, William Borrell, and another knight, Baldwin de Carron, a friend of King Richard and one of his retinue, a man as black as darkness where William Borrell was shining as daylight, wheeled their horses suddenly, and, calling on the name of St. George, turned on the enemy, the wall of infantry parting gladly before them. Immediately, with a shout, both horse and foot in a body followed. Afterwards nothing could hold our men back. In a moment the whole line was in movement against the enemy. At once King Richard ordered the trumpets to sound the signal agreed upon for the attack. And the battle that was, we believed, to decide the future of Jerusalem was at last joined.

I do not know how I bore myself nor what I did : I know that I was one with all the many hundreds about me, that I struck blow for blow and received them again, that Everard fought beside me on foot, both our horses having been killed. I heard myself shouting but did not know what I said ; I saw nothing, so thick and black was the dust about us, amidst the din and confusion I could glimpse only the Standard like a great wing above us, dipping and falling but curving upward again.

The dust settled a little ; the sun, orange-red through our cloud of dust, began to sink in the sky. The Turks, though their ranks were broken, fought on. They fought on, not as an army any longer, but as separate groups and companies of fighting men. Here and there numbers of them fled, hiding themselves in thickets, or climbing to the tops of tall trees, or tumbling hot-foot down slippery paths to the cliffs to find coolness and Paradise there in the depths of the sea. For two miles the Sultan's army could be seen in flight or in retreat, on foot and on horseback, on the backs of unwilling camels, astride vast trumpeting elephants. Their banners went with them, flaunting their bright colours as though defiant still. Truly, though the Turks fled, there was no humbling them. Whenever our men paused in pursuit they turned and came at us again. Last of all

Tak-i-ed-din, the nephew of the Sultan (some say his son), with a chosen band of seven hundred Turks attacked the Standard itself most unexpectedly. Their colours were yellow ; a pair of baggy yellow breeches was embroidered upon their banner for a device. Hard pressed though we were by Tak-i-ed-din on one side of us and the great weight of our own men upon the other, we could still laugh at so odd and comical a device. From the very audacity of the attack we might indeed have been overwhelmed had not William des Barres, whom I had not seen since the King's encounter with him in Sicily, come to our rescue and the King himself, mounted upon Fauvel, followed with fifteen of his own company. It was only then that Tak-i-ed-din, or Emir Baggy-Breeches, as our men were already calling him, broke off the battle and rode off finally into the hills.

We pursued them until pursuit appeared dangerous. At the foot of the hills we left off our pursuit and returned to the plain. No more than fifteen men at the most from so vast an army continued to fight still around the Sultan's standard ; in their midst a little negro lad, a scarlet turban on his head, beat valiantly upon his drum. We took him prisoner and spared his life, and afterwards King Richard sent him to London to his palace of Westminster. There he died, of loneliness, I think, as much as from our English fogs and damps. He was named, he answered when we questioned him, Mansour, and was born beside King Pharaoh's Nile.

The fighting over, I sought my friends. I found Brand and Giles with a number of English archers and foot soldiers in an open courtyard. Two peach trees grew within the court, and a goat and her two kids were tethered to one of the trees. I stood to one side. Brand was milking the goat ; Giles, a panikin in one hand, was protesting all the while : " I like not goat's milk, I say, nor goat's milk cheese either. It is musty-tasting and heavy on the belly also. And it does taste, I say, of what a goat smells of."

" Goat or not, taste or smell or not, I have set my heart on her," Brand affirmed. He went on milking.

I met Baldwin de Carron next. I was seeking Robert of Kinwarton, I said. He looked kindly at me and waved me on. I hurried and found Robert lying beside other men under an awning beside a pillared house. The Hospitallers—their Grand Master, Garnier de Naplous himself, was there —tended him. When I saw him I wept, and all relief and all gladness left me.

He saw my tears. Moving the one hand he had left, he said : " What, man ? I vowed all my body to the Cause."

I stayed beside him all that night while he tossed in fever and raved brokenly of Kinwarton and Oscar and Jerusalem, but not a word that I could hear of Melisande. In the morning they took him with other desperately wounded men by ship to Joppa, while I, with the rest of the army, passed on by road to the same place.

PART FIVE

THE SHADOW

1

AMBUSH

MIRACULOUSLY Robert recovered and yet, in some sense, the Robert of Kinwarton whom I had known did indeed die at Arsur. From now on he was changed ; from now onwards his will over-mastered him. More than ever by the isolation of his own spirit as much as by his injury, he was cut off from us ; even more than before he carried himself like a man in whom some sole purpose burned. Scarcely recovered, the stump of his severed wrist not yet fully healed, he obliged himself to wear armour and ride out again. When first he tried to do so I pitied him : he directed so bleak a gaze upon me I turned away. He made no complaint, struck no obvious poses, did not cry out in despair. Rather he turned forbidding ; he made himself inviolate and strange. All but broken by events, he exalted himself above them and above us all. He burned with a pure flame, Anselm, the King's chaplain, declared. But I, who never dealt in extremes after Robert's fashion, nor in words as Anselm did, dreaded the course Robert's resolution might take.

Joppa, set high above the sea among orchards and date palms, appeared a pleasant place to us after so many miles of scorching plain. And yet, as I write, though I remember the languor and the pleasantness, the songs behind shutters, the shiver of date palms, and the crisp exulting of the giant waves, I remember my own restlessness even more. For the first time in my life I slept badly, and what shallow sleep I had was full of shapeless dreams. I was solitary in these days and perhaps for this reason oppression weighed all the more heavily upon me and a sense of catastrophe to come returned again and again to my mind. I spoke of my fears to Anselm, the King's chaplain. He enquired if I had been in the company of loose women, and when I answered, " Yes," he bade me fast and pray. I confided in Everard. He favoured me with a clear gaze and declared, with a turn of wit I had not expected, that I was like the man who could not enjoy a winter's day because it was so short. Everard had that gift, so useful in war, of never looking towards to-morrow. He had another gift also : he could put his love upon a high shelf and appear to forget it until the time came to retrieve it again. When he was melancholy he would take a purge and afterwards lie out in the sun for a long while, perhaps for a whole day. This, he said, he found better than fasting or prayer. " Indeed," he enquired, and surprised me a second time, " what are praying and purging but the same thing? Be merry, man," he bade me then, and left me.

Joppa was gay and merry enough also in these days; too gay, the straiter among the Knights Templars said. Hardly had the echoes of the fight died away, hardly were the dead counted and buried and the thanksgivings said, than the Court and all the ladies of the Court arrived from Acre like a gay visiting swarm of butterflies. I danced and feasted with the rest of the King's men; I made a number of false speeches and a little light love. It was to small purpose; whenever I paused restlessness overtook me again.

No news of the Lady Melisande came from Tyre. The Marquis Conrad waited like a garden spider meanwhile in the safe web of his own territories. Every week more of the discontented men of both parties stole off to join him. The Marquis welcomed them. The great Saladin had conferred with him, rumour said, and the Marquis himself had sent an embassy to the Chief of the Syrian Assassins, the Old Man of the Mountains. Many Frenchmen, after having declared that it was no part of their duty to add to the renown of the King of England, exchanged their steel helms for rosy garlands, and they, too, went off to Tyre. In the midst of so much Christian concord, news came, scarcely to be credited at first, that Saladin was reducing the proud city of Ascalon to ruins rather than allow it to fall into King Richard's hands. The King was for an immediate advance upon the city, but the French, and many of his own followers also, counselled differently. Better rebuild Joppa, they declared, and march upon Jerusalem by the short route from that city. So, unwisely as it transpired, it was agreed.

So many differences between friends and allies left their mark upon us all. Though we grew wiser our wisdom soured us, I think. Alliances, I would tell myself, were only animosities disguised; war was half a matter of waiting; treachery was as common as loyalty. At the same time old spectres re-visited me. I found myself remembering de Passy and no longer condemning him; I began once more to believe that I was suspect, not continuously suspect—I did not think that—but suspect now and then, never wholly absolved, never a full member of the King's brotherhood.

Alone, on the edge of the crowd, I brooded on this. A wrestling match between a sergeant of crossbowmen from Canterbury and a foot-soldier from Caen was in progress. The two combatants heaved and strained before a large part of the army, not a few pilgrims and priests, and the usual number of fat and lively washerwomen. From an upturned tub outside the circle of stakes which protected the wrestlers from the crowd, a hedge priest roared encouragement and advice to both wrestlers; in one corner a pilgrim squatted and, as if he could pray better here than elsewhere, told his beads. On our left was the fair plain of Sharon, before us were the mountains of Ephraim, the October sun scarring their sides with shadow. Within sight but out of earshot Robert practised his riding with Giles and Brand. Since I could do nothing for him myself I had lent him my two squires. They took their new mission very seriously and did more for Robert than I could ever have believed possible. They consulted in their own language and after their own fashion a smith from Birmingham called Ralph. He it was who devised a curious hook of iron which, fixed cunningly to the sleeve of Robert's armour, after a very rough fashion did indeed serve him in place of a hand. By means of it he could at least catch at his horse's reins and steady his shield. The three of them were out now, practising in a very comradely fashion, I did not doubt, the armourer's device, while I sat apart, solitary and out of humour, hugging my knees.

At this point the man from Caen threw the man of Kent. Immediately the crowd was in an uproar ; supporters of either party leapt into the ring and fiercely engaged each other ; in a moment insults and blows were thick in the air. The result might well have been a general mêlée if the hedge priest had not created a simple diversion by the loud ringing of a small hand-bell. I removed myself to a quieter place.

Here in a few seconds the Chronicler and Ambrose joined me. The former plied me with questions. How long would the army remain in Joppa ? What truth was there in the old tale that Queen Joanna had been offered in marriage to the Mahommedan Saphadin ?

I lost patience with the Chronicler. " Why ask me ? " I said. " Has no one told you that I have dwindled in stature of late, that I am no longer even half of the little that I was ? "

The two of them at once grew silent. Ambrose offered me a fig, in silence still ; I refused it passionately. They withdrew a step or two. A soldier asleep not far off groaned in horrid fashion. I was made acutely aware of other sounds, of the busy scratch of the Chronicler's pen as once more he began to write, of the steady, almost thoughtful movement of Ambrose's jaws. It was then that William des Préaux spoke to me. I had been aware of him for some little time but had kept my distance. Pointing to the wrestlers, he began easily : " They have finished a second round. Canterbury wins this one." He went on to speak of a hunting party King Richard had planned for the next day. Why could I not come ? I hesitated. He had caught—I was certain of it—the note of bitterness in my voice when I answered the Chronicler ; he spoke to me now, I told myself, out of kindness only. I wished to refuse him and yet, so much did I long for company, I could not.

" To-morrow, then," he said. He spoke of Robert as he turned to go, and praised his efforts to ride out again. I said I feared the effort was too much for him. " No," des Préaux returned, " there is great virtue in what he does." He waited a moment in an odd bashful fashion. Then, as I did not answer him, he went away. I looked after him. King Richard, it was freely declared, loved him too well. I could love him also, though differently, I thought.

On the next morning just before sunrise we set out : Everard and I and William des Préaux, with Sir Hugh de Winton and a few more of the King's company. The day promised well ; dew lay heavy on the grass, the mists were Venus draperies about the hills. Hubert, the King's falconer, rode beside the King ; Alain, his chief groom, rode a little behind. I looked at Alain with interest. Of all the strange figures that were about the King he was perhaps the strangest. He was small and brown and wrinkled as a dry plum-stone ; his legs and his back also were bowed. He had been born in Tyre, it was said, of a father from Yorkshire and a Syrian girl. He was credited with many adventures : he had been taken prisoner by the Turks and been returned, half-dying, with his throat slit ; he had been wounded more than once ; he had been almost drowned in a horse trough. He had, in fact, nine lives and had not reached—on this one subject he joked incessantly—the end of them yet. To-day found him happy, though he was by nature somewhat morose. He kept his head turned a little as he rode, as though he wished always to look over his shoulder. Men who knew him best swore that more than most men he feared to ride or sleep alone.

We had not ridden far in the direction of Toron of the Knights before a messenger, flourishing a roll of parchment in one outstretched hand, came riding fast after us. He was fully armed, he spoke in a muffled and fearful voice out of a large visor ; his surcoat bore the device of the Earl of Leicester, a white lion on a black ground. The Earl—so the parchment ran—begged the King for his own safety to return. He would certainly return, the King swore, and he clapped the messenger heartily upon the back and sent him away, still hiccoughing into his visor.

"I dreamed I found a red pepper in my good dirty-coloured porridge ; it was an Assassin, certainly," said Alain.

Everyone began talking of Massiat after that, and of the secret way underground to the heart of the fortress and the great fall of the River Orontes.

" And Sheikh Sinan is a little man," Alain said, " no bigger than I, Alain, am ; a little lame man, sirs, with grey eyes like frost flowers and a small white beard." He swore solemnly that he, Alain, had seen the sheikh. " I saw Massiat," Alain declared, " I spoke with Sheikh Sinan." A note of fear, I thought, crept at this point into his voice. " I, Alain," he said again, " have seen Massiat and returned. In proof here is my knife "—he produced it—" an Assassin's knife." He tossed it in the air and caught it again. We were incredulous and amazed, and he was pleased. He continued to talk.

We flew our hawks and called them in again ; we looked for signs of the enemy and found nothing more harmful than an eagle beating high in the air and a snake coiled upon a rock. At noonday we sheltered from the sun in a grove of oak trees at the foot of a steep hillside planted with vines and divided into neat terraced slopes. Small stone huts like round beehives marked the foot of the hills. They were empty, the ashes of their fires scattered long since. In all the countryside not a thing moved ; not a horseman could be seen. For all that, Sir Hugh de Winton went off to examine the hill slopes and William de Stagno and Hugh the Brown went with him.

The King lay in the deepest shade and slept, his long legs crossed, his sword-belt undone, his cap of Poitou over his eyes. Everard and I lay opposite him—I know we had hard work to restrain our laughter when the King snored, more particularly when he woke and, like any other man who snores, glared at us suspiciously. William des Préaux kept guard, fully armed, beside the horses, sometimes humming, sometimes singing to himself a snatch of a love song. The lady was faithless and fair, I remember ; she came over the sea ; she had mermaiden's eyes. Alain kept up a low running patter of talk in his cracked voice—afterwards it seemed to me that even while he talked he was afraid.

Presently Hubert tied his falcons to the branch of a tree and Alain and he went off to forage, or so we suspected, for themselves. The quiet grew sleepy and heavy as the drone of a bumblebee ; I lay with closed eyes and dreamed, half awake at first, of how I might improve my fortunes and greatly serve the King. It was an old dream of mine. Gradually a scene shaped itself before my eyes. In a narrow place fit for an ambush a band of Assassins appeared. I saw their red girdles, their white robes, their impassive—so I imagined them—faces. And the King slept still and snored. The Assassins moved so smoothly in my dream they scarcely appeared to move at all. But I, John of Oversley, was as quick and as silent. What followed I did not see. In my dream still I saw only my blood leaving scarcely a stain upon the sand ; I was aware of the King, awake by this time, and leaning over me. He reproached himself. " And I mistrusted you ! " I opened my eyes. Foolish though my dream was, I felt myself filled like an echo with a trembling worship of the King.

I was scarcely completely awake before the terror and the ambush of which I had dreamed were in truth upon us. I heard first a beating and flapping of the falcons' wings and their shrill reiterated cries. About a score of men, their faces muffled, their horses' feet muffled also, faced us in the narrow track. I saw their white cloaks, the blue and crimson trappings of their brown horses. They appeared to me of more than human size poised motionless against the blue of sky, the green of the plain. Their leader threw up his sword-arm as if for a signal; it was then that I heard William des Préaux cry out. Even while I leapt for my horse I remember thinking that these men were queerly slow, that it was almost as if they meant to capture rather than to kill. William des Préaux was mounted first. "I am *Melek*," he shouted, and rode at them. "I am King Richard." I saw the Saracen horsemen close round him, then turn and wheel suddenly, and speed as fast as Emir Baggy-Trousers himself, away. The thing was gallantly done on William des Préaux's part. It was better a thousand times that he should suffer rather than King Richard, and yet Everard and I remained uneasy at his sacrifice and ashamed that we should be condemned, for King Richard's sake again, to so inactive and inglorious a part.

One last sight was allowed us of William des Préaux, his body turned halfway towards us, his arm raised in greeting; then the white cloaks of his captors wrapped him about, their long arms like swans' wings beat about him. Afterwards we saw only a scuffle of hooves and a cloud of dust and a knot of what might have been any group of horsemen, William des Préaux in their midst, riding away.

Even so, William's sacrifice might have been useless if it had not been for Sir Hugh de Winton. It was he, returning only a moment or two afterwards from a different direction, who struggled—something Everard and I could never have done—man to man, with the King. "Let him be *Melek*, Richard," we heard, "for the Cause and for all our sakes." The old knight was no more of a brake at first, as he struggled and grappled with the King, than a waggon weight is when the waggon runs downhill. On his back, purple of face, the King bending over him, he delivered himself finally: "Those were the Sultan's men. They will take ransom for des Préaux. He will not die." Then, and only then, did the King listen to reason and agree not to attempt the rescue of his friend.

When we were armed and mounted again and old Sir Hugh was once more upon his feet, Hubert the King's falconer came towards us out of the vineyards at the foot of the hill. He was sullen with anger and yellow-faced—he was of a sallow complexion—and limping and bloodstained besides. He dribbled words: "Two men came out of the vines and stood in front of Alain. 'Hail, master,' one said, and raised his hand. He'd a knife in it. When Alain leapt on him I saw death sickly in his face. I could ha' died, sirs. But in a moment Alain was as good as dead, and life is sweet. They that killed him had no thought for me; they were come and gone, sudden and quiet, like an adder striking. I stayed with Alain ; I had his last words. ' A curse,' Alain says, ' a curse on all forked beards and lame legs.' I left him by the crooked pole in the vineyard with a dead bird swinging from it, him that is no more now than a dead bird."

Sir Hugh turned fiercely upon Hubert. " Why should Alain die ? "

" A' swore a' would never die in his bed," Hubert answered, shivering.

I said quickly : " I have heard the Frenchman, de Passy, declare that the Assassins would allow no man to live long who had left Massiat without their consent."

Sir Hugh de Winton and the rest stared at each other and then at me, and the King said quickly : " God rest Alain."

We left Alain where he lay in the vineyard under the dead bird, and returned.

The affair was a nine days' wonder in the camp, then forgotten. A double guard, unknown to the King, was placed about his tent ; a great search was made throughout the army for traitors, though none, of course, was found ; finally, so that the King might be assured of the identity of Alain's murderers, a hunt was set on foot for Bernard, the King's spy. But Bernard, with that complete freedom King Richard allowed him, had vanished once again.

October crept on, and the walls and towers of Joppa rose as though by a miracle from the dust and rubble Saladin had made. Delaying offers were sent to the Sultan by King Richard through the Sultan's brother, Saphadin ; reproaches and commands to the stragglers and wine-soakers among the knights at Acre ; soft silvery words to the Marquis Conrad at Tyre. And all this was necessary, since the army, we knew, must set out shortly for Jerusalem, that city which all Christian men declared that they desired.

Meanwhile, for all my argument with myself, the dread I had of some danger still to come would not leave me. By day I could laugh at my fears ; by night they returned. I dreamed repeatedly the same dream : I looked for Robert and found only his footsteps and a trail of blood over white stones. I followed the trail, and in the distance I saw him, a small figure moving among the sand-dunes like a man asleep. In a country of mountain peaks suffused with rose I waited for him, while beside me a smooth sheet of water fell into an abyss. My search might vary ; the mountain peaks and the smooth water falling and my own torment of mind did not change. It was something of the same dream I had dreamed of Robert on our setting out, but sharper now and, like Robert, subtly changed.

I spoke to Robert of the strange country through which in my dream at least I followed him. At first he gave me an odd answer : " I do not

know the place." Then, as if he were aware of my astonishment, he said :
" I dream, constantly."

" But these are nightmares," I said.

He laughed at me and moved the stump of his severed hand. " Sometimes my dreams are nightmares also."

2

THE SIN OF LOVING

ONCE more, for what precise reasons I shall never know, I was included among the King's esquires. As one of the King's company I saw more than I had seen yet of Jean and Pierre des Préaux. Of the two Pierre was the more like William. He had the same freshness of face, the same quickness and charm, but he lacked, I think, the younger man's passion for life which made him so memorable ; he lacked William's gentleness also and what was simplest in him, his courtesy. Pierre would never win his way by plain goodness of heart ; if charm would not serve him he would try bullying. Jean was different again. While William and Pierre were reckless and open in manner to all the world, he was careful and reserved in all things, so contained within himself that to an ordinary observer he appeared lumpish and dull. In an argument he was one of those who listen and wait, in order, or so it always appears, to have the last word. He was reported, though I could scarcely credit it, to be well versed in philosophy and medicine, both of which he had studied under an Arab teacher from Seville. Certainly, if he did indeed possess so much knowledge, he concealed it well. He had large feet and would often stumble over the most obvious stones, and look back, and appear surprised to see what stones were there. And this, the Chronicler declared, and I pretended to agree with him, was a sure mark of a philosopher. For the rest Jean was courageous and a good knight ; he liked plainness and plain dealing and plain words, plain women also, the gossips said, though the Countess of Leicester, who was his friend, was removed a thousand years from any charge of plainness.

William des Préaux's capture was a fortnight old and the consternation it had aroused had already died away when Brand and Giles and I were riding down the Joppa road towards Arsur between the orchards.

As I rode I looked about me. Little trace of the battle remained. On one side were the fields over which Emir Baggy-Trousers had galloped his white Arab horses and galloped them back again. But already two small oxen were dragging a ploughshare over the trampled stubble while a man not much taller than they were goaded them from behind. A tall camel stalked ahead, burdened, it appeared at this distance, by nothing weightier than its own shadow. The road so great a host and so many furies had travelled so short a while ago was empty now except for a small gesticulating group of women, whom I took at first sight to be drabs of the camp, and one or two men, whom I took to be stragglers from the army newly arrived from Acre, and a couple of half-naked dancing beggar boys besides. We could hear voices and laughter and a plentiful sprinkling of oaths, and one other voice, not loud, but raised above the rest on a haughty note. We drew nearer. Said one of the drabs, belly thrust forward, a hand on her hip : " She swears she is a gentlewoman, Baptiste, and by the Cross, I do more than half believe her, for her toe-nails show as fair as the Virgin's."

" So it is with the toe-nails of Turkish harlots, I tell you," Baptiste, whom I took to be a Genoese, answered in a surly voice.

Giles, always curious, pressed nearer. Brand and I followed.

The flimsiest of the three women detached herself from the rest and spoke haughtily again. Thrusting the others of her company aside with her staff, she cried out : " Give me room, good friends and fellow baggages, I would speak with this esquire."

Holding her green cloak about her, she came forward, stumbling in little steps as she came. Her hair was bleached and dry, her feet bleeding, her face when I looked upon it seamed with dirt. There were blue hollows as though they were painted there beneath her eyes.

Amazed and dumb, I stared at her. It was Melisande.

She stopped short ; she accosted me. " I had planned to make a brave entrance, but at Tyre I lost my modesty, at Arsur I lost my shoes."

Bareheaded, in silence, the three of us greeted her.

The women screamed to each other : " See how they reverence her."

Melisande called over her shoulder to them : " Farewell. I thank you. Farewell."

Baptiste grumbled and swore. Like farmyard ducks the women waddled past.

I looked at Melisande and still I could not speak. Here was another, my mind went, whom I had loved, who had been changed.

As if she guessed my thoughts Melisande mocked me. " I have lost much more even than this, much more, as you can see, John of Oversley." Even then I could not speak.

Brand said patiently : " Master, will the Lady not ride ? "

I came to my senses. " Forgive me," I said, " I was amazed."

She turned quiet ; she shed a little of what she had brought back with her from Tyre. Her eyes met mine. " Why should you not be amazed ? I have come on foot from Acre whither a ship from Tyre brought me, through the dregs of several great armies. But if you will not speak, spare me your chivalry."

I said : " Do you not see I cannot speak ? "

Mounted upon my horse, I upon Brand's, Brand and Giles following, we rode on. At one point by the roadside we encountered a small congregation of lepers. Blind eyes and fleshless faces upturned to the light, fingerless palms stretched out, they begged for blessings and for coins.

Suddenly Melisande said : " I have kept company with lepers also. They are not lecherous as most men are." She turned in her saddle before I could speak and looked at me. " Though I am brazen to-day, to-morrow I shall be ashamed."

I recovered my tongue. " So you should be," I declared roundly. For she had worked havoc in more directions than one, I thought.

She begged for news of Robert. " If harm has come to him because of me I could not forgive myself."

" Harm has come to him," I said. I told her of Robert's injury and how it seemed to me that he had changed.

" Then we are both spoiled," she answered. As she spoke her courage, which at this moment was perhaps no more than a high gesture, left her. She drooped in her saddle. I spoke savagely then, I do not know why, unless from pity and sudden resentment and an odd sort of jealousy. " Truly, I agree with the priests that women are vain and viperous and all the beauty of women is no better than a snare."

She straightened and, looking away from me, spoke calmly. " With the priests this scorn of women is no more than sour grapes and Holy Writ ; with you it is no more than sour grapes." She turned to me again. " You see, if you attack me I shall defend myself."

" That is the des Préaux motto," I very dryly said.

Her hood pulled closely about her face, she rode on beside me in silence. Whispers and hard stares followed us as we went. One or two curious people trailed behind. Someone, a little distance off, guffawed loudly.

" Holy Mother of God, I cannot bear it," I heard her say.

I might have pitied her but hers was always a weathercock mood, her impulses tossing her this way, then back again. She was not humble enough even yet ; she was too ready of speech, I told myself, and too shrewd also.

As she dismounted before my tent she stumbled heavily. " You see, I cannot keep from falling," she said. She moved on into the tent and I followed her. While she ate and drank she talked flickeringly and fast like someone light-headed from fatigue. I listened unhappily. She spoke at last of William des Préaux. "Above everything else I must see William."

I forced myself to answer her stolidly. William, I told her, was away upon the King's affairs.

While her eyes sought mine for the truth she said again—it was a speech she had made more than once in my hearing—"William is a child. He will never grow up. He will never weary of killing and fighting." I made no answer. Like a child herself she repeated her question, one hand in a tired gesture plucking at her hair : Why might she not see William ?

When at last I told her why, she covered her face and wept very piteously. "Oh, William, where are you now ? I have so longed for you."

I would go and find Pierre, I said.

She took away her hands. "If it please you, let it be Pierre. Not Jean. If you ever had any kindness for me, let it be Pierre."

"You know well how much kindness I had for you," I said.

Though I went in search of Pierre, I found only Jean. I returned a little ahead of him to Melisande.

"Is it Pierre ? " she greeted me.

"Jean," I said.

Jean des Préaux came in. When I would have left them together he motioned me to stay. He spoke at once to Melisande. "So you have returned. Why ? "

I could see her gathering all her courage to answer him. "Because he was even hollower than I had thought. Because he intended only humiliation for me. And you know," she added, "you know well I would not be humbled by anyone."

"You have humbled yourself," he said, "and brought shame upon us all."

"What have I done," she asked, "that you have not done ? And Pierre ? And even William ? "

"Even William ! " he said, a quick spurt of anger showing for the first time in his heavy face. He lashed out at her then. "At least I have kept my word."

"And I," she said, white-faced.

"You did not consider Fitzgerold," he returned, "much more than a man considers an ant under his feet."

She answered him indignantly. "That is not a good comparison. He is much too stout for an ant."

Everard came in at this moment and stood as though invisibly to one side.

"Like all women," Jean said, "you are without reason or conscience."

"And I," Melisande said, "think it great grief that there is no safety for women except with men like you, Jean, who speak so foolishly of them."

Jean leaned forward. " You are too pert. And too impenitent."

It was then, when the silence between them was so full of danger, that a pariah dog, one of several hundreds about the camp, burst in, paused, yapped fiercely, broke off as though in surprise, then fled. The blood that had burned in my cheeks ebbed ; I shifted my weight from one foot to another ; Everard's hand stayed still once more by his side, and Melisande said weakly : " I told you, Jean, that I would never keep faith with Fitzgerold."

" Who are you ? " he asked, his voice thick.

" We are of the same kind, you and I," she said. She went on as if she were afraid. " I told Pierre I would not. I told William. Oh, Jean, where is he now ? I have so longed for him."

Surprisingly he answered her. " He is alive. He is a prisoner of the Sultan's, not, as we feared at first, of the Assassins. He would be angrier with you," he said, " than I am. He would know better than I do how to punish you."

She stared at him, dry-eyed.

" Who will wed with you now ? " he asked. " I would not."

" You know I never wished for a husband," she returned.

" You should be beaten and put into a nunnery," he said.

" I will be beaten," she said, " if you wish. But not in a nunnery." She thrust her hair out of her eyes. " Indeed I do not mind being beaten in the least," she assured him.

" Pray, what will you do now, short of marrying ? " he asked, and stared.

She sat down suddenly on the rough stool I had set for her. " I will sleep a great deal. After that I will think again. For now you see me not one but half a dozen different selves : I am afraid and confident in turn, pert and sad, brazen and ashamed."

" You are everything in turn," he said bitterly, " but never wise."

" Jean ! " She got up and came nearer as if she would plead with him. He hardened and did not move.

When she spoke I thought her too subtle for her purpose. But gradually her voice more than her words, I believe, won upon him and softened his mood.

" You were never angry with me before," she pleaded. " Do not be angry with me now. Do you not remember how we rode the bull together, you and I, when I could scarcely walk, and how Pierre fell off his horse from laughing and you held me and I was not afraid ? "

He spoke through thin lips absently. " Isambeau always said that I should have beaten you."

" Isambeau ! " She broke off in exasperation. " Sometimes I despise Isambeau."

He looked steadily at her. " There must be some virtuous women in the world."

" Ay," she said, " and plants with no sweet perfumes either. Who has ever tempted Isambeau ? Who would tempt her ? " She moved both hands. " She has never truly loved me, never advised me well. I have never had anything from her but this talk of beating and nunneries. I think it had no purpose except to make me rebellious and afraid." She paused. " I think Isambeau is one of those plain women who only wish to punish and oppress."

" All women should be plain," Jean said, " so that men might be less vulnerable."

She swept all that he had to say aside. " Be good to me, Jean," she pleaded again, " now that William is not here. You used always to be good to me. Do you remember—I remember if you do not—when William and Pierre tossed me in the skin rug from Pierre's bed and it burst and I fell in the gorse bushes and was sharply pricked and did not weep ? And you comforted me again by praising me ? "

He interrupted her harshly. " You are a jade, Melisande. If you had been bred less like a man you might have been more virtuous. I remember the dowry I must render Fitzgerold as forfeit for broken promises. You must wed soon, I say, and whom you please. But you will have no dowry."

" I never cared so much for that dowry," she answered in a tired voice, " since it brought me only Fitzgerold." She waited. " Jean, may I go now ? " Her face was upraised and pitiful enough all at once, her voice falling away.

He nodded and half-turned from her.

She moved unsteadily towards him. " Jean, will you not come with me ? I am afraid to face them now, without you and without William." She crept nearer and laid her cheek against his sleeve. " Do with me as you wish, but do not be angry with me always."

She had spoken to him as if he were God. He stirred uneasily, I thought. " God will punish you," he said.

" I am punished," she said. He looked down at her. " You do not know," she said. " You will never know." I saw her head thrown back, the curved line of her throat, the slow tears oozing between her closed lids. " I meant only love," I heard her say. " Why should I weep ? "

He took off his cloak slowly and put it about her. It was black, I remember ; it reached to the ground and almost hid her feet.

She shivered into it though the air was not cold. " It smells of you," she said, and began to weep. " Now that I am fallen how they will look at me ! " She sobbed, then clenched her hands. " I will not be fallen for long, Jean, I promise you."

" I can do nothing against what is spoken behind my back," he said. " But you know well no one shall mock you to my face."

Her hand on his arm, they went out together. I followed them and Everard, who had scarcely stirred all this while, leapt suddenly to life and came with me.

With the gesture that might have been expected of her Melisande had chosen to submit herself to the mercy of the King and to the more doubtful mercy of all those who had known her about the Court. Two days after her return the King himself was to hear her case. As her self-appointed champions Robert and Everard and I waited for her on the day appointed, in the ante-room to the pillared hall of the merchant Hakim's palace at Joppa which King Richard had taken for his own. Melisande's two brothers were to attend her also. For the rest, Jean des Préaux had seen to it that she should be presented by no less a person than the Countess of Leicester.

The first charge against her, that of deserting the King's Court, was self-proven ; the second, that of cleaving to the King's enemies in Tyre, could not, everyone was aware, be pressed too closely since the Marquis Conrad of Montserrat, Lord of Tyre, once more called himself the King's ally. Although no death sentence threatened and even a decree of banishment was considered unlikely, all the Court and all those other persons who felt they belonged to the Court, from the wife of the King's kennel-man to the cousin of the King's groom, would be present, we knew, to whisper and stare and pity and condemn. There is nothing more appetising than a scandal ; and a fall from grace, as all the world knows, is more resounding than a victory. Every moment fresh numbers of spectators arrived ; every second, both inside and outside the hall, the twitter and stir grew.

Ours, I think, were mixed feelings. The situation in all conscience was ironical enough. Here was the Lady whom we had all in different degrees loved, and to whom with more or less seriousness we had all paid court, in need of our help ; in need, it appeared likely also, of one of us for a husband. So much of a whirligig is fortune, no one among us was transported with delight ; everyone, if the truth be told, was somewhat dismayed.

We had discussed the affair until there was no more to be said.

" When I look at her I see only his face, God comfort us both," Robert said.

" I could not hold her in marriage," I declared. " No, nor any woman like her."

Everard, who had been silent until this moment, burst out then : Did we love the Lady not for herself but only for the image of her each one of us had made ? " The truth," he said, " is that we reject her. She is changed, we say. It is we who have changed." He flung out from us then, and presently returned.

We continued to wait in the ante-room while from without came the tread of armed feet and whispers and the rustle of silken gowns and words of command. Among all the stir I believed I heard the jingle of silver bells and the light tapping feet of mules and Jean des Préaux's voice. There was always a hesitant quality about it except when he was moved, and he was seldom moved, or enraged, and he was rarely enraged. Perhaps at heart he was a philosopher, I thought idly, perhaps for him a divine harmony did indeed rule the world, and all things, like the stars in their courses, kept each their separate and ordered place. If in fact he thought so I disagreed with him. Our own fates laughed at us, Ambrose had said, and led us on, and emptied us of zest and of desire and made us blind, until at last the longest part of time for us was night and what remained of our short day no more than an encroaching shadow. I was no judge yet of life, nor was I old, and yet I thought that I agreed with Ambrose. In things and in events it seemed to me only a half-rule showed ; the rest, like the dim edges of the world of which travellers spoke and dreamed, was full of tumult and the echoes of the dark ; even the stars, hung for an eternity on high, reached their eternity's end and fell at last.

I roused myself to listen again. Robert stayed unmoving and tense, resting, as he so often did, his injured arm upon his other hand. Everard, the laboured squeaking of whose pen had long been distracting me, finished his writing with a cheerful flourish and got up, parchment in hand.

I looked at the parchment. " My forty-acre field," I read in his ungainly script, and " my little manor of Kingleigh "—he had, for what purpose I could not guess, been compiling a long list of all his properties. He laughed shamefacedly, dropped his pen, flushed red and stooped and picked it up, dusting it again. Then, to my astonishment, he went out.

" Young Bogis," I said, looking after him, " is clean out of his wits." I doubt if Robert heard. He did not answer me. We waited still.

Jean des Préaux was the first to enter. Pierre followed. Pierre's fresh-coloured face was puffy with anger ; head down, he glowered at us all. He swung round more particularly upon me. " Why are you here ? All the army knows you were the Frenchman's friend."

" I need not be here," I assured him. Jean motioned him to be silent and signed to me not to care. That day I was beyond caring what Pierre or any other man might say of me ; the day after might be different, for slights and suspicions, like small poisonings, grow worse overnight. As for his anger, I was indifferent to that also. I had been bred up on angers ; anger has never impressed me. I looked away.

The arras lifted and Melisande came in. She was in white, her hair in a snood of gold. There were triangles of colour like scarlet banners in her cheeks.

Pierre greeted her roughly : " Have you no other gown ? Already they are laughing at you."

" It is my best, Pierre," she said. " I left it, perhaps so that I might return and find it again."

" You will never be pure again," he said.

She answered him, a tremor in her voice I did not care to hear. " In that I am no different from other women."

When Jean rebuked him for the second time Pierre turned and, like a bullock through a thicket, charged out again.

Melisande spoke at once while the arras swayed behind Pierre, and Robert went down on one knee. " More than for any harm I have done myself I could weep for you, Robert of Kinwarton."

Like a man lost in his own pain he looked at her while the traffic went on outside and small stirs and spent airs from beyond the arras moved, fugitive as motes of sun, within the room.

" He was not worthy of you," at last he said.

" When you love, who thinks of worth ? " she asked. " You once loved me."

" Once." Robert seemed to brood, his head bent, his one hand covering his face.

I do not know what moved Melisande then—she was not easily moved. Suddenly she bent over him. " Do not grieve, Robert," she said, " oh, do not grieve, for our day, past now. Oh, do not grieve."

" How can I not grieve ? " He was on his feet. " I may not be with you," he said, " nor serve you, now, or ever in my life. But I would have you know that when I die in all God's holy angels I shall see only your face."

" Robert. Robert," she cried then, her face as bright as April and as near, I thought, to showers.

He drew off from her. To me he seemed to draw altogether away.

Her face quivering, Melisande turned to me. We were her Court, I thought, and she was always Queen. My hands trembled as I spoke. " I would be your friend always, as I promised," I said.

" I had not hoped," she said—she seemed lost a little—" for so much courtesy."

Bogis returned. He appeared over-large, over-solid in the small ante-room. Only his forty-acre field would contain him, I thought, or his little manor of Kingleigh.

Melisande looked doubtfully at him for a moment. Then, half-hesitating, she said, " Bogis—messire Everard," and waited.

He spoke stiffly. " I would be private with you, but there is no time."

" Do not speak to me, messire Everard," she said. " Truly, truly, I am not worthy."

He came nearer her. " When I was sick of the fever I dreamed of you."

" And now ? " She waited, breathless a little and as though once more she were afraid.

" Now I would no longer dream of you." He looked at her straightly. " I never loved you so well as now that you are of less account and therefore nearer me."

" Are you so large, messire Everard," she asked, " that you must pity where you love ? "

He caught the edge of pride in her voice and was almost aggrieved. " I do not pity. I love, and that is enough. And I am not so large."

" Would you take such as I am," she asked, " cast-off and blown upon, a beggar and quite unskilled, to England for a wife ? "

" I will," he said. Down on one knee at last, stumblingly, her hands in his, he said : " Body, heart and hand, desire and truth, I offer you humbly, if you will have me, Peter Everard, for husband." He waited—for my part I had not thought to hear so much poesy from Everard—and then he said, surprising me again : " There was more that I have forgotten, fine cobweb stuff that the Chronicler taught me. But this that I have remembered is truth and my own."

He paused again. " I would have you for my wife and lady," he said patiently when she did not speak.

" Oh, Bogis," she said in a rush, half-weeping now and turning away her head. " Are you like this ? I had not known you before. Forgive me," she said.

I looked at Robert. For a moment I could no longer look at Everard or Melisande. Robert's face gave no sign, only the stump of his maimed arm twitched unbearably for a moment as if the ghost of his dead hand were moving there.

I looked at Everard. His was an archangel's face, solemn, and important a little, I thought, and marvellously clear. While I looked at him, like an archangel who still has flying work to do, he was on his feet. " I will speak to the King." Dusting his knees, which was something he seldom remembered to do, he went out. As he did so I noticed for the first time that surcoat and armour, cloak and shoes were bright and bridegroom new.

Two page-boys held back the arras. We stood to one side. To a fanfare of trumpets the King and the two Queens in scarlet and ermine came in, the heralds stepping before them like dancers in pointed crimson shoes under their stiff gold tabards. And Melisande caught at Jean des Préaux's hand while the rest of the Court, the Queen's ladies, the King's gentlemen, the lords and knights and esquires, the grooms and the chamberlains, a long serpent-like train, wound slowly in.

The first astonishment at the result of the Lady's trial had died away. The streets of Joppa were patterned with shadow; far-off, the first stars hung like lanterns of yellow upon the peaks of the mountains; near at hand the masons and carpenters were making their way, ochre-coloured and bent like gnomes in the dusk, from Joppa's new walls. It was then that the Chronicler accosted me.

"How went it?" he enquired. "It was a long speech, I flatter myself."

While I looked at him uncomprehendingly he pulled at one of his long ears. "Messire John, I who am as chaste as an eunuch, and for much the same reason, have yet made some very excellent loving speeches. How went that line—'Your cheeks like the petals of a rose' and that other, beginning 'My heart's passionate constancy'?"

I came tumbling to my proper senses. I pretended a heartiness I did not feel. I clapped the Chronicler resoundingly upon the back—he looked startled, then beamed at so much comradeship. "Forgotten, man," I said. "Vanished clean out of mind. All excepting his truth, and his desire, and other such poor simple stuff."

The Chronicler began to shake his head. "Without doubt, messire John, there is something poetical about a man who is in love."

"I tell you," I interrupted him, "he forgot your rose-petal stuff; he remembered only the heart's good homespun."

"So, so," the Chronicler nodded again. "Well, messire John, one ounce of fine feeling, they say, is worth a peck of poesy."

My false heartiness, like a mummer's beard, dropped off me. "True feeling—he has that," I said. "While I thought only of myself, messire Everard thought only of the Lady. For that reason she was most wise to go with him."

"Then they are man and wife, no doubt upon it." The Chronicler clapped one hand eagerly upon another.

"I never saw so hasty a wedding," I said, "nor such a crowd of witnesses."

"She was too pretty a lady to suffer long for so brief a sinning," the Chronicler said. He turned to go, then paused for a moment. "Well, well," he spread both hands, "who knows where life leads?"

I watched him go. For an instant in my mind's eye I saw again the scene in the King's audience-room: Melisande in her white gown standing before the dais between the Countess of Leicester and Jean des Préaux.

I heard the heralds from the gallery cry out her titles and names, and the clerk of the King's office recite in a voice, toneless as water, her offence. Traitress, he termed her, and adulteress. I saw the Countess of Leicester and Jean des Préaux fall away from her as the King spoke, and the Lady herself drooping in the cool greyness of air among the tall pillars that seemed to me like frozen trees. On the Persian arras behind the King's chair I saw the leaping hounds and the spotted panther springing ; I heard Melisande's voice, unwontedly strong for a moment and clear ; I saw the King's face, haggard before, quicken as she spoke. In the enclosed space of the audience-chamber I heard the Lady Melisande's answer to the King's question : " Guilty of the sin of loving, my lord. But not of treachery, never of treachery, my lord. I swear it, by my soul's life."

I remembered how Queen Berengaria's pursed mouth trembled, then hardened above her small childish chin, while the King's eyes sought Melisande's face, so like and yet so unlike that of William des Préaux. The sin of loving, I thought—I was not alone in the thought—the King should know.

I remembered again how the King spoke after this, looking about him : "My lords, forgive me that I cannot find it in my heart to decree any punishment for the sister of that good knight and servant of the Cause, William des Préaux, and of the Sieur des Préaux here. The Lady returned to us of her own will, at peril of her life. If any one of you present believe her guilty of treason, let him speak."

I saw the half-smiles, was aware once more of the scarcely perceptible shrugs, and that Melisande knelt still. I heard the King speak to her while Jean des Préaux waited, an odd stretched look about his mouth : " Lady, will you take Peter Everard Mortebois for husband ? "

As I write I can see the two upraised fingers of the Archbishop's hand as he blessed them after their marrying, hear his cracked thin voice : " Daughter, sin no more." I remember how stiffly Queen Berengaria sat, half-hidden like a tree in a rainstorm in her own crimped fall of hair, how Queen Joanna wept as if she enjoyed weeping. I can hear the King's voice even now : " Lady, where will you go ? "—" I will go with my husband," I can hear Melisande say.

I looked for Robert and found him, stretched out, face downward upon the floor of his tent. He wept, I thought then and think now, for lost familiar things, for his old life not yet finished, for the new life he had yet to live.

Unheard I came away. I waited outside the camp, moved as I had never yet been moved, for that moment when, as though heaven let down a curtain from on high, night would come on. Here was a twist in Robert's affairs and mine, of which I had not dreamed, an end—I realised this also—to a part at least of what was green and precious in me. I would have rejected sorrow if I could, but its print was there, in all my mind. It was then, as I remembered Robert, that I remembered also the words of Ambrose's song, "O the scars that life leaves," and it was then also that the Chronicler came to me, scarcely moved at all, and all agog for news.

3

A FEW ROCK PIGEONS

Y the end of October Joppa's walls were re-built and the march towards Jerusalem begun. Once more all was relief and thanksgiving among us; once more as on our departure from Vézelay no one dared to voice the doubts that lay like water weeds at the bottom of every man's mind. A vast host almost three hundred thousand strong once more, we set out to the sound of trumpets and the faint throb of distant drums, to the far-off chanting of the monks and the songs of the pilgrims. Our lance-heads flashed back a thousand points of light, our banners and pennons were over us like a ceiling of bright falling leaves. If Jerusalem could have been reached that week, or even that month, if nothing more had been asked of us than marching and fighting, I, John of Oversley, might have a different tale to tell. But Jerusalem lay not so many miles as arduous weeks of toil away. Since every step forward our armies might take must be made secure our march could not be the magnificent sweep towards victory of which I and thousands more had dreamed. It could be no more than a slow progress from one obstacle to the next, from one difficulty safely surmounted to another.

As we had paused to make Joppa safe against attack so now, only a few miles from Joppa, we were obliged to halt again in order to re-build the strongholds of Casal Maen and Casal of the Plains, which the Turks had first abandoned and then thrown down and which guarded Joppa itself. Every week-day we laboured to re-build the walls, but on Sunday, although each day lost was a gift to our adversaries, the Sultan and the Devil, no work, except by the priests at their masses and prayers for the saving of souls, was done. Sunday was a day of rest for us, therefore, on which to do as we pleased.

I was happier in these days. Since we had left Joppa Robert and Everard and I had come together almost as bachelors again. If Robert and I thought of the Lady Melisande—and we did think of her—and of de Passy, we did not speak of them. Here, on the road to Jerusalem, what had been recent history at the Court no longer filled the forefront of our minds. Love itself seemed like something small set on the top of some distant hill. We had left it behind us : we would return to it again.

On this particular Sunday, November the fourth, the three of us had decided to go off in search of rock pigeons. We were tired of horse-flesh and dog-flesh and salt rancid bacon and beans ; if the pigeons failed—and that, we felt, was unlikely since they abounded in these parts—we were resolved to bring back what we could of forage and provisions, or even, more ambitiously, of plunder and prisoners. The suggestion was mine, agreed to eagerly by Everard and somewhat unwillingly by Robert. We would go out lightly armed as for a skirmish. Brand and Giles and three or four mounted men would go with us. Setting out at dawn we should, with good fortune, be back before sundown and would sleep that night well-fed and content.

I think Robert was undecided until the day dawned. It promised to be the sort of day for which a man longs when he is sick and fevered : a day of quick moving air, of warm sun and light shifting shadows, when earth and sky seem in unity together and all creation seems to share in the same peace. The air indeed was so pleasant and so free we might have been in England, no longer in Outremer. It was as if presently church bells would ring for matins from some church tower behind a grove of oaks on some round hill, or in some long hollow between the sandy dunes. The camp as we rode out seemed full still of the dreams of sleeping men ; the long lines of washing strung out overnight stirred in the first morning airs and, alone among other sounds, a little bell tolled as if it would never cease.

Our talk, in which Brand and Giles and the four men-at-arms joined, was all of the reports brought in overnight to the camp by the King's spies of new treacheries of the Marquis Conrad and new plots of the Sultan Saladin. The Marquis had bought much more than time, it was said, of Saladin, and sold much more also. Even at this moment the Sultan was entertaining Reginald of Sidon, Conrad's messenger, most royally within his tent.

What, asked one of the men-at-arms, a Gascon called Henri, was the meaning of it all ? " I cannot fathom so much treachery," he declared.

Everard answered him kindly : " The Marquis Conrad has offered, not for the first time, to join the Sultan against King Richard and against Christendom. He does so because in time of peace Tyre grows fat from trade with the East, in time of war it is stricken and grows lean."

" If the Marquis had been Brand he would be dead bones by now, certainly," Brand said, nodding.

" I do not believe," I declared, " that Saladin will dare to trust Conrad for all that he feasts Reginald of Sidon."

" They be all Judases," remarked Giles piously.

" We make too much of Saladin," Robert said. " It is as though the English must always have an enemy for a hero."

So the talk went on, moving between long pauses from one topic to the next, always tending to return to this same question of Conrad's treachery. We talked, but as yet we were not greatly troubled. Treachery of some sort was part of the air the armies breathed in Outremer ; plots and counter-plots succeeded each other like rainy days. If there were always plots they were almost always discovered ; if there were always quarrels we expected nothing different. It is even possible that quarrelling may have helped in the monotony of the camp to keep our minds alive.

We rode on past Casal of the Plains towards Bombrac. Larks with crested heads rose and sang and fluttered from bush to bush as we passed ; yellow-winged creatures like locusts tossed by in the tail end of a wind ; flocks of rock pigeons flew up behind us with a stiff whirr of wings. Two eagles wheeled as though in some aerial play high up over our heads. We moved on beyond Bombrac towards the foothills of Samaria where the land falls in craggy terraces beloved of fat lizards and of rock pigeons also.

Having set our bait and laid our nets we waited on a wide platform in the sparse shade of one of the terraces for our birds to come in. Below us the plain shimmered in the light ; behind us the rocky terraces showed harsh in the glare. While I lay on our high platform I began to wonder idly how easily and how far a man might fall from the edge of one terrace to the next, how long lie undiscovered in the shadow of some boulder, or beneath some twisted juniper or thorn. From where we were I could distinguish the white mosque-like dome of the well at Bombrac, and the cluster of huts around the well, and the fringe of date palms, ragged as the edge of a monk's robe, that encircled them. In the farthest distance Joppa showed white and shining behind its new walls ; beyond, in a faint rainbow-coloured mist, I believed I saw the sea.

We had not been stationary long when Brand and Giles and the four men-at-arms left us with a stealthy air, intent, we could only suppose once more, upon some errand of their own. They declared they were off to watch the nets and afterwards bring in the birds. On the contrary, Everard declared, they were off, he believed, to play at draughts among the rocks. I thought differently. I said I knew what they would do. The Pisans would catch lizards and roast them in their skins as we roasted hedgehogs in England and Brand and Giles would eat the lizards. Everard turned over on his side. " Jeroboam," he said, " will be dead by this time." I thought he sighed again for his lost lizard. "Jeroboam will be a grandfather by this time. Would you deny him his pleasures?" Robert enquired.

"No," Everard said. He smiled so simply and suddenly we laughed at him.

We stayed sleepily where we were. Robert alone had kept his sword beside him and with his one hand, which was seldom still, played with it constantly. I looked away. Robert's restlessness in these days bred a strange fidget of pity in me. I shut my eyes. The sun rose higher, the air was spiced with juniper and thyme; it was very quiet and, I remember also, most unnaturally still.

The twelve men came on us as suddenly as figures in a dream. They appeared as stark and as unreal, standing silently to the left where the platform upon which we lay narrowed to the downward track again and the gully between the terraces sloped steeply down. They had brown faces like Beduins; their robes were white, their horses' feet, I saw, and could scarcely believe what I saw, were bound in felt. It was like, and yet unlike, the ambushing of King Richard, for though the method was the same these men appeared swifter and more full of purpose than Saladin's men had been. We scrambled for our weapons; swords out, they were on us. The nightmare quality held; even the silence held; even this moment of time, like their swords, had a keen edge. This was violence, I thought as I struggled, this was evil, I told myself, my back against the rock. In the next instant I saw that they came at us with the flat of their swords only as if once more, as in the Sultan's attack upon King Richard, their purpose were to capture rather than to kill. I saw Everard at grips with one of the twelve. He had hold of the other's sword-arm and was twisting it while striking at him with his fist repeatedly under the chin. They were too closely held for any other man to interfere, then down and rolling over to the edge of the platform and back again. It was then that Robert, who had waited beside me until this moment, cried out sharply and bitterly, "My God, my God," and started forward. I know that I followed. I felt myself struck from behind, so shrewdly that I fell to my knees. I stayed bent forward upon my knees like a calf, my head nodding as if it were not mine, my senses leaving me while my hands and arms were twisted and tightly bound. I saw Everard on his feet again pressed backwards most dangerously, and struggling, then gone, with a long slither of stones and no other sound, into the abyss, his enemy following him. Robert, having no one any longer to guard his left side, was overpowered.

I waited dully for the next thing. They had bound Robert. At a signal from a tall hook-nosed fellow who appeared to be their captain and who had held off from the attack, they circled Robert's waist with a rope, and, leaving his feet free, prepared to lead him away. Anguish, I think, restored a part of my reason to me. I know that he went uprightly between two of them, a quietness upon his face and, unless I dreamed it, a faint smilingness as well. Maimed as he was, set on martyrdom as he was, now, he may have thought, was a good time to die.

I roused myself; I cried after him: "Farewell." He turned his head, but was struck again, quietly and brutally once more, so that he stumbled and almost fell. My eyes followed him. He went to his death, I thought, in some gully between the rocks. Even while I looked he was gone from me. Never, either to be glad of his company or to be vexed with him, should I see him again. I wept then as suddenly as a child, but brokenly, as children seldom weep. I recovered myself; I prepared to go with him.

Astride one of their horses, my hands tied, my feet tied under the horse's belly, roped between two of my captors, I was led away. I looked back. This was the country of my dream at Vézelay : the craggy peaks, the desolation, the featureless plain. We climbed higher. The peaks grew sharper, lonelier, like the peaks of the spirit, the deserts of the mind. As we climbed I thought I saw Brand and Giles and the rest on a terrace below our path, small as farmyard fowl, their heads together among the stones like hens pecking. They stood up, it seemed to me, and looked upon us as we passed, high up and far from them and beyond distinguishable sight, then crouched comfortably to their game once more. In the next turn of the track they were lost to me and I was beyond their range.

My nightmare of mind and body endured, it seemed to me, interminably. We rode on and no one offered me violence, or food, or drink, or rest ; no one spoke to me. The two men who had led Robert away did not return. Whether to hope from this that they were dead and Robert alive still, I did not know. It was possible that Brand's party had caught up with them ; it was possible but not likely, I thought. The sky flowered to flame, the mountain peaks were cones of fire ; the day lingered before it died. Now, in half-delirium I believed I saw the bearded stranger whom I had allowed to pass on his way beyond Acre many months before. It was the purest fancy of a disordered brain and yet I saw him very clear. He rode ahead of our company, I thought, and turned every now and then to smile at me. And, smiling, touched his beard. Though there was no benevolence, I felt, in his smile or in the touching of his beard.

We rode downhill, a lantern slung on the saddle of the foremost rider showing the way. Presently the shadows darkened, the leaves grew still. As if only night were dangerous two more men held me then. I hated, as I have never hated anything before, the touch of their hands. We rode on tirelessly. Gradually all my pains and dreams, all the confused workings of my mind turned back irresistibly to sleep.

4

THE MOUNTAIN AND THE FORTRESS

How long the darkness lasted for me I do not know : I think it lasted for many days. The blow I had received before I was overcome was shrewder than I had thought, shrewder than was perhaps intended. I have only a confused memory of what happened after that first day until the last stage of my journey to the mountain and the fortress to which, though I was ignorant of this also, I was bound.

I remember how I burned with fever, how pain thrust dagger-like through my temples ; I remember the slow progress we made, moving on and for ever on, the rough joltings on the backs of mules and horses, the lurch and sway of the rude litter in which finally my captors carried me ; the almost trackless ways, the perilous roads. I remember how, from the drought of fever and the pain of constant movement I longed to be cool and to be still, and how, as if I were in some thirsty precinct of hell, I was never cool and never still. Between one swoon and another I was all the time aware of the harsh pressure that drove us on ; dimly I felt that though I was a prisoner my captives themselves were not free, but all of us alike subject to the same arrogant will. It was plain even to me that the tall fellow who had commanded the fight and whose features, now that I could take note of them, appeared as keen and void of pity as those scratched on some old Roman coin fallen out of Acre's walls, was for the space of our journey absolute lord of us all. Though I might have died from so much travelling, though my life appeared for some reason to be valuable to my captors, by this man's ordering I was forced to journey on with scarcely a pause. I know that in a fit of unbearable weakness I raved and cast about me wildly, that when my madness had given way to weakness once more, someone brought me a cup from which I drank unwillingly. The potion appeared bitter at first, then cloying and sweet. It bred strange fancies in my sick brain : I felt my mind buoyant at first as a ship on a freshening sea, then, like a ship again, I felt myself fallen into a great trough of calm.

I do not know how things real are joined with things imagined in a man's brain, nor how between the two, often enough, nightmares and monstrous shapes are born. I only know that my nightmare, that had endured so long, broke at last. I woke first, and this again seemed strange, to the actual sounds of some quayside, to a visible sea smelling, as the sea always smells at any portside, of freshness and filth, of seawrack and garbage and decaying fish. I parted the curtains of my litter and looked out. I was unattended and stationary at the quayside. A great bustle of preparation was to be seen on board a tall galley anchored near the quay. Sails were being hoisted, decks scrubbed, stores and water taken on board ; a flag I had never seen before, half-red, half-white, was being run up to the masthead. I watched curiously for a moment and then grew tired. Other ships also were lined along the side : fishing boats shaped like fish with the eye of Isis painted in bright colours on their sides ; small fishing smacks with red canvas sails, and stout dromons stuffed with cargo for the far lands of India and Cathay. They, and the tossing waste of dark blue waters beyond, were a sight to lift a man's heart. Beyond the quay on a stretch of sand, a town with white flat-topped houses and tall Saracen towers could be seen, carved into pleasant squares by lanes made luxuriant with flowers and shrubs. Tall cactus hedges ran down to the waterside, beyond were grey-green olive groves. It was noonday, and suddenly, though I could no longer hear them, I remembered how the cicadas had filled the air with their rasping as we rode in. I closed my eyes, and memory stirred in me again. This, I told myself, was surely the city of Sidon. I remembered its white towers, its tall cactus hedges as they had appeared to us from the sea as we passed that first time with King Richard and the King's fleet to Acre.

At this point someone came and laid a cloth steeped in some sleepy brew of herbs over my face, twitched my curtains together angrily again, and waited. I could see his shadow solid and dark through the thin curtains of my litter, and on either side of his dark shape the noonday light. I woke in darkness to the patter of bare feet on the boards above my head, to the creak and strain of sails, the splash of oars and movement again, the movement of a ship under me. I was in some ship's hold and we were running out to sea, to what place, and why, once more I did not know. But the fumes of the drug were still heavy in my brain. Like a man scarcely concerned for his own safety I sank back once more into my private darkness that, like a quilt of down, had so far covered me. I think we voyaged for a week, or perhaps for no more than three or four days. In the darkness of the ship's hold it was not easy to measure how time went nor tell the difference between night and day, and yet I believed I could distinguish both from the greyness that seeped down with each new dawn and the faint rosiness that followed the coming of each day.

I was never alone in my hold. My attendant was there, a white huddled shape clasping his knees, or a long figure stretched out not too far off nor yet too near my head. At first I would call out to him, " Why are you on guard here ? " I would abuse him also ; I would even plead with him. Not once did he answer me. On one occasion I hoped to provoke him to speech by swearing aloud to myself that he was a deaf-mute. He laughed at me and made sounds and gestures like a man mocking a deaf mute. I laughed in return. At that he withdrew himself utterly. I thought of him in secret as the Cat. He moved like one, halted like one, as suddenly and as smoothly. If he had shown any sign of friendliness I was so much alone I might have loved him as men in dungeons have been known to love rats and mice and swallows. He showed no friendliness and no hostility either ; he appeared to be wrapped always in his own neutral silence. For this, and for his constant watch on me, I hated him at times. I could never hate him for long, for it was he who tended me ; he also spent every day as I did, cloistered within the dark. He had, I remember, a queerly bent back and tender hands.

I grew to know the shape of him and the touch of his hands, but during all this time I never saw his face. Only occasionally, by the light of the shuttered lantern that he held while he tended me or moved about his tasks, I saw his feet. They were slender and long, ringed about each ankle with a deep groove-like scar. It was the strangest scar I had ever seen, though no man can come to Outremer in time of war and not see many strange and fearful marks and scars.

For almost the length of the voyage I lay passive within the hold, pretending less life than indeed I felt. I do not believe my enemies were deceived, for on the fourth day or thereabouts after we had set sail the trap door leading to the hold was thrown open, and for the first time since our setting sail the full light of day poured in. While I waited a Saracen in a black caftan and Arab doctor's robes climbed carefully down the ship's ladder, revealing as he did so to my admiring eyes a very ordinary and hairy human leg. The leader of my captors followed. Having conferred together the two of them stood one on each side of my bed. The learned doctor—I took him to be still another doctor of medicine—peered into my eyes, looked into my mouth, held my wrist between the finger and thumb of one hand, then laid his ear to my naked chest. His hair was curiously silken, I remember, and tickled unbearably and smelled of sandalwood. For both these reasons it was peculiarly offensive and yet queerly exciting to me. His examination over, my doctor stood up and washed his hands with a finicky delicate air in a metal bowl which the other man, very negligently, I thought, held for him. Once more the two of them conferred. Then, still without a word to me or my attendant, who had been hovering broodily like a moth at egg-laying time within the shadows, they withdrew again. I looked for and beheld the learned doctor's other leg : it was as hairy as the first and, which appeared to be more remarkable, was circled below the knee with a jewelled band. Idly once more, I wondered why. Here, in solitude, among my enemies, much of what I saw eluded me. Both pairs of legs vanished, the trap-door shut. No more than at first was the darkness of the ship's hold completely mine. Quietly, from the shadows at the other end of the hold my attendant returned.

On what I judged to be the next day my circumstances, perhaps because of the learned doctor's report of me, changed. At daybreak I woke to find myself on deck, an awning over me to shield me from too many curious eyes, from my own looking out, and a little also, I do not doubt, from the sun. Here, for the first time, with the dawn flushing all the western seas with light, with the wind fanning my face and moving always on, I felt some glimmer of strength and hope return. I stayed on deck. All day the life of the ship went on around me ; the sun shone gently, birds flew overhead and perched upon the mast. Like Noah's dove that rested on the ark, one had a tiny sprig of green within its beak. Like Noah again we sighted land about noon, faint and unreal and almost lost yet among the waters. By sundown we had once more put into port. I sought my memory again for any recollection of the place. None came ; it resembled almost any other place along the coast of Outremer. That is to say, there were mountains beyond the town and a wide plain beyond ; the town, built of white stone, was lit with cypress trees. There was the same sparkle in the air, the same riot between tall prickly hedges of vivid-coloured flowers.

Like an Irish poet composing in his cell I closed my eyes and looked within my mind. From out of the dark some sort of recollection came. This might be Tripolis, I thought. From Sidon we had sailed due north. At once an intimation as sudden as it was alarming visited me. From Sidon to Tripolis—so much, I thought, was clear. From Tripolis on-wards in what direction, bound for what place ? I held the question poised unanswered in my mind.

Of one particular at least I was not left long in doubt. A galley, her sides hung with figured cloths of Egypt in white and green, drew in beside ours. Our men hailed her with speech and gesture. I believed they asked her from whence she came and whither she was bound. An African, mother-naked and glossy black, squatting cross-legged upon a round embroidered mat and combing his dense thicket of hair, paused, comb in hand, and answered briefly. " Cleopatra," I thought he said, and " Alexandria," and " Tripolis." Still one more question was shouted to him. He answered silently with gesture only. He clasped both hands before him, then looped the fingers of both hands about wrists and ankles as if he were manacled and chained. Then he, in turn, shot a question at us. Were we a slave-ship also ? I thought he enquired. In recklessness and excitement I answered loudly in English, " Yes, yes."

At that my guards rushed on me and pummelled and bound me, bandaging my eyes and my mouth while my African turned his back and sang, or rather chanted, some melancholy ditty of his own race. It filled my ears strangely at the time and the recollection of it comes back to me still when the wind soughs in the trees or hawks down our long passages at Oversley. For it was a song, I thought, of slavery—there was so much of lamentation in it, so much of acceptance also.

When our ship had put first into Tripolis I had already some inkling of what manner of men my captors were and to what place we were bound. When finally our small company wound out of Tripolis into the Aleppo road I think I knew. From this time onwards, my eyes and mouth free again, I resolved, all my senses sharpened by alarm, to keep careful note of the way and of the country that lay ahead.

We travelled on, always under pressure of the same will, always with the same apparent urgency. We halted for food and sleep only ; if we met other travellers we passed them without look or greeting ; we skirted houses and villages, moving wherever possible by tracks and unfrequented ways, keeping among ourselves an all but absolute silence. If I spoke no one answered me ; if I continued to speak and held, as I did on one occasion, a pleasant conversation aloud and with myself, my mouth was stopped a second time, and that not gently. Loosely bound between two of my captors, never for two days together the same pair, I rode horseback once more. In spite of my resolve to keep careful note of the way, from the monotony of so unbroken a silence I often slept as I rode, only waking to an ill-humoured tug of the rope that bound me, or to some sudden jolt when my horse—normally he stepped with the utmost precision—chanced to slip upon a stone. I slept so much it was as though I journeyed through some silent country of the mind. Even those stretches of our journey which I remember most clearly possess for me as I look back upon them the over-sharpened quality of a dream. I have tried to account for it in other terms and cannot. Though I gained in strength daily I was sick in body still, haunted in mind for all my surface calm by my own imaginings of Robert's death and the ordeals I myself had still to face.

If I had yielded in spirit to my captors or even remained passive under captivity I think I could scarcely have survived. But in every silent way I could I resisted my guards, always encouraging a certain scorn of them in myself and showing it in my manner as much as I dared. For these and other reasons I do not doubt the captain of our band would have killed me joyfully. Since he did not as yet dare to take my life he did his utmost to break my spirit. I was struck and pummelled upon the smallest excuse, denied food, and what was worse, denied water. I was kept under constant watch by day and by night and sometimes robbed even of the solace of sleep. I revenged myself by looking as closely and as contemptuously as

I dared at my tormentor's face. It was, as I think I have said, handsome enough but ravaged as though from within : a Medusa face. I would look with greater charity at my attendant with the scarred ankles. His face which might once have been gentle, was now overlaid by a purposeful vagueness as if he no longer had any wish to be liked or disliked and dreaded, for fear of what he might reveal, even to be known. His gentleness, I believed, was no more than skin-deep. On the surface he was very much as he was made ; beneath the surface the Assassin showed. There were occasions when he would give way to devilish furies and fits of malice ; there were other times when he would fall into long brooding silences. My other guards were less notable : expressionless mutes with blind masks for faces and balls of hangman's hemp for souls. Permanent sleep-walkers, without thought or knowledge or even instinct, they amounted to less in the scale of things, I would assure myself, than animal or bird. Since prisoners must despise their captors or yield to them, it was necessary for me, as I have said, to practise being scornful at their expense.

I knew nothing of the country through which we passed. Since I had no speech with my captors the villages and townships, the foothills, the mountains and streams were alike nameless to me. And yet, from travellers' tales heard sleepily over camp fires or within our tents at Joppa or Acre, I believed we were heading for the highlands of Northern Syria, that the great river winding before us in the distance in a hundred curves was the far-famed Orontes, that the high range of mountains running beyond the limits of the plain almost to the sea were the mountains of the Lebanon. From the plain we passed eventually into hill country and from thence into a mountainous region of small infertile fields, of squat villages sheltering in the base of the foothills, of deep gorges and noisy torrents of still reflecting pools lost in some hollow like the eyes of the quiet moon. I remember plants green for ever in the spray of waterfalls, mists coloured like the gauze wings of dragon-flies. By day the air was clear, at night white mists like enemy shapes came stalking the steep sides of the rocky terraces ; overhead flowed cold waves of wind under the piercing silence of the stars. By day the shadows of the clouds moved majestically over this quiet land. Small forests of cedars and cypresses overhung the precipices ; below were falls of rock, deep gullies filled with stones, filled with bones also, I did not doubt, of horses and of men ; while every crack and cranny of the rocks thrust out thick cushions and pads of flowers. I would look at these and wish I knew their names.

We met strange weather. Freak storms came on us suddenly ; then, like April showers, swept suddenly away. A great tempest of rain and lightning overtook us in the mountains about nightfall one evening and raged until the first light of dawn. Huddled together like a covey of wet birds we watched through the long hours from the shelter of an over-hanging rock while lightning like a messenger of perpetual flame still came and went through the open cave of the sky. From the rain that fell upon us so violently and the torrents of water pouring down the rocks we were almost swept away. Then, towards dawn, suddenly once more the wind ceased to blow, snow fell gently and silently with its soft gradual motion and all the falling water was overlaid in the light of the waning moon with a thin film of ice. We had been ravens before in our dark cloaks ; patched with white we resembled plovers or magpies now. I was not numbed in sense by the fury of the spectacle as my guards appeared to be ; rather the storm answered some deep need in me, echoed a part, I think, of the strife within myself. For I had much to forget, several wrongs stifled too long to requite or forgive. With dawn the snow ceased to fall ; ice turned to water once more and the sun shone out in a vaporous world that for an hour or so was magpie-coloured too. The captain of my guards stepped out with a swagger from the shelter of our rock ; my attendant with the scarred ankles, who had held himself knotted and tense all night, untied himself as I have seen an old shepherd do after a long February vigil with creaks and stifled groans. We lit a fire and in this changed world of steaming mists and falling waters worshipped it in silence for a while, then went once more on our way.

Now that I had fully recovered, my mind began to turn more constantly to thoughts of escape. I was riding with my captors up yet one more winding track revolving some far-fetched plan in my mind. I know my plan involved a fortress, a devoted Turkish maiden with a pleasant English face, a scaling ladder and a long rope. The night was dark but not too dark for my project; all my plans, I remember, promised well. The suspense, imaginary though it was, was so painful I could scarcely bear to ride on.

I turned my head. On a lower track on the opposite hillside reality faced me. A party of Templars stayed motionless upon their horses in the hill track and stared at us. Their white cloaks, the red crosses upon their shoulders could clearly be seen. I jerked suddenly in my saddle as though convulsed, I wished to cry out to them, to give them their own war-cry of " Beauséant " so that they might know me for a Christian, sworn as they were to the Cross. But though I opened my lips no words came. My guards were quicker in action than I was of speech. While the Templars turned to one another, doubt and questioning in all their gestures, a cloak was thrown over my head, then drawn closely over my face. I was sur-rounded and hustled on up the steep track, and on, until I could only suppose I was out of sight.

Of all the disappointments I suffered on my long journeyings this that I suffered then was the hardest to bear. To be shown friends and safety, only to be snatched instantly away from both, held a peculiar anguish for me at this stage of our journey when the mountain was closing in upon us and the fortress was almost within sight. I continued to cry out and to struggle. To do so was quite useless, I knew. And yet, even though my life had depended upon it, I could not have been silent. I was not only beaten, so alarmed were my guards that I was even pricked with daggers. For a time while my fit of rebellion lasted, I experienced a new strange pleasure from so much added pain. But afterwards when we halted that night, I leaned my head on my knees and wept secretly from exhaustion and the humiliation and disappointment that I felt. At the back of my mind also was the realisation, and the added fear it brought, that I was not after all the favoured prisoner I had appeared at first to be.

It is difficult to weep and not to sniff. I sniffed, then looked up to find the eyes of my attendant with the scarred ankles fixed upon me, an odd kindling in their brown depths such as one sees in a dog's eyes sometimes. Immediately he looked away. I learned afterwards that there was a streak of madness in him, and that sometimes he would bark and even frisk like a dog.

One of my chief complaints in my captivity was that I was most desperately cut off from friendliness or speech and yet was never truly alone. It was a special torment to me, when I had a mind to feel torment, to be unable to keep company even with myself. I waited, my limbs twitching, my mind on fire. Presently my guards, one on each side of me, slept. I looked about me. All the wild hill country lay bare in the light of the moon : hill peaks like mountains, rocky terraces as steep as castle walls. Below, far-off, the Orontes flowed, winding in faint silver coils between banks of mist. Gradually this world of stars and silences, so deep in shadow, so full of the moon's light, took me, majestic as it was, a little to itself. My senses, over-sharp before, dulled ; my brain worked coolly now. From our encounter of the morning I was driven to ask whether we could not be far removed from Krak of the Knights, the great fortress of the Knights Hospitallers nearest to the Moslem territory of Hama and the Assassin fortresses ; whether the party of Templars I had seen might not be visiting that place ? Could it be that we were within reach of Massiat itself, the chief seat, or so I had always been told, of the Assassin power ? I cursed my own ignorance that both Krak of the Knights and Massiat alike were no more than names to me.

At what stage in the midst of so much conjecture and vexation I fell asleep I do not know. When I woke the dawn was opal-streaked and cold, and my attendant of the scarred ankles, his cheeks puffed like those of a cherub in the carved altar screen of Alyncestre church, was on his knees, blowing warm embers into flame. Beside him on a dish of plaited rushes, a heap of trout lay. I watched while he wrapped them, one by one, in wide wet leaves, I think of bay, and roasted them on the cooler side of his fire. We ate them afterwards. As our encounter with the Templars had been the worst part of my captivity, so my Assassin's trout, freshly roasted and eaten, were the best. They did something, though I could scarcely say what, to console me for my misery of the day before.

It was on that day that both observation and instinct told me we were not far from the end of our journey. The bearing of my guards changed ; from now onwards they appeared a little less like sleepwalkers, a little more like ordinary careless men. I thought their manner betrayed a certain eagerness also. Weapons and gear were furbished up, horses groomed. The lesser sort of my company of gaolers put on clean linen robes ; the captain and my one-time attendant added girdles and shoes and turbans of scarlet to their white garments. I watched unmoved. I was at last certain of what I had suspected almost from the beginning, that I was in the hands of men of the Order of Assassins. It was all one to me now. Since my fit of rebellion and the exhaustion that followed I was no longer greatly concerned for myself or even unhappy for my friends. I lived for the day only and for the next thing.

We journeyed on through country that grew wilder with each half-hour's travelling, up rocky ledges so steep we looked and felt, I think, like flies walking, over paths winding like steep stairways over shining slabs of rock upon which our horses could scarcely keep their feet. I saw the stars that night, piercing and greenish-bright, and the mists rising under the moon. From the ridge on my left I heard a lion roar as loud as if he lay under my hand. The lion roared, and then the silence, like a peaty bog, closed up again.

The fortress, invisible before, could clearly be seen in the light of the next day perched high upon its tableland of rock. Around it ran a great wall ; below, caught like a bird's nest within the foothills, a walled town lay. From a mingling of excitement and fear I spoke sharply and suddenly to the captain of my guards. " What fortress is this ? " He was surprised into answering me. " Massiat," he said, and returned me a look as fierce and uncomprehending as a hawk's.

So now, after days of conjecture, I touched certainty at last. I could no longer doubt that we had arrived, not at the fortress of Qaf, nor at any other of the half-dozen Assassin strongholds in this part of Syria, but at Massiat, the most formidable of them all. Here the Old Man of the Mountains himself, Sheikh Sinan Rashideddin, Lord of Massiat, Grand Prior of the Syrian Order of the Assassins, was to be found for the greater part of the year. I looked again. With its courtyards and walls and towers, the fortress appeared vast in extent ; perched high amidst the hill peaks it appeared impregnable. Though I was aware of a sick feeling at the pit of my stomach I did my best to appear unimpressed. I turned of my own accord—for we were dismounted by this time—and plodded on up the steep incline.

In the distance a man in a white robe could be seen descending the same hill peak on which we were. He drew nearer, stepping smoothly and swiftly. I took him for another of Sinan's messengers. Messenger he was, but not for us. His eyes fixed on the way before him, he pressed on without look or greeting. Every week, or more frequently than every week, I had been told, Sheikh Sinan's messengers went out from Massiat into the world. In one or more of a hundred disguises they would wait for weeks, for years if necessary, for the right moment in which to strike. If one of their number failed another took his place. His mission completed, not one Assassin in twenty returned by the way I trod now. They were murderers, and yet, in return, they themselves died every kind of painful death. Why was so much demanded of them ? I wondered. And what monstrous travesty of faith was this that thousands should die in order that one old man might rule ? Patient as God, pitiless as Moloch, Sinan waited sometimes in Qaf, men said, sometimes in Massiat, and walked in his delectable gardens there—both places were graced with gardens unequalled in all the East, report said again, for beauty—and lived simply and cleanly, and thought calm thoughts and holy thoughts, while sending his men to murder wherever murder would serve his purpose, whether that purpose were for revenge, or power, or gain. What considerations, I asked myself again, ruled Sheikh Sinan, who himself ruled so many other men's lives and minds ? Love of the fear in which he was held ruled him, it was likely, love of his own almost godlike power ; in the end, love of himself, of Sheikh Sinan Rashideddin. My head bent, my mind busy, I toiled on. And this man, I continued, for I wished to have everything clear in my mind, had sent his messengers to snatch me from my fellows and transport me, John of Oversley, John of Nowhere, Lord of Little, to Massiat. Again, for what purpose ? Either Sinan was mistaken or mad, or I was mad, or else I dreamed.

Once more I raised my head. The fortress stood solidly before my eyes against the noonday sky ; it showed as clear to me, as dark against the light as the citadels and walls of Hell do, it is most likely, to the damned. I could see sentries in their watch towers looking out and men running to their posts along the walls ; as I watched, a flight of pigeons took off from the nearest tower, wheeled in concerted movement in the air, then veered sharply once more and headed west. A man signalled to us from the castle walls ; our captain, with whirling movements of his arms, appeared to signal back.

At the foot of the last ascent we halted by a still pool. It was ringed by rocks ; the water, which was deep and milky rather than clear, mirrored only dimly the flight of birds, the passage of the clouds, and my own strangely bearded face. I could hear the fall of water close at hand but out of sight. While I gazed about me and took note of the pool and every neighbouring shrub and tree, my guards came and covered my eyes once more and bound my hands. Held fast between two of them I was thrust on up a narrow stair, then on again. Presently, instead of smooth rock, uneven paving stones lay under my feet ; no wind touched my face ; the air was dank and as though unwarmed by the sun. Our feet, lightly shod, made scarcely a sound. On a sudden decision I cried out. As I had expected, the echoes of my own voice answered me. Although I was struck instantly across the mouth, although in revenge even my lips were bound, I cared little. We were in some underground passage-way, I felt certain now.

It was then that I began to be afraid. In the darkness I could hear the faint deep flow of water on every side ; I could smell—I knew the smell of old from our deep cistern at Oversley—the odour of rain water, kept for a long time and stored within stone ; I felt myself shut in by walls, menaced, it might be, by a blind and therefore fearful end. I continued to advance between my guards ; the flood appeared nearer ; every moment it sounded louder. I saw it in my mind's eye, a smooth green tide, in its depths a brightness like emerald. Terror of water, terror of colour and no light, terror of darkness and the pit seized me for a moment then. For a little while I think my mind grew numb from so much stifled fear. But presently again reason returned. Why bring me so far to drown me here, I asked, when I should have drowned better in Orontes or the sea, or even by the pool ? Why drown me at all when one of a dozen drier deaths would serve as well ?

My fear passed. In the next breath we were out of the underground passage-way. Now a wind that was both dry and cold lifted my hair, tore at my cloak. I was thrust on between walls again, down echoing corridors, down yet more stairs. I was thrust in to another place suddenly, jerked down upon a stone bench—I could feel the cold coming at my limbs through my linen robes—I heard a heavy door thud to, an iron hasp clamped down ; now someone came behind me and untied the bandages from my eyes and mouth. I was in a monkish cell of stone, lit by two small lancet windows set high under the groined roof and a flickering solitary taper's light. I was not alone. Crouched by the lighted taper, staring like a hound at the flame, was my former companion in the ship's hold.

5

FROM NIGHT TO DAY

I CONFESS that when I set eyes on my Assassin of the scarred ankles and the apparently gentle face within my cell I was disappointed. I had seen a great deal of him already and heard nothing. A bent toadstool leaning over in the wet grass would have been as companionable. From disappointment my mood changed cloudily to resentment, and then swiftly to anger. What had I done to be transported to this place, condemned for days and even for weeks together to the company of a half-crazed mute? I addressed my companion harshly : " Why are you here with me? "

To my astonishment he looked up. One hand touching his dagger hilt, he said : " If you try to escape you will die."

" I could strangle you, bent as you are," I said, " with my bare hands."

He answered me calmly : " You would still die."

I pressed him, perhaps foolishly, to tell me why I was in Massiat and what it was intended to do with me.

He returned me a blank look ; then, gazing once more into the taper's flame, said : " If I were to tell you why you are here, and for what purpose, I also should die."

" You are over-fond of death in Massiat," I observed.

He said coolly : " Death is the other side of life."

I answered him fluently, for since he had obliged me by speaking at all I had some faint hope of winning him over to my side. " I know that death is likely to be the last answer to every man's questions. But no man or woman is happier for making a commerce of death as I think you do upon your mountain here."

He spoke, as I might have guessed, with a gleam of pride : " We are no more than our Lord's servants, and he is most akin to God since he has power over life and death."

" And all this by murder," I interrupted him.

He corrected me. " Not by murder as you think of murder. We teach that all measures are lawful if they lead to the end our Lord Sinan desires."

When I declared that Sinan's purposes must one day fail since all men would end by being opposed to him, my companion did not appear to disagree with me. " It has been foretold of us," he said, proudly once more, " that we shall be like the hunted fox in the brake." He shrugged. " I

226

do not listen to prophecies. They are often no more than passionate and revengeful wishes."

" Who are you," I pressed him, " to set yourselves against so many better men? Are you not mortal? Is not the Sultan of Egypt, Saladin himself, your enemy? And King Richard, my master, also? Only the Marquis Conrad is your friend."

" All men are mortal," my Assassin declared. " And my master Sinan desires no friends."

" Sinan also is mortal," I reminded him, " and must die, and come to judgment."

My attendant turned a still look upon me. " It is you who will die and, before dying, come to judgment."

" I will not die easily," I declared. Even as I spoke I felt a faint shiver of cold. Death after all is not a warm thing to think of.

" Our Lord Sinan," my guard continued, " has only to lift a finger of one hand and we of the Order go to our deaths for him as willingly as upon any other errand. In an instant of time we die. Indeed there is nothing in all our lives so quick as our manner of dying."

" What death does Sinan choose for you then? " I asked curiously.

My guard answered me half in metaphor. " Like Azrael we leap from heaven and fall, and are not mourned, or remembered. For us death is another potion which we must drink when our Lord commands."

" Surely," I exclaimed, " surely this is only one more bloodthirsty tale with which to frighten strangers ! "

" You will see. I think, since you are here within the fortress, that one day you will see."

I enquired carefully : " How often is this judgment of which you speak given among you ? "

My companion looked searchingly at me as if he would read my thoughts. Then, stretching out his hands as if for warmth towards the taper's light, he answered : " It is for Sinan Rashideddin to say when there shall be a judgment, for only he is Lord. Though we do not speak of it the thought of judgment is never far from our minds. When we shut our eyes we see not the steep rocks and the precipice only, but the moving air and the sharp leap between. Yet we do not complain. For fear is necessary and all Islam lies beneath the shadow of a sword. After a judgment we are full of joy and gratefulness to find ourselves alive ; the air breathes sweeter, even the commonest things of earth appear blessed ; we feel lighter, like men who face the spring and have been purged."

As he spoke I recalled how uncontrollably the executioner at the camp would yawn after his work was done, and how our men slept after the slaughter of the Saracen prisoners, not from fatigue only but like lions after a kill.

I reviled him. "You love nothing. You do everything but drink blood."

He turned on me. "Love is no better than folly."

I had not wit enough to answer. While I hesitated our door was thrust open and a rough fellow whom I judged to be a servant entered. After salaaming he set two platters of bread and dates and honey before us and a flagon of wine. At sight of the food we put argument aside. Casting all my fears of poison over my shoulder as if they were a handful of salt to the devil, I fell to. My Assassin followed. He chewed steadily while regarding me all the while out of melancholy red-dark eyes. When I had eaten, my hand moved towards the flagon of wine. On a second thought I half withdrew my hand. My companion waved encouragement to me. "Drink." He drank generously himself.

The wine when I tasted it was too much like syrup for my palate. I did my best, therefore, merely to sip and taste my portion. While my companion drank I spoke deliberately once more of Sheikh Sinan. What manner of man was he? I enquired. Was it true, for example, that he had come to so much power by subterfuge and deceit? Here my Assassin frowned and pretended not to understand. He made no bones about answering all my other questions. This surprised me until I reminded myself that no man is so unnatural as to wish to be silent for ever. We were both, I realised, as though drunk with speech after so long and enforced a silence. I know I was unwontedly fluent in my questions, while he, I felt certain, was more than usually flat in his answers.

I spoke of Sinan again more simply. What was he like in appearance? For I wished to have a picture of the man in my mind.

"He has the face of a saint," my companion answered.

I started. Then you yourself were once a Christian, I almost said. To cover my confusion I drained my cup and went on quickly to ask how that could be?

"All Sinan's thoughts," my Assassin solemnly said—here I almost laughed at the floweriness of the answer—"are gentle like the padded tread of a tiger's feet."

I spoke quickly again, my hands shielding my face. "I would know more of Sinan, so that I may understand the worship his followers have of him."

Rocking a little before his taper's flame, my Assassin related a stranger tale to me than I had heard yet.

Not so long since, in the year 1162, a Syrian stranger came to the fortress of Qaf among the mountains not far from Massiat. He was thin and spare of figure and was dressed in a rough striped cloak such as men of the Yemen wear. For seven years he stayed at Qaf, a member of the household of the old Lord of the Assassins in that place. During all this time he bore himself with piety and modesty and passed among all men who knew him in those days for a saint. How much greater then was the surprise of all men that on the death of the old Lord of the Syrian Assassins this stranger should present his fellows with a paper from the Grand Master of the Order naming him as his lieutenant in Syria and successor to the old chief? This stranger who had borne himself like a saint until he came to rule was no other than Rashideddin Sinan, Grand Prior of the Order of Assassins now and Lord of Qaf and Massiat and all the other Assassin fortresses in Northern Syria besides.

From this time, my companion continued, Sinan's followers greatly increased in numbers and his power grew until he was in all but name an independent prince. To the mountain folk he was the One who must be Obeyed. He was immortal, my Assassin declared, and as he spoke he looked inscrutably at me.

I stayed silent. My companion went on to give me instances of Sinan's supernatural powers. Sinan was aware, he declared, of news before his messengers arrived, and, having heard them patiently, would often correct their reports down to the smallest detail. Surely this was miraculous, my Assassin asked. Once more he gazed at me. I opened my mouth, swallowed my words, and did not speak. Sinan, I had almost said, learns by pigeon post, as Conrad does, as King Richard does also.

My cell companion, as if he were waiting for me to speak, still kept his eyes on me. "How came Sinan to be lame?" I enquired next.

"An earthquake," my Assassin simply said.

"Then how is he immortal?" I could not help but ask.

My companion stayed silent. I asked again: "How have you built up so vast a power for Sinan?"

"By obedience," he said. He turned on me. "Have I not told you so a score of times?"

Having begun to speak, once more he continued. Though a mounting excitement possessed me, I obliged myself to listen. My Assassin would have made a scribe like Ambrose, or like Richard the Chronicler. His words came in rushes, quickly dammed, then again in freshets and streams, in statements hard and smooth as altar slabs, or flat and colourless as plain stones. He held himself tensely, feet crossed, long knobbed fingers clasping his knees. Two fever spots burned high in his cheeks. I listened, and heard again a set of strange half-truths recited, rather than spoken, in a harsh monotone. I heard enough of the precepts of the Order of Assassins to fill me with distaste and almost with fear; I heard much more to make me vexed and inflamed. For all that I could hear was clean contrary to principle or truth and to the known and tested ways of men. It was not possible, I learned, to turn young men into Assassins overnight. A Rule was necessary and a Discipline within the Rule ; an Order of Progression must be observed. For a learner progress was by slow stages : belief was first confused, then undermined, then broken down. This done, the new gospel of nothingness, of no truth, no goodness, was poured, like wet mortar into a master builder's mould, into the learner's ears. Young men, outcasts of all creeds and all races, came to Qaf and Massiat to learn the Assassin's creed : men who were rebels and heretics, men guilty of foul or merely of unnatural crimes.

" And their reward ? " I asked at last.

Still clasping his knees my companion was silent for a long time before he answered. " The reward is Paradise," at last he said.

" This is madness of the first order," I declared, " it is so near to being sane."

I asked again : " If your Assassin's will fails him, if he forgets the Rule to which he has been trained, what then ? "

" There is the Potion to remind him and compel him also," my companion said.

It was all matter for some mummer's play, I thought. I shut my eyes and brooded as deeply as if I were alone. I had heard—was it at Acre ? —of this brew, part hemp, part henbane, which Sinan's young men drank to nerve them for their work, from which, since the brew was called " hashish," they took, it was said, their name. What else I had heard I could not remember. I let it pass ; I listened to my companion again. Much of what I heard I have forgotten ; much more was too subtle and fine for my blunt and clouded mind. I know that there were differing ranks of high and low among the Assassins as with us in the West ; I know that for the main part the followers of Sinan could be divided into the Learned and the Learners. There were, for example, the Fedavi, or Faithful Ones, who had survived all the rigours of their calling, and there were those who as yet were mere learners or apprentices. Only the Fedavi, the fledged masters of their craft, were entrusted with Sinan's messages. It was all very simple, yet diabolical also.

I addressed my Assassin : " You are an initiate then ? "

He touched his red girdle and shoes. " I am a Fedavi."

I leaned forward into the dusk of the cell. " And the reason for all this mummery, man, in Jesu Christ's name ? "

I thought his face blanched a little as he answered me. " His name, His power."

I drew back again, and then he said what seemed strangest of all to me, that in the beginning of their Order another and wider purpose had been served, but now both he himself, and he believed everyone in Massiat, had all but forgotten what that purpose was.

We had talked for a long time. And suddenly the taper's flame that had been low sank silently before my eyes, stayed like a red berry of fire in the dusk, then died. As suddenly the strangeness of my position came home to me. I took hold of the flagon of wine before me and drank again. Now for the first time my Assassin's words affected me deeply. When I remembered them, the subtler portions of the Assassin creed came near to maddening me. Sinan's followers were not content to be infamous ; they must make a tricky maze of infamy for their own delight and the confusion of other men. On the face of it my Assassin's story appeared as strange a tale as a man might dream of on a dark night. It was sober truth. I, John of Oversley, was here, a prisoner in Massiat, in the mountains of Northern Syria, in painful danger of slavery, in danger also, it might be, of death, with no friend, with nothing but my own conscience and my own wits—and I wished I had more of both—to guide me. Here for no good reason, for no evil that I knew of, for nothing that I had willingly done. When I recalled my own innocence, a new recklessness possessed me. Dark thoughts swam up before my mind's eye and vanished again.

Like a man drowning, I cried out : " You are infamous, every man Jack of you. All your cleverness is cunning and trickery. You deceive only yourselves. You have cast out God ; you deny even Mahommed, yet your consciences cry out like empty bellies to be filled. You are like other men ; you must believe, you must worship as other men do. So you turn to Sinan ; you see God in all his tricks and subtleties. Oh, you fools ! For he is a man as you are and will die and come to judgment as all men do. Daggers and poisons and fevers and the slow decays of age will work on him as upon you or upon me. Dead he will smell no more sweetly than a Beduin. Even though you fill him with spices and make a long hollow shell of what was once a man he will not endure for ever. For he is mortal, I say, mortal—" I halted my rhetoric. I saw my Assassin's face—" mortal, and I believe you know it," I said.

My Assassin was on his feet, one hand to his dagger. " You blaspheme and force me to blaspheme also."

" If you did not doubt already, I could not force you to blaspheme," I returned.

For answer he hurled his dagger at me. Nimbler than any Syrian goat, I skipped aside ; the dagger fell harmlessly to the stone floor. I stooped and picked it up. A Crusader's cross and certain blazonings I could not read were engraved upon the hilt. I stared at my Assassin. It was possible that the blazonings were not his, that the knife was not his either, and yet I did not think so. I never saw a face so changed by fear, or ravaged by guilt. Now, looking at him, I believed I knew the secret of the scarred ankles, the strong bowed back.

I accused him. " You have served in the galleys of the Turks. You have been scourged by the Turks and have worn their chains even to the bone."

At that he sprang on me. He was strong and used to scuffles of this kind. But he was not so desperate as I was, nor so young.

Warding my hands from his throat, he said : " I bought this freedom."

" I think you sold your faith." I took away my hands. I withdrew from him. " Who am I to blame you ? " I asked. " I go in dread of the same choice."

Free of my hands, he scuttled away from me like a beetle into a dark corner, and, having found his dagger, nursed it passionately between both hands.

" Do not think I regret my denial," he said. " Do not believe when your time comes that I shall pity you. There is no true faith ; there is neither faith nor truth anywhere under the sun." As if this were not enough, he continued : " This life is animal and vile, like this body. Earth and the flesh are real ; God is only a name." Calm of face now he looked at me. Here was another saint turned devil, I thought.

I had tempted him to blaspheme, he declared. In return, for a moment only, his words tempted me. I hesitated, then reacted violently to my own doubt.

" This place is evil," I cried. I moved towards him. At what point I was seized with dizziness I do not remember. I know that I sank down upon my stone bench, that in a last clarity of thought I cried out again : " What is this potion which you drink, this brew of hashish from which you take your name ? "

He came near me. He thrust his face close to mine. " You have tasted it," I thought he said.

I thought his eyes so near to mine shone with a red gleam ; I thought he leaned back upon his heels within my cell and barked like a dog, and that in between barking, jaws open, he laughed silently, tears of laughter mingling with the foam flecks on his cheeks.

I slept then and dreamed of a world peopled with giant contending shadows. There was no peace as there was no charity in my world of sleep, only confusion and chaos as in that time before the long day of the world of men dawned.

After what seemed only a little while I came to myself. I saw the burned-out taper end, the overturned cup and flagon, the spilt wine. The thin light of early morning filled all but the dim corners of my cell; a wisp of cloud in a milky sky striped my lancet windows' narrow points of light. My head felt thick and curiously cold, my tongue appeared swollen in my head. I looked about me. My Fedavi of the scarred ankles was gone. But still I was not alone. Another Assassin waited, head bent, his back towards me. He turned. Even as he did so I knew whom I should see. Guy de Passy turned towards me.

I was not greatly astonished: perhaps I had always known that I might find him within my cell. He looked at me as if I were a stranger. I spoke like one. "Why are you here?"

"For the same reason that you are," he answered.

"I do not know for what reason I am here," at last I said.

He waited and did not speak. Two more Fedavi entered, bearing between them a bundle of white robes. I was to dress in these, it seemed. When I refused, at a sign from de Passy the newcomers set on me. It is a deadly thing for a man to be overpowered as I was under the eyes of a friend. I remember my gaolers' hands now, cool and dry and smooth-skinned. I was reminded of my uncle Raymond's hands; I remembered how I would stand like a great calf before him when he beat me, naked and sweating as I was now, and hating him as I hated these men for their power over me.

"Traitor," I called de Passy when they had gone, and a good deal more that was worse. But a naked man is in some sense a defenceless man. Even as I abused de Passy my mind was turning back towards shrewdness and good sense. In order not to shiver more than was necessary I put on the clothes, a white robe of wool reaching to below my knees, which felt instantly comfortable and warm, a dark girdle and dark sandals, and a white burnous.

"Here, you see, you are compelled to obey," de Passy remarked, watching me calmly all the while.

Two youths who could only be learners in the Assassins' trade brought food to us: fermented asses' milk, and honey, and coarse bread. I ate, and reminded myself that I was always twice as brave when I had eaten.

Before long I repeated my question: "Why am I alive and in Massiat?"

"They have work for you to do," de Passy, munching calmly, replied.

"And if I will not do it?"

He wiped the corners of his mouth with a napkin delicately. "No one lives long in Massiat," he said, "who does not serve Sinan."

"You have served him?"

"I have served myself." He leaned towards me. "You are a necessary part of a great plan that Sinan has made. You yourself are required to do nothing. You need only allow, while appearing ignorant, other things to be done."

I pondered for a moment while he watched me closely. I asked, " Whom will you murder now ? "

He replied carelessly : " In the year 1100 the Lord of Hama died ; in 1149 we slew Count Raymond of Tripoli at his prayers. Between those years and since then many men have died at our hands."

I cut him short. " I will have no part in it."

" Your life, and perhaps mine also," he declared, " depends upon your consent."

" Not your life, I think." I had the assurance to laugh at him.

He controlled his anger and spoke quietly. " I repeat, your life depends upon your consent. And mine also. Does that not move you ? "

" No more than my own life," I answered. My thoughts swam dizzily for a moment, as though my brain climbed a winding stair. " Why should I be chosen ? " I asked again.

Even while I spoke my brain cleared, and I knew. I was needed to help in the betrayal of one infinitely greater than myself, whom I served, whose servants knew and trusted me. I, John of Oversley, nobody though I was, because I was nobody, was intended to act as a cloak for the murderers of King Richard. And among those murderers, perhaps the chief Assassin among them, was Guy de Passy. Even our friendship, it was likely, had been only a means towards this same purpose. Much that had appeared mysterious to me hitherto appeared clear now ; much more began to show plain : the flattery, the subtle charm that had worked upon me and not only upon me, the subterfuge, the patient waiting, the ambush itself.

I cannot tell how time went with me then, whether minutes passed or seconds only. I was as though frozen and sick with the realisation of it all and the fear. I looked up at last : I spoke stupidly enough, I do not doubt. " Go your own way. Leave me to go mine." For de Passy's way was the way of treachery and murder, I thought. As yet I did not know the truth or even a half of the truth.

" Unhappily we go together. That much is certain." De Passy turned from me in that light assured way of his which at one time I had so much admired.

" Leave me," I said.

At the door of my cell he paused. " Consider the matter. You will not be allowed to consider long."

He left me, and the fearfulness of what I had heard filled my mind to the exclusion of all else. There was much that I desired to know, much more that I feared to hear. If I were to keep my reason under so great a burden of decision all this, I was aware, must wait.

6

THE WEB

I was allowed more time in which to make my decision than I had thought possible. De Passy appeared to be too occupied to pay me very much attention and not one of all those other Assassins who spoke to me referred to the reasons for my captivity. I say captivity, but in all except reality I appeared free. I was permitted to move at will within the fortress and outside it. Only occasionally was I made aware that I was being watched and followed. Even as I lay beside the pool before the northern entrance to the fortress and considered my situation, I was aware of my Fedavi of the scarred ankles sitting, it was true, far enough from me, brooding as I was, full of savage discontent as I was, yet never allowing me for a second to move out of sight. Though the chains that held me were of the slightest I could not doubt their strength. The delay in forcing a decision upon me sprang in part, I concluded, from the general subtlety of the Assassin mind. I had been tensely determined on resistance, resolute for sacrifice and, if need be, for martyrdom. After days and weeks of waiting uncertainty had clouded my mind. My resolution had weakened, and the long period of waiting had allowed me to be in two minds once more and taken some of the stiffness from my knees.

I marvelled again not that I should have been shown so much of the fortress of Massiat but that I should have been permitted to discover so much more of its secrets for myself. Either I was reckoned a great simpleton or, and this on the whole I considered more likely, Sinan had determined, even if he were successful in using me, to take my life. If this were not so I did not know how to account for the fact that my Fedavi of the scarred ankles should interpret his role of guard to me with what on the surface appeared a most dangerous licence. By his side I had witnessed all the life of the fortress : the manning of the look-out posts along the battlements, each one no more than a bowshot from the next. I had assisted in the hand signalling by day, the signalling by beacon at night. I had witnessed the arrival and the regular despatch also of Sinan's pigeon post ; I had even helped to feed these homely and yet, I could not help but feel, sinister birds. Not two days before the events of which I write, after my Fedavi and I had spent a pleasant mid-morning feeding the pride of lions which Sinan kept at Massiat as at every one of his other fortresses— for what purpose I could never guess unless it were for the mingled pleasure and the terror of their roaring—I had watched the arrival of Saladin's messenger to Sinan. He had toiled on foot up the steep slope as I had done ; he had mounted, on all fours sometimes, the slippery stairway. At last, almost exhausted, he had arrived among us to be greeted by a fanfare of trumpets, a bushel of salutations and a vast deal of silent curiosity. No secret of his identity had been made. Indeed secrecy might have been difficult, since he wore the yellow and gold livery of Saladin. On the same day from the same watch-tower, I had witnessed the return shortly afterwards of a successful Fedavi. The pigeon post had heralded his coming ; when he arrived all was in readiness to welcome him. Breathless and alone, and as though half-dead from wounds and hardships, he also had toiled up the steep slope. For him and for the success of his mission the kettle-drums had been beaten and the cornets sounded all day until after sundown. At sundown Sinan's lions had added their voice to the rest, until the din, from the repeated echo among the precipices, was as deafening as if a hundred lions had roared and every kettle-drum and cornet been sounded in Mahommed's Paradise.

Since the arrival of these two messengers a mounting excitement could be felt within the fortress, as if some new enterprise of murder were begun, some new villainy born. Under pressure of the general excitement a curious licence had reigned. Too much hashish had been drunk, there had been fighting with daggers among the faithful, arrows had been shot wildly into the air. Many of the faithful, after having eaten pork, in deliberate defiance of the Prophet's rule, had retired to cold corners to nurse their overburdened bellies and their too easy consciences. My particular Fedavi, after having slept for several hours in the shelter of the battlements, had arisen cramped in limb, it is true, but warmed, most unusually for him, by something like affection. Taper in hand, he had conducted me into the centre of Sinan's fortress. Once or twice I had paused and counted somewhat anxiously my chances, under so mad a guide, of coming forth alive. Always he had beckoned me on, always I had followed his bent, swiftly moving shadow. We had made our way along stone passages, down crooked stairways ; we had described as many loops and twists as the River Orontes ; we had descended deep into the solid rock upon which the fortress was built. We had paused finally before a vast doorway of stone and, after much thrusting back of bolts and bars, each one of which sounded loud as a separate thunder-clap in my ears, we had entered Sinan's treasure house. The walls of the chamber were of rock, rough and unhewn and dry. Low benches of stone were ranged along each side. Upon them tall earthenware jars, like western porringers, were set. There must, I think now, have been close on two hundred of them. My companion had beckoned to me and I had followed. Like a cellarman examining his casks of wine he went diligently from jar to jar.

Each lid on being lifted revealed in the light of the taper a vast treasure beneath. One jar held gold coins thinner and finer than I had ever seen ; another, on being opened, was brimful of jewels of amber and turquoise and pearls and emeralds. All Sinan's wealth and all the treasure of the Syrian Assassins lay here : the ransom money of Turkish emirs and Christian knights, the rewards of a thousand crimes. My Fedavi, like a different Delilah, tempted me. He held a pearl glowing like a small milky moon in the taper's light before my eyes. His own eyes glittered with greed and grew broody, I think, with love. I also loved the beauty of the pearl and longed for a moment to have it in my hand. But then I grew afraid. I grew afraid of the excitement I felt within myself and of the strange spell of so much beauty and so much wealth within so odd a place. I took rough hold of my Fedavi's arm and shook him. By some means I communicated my own fear to him ; I persuaded him at last to come away. Only when the walls of the outer passage-way were about us and the stars showed in the sky within the frame of the open arch ahead, did I breathe easily again.

I had often wondered at the deep flow of water that could be heard within the fortress on rainy nights ; I had often asked myself how a fortress perched as Massiat was upon the barren rock could be provisioned and watered sufficiently to withstand a long siege ; I had wondered a hundred times precisely where the covered way led down which I had been hurried blindfold on my first coming to Massiat. My companion seemed to be at pains to make all this clear to me. Later that same day, on a pretence of feeding Sinan's lions on the western and most precipitous side of the rock, we had traversed the citadel from end to end.

We had climbed as far as the pool, and while I was asking myself how, burdened with sacks of meat as we were, we should mount without mishap the rest of the steep stairway, my companion halted at the foot of the small round watch-tower that in one place marked the steep path, and, eager as a dog, vanished inside. Once more I had followed. We were in an underground passage-way, not more than three feet wide, which climbed in rough steps to the height (or so I guessed) of the citadel above. An Assassin learner passed us, driving a small flock of goats before him up the rough steps. We pressed close against the walls to give him room. I remember the rank goat smell that came to us as we did so and the patter of the goats' feet on the stones. The passage-way led us eventually to the centre of the fortress, to a covered space a hundred feet or more in length. Some little way beyond were the water cisterns. There appeared to be a great many of them, some as much as forty, others no more than six feet in length. The water was greenish-dark like the water in our deep well at Oversley. It gave out the same faintly smoky smell. I had washed in water like this ; I had swum in it, and drunk it also ; I had had it under my nose in half a dozen different ways for the greater part of my life. The look of it and the smell of it had swept me back as it were a thousand years in thought. We had gone to the westerly side where castle wall and precipice are one, where below only the jagged points of the rocks could be glimpsed and the abyss between. Here, bounded by the walls and the precipice, Sinan's outer Hall of Audience lay. I had taken curious note of the place. It was wind-swept and bare, an island of flat stone thrust up nakedly against the sky.

On our near side were the lions' dens, barred with iron, and hewn like the water cisterns out of the solid rock. My companion, who was some-thing of a lion-tamer, had disappeared within the dens for a while. I had waited, watching the movement of the clouds, the infinite changes in the smooth depths of the sky and a solitary eagle's flight. When he had fed the lions, my companion returned, Sabbah the lion cub—who was as tame as a dog with us both, whose broken paw I had helped to mend, whom I looked upon in part as mine—running beside him. The lion cub, my Assassin and I had made our way back together by the same road to the pool where I was now.

I stirred where I lay. Made suddenly aware of my own solitariness I looked round once more for my Fedavi. He was stepping with extreme delicacy along the rocky edge of the pool and peering in. At a sudden movement on my part he started, lost his balance momentarily and fell. With no more feeling than one has for a frog moving upstream and battling manfully against the small waves, I watched. He made little progress. Head thrown back, dark goggle eyes fixed as though despairingly on me, he did indeed look very like a frog. The current that flowed strongly here beneath the double shelf of overhanging rock held him. His mouth open, he called to me. Drown, I thought. To Paradise with you, and one Assassin the less. I looked away. I saw the abyss below and, far off, the Orontes winding to the sea. The cones of mosquitoes danced their puppet dance in the nearer air, the carrion crows weighed down the frail branches of the cypresses, and high overhead the clouds moved, looking as innocent of harm as the foolish faces of Easter lambs. It was then that I heard de Passy's voice calling my name, then that I caught sight of him leaping down the stairway of rock. Any thought of revenge upon my Fedavi I might have had left me then ; I remembered only Christian charity.

The current, when I dived in, I found to be indeed strong, and the pool full of swirls and eddies by the overhanging shelf of rock. How I seized hold of my Assassin and fought my way clear of the current I scarcely know. My Fedavi was limp and drooping as a withered cyclamen flower when I pulled him ashore, and petal-white. I looked down at him and almost regretted my Christian charity. Dripping water as I went, I made my way alone up the steep stair—I had no mind for the underground passage-way—to the fortress again. It was with a sense of something like relief that I did so. Any place becomes home to a man after a time, and to be so near the sky, so high above earth, was often very pleasant to me.

I had need after all for some consolation. There were days when my mind was filled with unease ; there were other days when nothing that threatened me appeared real, when like a hedge-pig in winter I seemed more than half asleep. I had come near to feeling some sort of calm ; suddenly, for what reason I do not know, my calm fled. My mind turned restlessly upon the same thing, once more I was all but overcome by the weight of the decision I must make. I sought—for the place exercised a curious fascination, understandable in my particular circumstances, upon me—Sinan's outer Hall of Audience again. My head folded in my arms, I sought to discover what lay hidden at the bottom of my mind. To die was perhaps a simple thing. Yet I did not think so, and I did not wish to die. But for me to betray King Richard was impossible. I could not over night turn myself into a traitor. I was as certain of this as I have ever been certain of anything in my life. And yet, if I did not at least appear to consent to what Sinan desired, I was clearly destined for eternity. I lay with my face hidden for what seemed to me to be a long while, for what may have been a few moments only. This business of deciding would be soon over, I knew. I had only to refuse, all the rest would most quickly follow. I looked up. I could see only the sky and a half-dozen of birds flying low overhead. I watched them. Sinan's pigeon post, I realised, was coming in. And suddenly the thought came to me : Why should I not pretend to play Sinan's game ? Why should I not do my best to deceive him and—by what means it was beyond my brain to imagine as yet—contrive to warn King Richard ? My death alone in Massiat might further my hopes of salvation ; it would further nothing else, nor would King Richard be any nearer safety. In this as in many other similar affairs Sinan would spend a hundred lives rather than fail in his purpose. If I resisted him, another of King Richard's company might be found who would be more malleable. Other smaller voices spoke to me. What folly, they said, to attempt to deceive Sinan ! I acknowledged the folly of such a notion, and yet, since no better expedient offered, I resolved to persevere in it. In coming to my decision I fell into an error which after-wards was almost fatal to me. I did not take sufficiently into account the certainty that my motives would be misjudged and my story discredited. I did not think it possible at the time for a man to be proclaimed a traitor in spite of himself. In my simplicity I did not realise that the steps I must take to deceive Sinan would afterwards be offered as proof of my own duplicity. But even if I had realised every part of what was to come I do not think I should have decided differently.

From this point my mind moved off by way of relief into a pleasant day-dream. In imagination I heard the jangling of Alyncestre bells and the children's voices at their high singing. So sharp was the vision my eyes filled with tears ; I blew my nose and resolved I would lay all my wreaths of welcome as a thank-offering upon Raymond's tomb when I returned. I felt a flutter of robes beside me ; the tears still wet on my cheeks, I raised my head.

De Passy looked down on me. I believed, though this may well have been a last quiver of sentiment on my part, that something of his old kindness for me showed for a second on his face. Abruptly he turned his back. As I have said, the precipice and the abyss below fell away from the point where we both were.

Turning towards me abruptly once more as if he did not greatly care for the view, he said : " I have no love for Massiat. Rather I hate it."

Partly in order to hide my own distress I scoffed at him. " Do you fear," I asked, " that Sinan may one day declare a judgment upon you ? "

" Sometimes I fear it." He spoke simply and unlike himself, then paused. " Why do you pretend a hatred of me you do not feel ? "

" You are a traitor," I declared, " a liar, and faithless, and several times a murderer. Is this not reason enough ? "

" I did not dream you had so much power of abuse at your tongue's end," he said, and spoke lightly.

I did not answer him.

He went on in a softer voice : " Why are we enemies ? I would serve you if I could."

I found my tongue. " You are faithless even to Sinan." His face darkened. I could no longer even guess his thoughts. Only half expecting an answer, I continued : " If indeed you wish to serve me there is one matter of which I have not dared to speak."

He encouraged me. " Proceed. Though you honest souls have an odd way," he said, " of asking favours."

" Did you not order the ambush," I asked, " and arrange that only I should come out alive ? "

" I ordered the ambush certainly," he answered.

" Then you are guilty of Robert's death and of Everard's also ? "

He laughed at me. " I understand that Everard Mortebois fell into the ravine. Am I to blame ? " He turned on one side. " The Lady whom we have all adored should thank me for saving her from so much tedium."

" Do not speak of her," I said.

" The Lady," he reminded me, " once did me the honour of loving me."

" I tell you again," I said, " do not speak of her."

He shrugged angrily. " This chivalry makes fools of us all."

I said : " There are many different sorts of fools." I went on to accuse him. " You were always Sinan's man."

" I have told you, I serve myself."

" Have you served yourself so well ? " I turned on him and saw that my words had touched him in the quick of his pride. " Why did you kill Robert ? " I demanded.

" Why ? " He roused himself. " Did he not despise me," he asked, " among his own kind first, then for all the Court to see ? Why should I not hate him who sought what I sought, glory and greatness, who desired even the same woman—a man so different from myself ? He was more righteous than I was, he was too righteous. I believe it was chiefly on account of his righteousness that I hated him. There was no weakness in him. There was none even when he faced what to other men would have been a continuing martyrdom." De Passy broke off here as if he had said too much, then went on quickly : " I would not have ordered his killing for any frivolous reason. His death was necessary and part of our plan."

" If there was ever any kindness between us, tell me truly," I said, " is Robert then alive ? "

I never encountered so deliberate a silence as now, never saw cruelty grow so surely upon any face.

He spoke softly at last : " I believe so. They put out his eyes. They blinded him and sent him wandering."

I cried out at that. I covered my face.

" Even I," de Passy said, " cannot hate him now." He turned. " What is there left," he asked, " to hate ? "

" Robert is left," I cried after him. I put my head down and grieved like a woman for the love and the misunderstandings also that had endured for so long between Robert and myself.

While I lay and grieved, Sinan's messenger, a tall Assassin with curiously marked and pitted cheeks, found me. " Our Lord Sinan commands you to come."

I followed him.

A man's memory must, I think, always work unequally. At this distance of time—though it is not, perhaps, so long—I am unable to recall all that happened to me with the same detail or with an equal intensity. Some things I have forgotten ; others return to me as it were only here and there. My mind, dulled by anxiety and grief, recorded only a part of my talk with Sheikh Sinan.

I followed my guide in silence by a deliberately circuitous route through a labyrinth of passages, until finally we arrived at a fairer corridor than the rest, its floor of mosaic, its walls of some smooth and shining green stone. We passed, as though to the presence of some High Priest of Solomon's Temple, through a succession of arched doorways screened by curtains first of black, then of scarlet, then lastly of white. The white curtain was drawn aside ; my Assassin prostrated himself. I went on alone.

Sinan's inner Hall of Audience was hung with scarlet hangings here and there ; all else was shining and white. At the far end a figure that was both stooping and frail rose to greet me from a curved chair. He bowed ; I bowed in return. Sinan's eyes were grey ; his beard, which he touched as though absently with one hand, was bluish-white. I stared at him, and memory stirred suddenly in my dulled mind.

I spoke without preamble or reverence. I said, " You are the learned doctor whom I met beyond Acre, to whom I granted right of passage."

Sinan answered me calmly in good Norman-French : " Fortune arranged it so." He went on speaking. His manner was mild ; he appeared neither formidable nor remote, and yet I felt no warmth and scarcely anything of humanity in him. While he talked I believed I could detect a greater weariness in him than had at first been apparent. The power he wielded had become a habit with him, I thought, of which perhaps he had grown tired. I felt an absolute control in him, not of the body, for the body goes its own way to destruction, but of speech and mind. I looked at him again and reflected that vanity had been my ruin. Here before me was the man most feared in the East whom I had allowed to go free out of a foolish love for a vain gesture. I had done this, it seemed, so that Robert might suffer and be maimed a second time, and Everard die, and King Richard be in danger, and I myself in the most fearful case in which any man might find himself.

I listened dully. Nothing that Sinan said, speaking so gently and so precisely, held any surprises for me. I was to serve King Richard as before ; a chosen number of the faithful, Assassins every one of them, would return to the camp with me. If I betrayed them I should die ; if I refused my help I might die now. Sinan's messengers, not I, had work to do ; my part was to do no more than make it possible for them to strike. I was to choose, Sinan declared, and paused.

I neither consented nor refused. Looking—I intended it—as stupid as any man of Oversley may look, I did not speak.

Sinan was at pains to make himself understood. He did not need me, he declared ; his purpose could be achieved without me, perhaps at greater cost, perhaps at the price of some delays. I had nothing to bargain with—I must see that. Since there was some need for haste in the matter, he, Lord of Massiat, had thought to use me and my friend.

Here I spoke as vehemently as any man could. " Never my friend," I said. " Never."

I turned silent and brooding. They would use me and afterwards kill me, I was certain.

Sinan leaned towards me. " You are afraid."

I answered him : " I do not wish to die."

He put the tips of his fingers together, then parted them. " Then obey."

Once more I was silent.

From beside him Sinan took a cup of gold most curiously wrought and filled with wine. He offered it to me. " Drink, messire."

But I who could never drink straightway of any bitter draught of herbs my mother gave to me in spring, who would carry the cup to my lips two or three times and set it down again, untasted still, could not drink now.

Stooping and limping as he went, Sinan moved away, and the white curtain fell once more into place. I watched him go, and then, quite steadily, I drank. The cup, I thought, fell from my hands ; I saw it roll away. Whether the rest will pass for truth or for some strange figment of the brain I do not know. Travellers with whom I have talked since have sworn I did not dream, nor, they say, was my mind confused. The wonders that I believed I saw did indeed exist, they affirm, and have been seen by other men, captive as I was, at Qaf or Massiat or some other Assassin fortress. I can only say that the marvels that I saw on that day are as vivid in my mind's eye still as the green pleasaunce of walks and flowers I made for Elfrida out of a portion of the waste at Kinwarton when I returned.

I woke to the sound of birdsong and the play of fountains. I was in a wide space filled with gardens. Around me were green arbours and walks overhung with flowering clematis and vines. Beds filled with flowers so bright the eye ached from looking upon them stretched on either side and here and there were little streams, so cool the eye when it fell upon them was refreshed again. Persian roses, yellow and white and red, bloomed there, lilies bending like courtiers might be seen, and cyclamen plants, their flowers like resting butterflies. Small temples of bright painted porcelain, like the porcelain cups and dishes the Sultan Saladin had sent to King Richard from far Cathay, adorned the walks. From these, scarcely heard above the sound of birdsong and the fountains playing, came the twang of lutes, the tinkling of guitars. Beyond were wooded glades and vineyards and small orchards of fruit trees. I walked down pillared colonnades, hung with Persian carpets and Grecian stuffs, furnished with long trestles set with sweetmeats and wine in dishes and cups of gold.

Beside two porcelain temples stood two trees of gold adorned with jewelled birds. By some miraculous device the jewelled birds sang, the gold leaves stirred. I stood and marvelled at them. Then the wine and the sweet-meats and the low couches tempted me. I looked for houris and found none, and this I considered somewhat remiss of Sinan. I lay down upon a couch spread with a shawl embroidered (most scratchily for my bare heels) with metal threads and gold. I slept again and dreamed of golden singing birds, and houris with limbs so supple and so small a man could pack a complete houri in a jar, and with a simple shake spill her forth when he wished again.

I woke by Sinan's side. The gardens and the singing birds were gone. My head felt crowded and thick ; my heels that the embroidered shawl had rubbed itched hotly. Sinan sat as if he had never moved from his curved chair. I leaned upon one elbow, then—for this man exacted homage—struggled to my feet.

He said courteously, one finger poised upon another, " You have seen and you believe ? "

I answered stiffly : " I cannot believe."

" Nevertheless," Sinan said, " you will obey. You will see nothing but the way and follow it."

Lifting a hand in dismissal or farewell, he moved slowly away.

Once more I returned with my Assassin along the way I had come. Outside the door of my sleeping chamber my guard left me. Though I had promised nothing I was free, I thought, free to carry out Sinan's commands, free to perfect any plan of my own in secret as I had wished. Gradually an absolute confidence possessed me. I was certain that I could carry out my task, certain, though Sinan had not deceived me, that I could deceive Sinan. In my new mood of confidence I sought out de Passy. I found him asleep beside the pool, one arm flung out, the other covering his head, his dagger out of its sheath and lying beside him. I do not remember picking up the dagger ; I only know that in the next instant I was leaning over de Passy, his dagger in my hand. I would have killed him then, I think, for Robert's sake, if he had stirred. But, smiling, he lay still. Odd thoughts and images ran through my brain : I was aware of the last of the sun's beams warm upon my back ; I thought how they would never pierce the darkness behind Robert's eyes ; I remembered Brand's face when it was solemn and the coarse hairs that sprouted from the bridge of his great nose ; I wondered where it would be best to strike and how. Last of all, and suddenly, and for no reason, I recalled that King Canute the Dane had forbidden the killing of a sleeping man.

De Passy opened his eyes, and without moving looked at me. " We are both in the same web. Why kill me ? " Like a deaf-mute I stared at him. He rolled over, away from me, and got to his feet. I might keep the dagger, finally he said. Without even a glance over his shoulder he went away. Humbled and angry, I looked after him.

From that point it was as though all the small demons that line the path to Hell tormented me. A stranger and hateful to myself, I was possessed by miseries. I am not certain where I went nor what for a brief space of time I did. I fetched up at the pool again. We are earth and air, fire and water, men say; and yet I think I am more water than earth or air or fire. For me there is a depth in water even at its shallowest, a shiningness even when it is most dull, a fluid everlastingness. I remained by the pool for how long I do not know. Dusk deepened into night, the hills and mountains grew cold; while I watched, the clouds, gathered up before, came out again and spread like flocks of sheep over the pastures of the sky. I waited while rocks and trees, shapeless in the dusk, grew separate before my eyes as though in their own space, and still. Gradually the fever in my brain cooled. I heard the slight sounds of the water, the clash of wavelets like small fish leaping in the pool, the deep flow of the current under the rocky shelf. I had been as though deaf before. Gradually, as sense and feeling returned, my plan took shape within my mind.

As I moved a second time towards the steep stairway leading to the fortress two Fedavi, who had all this while been hidden in the shadow of the rocks, stepped out, and, one on each side like attendant demons, kept pace with me. I was a prisoner and guarded still.

7

ESCAPE

THE weeks went by and spring came, and still no opportunity of escape offered. While my desire to be gone grew daily, my life at Massiat stretched on, uneventful, orderly and unreal. Sometimes the very uselessness of my existence sickened me, for I was not useful even to myself; at other times I contrived by some means to be patient. My lot was no harder than it had been, nor were my movements unduly circumscribed. Yet still, wherever I went, my guard followed me.

Though I grew sick in body and in mind I continued, with more resolution than I had known I possessed, with my plan. It was after all not so much a plan as a hope of freedom. From the beginning of April I made very secretly what preparations I could. Whenever names of places or routes to the sea were mentioned I stored whatever I considered might be useful in my mind. I took from Sinan's armoury a second dagger, and afterwards a short Frankish make of sword ; I hid a change of robes, securely bound in skins, between the boulders and a crooked thorn bush on the slope below the pool ; I even concealed bread and a rude jar of honey similarly wrapped under the same boulders, though I had little hope of finding bread or honey fit for eating again. I contrived all this at great danger to myself in between performing my tasks for Sinan. It amused me to think that while I appeared to be furthering his plans I should be assisting my own ; that while I toiled, now and then out of sight of my guards, at hewing and rolling stones for the repair of Sinan's fortress walls I should be providing for my escape from them. I do not believe I was observed in any of my preparations, but I could not be certain of this since it was never Sinan's pleasure to pounce at once. There were times when all my efforts appeared like a child's game of make-believe to me. Yet I was engrossed in them ; they consoled and entertained me and, I believe, kept me sane during all that time.

Here at Massiat this year's spring was almost as scorching as midsummer. High up though we were, this morning no wind stirred, the young leaves of the wild pear trees upon the slopes hung limply ; the rocks showed smooth as glass. I watched my companions at their chess : de Passy smiling and deliberate, my Fedavi of the scarred ankles crouched over the board and fanatically intent. It was as well for me, I reflected, watching them, that I was not compelled, as Huon of Bordeaux had been compelled, to play and stake my life upon the game. Huon of Bordeaux, a cool one-eyed giant of a man, had won his game and the Sultan's daughter for a wife as well. I desired no Sultan's daughter. I would as soon, I thought, take a slim brown serpent to my bed. Nevertheless I was worse placed than Huon, for while I only played at make-believe Sinan played cat-and-mouse with me. And so far Sinan had won. In order to keep up the pretence I had set before myself, I had been obliged to give to the Assassins much of the information they needed to aid them in their attempt upon King Richard's life. I had given as little as I dared. Even that little, I owned now with a sick heaviness, was too much. I would have lied to any lesser man, but I had not dared to lie to Sinan. I had told of the King's tent and of his habit of sleeping unguarded within his tent and alone ; I had listed the men about the King and spoken of what I knew of them ; I had named a few of his servants : Anselm, his chaplain, Philip, his crier, John d'Alençon, his clerk. When I was asked to speak of King Richard's plans I could in all honesty plead ignorance ; when I was questioned most closely concerning the identity of Bernard, the King's spy, I could safely appear as ignorant as Sinan. I had told nothing, it may be, that Sinan could not have discovered for myself. Yet this, I owned, was no excuse.

Simpleton as I was, as in many ways I remained, I could not help but wish I had chosen the more heroic part.

In the hope of saving King Richard's life I had done everything a man could do so far to save my own. In intention I was honest, but who would at this stage believe in my intentions? Who would not whisper when I returned that I had been bent on saving myself? Here—I realised suddenly—was the web Sinan had woven for me. Whether in Massiat or outside it I might not be able to prove my innocence; I might not be able altogether to break free of the web. Now that the full realisation of the risks I ran was borne in upon me the sweat broke out on my forehead. I leaned forward, I held my head in my hands.

I felt de Passy's eyes upon me and looked up, something of the horror I felt reflected, I am certain, in my eyes. He stared, then with a faint show of contempt looked away. Contempt has always been a spur to my own vanity. My head on my arms again, I thought differently once more, and to better purpose. Honesty, I told myself, like murder, would out; in the end even those who would be most inclined to condemn me for a traitor would come to believe me. I was no Bohemond, nor Sir Lancelot either—though both heroes were far from perfect—but I was not altogether foolish, not altogether hesitant or a coward. I was aware, among so much else, of an unyielding stubbornness in me. I had won everything so far upon which I had set my mind: health and bodily strength after a short lifetime of sickness; the rule of my own person and my own lands in spite of all that my mother and my uncle Raymond had done; the opportunity to ride out with King Richard and to serve him. I had not been unsuccessful so far. Why should I fail now? I had always feared the unmeasured ways of my own mind, just as I had feared at the beginning of my recovery to set foot upon solid earth. The journey from the fortress to King Richard's camp would be a journey by paths I did not know into my own mind. Upon this journey who knows, I asked, what discoveries I might not make?

De Passy was on his feet and pointing exultantly ahead. "Look, the messenger!"

A messenger could indeed be seen making his way up the steep track. He also, like so many of Sinan's returning messengers, moved only with pain and difficulty, like a man whose will alone drives him on. In a few moments the alarm spread, the turmoil and excitement increased. Before long every Assassin within bowshot was tumbling pell-mell towards the battlements and the Northern gate. The trumpets and horns were sounded, the kettle-drums beaten, and Sinan's men once more abandoned themselves to a day of feasting and forgetfulness. There appeared to be no limit to the extravagances Sinan would allow for this day only: the flagons of wine, the feasting, the couches, the music. The fact that the messenger was not expected to outlive the night was a matter of indifference to Sinan, as perhaps it was to the messenger himself.

I had sworn to show no interest in the affair. Nevertheless I could not prevent myself from enquiring curiously of de Passy the name of Sinan's latest victim. He answered me in roundabout terms. " An enemy of our Lord Sinan's who robbed and afterwards put to death a member of the Brotherhood shipwrecked upon the coast of Tyre." He spoke, I thought, as if he were repeating the day's lesson.

" Not Conrad ? " I asked. " Not the Marquis Conrad of Montserrat ? " De Passy did not answer me.

Towards noonday the lions—for no one had fed them—added their voices to the din. Sullen and angry, I lay alone, my fingers in my ears. The air was feverish with noise and as though thunder-thick ; the trumpets and the horns were lightning strokes of sound. Imperceptibly at first my brain cleared. Gradually all that I had seen since I came to Massiat, like the irregular pieces of a painted window, began to take shape and pattern in my mind. I remembered the arrival of Saladin's messenger and Sinan's flattering reception of him. The Sultan Saladin, though chivalrous enough, remained, I reminded myself, a Turk and an infidel. To the mind of a follower of Mahommed the use of poison and the dagger carried no reproach. Saladin was hard-pressed as King Richard was by ill news from home ; his dominions were as rebellious in his absence, his armies also threatening to fall away. What more natural than that, having suffered defeat at Arsur, he should now with the help of Sinan contrive a new and simpler victory? To deprive Christendom of King Richard of England and Conrad of Montserrat also would be victory indeed. Schemer though Conrad was, after King Richard he remained the ablest captain in the Christian host. If Conrad were indeed dead it seemed to me that the attempt upon King Richard's life could not long be delayed. It appeared all the more urgent, therefore, that I should be gone.

I grew both cool and reckless : reckless as to my own fate, cool in calculating the hazards against me. Some little time after noon de Passy joined me ; shortly afterwards—the two were seldom far apart—my Fedavi with the scarred ankles followed.

I set myself to carry out the first part of my plan of escape. I pretended a despair I did not feel. My head uplifted for a moment from my outstretched arms, I said : " I cannot bear my life." De Passy looked at me, contempt again, and something like pity also upon his face. I said : " I have destroyed myself." The two of them thrust a jug of wine towards me and bade me drink. I did so, and presently the three of us slept. I woke first, a notion born perhaps of sleep quickening in my brain. I carried it out. Unobserved, I left the lions' dens; unobserved, I returned and, so powerful was Sinan's wine and so peaceful the state of my own mind, slept again. De Passy woke me. Stripped to his tunic, he invited me—and here my pulse leapt suddenly—to bathe in the pool. I had always heard that Providence aids conspirators at first only to flout them in the end. Certainly Providence, or some heathen god of chance, aided me then.

While the sun set the three of us bathed in the pool. The water was milky and full of reflected fire; the mists hung roundabout and hid the hills. Darkness is never more than a step or two behind dusk in these regions of rocks and deep ravines and cool shadows. Deliberately I delayed entering the pool; as deliberately I lingered in the water long after my companions had finished their dressing on the shore, and while I swam or floated in the pool I kept my eyes upon the dwindling space of open sky and the descending sun and prayed the lions would not discover they were free too soon. I laughed to myself to think that after so much care on my part I might be waylaid and eaten, most loyally, by one of Sinan's lions. If there were light enough left I swore de Passy and my Fedavi should see me drown. I swam silently in the pool like a man bewitched. In all the world, I told myself, there was nothing but myself and the milky water and the sun's strange light. When the sun seemed on the point of vanishing I vanished also. I shot up my arms and dived silently; the current took me, I all but drowned as before, and as before I was washed up under the rocky shelf. I waited there like a water-rat and stirred no more than a water-rat would have stirred. From my hiding place I heard de Passy and my Fedavi calling to each other, calling for helpers and ropes, for flares and torches. When I was numb with cold and half drowned from so much watery waiting, I heard them move away up the mountain once more. I thanked God and sought among the bushes for my clothes and weapons. I sought for five minutes, and, while I sought, every thorn tree seemed alike and every tree a thorn. While I wasted precious time in search my stratagem served me well. My body pressed close to earth, my teeth chattering, I saw a great tossing of torches about the battlements; I heard the roaring of Sinan's lions. I laughed silently and helplessly to see my late guards leaping here and there like Saladin's witches upon the battlements in their attempts to escape Sinan's playthings. With laughter my wits returned. I was able to find my dagger and sword and clothes. While I dressed I prayed—it was after all no laughing matter—that I might not myself meet with one of Sinan's lions.

The night again favoured me. The moon—I waited for her light—rode high; the sky was thick with stars, earth chequered with moving shadows. All night I journeyed, never once following any but the roughest paths. Sometimes I fetched up at an abyss or faced a rocky peak I could not climb. Though I did not pause for rest, I followed such circuitous ways I do not think I travelled far.

Towards morning I was aware of some wild beast following me. When I paused he paused also, when I continued he followed. I fled at last from the soft pad of his feet; as I fled, other smaller creatures shared my fear and my flight. A hare scudded, white tail showing, before me; a mountain deer started up, so trembling and so sudden he seemed like fear itself. I waited in the first showing of day for my enemy to appear. Nothing moved nor came; no other creature than myself appeared disturbed. A lizard came out and lay upon a neighbouring rock; two conies chewed on the same green grass blade in the entrance to their burrow. Their whiskers gleamed, their full round eyes shone. I looked at them and wished that, like Nebuchadnezzar, I also might eat grass. For the ants had made a feast of all my food and now, as if that were not injury enough, were industriously feeding upon me. I was too weary to care over-much for ants or wild beasts. I found a penthouse of two rocks hard by a stream and slept there. I woke as though to some new danger suddenly. It was broad day; some sweet-voiced bird sang. Couched on a shining slab of rock my lion waited, I thought, for me, his head majestically between his paws. My hand on my dagger, I also waited. My lion turned his head and, submissive as any hound, came shambling towards me.

From this time Sabbah the lion cub was of service to me. While the fortress could be seen perched on the wild hills I moved by night and scarcely dared to show myself by day. The cub and I moved together; when he was gorged, but not until then, I shared his kill. Time passed, Massiat was behind us and out of sight; the valley, threaded with streams shining most peacefully in the sun, appeared not too distant. I hugged myself and scarcely dared to think as yet how fortunate I had been, for in this wilderness of shrub and rock I had encountered neither enemy nor friend. At this rate of progress I could not fail, I judged, to reach the plain and comparative safety. But this was barren country. Short of food and sleep, short of everything except water, I started at every sudden looming shape, my pulse leapt at every shadow. I was afraid, for it seemed against all reason that Sinan should make no effort to overtake me within his own country.

So it proved. Sinan, who thought himself like God, like his master the Devil, sent many messages. A poisoned dagger, a book of verses and a loaf of bread to the Sultan Saladin; to me only a bloodstained hunting spear and a dead lion cub. I woke and found the cub stretched across the rough track. He had not long been dead. From that time I fled, as if all the demons that mobbed Saint Bernard on his heavenly way were after me—indeed I would have preferred a hundred demons to one Sinan.

When I remember that time I marvel how I lived and how I journeyed. My senses grew needle sharp ; I was hungry all the while and afraid all the while, and angry because I was afraid. In the end, from fear and hunger and solitariness I grew so light-headed that at times it seemed to me I must be mad.

So I feared until I met madness itself confronting me in the midst of a parched wilderness of rock. At first I believed the face I saw peering at me from behind a boulder was a figment of my own brain. While I waited the creature came on all fours towards me. I leapt to my feet ; the stranger, upright now, swayed upon his. A man, taller by a head than I was, burnt to a dry sandy colour by the sun and gaunt beyond belief, stood before me. Through a tangled fuzz of hair two small mad eyes, blue as King Richard's eyes, looked out. The cracked lips opened, but in all the torrent of sound that issued from them I could catch no intelligible word. I spoke to him in English, then in Norman-French. His face, that had dripped with foolish smiles, sobered ; for a moment he became bewildered and anxious like a man who tries desperately to summon his senses to him ; next, his hands came up, one fist sought his mouth ; he howled and wept before me then most pitifully and most revoltingly also. I was hungry, worn by days and nights of watchfulness, assailed by short fits of heat and cold, darkness and nausea. I sat down and held my head low down between my knees. My stranger thrust it further down, roughly, then stood off and laughed at me. He vanished, then returned, a speckled trout, broiled and cold, upon a platter of leaves between his hands. I ate and my hunger appeared to amuse him. If I was starved of food he was starved of laughter, I decided. He rocked to and fro upon his heels and laughed immoderately, his tears of laughter, like November dewdrops, spangling his fuzz of beard. When I stood up he beckoned me to follow. We arrived at last at a rocky dell through which a stream that could only be a trout stream flowed. Here my hermit, if hermit he was, lived in a rough and evil-smelling cairn of stones. He paused before the entrance to his cave and, with the same look of anxious remembrance upon his face, stooped and drew with one finger a rough crusading cross on the bare ground, then paused and looked up at me. I made the mark of a Templar's cross upon his shoulder. He stooped again, and in a kind of frenzy drew crusader's cross after crusader's cross wherever a bare patch of earth showed.

I spoke loudly. " Who are you ? "

" Bertrand," I thought he said. And then he looked at me as if he, Bertrand, were no longer mad.

From this moment I knew I could not leave him. The knowledge angered rather than pleased me—I took no credit for it at the time, I take none now, for I would have abandoned him if I could. To saddle myself in the pass in which I was with this wild man of the mountains must by any other reckoning than mine have appeared the purest folly. And yet, sworn to the Cross as I was, I could not bring myself to depart without him. By speech and signs I at last persuaded him to follow me. He did so with the same anxious look he had worn at first. We had progressed no more than half a mile when his bearing changed. He turned abruptly and, like a dog running home, headed faster than I could follow for his cairn of stones. After another sharp struggle with myself I went in search of him. I found him, as I had found Sabbah, dead, stretched out, arms spread, as if in truth he lay upon a cross.

I left Bertrand. I fled again. As I fled the air itself seemed full of stealth ; even the wind that followed me after sundown seemed muffled, as though it came swiftly on sandalled feet. I did not rest that night. The darkness was patchy about me like an old black cloak, thick clouds hid the moon, the wind still followed me. I know that I encountered and survived many dangers from water and rocks and small precipices, that, forgetful of all else, I still ran on. It was broad daylight when I returned fully to myself. I must have fallen and been struck senseless as I fell, for now I woke to find myself outstretched upon a wide slab of rock. Below was a fall of stones and an abyss whose sides were set with tufts of small brilliant flowers. Beyond lay neither hill nor mountain, but, half-hidden in a comfortable mist, a fertile plain. When I looked at the abyss my head reeled ; when I saw the plain I did not dare believe my eyes. While the sun warmed my limbs unexpected sounds of voices and the jingling of bells stole in upon my ears. I disregarded them. They persisted. Other sounds, of shouts and the cracking of whips and men's voices singing, were added. I could not, I was certain, be deceived. Full of hope I ran on down what remained of the steep track to the plain. Where a road skirted the foot of the low hills I paused. The sound of bells grew louder, as did the voices. I could almost distinguish the Arabic words of command, could hear the high-pitched and, to my ear, monotonous singing of the muleteers. While I waited, a long caravan of mules and camels, riders and footmen and muleteers, wound into sight. They came on to a great shuffle of dust and a cracking of whips. Summoning all my senses, I waited, then stepped forward and accosted the leading muleteer. I spoke in Norman-French—a tongue many Syrians and many muleteers who move up and down all the Syrian country are at least able to understand. I was a stranger, I said, while the muleteer eyed me curiously ; I came in peace.

" Peace be with you," he returned. He waited, twirling a long straw from one end to the other of his large mouth.

For a Mahommedan he had, I thought, a mocking look. I wished to follow the caravan, I declared. I would tend mules, carry fodder and water ; I could use a sword ; I could fight. I gave him the signet from my finger that I had from my father. It was of gold and enamel of Limoges : it bore our device, a black corbeau on a blue ground and a small lily of gold, upon its face. He rubbed it against his foul shirt and grumbled a little in bad Norman-French : " This Frankish stuff is of no use to me."

I said : " I have no other."

" Then come," he said, " but let it be in peace."

I walked beside him ; the caravan that had creaked, like a long litter, to a standstill, creaked on again ; my muleteer cracked his whip and broke out as suddenly as a linnet into song, of which I understood not one word. He was gross and merry and swarthy as a Beduin. Gold ear-rings swung in his ears ; his turban was of some tarnished stuff of red and gold ; he carried a great paunch bravely like a round barrel before him.

I said as loudly as I could, for suddenly faintness, with the surrounding earth, came up to meet me : " For the love of man if not of God, give me bread."

My muleteer stopped his singing. Thrusting a hand into his saddle-bag he presented me first with a handful of dates, next with a round hard cake of unleavened bread.

When I had eaten and my belly no longer murmured at me like the sea in a cave, I questioned him as much as I dared. Cracking his long whip once more, he answered me frankly. They had come, he said, from far Cathay, through Ind, over the high mountains that are the roof of the world to the land of Persia, and the great city of Baghdad. From Baghdad they had made their way to Hama, and now they would journey on to all the ports upon the Syrian coast, leaving merchandise at each place of call and collecting fresh merchandise again. What merchandise did they carry ? I enquired, glancing behind me at the long moving line of baggage beasts and panniers, at the dark faces of the Mahommedans, the pale delicate faces of the Persians and the faces of those others from Cathay, so yellow-skinned, so slant-eyed. My muleteer reeled off a long list carelessly ; ginger and spices, he said, and precious musk and frankincense and myrrh ; from Cathay dishes and vases of the new enamelled porcelain similar to those Saladin had given lately to King Richard of England. From Ind they carried silks, he went on, from Persia fair carpets and jewels of tur-quoise and rubies and white diamonds, precious woods of ebony, ivory of elephants' tusks, gold dishes of filigree as fine as spiders' webs. Here he stopped short and laughed at me. I closed my mouth, which was gaping a little ; I swallowed quickly and enquired what merchandise they would carry back with them again. He recited another list : from Tripolis cotton cloths ; from Beyrout goods of iron and wrought smith's work ; from Tyre dyes of purple and yellow and blue and light transparent glass ; from Naplous oil for lamps and soap to take all foulness away ; from Tiberias sugared rinds of citron and lemon and bitter oranges, dried figs and sugar cane. Once more he halted. He said he wished he had some sweet sugar cane with him at this moment to cool his mouth that tasted of nothing sweeter than dried camel dung.

He grew quiet and my mind turned back once more to the urgencies of my own case. I could, it was likely, travel with my companion, the muleteer, for as long as I wished, to Tripolis, it might be, and from thence take ship to Joppa once more. But haste was part of my purpose and a caravan moves no faster than a crocodile upon dry land. And Sinan's men at least would not put off their plans against King Richard or their pursuit of me.

That night I lay beside my muleteer upon his saddlebag under the stars. The camp fires of wild sage bush and thorn glowed like animal eyes in the dark. All around me was the silence, that yet is not silence, of sleeping men. Over all was the greater silence of the wide air, the deep arches of the sky, the broad earth. Over all was God, I thought, a simple, comforting and ancient thought. The air was searching and cold, the stars grew green and sharp, a small wind leapt like a grasshopper over the dried blades and crouched like a grasshopper again. My muleteer threw a fleshly arm lovingly over me. I drew nearer him. In the shelter of that great paunch I slept and dreamed—what a caravanserai of assorted merchandise is a man's brain !—of May Day feasts at Oversley. I had two handkerchiefs of red and yellow in my hands ; I leapt like David, I thought, and was equally mettlesome and twice as brave ; the sun shone, the may trees were in bloom, and Raymond, a bright halo round his head, stood by and—something in life I had never known him do—applauded me. I woke : it was morning and my muleteer was shaking my arm.

If a man has once known fear, fear, I think, always returns. I had grown somewhat easier in my mind when two newcomers at our next halting place joined our caravan. It was a usual enough occurrence and there appeared to be no obvious reason why I should turn uneasy. These men were harmless enough in appearance, seedy travellers, metal workers from Baghdad, loaded with jugs and pots of their own making which, like pedlars, they would sell when and how they could. And yet I could not help but be suspicious of them and a little fearful also. Their hands, I judged, were not the hands of men who made pots and jugs. They moved always together ; they kept too close to me. I was sometimes aware of their eyes on mine, eyes as expressionless and dark, as devilish also as a swan's or an adder's eyes. I stayed for my own protection beside my muleteer. With a kind of malicious and lecherous regard he welcomed me. I must keep beside him, sleep beside him also. " Come, share my coverlet, boy," he would bellow when it was time for sleep. There were times under his close scrutiny when I would realise he was neither so great a fool nor so gross a fellow as I had believed, when I would for a moment speculate very curiously in my turn upon him. But this again was nothing. Our caravan was a moving city : in its queer masterless world men's fortunes were as variable as the tides, and the same man might in one short life have followed a score of trades.

As the days passed my two strangers appeared to follow me more closely. Their very impassivity filled me with alarm. I thought I detected a certain desperateness about their approaches, as if time for them, and for me also, were running short. My muleteer began, for reasons of his own, to abuse them roundly. He did not like their faces, he declared. When they came near he would crack his whip too close to them, or—which appeared to annoy them most—drive them away with flappings of his saddlebag as if they were inquisitive farmyard geese. I had told him that these men meant evil towards me. His answer, delivered with a great deal of cheerfulness, filled me with laughter at the time. I have laughed over it on many occasions since, but I will not write it here. I deliberated whether to tell him more of my story and what lay behind my fear. But I did not dare confess myself a fugitive and therefore a possible cause within the caravan of strife. For it is a rule of every caravan that all its members should live together in peace.

While I was still hesitant in mind, my adversaries came at me. We had enjoyed many moonlit nights, so shining I confess I loved the moon and slept the better for her bright silver light. But on this night of which I speak the moon was on the wane and the night skies overcast. I had stayed tense and wakeful beside my muleteer ; then, worn out by too much watchfulness, I had slept. I woke and stiffened again, my companion's hand, large and more malodorous than a rancid ham, over my mouth. Now that the moment had come my mind worked quickly, I felt no fear. The two fell on us silently. As if a mountain moved, my muleteer fell on one of them. The other grappled with me. I remembered the shirts of mail Sinan's Assassins wore and struck at my assailant in the neck and groin. And yet I do not think I struck deep enough, for my man, like some old mastiff, held on. I was half strangling when my muleteer, with a mountainous heave, moved to my aid once more. It was an unequal struggle from this moment. Released at last, I rolled over, picked myself up and held my throat. My muleteer was shaking my particular enemy as a dog shakes a rat and cursing riotously all the while. " By the Name," I heard, and, to my greater astonishment, " by the Bread."

The last was an oath I had heard before only from King Richard's lips.

By this time every neighbouring sleeper was awake and crowding round. One Assassin—not mine—appeared to be dead. The other—my muleteer had not yet ceased to shake him—must by this time have wished that he were dead. I held my throat and stared at the glare of the torches and the velvet night and felt thankful and queerly empty also. Finally, the muleteer having grown tired of him, my adversary was led away.

A lump of mutton fat tied by my muleteer about my aching throat, I gazed upon my protector. For his part he appeared as gleeful as if he were about to attend a feast.

I said, and spoke with difficulty : " Surely you are a Christian Turk? "

He beamed delight at me. " Friend, I have served many masters."

I spoke again, not very sensibly. " These fellows were after one of us. Or both."

" Both," said he, " by the Bread." He winked, and then, for my greater mystification, let loose a string of oaths in more tongues than one.

I began formally again : " I am obliged to you for my life."

He winked a second time. " You may call me Suleiman."

I said, for I wished above all now to be honest with him : " I should tell you that I am of no importance. I am John of Oversley, an esquire of King Richard of England's company and a fugitive for King Richard's sake from the fortress of Massiat."

A hint of courtliness about him for all his grossness, he bowed. " Messire John, your servant, Suleiman."

We parted after that. For the rest of the day I nursed my injured throat while considering what I must do. A dozen reasons suggested to me that I must wait no longer but go. Though two Assassins were dead —my second assailant had been promptly hanged—more would pretty certainly succeed them. I had told the half of my story, I was reluctant to tell the rest. I was wise, I felt, to trust no one. Even Suleiman, if he were pressed to do so, might betray me. I was ignorant of the way to the Christian camp and fearful of the journey, yet the desire to warn King Richard possessed my mind to the exclusion of all else. I decided, therefore, as soon as opportunity offered, to leave the caravan and set off, alone, for the Christian camp.

Our caravan moved on its way, and everything was cheerful and laboured and monotonous as before ; the air was as full of dust and singing and the cracking of whips and the sound of bells ; the smells did not vary nor the coarse food. Everything was the same, and yet I went as painfully as if I trod upon thorns. On a night almost as overcast as the night of the Assassins' attack upon me I left Suleiman's side ; I abandoned the caravan.

I took the muleteer's dagger ; I left him with one of mine ; he had my signet ring. He did not stir when I left him, and yet I think he was awake, he lay so unnaturally still.

My departure was not so reckless as at first sight it may appear. We were in Christian country and Crusaders' castles lay all about us. From all that I had heard in King Richard's tent I knew that parties of Christian knights were occasionally to be met coming to or going from one or other of the Christian fortresses ; I knew also that King Richard himself was in the habit of sending out long-range scouting parties whose duty it was to report to him any movements of Turkish arms, or the passage of rich merchandise and richer caravans.

It is strange to reflect now how fortune favoured me at first only to turn against me in the end. About noon on the day of my departure from Suleiman I caught up, as I had hoped to do, with a crusading band. I had kept to the lower foothills in order to proceed more safely, and in order to observe any movements on the plain below. I came upon my party of crusaders as unexpectedly as a man falls into an ambush. Hidden by a shoulder of earth, they appeared almost to wait for me at a point where the narrow track upon which I was once more joined the plain. There were not more than six of them : a sergeant of mounted archers and five men-at-arms. I shouted to them in English and then in Norman-French. I waved both arms and ran to meet them. They faced me stolidly. I related a part of my story, incoherently enough, in a delighted rush of words. They looked at me, then at each other. They had some excuse for suspicion. I was burnt brown as a Beduin ; I wore Saracen robes ; I carried no signet ring, nothing with which to prove the truth of my tale. One of the men-at-arms guarded me while the rest consulted together. In a few moments I was questioned again.

The sergeant of mounted archers, a thick-set fellow of the stamp of Brand, addressed me in the cross-bred Mercian speech of Severn and Avonside. What business had I in these parts ? he enquired.

I related my story more coherently. My sergeant heard me out, stolid as only a man rooted in Midland clay can be. He asked my name and place. I gave him both. Next he enquired what proof I had. " My word," I said.

He looked sceptical. What were the blazonings of my house ? he asked. ·

" A corbeau on a blue ground," I said.

He looked cunningly at me. " You are from Oversley ? What would a stranger see first on Oversley Hill after the castle of Oversley ? "

I laughed at him. Here at least I could make no mistake. " Twelve oak trees," I answered. " The Twelve Apostles, stepping down the hill."

"Sir Esquire," he said then, "how came you to be so safe among that murdering white-smocked lot?"

I waited, sweating as I did so. Here, at my first encounter, was the suspicion I had feared and scarcely knew how to meet.

After a moment I said : "That, sergeant of mounted archers, is for your captain to hear."

I went with them. To my surprise—though why I should be surprised I do not know—their captain was no other than Hugh the Brown, whom I had known in Messina and in Limasol also.

He greeted me only coldly, I thought, and heard all that I had to say silently as if he withheld belief. Even while I spoke the eagerness with which I had begun changed to diffidence and stumbling. I turned cool in my turn. Either I must be conducted to King Richard with all haste, I said, or I must be given horse and weapons in order that I might make my way to him alone.

"Not alone," Hugh the Brown answered.

"Will you make haste to return for the King's sake?" I asked then.

"For the King's sake," he said.

We made great haste, travelling by night and by day until at last we arrived at the Canebrake of Starlings, on the road to Jerusalem, where the King and the army lay.

8

THE CANEBRAKE OF STARLINGS

I DO not know whether there is any torment comparable to that a man suffers when he tells the truth in a matter of life and death to himself and is not believed. If he has never known loneliness before, nor despair, for the first time he becomes intimate with both and the misery that falls on him then holds scarcely a glimmer of light.

It was towards the end of May that I was brought once more into the Christian camp, which at that time, as I have said, was at the Canna des Etourneaux, or, in English, the Canebrake of Starlings. Here, during the last week of May, King Richard had encamped, having previously taken by storm the great coastal fortress of Le Daron.

The Canebrake was a strange choice, I could not help but think, for a camp. The country was low-lying and open, except for many tall thickets of reeds. Their criss-cross blades shone blue-green ; they made a sound like thin organ pipes when the wind stirred, and hosts of starlings, encamped among them like another army, kept up a continual murmuration and movement among them which, though I found it pleasant at first, became wearisome after a while.

I had told my tale on my arrival as simply and as clearly as I could, first to old Sir Hugh de Winton, then to William the Marshal, and then again, the matter having become official by this time, to Leonard, the King's chief scribe. From the beginning it was plain that I was not believed. Every time I told my story I did so with a greater effort and a determination not far removed from despair. In order to come to an end quickly, I found myself, as if I were indeed a liar, omitting details and circumstances which were vital; I changed the order of my narrative ; I broke off before I should ; finally I fell almost as silent as my questioners. I raged secretly ; if only men would listen, I told myself, they could not help but believe. I knew nothing at that time of the general distrust and suspicion among the host following upon the French treasons and the murder of the Marquis Conrad. I knew only that wherever I went—for at first I went everywhere freely—men appeared to move furtively away from me. Those whom I knew averted their faces as if they, and not I, were ashamed ; those who were unknown to me stared from a distance as if I were dangerous though not yet caged. Though I was scarcely aware of it I had become both famous and suspect. My friendship with de Passy was a prime cause, as might have been expected, of my misfortunes. Was not the Frenchman, Leonard the King's scribe asked, his quill pen poised, the chief among Sinan's captains ? And was he not known to me for a pretender and a rogue even before I had arrived at Massiat ? My story was not valued highly. I could supply no details of the plot against King Richard's life, only assurances that a plot existed. Why, I was asked, did I suppose my information to be valuable ? Every day, I was told, brought news of some fresh conspiracy from some different source against the life of King Richard. Next to my friendship with de Passy my own safety, as I had foreseen, counted for most in the score against me. Who was I, men asked, as the sergeant of mounted archers had asked before them, who was I to succeed in escaping from Massiat, a fortress and a power from which it was known that scarcely a man yet had escaped ? Surely, men said, there had been some complicity between de Passy and myself. If I were innocent, how did it come about that I alone of our small company of friends had been spared ? Did not that fact of itself argue that the French-man was confident of my complacence ? It was suggested that I had quarrelled with the Frenchman and afterwards, out of alarm for my own safety, had remembered my duty to King Richard. If I were not a complete traitor I was at least judged to be heavily tarred with treason. When I confessed that I had offered certain information to the Assassins which might be of service to them, my guilt was accepted as certain.

If only Robert had proclaimed his belief in me he might have done much to clear my name. But from the beginning he held cursedly aloof, nor once, though I sent him many friendly and desperate messages, consented to come near me. Nor, since I was by this time confined to my tent, could I obtain leave to seek him out. In this manner a new torment was added to those I already suffered : the thought that Robert of Kinwarton, of all men living, should hold me guilty with de Passy of Everard's death and his own blinding. In all the many thousands of the Christian host I had not left, I thought, one friend.

As if the case against me were not black enough, the misfortune that continued to follow me contrived to blacken it a hundredfold. An armed stranger, who had been caught trying to enter the quarter of the camp where the King lay, declared, on being questioned, that he had been sent by Sheikh Sinan to find me, and that I was indeed a true partner in his master's plan to murder King Richard. When the King's scribe and the Marshal, who together acted as prosecutor and judge in the case against me, related this new piece of evidence, I cried out at once : " Do you not see that Sinan has sent this man to secure my death at the King's hands ? " For all that I might say I was looked upon only as a new serpent from Eden. Sorrowing over me a little, the two of them left.

The camp executioner, Master Dick Moxon of Winchester, appeared next, followed by a smith with a brazier and all the implements of his trade. I must confess that when I saw the brazier of burning coals I flinched. The two did no more than fix light chains upon my wrists and ankles, doing all this as impersonally as if I were a calf, or hanged and dead, or, what I dreaded most, already buried up to my neck and alive. Their work done, like good workmen—they were no more—they went stolidly away.

Alone, my tent guarded by archers and foot soldiers, I tried to turn my thoughts to death and punishment. I could not ; my thoughts would not rise ; my mind remained miserably earth-bound. I recalled, for instance, how I had been weak and sickly for so long and denied life, and now, it was likely, I must lose in a cold-blooded fashion the life I had so newly won ; I reflected how I, who had for so long not known how to live, must shortly find a way to teach myself to die. In the closeness of my tent I remembered how upon the mountain the fresh wind came leaping after me, and how I fetched up suddenly, it seemed, on the smooth slab of rock and how when I awoke night seemed at once to have been transformed to day. And I reflected how joyful I had been afterwards and how that might be the last of my joy. And I hoped soberly that I might hang, or die of the sword, and not be buried, as many traitors were, chin-deep in the hot sand.

Light though they were, my chains moved as though in response to the shiver of fear that smote me then. I turned, and under the stuff of my tent—it was by this time almost dark—I beheld, sudden as any apparition, Giles's squirming head and queerly contorted face. I might have cried out, for no man loves a spectre, had not Giles croaked hoarsely : " Master, this accursed tent rope is fair strangling me."

In spite of my chains I released my poor Giles as if he were a rabbit in a snare. He shook his head and crawled in between tent and earth most gingerly.

Next I heard snorts and loud breathing followed by a hoarse cough as though some young bull, as had happened to me once in my tent at Oversley, were nosing a way in, and Brand appeared.

Proud as if they had captured a Saracen citadel the two of them beamed upon me. I opened my mouth, but my throat had contracted suddenly and I could not speak.

Jerking a thumb over his shoulder towards my guards, Giles said : " Master, we ha' blessed them with a little somewhat to keep 'em blind."

" But they will hear everything, master," Brand added. " They conditioned that."

I said as nobly as I could that the two of them should not be at any risk to themselves for my sake. My gesture appeared to be wasted, for Brand merely sneezed loud enough for twelve men, and one of my guards thrust his head protestingly within the tent. " In the Blessed Name," he said, and withdrew, only to reappear in the next second, and thrust a lighted torch into our midst.

" Brother Brand has a monstrous ague, master," Giles declared. " He has had it ever since that pesty march we made from Ascalon."

I knew nothing of Ascalon, and said as much and could not keep the longing from my voice.

I looked at them afresh, and when I saw the affection unchanged upon their faces I was greatly moved. Alarmed even yet for my own dignity, I looked away.

Brand said, " You were ever a simpleton, master. And you have been deceived." He went on more quickly : " Do not be so cast down, young master. If 'tis to be henbane in Master Moxon's porridge, henbane it shall be, or laburnum seeds, for there is plenty o' both hereabouts."

" Quiet, brother," said Giles, looking about him nervously.

" I am past such help," I said, " and would not have it if I could. If one executioner dies of eating sour porridge, do you think another would not at once be found ? I would have you safe," I said. " I would not have you die with me, if indeed I do die."

" There's reason in that, master. For you are not dead yet," said Giles, heartily. " Not by a long way you are not."

" To speak plainly," Brand said, " I know not how you will fare, young master, if you do not contrive to see King Richard."

" I have seen his scribe, master Leonard, several times," I said.

Brand described Master Leonard pithily, and for a moment I felt the better for hearing so many good Mercian oaths.

I said at last : " Do what you can for me. But always without risk to yourselves."

" Master, how may we speak to King Richard ? " Brand asked.

I thought quickly. " Speak to the Lady Melisande for me if she has any belief in my innocence," I said.

" 'Twas the Lady that sent us and gave us gold, master John," Giles declared.

" Tell her," I said, more moved than I had been so far, " that I am not guilty except of more of my old foolishness."

" That is what the Lady did herself swear, master," said Giles.

" By the Lord," I exclaimed, " I begin to see myself with all your eyes."

" Giles, hold your peace," said Brand. " And master, do not be angry. It was from service to you that the Lady sent us and because we greatly desired to come."

" Then speak to her," I said again. " Bid her beg an audience for me of the King. Say I would speak to him alone if I might."

" Would it not be good to have a second string to your bow, master ? " Brand continued cautiously.

The torch burned lower and I spoke slowly, my eyes on the flame. " There is Robin de Herdecourt," I said, " he who was with us at Limasol. Would he not ask Sir Hugh de Winton to speak to the King for me ? For the King will not listen to women only," I said, " not even to the Lady Melisande des Préaux."

My two worthies looked at each other. Said Giles : " It is the gallant with the seaweed tail."

" Master," said Brand, " it was he who declared in my hearing that he would never believe a man to be such a fool as to be guilty and return. For then the Old Man of Massiat would be after him, and Master Moxon would be after him also, and such a man would have two millstones hung about his neck."

I spoke shortly. " That is not any great declaration of belief, but speak with him if you will. And go now." I blessed them, and thanked them both.

"Farewell, master, until we meet again," Giles said. Outside Brand sneezed loudly. Lumbering creatures though they were, they were gone very silently.

Within my tent the torch still burned. Like hope, I thought—a man in danger of his life, I believe, thinks nothing new. I looked steadily at my torch of hope. But soon that also burned lower and went out, leaving, in proof of the sad end that comes to every metaphor, a most unsavoury smell of tallow behind.

I had heard nothing all this while of Ambrose and Richard the Chronicler. I could not believe they would set me down as plainly guilty; I did not dare hope, on so short an acquaintance, that they would discount all the apparent evidence against me. Some days after the visit of Brand and Giles they came also. Whether they came of their own accord or whether they were solicited to do so by the Lady Melisande, or even by Brand, I do not know. They came, and that was enough. I even experienced a burst of light-heartedness on seeing them: Ambrose so much gaunter than I remembered him, the Chronicler grown small, I thought, and as yellow-skinned as if he were troubled with the jaundice or the stone.

Ambrose said: "You are in a sad case, John of Oversley."

"Messire Ambrose," I answered, "that is not news to me."

Between them they straightway gave me to understand, though without vouching for it, that the King would see me.

The Chronicler said, for he was always more full of curiosity than feeling, that he believed the King might consent to see me in order to hear from my own lips something more of the Old Sheikh of the Mountains.

I answered stoutly again that the King might at least see me out of a love of justice and in return for the service I had once helped to render him.

The King was sick, they informed me. "If you have suffered much, messire John," Ambrose warned, "so have we all. And so has the Cause."

I stared at them.

The Chronicler added, and I thought he watched me as he spoke. "Since the death of the Marquis Conrad we have in truth suffered much."

I enquired when the Marquis had died.

In April, they said. For a moment, both of them watching me, I was silent. Once more I heard the trumpets and the kettle-drums and the wild sounds of rejoicing in Sinan's fortress. I recalled that if it had not been for these rejoicings and their cause I might never have escaped, never have been asked to suffer the accusations I suffered now.

I spoke of Saladin's messenger to Sinan; I told Ambrose and the Chronicler what I knew of Conrad's death.

Ambrose said quietly: "All this may indeed be important. For there are many among the French and Austrians who accuse King Richard of the death of the Marquis. One of Conrad's two Assassins also confessed before he died that King Richard had hired him."

"He lies," I said. Once more I told what I knew. I spoke this time of Sinan's grudge against Conrad for the death of one of his Fedavi shipwrecked at Tyre.

The Chronicler shifted the roll of parchment which he always carried under one arm, and spoke breathlessly : " I think the King must see you, messire John."

They were in such a shuffle to be off they could scarcely bear to take their leave.

More confident than I had felt yet I called in my guard when they had gone. I greeted him : " You have heard all that has been said between us ? " He answered sheepishly that it was his duty to hear. " Then tell me," I begged him, " of Ascalon."

He told me plainly all that he knew. Gradually a tale more chequered than any Ambrose could have woven for me in his fine tapestry of rhyme was unrolled. I was reminded of the decision to proceed from Joppa towards Jerusalem ; I was told of fresh treacheries of Conrad of Montserrat about this time, and of continuing strife between French and English. My mind filled with pity and distress, I learned how the host on the first stage of its march to the Holy City was preyed upon by hidden bands of the enemy, how many thousands of our men perished. For the first time I heard how joyfully at last our armies had encamped at Beit Nuba, not four days' march from the city they so much desired, and how, having encamped there, all Hell, as it were, turned out to meet them, and Heaven grew blind, and the cold Syrian winter fell nakedly upon them, so that finally they were forced to retreat. Never since God made the world, my guard declared, was such deep grief shown, such suffering borne. Winds and tempests, torrential rain and hail tore up our men's tents, their armour rusted, their garments rotted, the biscuits and bacon upon which the army relied for food grew stinking and full of worms ; horses and men alike sickened and died, and in less than seven days the camp that had overflowed like a church at Easter-time with thanksgivings was filled with mourning. My guard related to me how many of the French, despairing of victory, had deserted the Cause, how some had returned to Joppa, others to Acre, how others still had betaken themselves to the Marquis Conrad and the delights of Tyre, how even the Duke of Burgundy himself, their leader since the departure of King Philip, had chosen a distant and more comfortable place than Ascalon for his retreat. I learned how King Richard himself had ridden beside seven hundred of the French knights, weeping bitterly and imploring them to turn back from the road to Joppa. And they would not.

On the nineteenth day of January, therefore, King Richard had led the faithful remnant of his army and all his sick and wounded back through the same evil weather along the coast road, deep now in swamps and mire, to Ascalon. When at last they arrived, they found not shelter nor warmth but desolation, the walls of Ascalon torn down, her buildings destroyed, the country wasted. Straightway by the consent of every man, the army began to rebuild the city. And in this task, so necessary for every man's safety, King Richard laboured as hard as the rest.

My guard finished his story. " And still," he said, " ill fortune follows us." For now, on the edge of summer, the rages of winter past, the great fortress of Le Daron in our hands, and Jerusalem once more within reach, King Richard was once again stricken by illness and beset by evil news from England as well as from Acre and from Tyre.

I pondered deeply for a moment. Small wonder that among so much distrust I was not believed ; small wonder in the general confusion that none of the King's men could spare time or patience to hear my case. From all that I had heard I could see what afterwards all men saw : a great army and a great cause perishing at the dead centre like a great tree.

And yet I could not bring myself to believe that we might fail. " Surely," I said, " surely, all this will pass."

My guard started up, overturning as he did so the rough stool on which he sat. " How, sir Esquire ? " he asked. He left me then.

As soon as it was light Sir Hugh de Winton himself entered my tent. He began without preamble : " The King will see you."

The old knight was unarmoured and unshaven. He glared at me out of bloodshot eyes, and said : " Whether you are knave or fool, John of Oversley, will soon appear."

I did not speak.

" I warn you, do not lie," he said.

I said : " I do not lie."

Someone struck off my chains. Without ceremony Sir Hugh stumped off ; without ceremony I followed him. Men made way before us, then stared after us ; in the mistiness of morning they seemed like their own ghosts. I know that the sun wore stilts of gold, that the east was grey filled with rose like a dove's breast. I remember that from a dense thicket of reeds as we passed a host of starlings rose in sudden darkening flight.

I stooped my head and entered the King's tent. It was small and confined and plain ; it was as small, I thought, as if the King and I stood both under the same cloak.

Leaning on one elbow the King stared uncomprehendingly at me.

I knelt on one knee and spoke to him. " Sire, I am John of Oversley, and I am no traitor."

He looked at me uncomprehendingly even yet. Then, with an effort, he said : " I think you served me once. I have forgotten when, or how."

" Sire, it is past," I said. " And it was Robert of Kinwarton who served you more than I."

" Every week," the King said—" have they not told you?—there is some new plot against my life, so much does Christ rule in his Holy Land."

" Sire," I answered, " this was no ordinary plot of which I spoke to your people. If Sinan has failed once he will continue for a dozen years until he does not fail."

The King said : " I can wait a dozen years."

" Sire," I reminded him, " you also are accused falsely. How if men will never believe you? "

" I made Conrad King of Jerusalem so that I might be free to go to my own people if need arose," the King answered and stared. " Why should I murder him? "

" Sinan Rashideddin himself has declared that you are not guilty of the Marquis Conrad's killing, sire," I said.

" But Sinan is a great and notorious liar. Who would believe him? " the King asked.

" I would return to Massiat if need be, my lord," I pleaded, " and bring sworn proof of your innocence from Sinan if you would order it."

" I must have messengers whom I can trust, John of Oversley," the King said.

I wept then, why I scarcely knew, for who knows why he weeps ?

" Sinan rules by murder ; I live by war," the King said. " Christ rules by peace." He spoke strangely, I thought. He looked at me. " Why do you weep? "

" I do not know," I answered and wept again. I grew calm then. Truth and untruth, everything alike would pass away. I answered the King. " I weep because when I was upon the mountain and fretted in mind and spirit I yet hoped I might be believed."

The King did not speak.

I said again : " Sire, if I know truth, all that I have told your men is true."

" We know nothing," the King said, " not even the truth in our hearts. I believed God's hand was upon me to win back the Cross and Jerusalem and the Holy Places. It was pride that was upon me and God has chastened me and my pride. What the enemy could not do some spirit of evil has done, changing victory to defeat, friends to enemies, truth to treachery, the love between brother and brother to a kind of hate. Everywhere plots, John of Oversley, plots and treachery. So Saladin is exalted, and the Christian King put down ; so now, though the sea coast is mine, Jerusalem is denied me. So that I feel nothing now, neither the faith within me, nor his Hand upon me, only weariness of spirit for the many men, gentle and simple, who have suffered with me, who curse me now. I desire nothing, John of Oversley, I desire only to be gone."

"My Lord, it will pass," I said.

I might not have spoken. "From God's tool," the King said, "I have become God's fool. I heard Sathanas laugh last night. I thought he stood outside my tent in the deep thicket of the night, a vast shape among the reeds, and laughed at me. 'Thou fool,' I thought he said, 'thou trusting fool. All Christian men are brothers in Christ, think you ? Think again, Richard. Dreams, Richard, cloud palaces of dreams. Go home, Richard Plantagenet. Go home. Or you will have no home, no place, no land to call your own either in France or in England, or in Poitou or Aquitaine or Normandy. You, and not Brother John, will be landless. Go home, Richard.' And then I thought I heard this fiend Sathanas laugh again." The King turned to me. "I am blessed by monks, washed by holy waters, but still the foul fiend visits me. You are tormented also, and you weep. What fiend is yours ? I ask you, John of Oversley, what shall a man who is tormented do ? "

I answered wildly : "Surely victory is of the spirit. Surely the truth is with God."

"You speak like a monk." The King was impatient suddenly. "More is necessary to Richard Plantagenet than the spirit or truth, or even the blessed name of God." He leaned towards me. "Men have put out their hands and cursed me that for my sake they ever crossed the seas. They have cursed me and died. But at Acre, and after Acre—did you not see them ?—they would have kissed my feet." He broke off and seemed to listen. Then, quietly but still strangely, he said again : "What is it I hear now from the same reeds ? "

I listened and heard the sound of felt-shod feet going up and down before the tent ceaselessly and a man's harsh weeping.

At a word from the King those outside brought the man in. A clerk in holy orders, pale-faced and young, his cheeks daubed with tears, stood before us and, wringing his hands, wept still.

"Who is it that weeps now ? " the King asked, courtesy and irony mixed in his voice.

Down on his knees the clerk went most awkwardly. He wept, he said, for Jerusalem.

Still with that same faint irony, the King said : "I have wept for her also."

Let the King not abandon the host, the clerk prayed.   Let him not for
any earthly cause abandon Christ's martyred city and God's Holy War.

"You are mistaken, sir clerk," the King returned, very courteous still.
"Not John of Oversley here is a greater fool of God than I."

In dismay the clerk forgot to weep.

"It is true," the King continued, "that all my soul's grief and my body's
pain has come at last to this, that I must return to my own country.   And
I take leave to think, sir clerk," he said, "that it is God's will that I should
return.   For no man has been tossed as I have been tossed from hope to
despair and back again."

The clerk spoke boldly and vehemently then.   "No King has suffered
less," he declared.   From one achievement of the King he went on to
speak cunningly of yet another, from the King's boyhood as Count of Poitou
to the day after the recent storming of Le Daron, through a hundred
exploits and as many dangers until at last—though these matters are
deceptive—it did indeed appear as if God for some special purpose of his
own had preserved King Richard.   "All men, Sir King," the clerk
finished, "will cry shame upon you if you desert them now."

The King was not offended, for plain speech never offended him.   Rather
he appeared thoughtful and curiously moved.   Peremptorily enough, he
signed to us to go.

I followed the clerk and the soldiers out.   The clerk, his moment over,
quivered like an aspen leaf.   Trembling still, he fell into another ecstasy
and began once more to pray : "Lord God of Hosts, Lord God of Battles,
suffer not thy servant Richard to depart from thy people."

I looked about me.   The soldiers' faces stayed expressionless as brown
slabs of earth.   The clerk prayed on, and now the large numbers of pilgrims
who had gathered together before and all around the King's tent took up
his prayer.   Never since the children of Israel waited upon the shores
of the Red Sea while the chariots of Egypt came thundering on them from
afar were so many tear-bedraggled faces seen, so many quivering uplifted
hands.   "Lord God, Lord God," I heard on every side while God's
own sun burned brightly down and the birds twittered and stirred in the
thickets and the world seemed full of fierce and burning joy.   The multitude
of sobs and prayers in so many tongues made a strange babble of sound
more like a gaggle of geese, I thought, than poor distracted men.

In the general ecstasy of lamentation no one even yet appeared to notice
me.   Foolishly perhaps, I began to hope that because I was forgotten I was
also on the way to being believed.   More like a free man than a prisoner
I returned to my tent.   The King, I told myself, had not cared greatly
whether I was guilty or innocent.   He had not even desired to hear more of
Massiat or of Sinan.   Nothing that was mine was of importance to him,

least of all my life. From perplexity and sickness he was like a man lost and wandering. I was a listening presence only, a mind that in some odd way, for I also had been lost and wandering, answered his. All this was flattering to me, and yet not flattering. Nor was it comfortable. The King had spoken to me as if I were another self, but still I could not help but wonder whether I was for Moxon in the morning or for Jerusalem.

Though I waited all day no messenger, whether good or evil, came to me. All day while I waited, the tumult without beat most devilishly upon my tired brain : the cries and weeping of the pilgrims, the thud of hammers and mallets, the constant shuffle and tread of feet as the bulk of the army, like a forest of tall trees, busily uprooted itself and prepared to move off once more towards Jerusalem. I lay full of sickness and longing within my tent, as I did not doubt King Richard lay in his also, while the army, squadron by squadron of mounted men, company by company of archers and foot soldiers, moved on for the second time in our Holy War towards Jerusalem.

9

THE ABYSS

I WAS scarcely awake, my mind still in the half-world of sleep and fading dreams, when I heard the voice of Philip, the King's crier, crying down the half-empty aisles of the camp. " Oyez, oyez," I heard, " gentles and commoners, holy pilgrims and sergeants, and all ye, King Richard's faithful fellows "—I tumbled from my couch, my dreams fell with a soft thud with my coverlet to earth ; I thrust open the flap of my tent. The dawn was streaked with grey, earth steamy as a new-baked loaf, and down the long aisles of the camp came Philip the King's crier, followed by two trumpeters. Their gold tabards glittered, their gilt trumpets shone and the long tassels hung red and blue and white. His cheeks plump and purple as a November fungus of the woods, Philip halted not far off and cried his message again. " Oyez, oyez," he cried, " in the name of King Richard of England "—I listened in suspension of belief, then in sudden credulous joy. King Richard greeted all his faithful fellows. It had been shown to him, the message ran, that he should not leave his people. God willing, therefore, he would abide in Outremer until the Easter following. Let no man doubt him longer. But let all good men make ready to follow him to Jerusalem.

His message delivered, the King's crier emptied the spittle from his mouth and passed on, crying the King's message in every part of the camp at the Canebrake of Starlings as it was certain it had already been cried throughout Ascalon.

Trembling, I dressed in haste. Bond or free I was determined that where all King Richard's faithful fellows went, I, too, would follow. I thrust past my guards, changed overnight since the beginning of the new march. These men were Turcoples; they were neither, that is to say, Christian nor Saracen, but half of each by blood, and closely allied to King Richard's cause. They followed me. All that remained of the camp, as we moved on, was in turmoil. Men, half-clad or not clad at all, poured out of their tents. Never before had I seen, and never again except at Joppa afterwards should I behold so many men looking simple and amazed in their shirts. Where there had been excess of grief before, now there was an excess of gladness. Those who were so disposed still wept, though now they wept from joy. Many clasped hands and formed rings and danced heathenishly. Others who had cursed before sang loud tavern ditties now in bawling tuneless voices. My ears were tender and I shuddered at the din they made and wished they would turn to cursing again. Soon the priests came, with books and shepherds' crooks, and rang their bells for seemlier songs and prayers. The dancing ceased abruptly; in sudden decorum men held down the tails of their shirts and turned good Christians again.

Within an hour all that remained of the camp was in motion. My Turcople guards signed to me to mount and make my way between them with the rest of the army towards Jerusalem. I gladly mounted the docile beast they brought to me; I remember thinking as I did so that though I had always possessed the voice of a crow I could for once have sung as tunefully as a thrush.

My joy changed before another morning. That night, while I slept, I was stunned, then gagged and trussed like a calf in a sack, and carried off. I had so little consciousness remaining I scarcely recall what followed. I remember only days and nights of constant movement like a repeated nightmare, and pain, followed by oblivion and pain and oblivion again. I remember wondering now and then if I were dead and wandering in some dim borderland between this world and the next. But the odours that assailed my nostrils, of horse-dung, and rude unwashed men, and thyme and sun-baked earth, were real enough. From all these signs I knew I was alive. By other signs I felt certain that Sinan's men had found me again, that I was captive a second time, that once more I should behold the fortress and mount with difficulty that too symbolical, that steep and slippery stair.

I was not mistaken. Again I saw the castle of Massiat, standing defiantly between the hard rock and the bright sky. Once more signals were given of my approach, once more the white-robed Fedavi came down to greet me. I, John of Oversley, who had been Sinan's prisoner, had returned. Once more I put hope, that frail taper, away. For whom did Sinan ever forgive? Whom had he ever allowed to return unhurt to the company of milder men?

This time I was allowed no freedom, given no companion, but kept in solitude within my cell. On the day following my return—as far as I could judge—de Passy came to me. He was as friendly, or as little friendly, as he had ever been; he appeared to feel no pleasure at my capture and no resentment towards me for my earlier escape. I was puzzled by so much indifference until I realised that Sinan's designs were no more to him now than King Richard's hopes had been. In other ways he appeared changed. He had kept, it is true, his old debonair assurance of manner. But under it I thought him uneasy and ill-poised. A fever of restlessness appeared to possess him. I had never seen him so self-absorbed nor so unconscious of himself. He had always been sparing of words. Words flowed from him now: ill-judged, boastful words. His movements appeared to match his thought. I had always considered him both determined and fanatical. I thought him queerly volatile now. Could it be, I asked, that he was out of fashion with Sinan, that he, de Passy, at last suspected that he was trapped and knew himself to be afraid?

While I speculated upon all this he spoke restlessly again : " If I could come near Sinan there is much that I might persuade him to do."

I said : " Sinan has finished with you, I think."

He answered with sudden venom : " Then I will finish with Sinan."

" You cannot change your coat so many times," I reminded him.

He dropped down beside me. " I am your friend."

I did not speak nor look at him. Perhaps, for fear that the old charm might work, I did not dare.

He laid a hand on my arm and spoke as softly as if I were a woman. " When you lay hidden in the pool I knew that you were there. For friendship's sake I spared you."

I found both touch and words distasteful. Watching my face, he laughed suddenly as if he were amused that after so affecting a speech I should remain unconvinced. " I tell you," he said again, " Sinan depends upon me."

" Then you are in great danger from Sinan," I answered. I went on : " You will deny it, but I believe the murder of Everard and the blinding of Robert of Kinwarton lie on your mind—on your mind, I say, not upon your conscience. They are on your mind because your judgment failed you at that time and has failed you since. Because what you did then in fact spoiled your plans, and made an enemy even of me. You are like a man who releases the flood gates," I said, " and forgets that he, too, may drown."

He looked blankly at me. " You are pleased to turn prophet."

" I think you have destroyed yourself," I said, " as surely as my own fever and Sinan's kidnappings have between them taken the strength from my limbs."

" You repay me evil for evil, like a true Christian," he said. He turned to leave me, then looked over his shoulder. " Are you content ? "

" No," I answered. With that, fever came on me again like a wall of marsh mist, and my hatred for de Passy and my momentary clarity of mind went also.

Afterwards Sinan sent for me. I thought I knew his habit of extracting whatever cool pleasure he could from every situation and from every captive brought to Massiat. A man so cloistered as Sinan must learn from whatever source he can, from men as well as from learned books or his own wisdom. For I would never deny, evil though his purposes were, that Sinan was wise. It was not without a certain pleasure even that I prepared to see him. He would delay torture or execution or judgment, I was certain, until he had practised a little of his philosophy upon me.

So indeed it proved. He received me in his great open Hall of Audience high on Massiat's flat eminence of rock. His Fedavi, motionless as statues, were posted at intervals along the walls. The sun was past its peak ; glittering particles on the rocks below threw back a thousand points of light ; the sky was cloudless, blue like an altar cloth, and full of peace.

I bent my head before Sinan. I would do no more than this ; I could do no less, for in his own manner Sinan was as great as was Lucifer, Son of the Morning among fallen angels, or Azrael, or Sathanas himself. And none but a fanatic or a boor—and I was neither—could remain altogether insensible of his power.

I waited, and the wind most irreverently parted Sinan's beard, the sun revealed impartially the bluish whiteness of his robe, the lilac whiteness of his hands. He did not speak.

I said, for it seemed to matter little what I said : " Sir, why have you brought me a second time to Massiat ? " He glanced at me. " Truly," I said again, " I do not know."

" Where all men obey me you have not obeyed," he said.

I said in answer : " Sir Sheikh, it is true the Brotherhood obey you, and the mountain folk, and all the princes of the East. But I am of the West."

He let that pass. Smiling faintly, he said : " Tell me why you, an unbeliever and disobedient, should not die."

Either there was a great buzzing in my ears or a great hum of flies coming from somewhere in the hollow of the abyss. For a moment I had difficulty in hearing my own words. At last I heard myself answer Sinan: "My belief is in Christ and His Church. My obedience is due, Sir Sheikh, to King Richard only."

Sinan bent his head.

I looked away. "I believe in my own people," I said.

Still softly, Sinan enquired: "Why did you escape from Massiat?" And one of the waiting Assassins posted along the walls slithered and from faintness or sunstroke fell upon his face.

"Because of my oath to King Richard," I replied. "And because I feared to stay and play the coward."

Almost deprecatingly Sinan's hand sought his beard. "Know," he said mildly, "that it is not our purpose to kill uselessly or without cause. You have already cost us gold for your life, which is worthless to us now. You took no oath of obedience, it is true, you were never a member of our Brotherhood." Once more, judicially, his hand combed his beard. "The Lord Richard," he declared at last, "shall ransom you."

"No one will ransom me," I cried loudly. As I spoke I watched two other Assassins carry my Fedavi of the scarred ankles—it was he who had fallen not two minutes since—past me and out of sight.

Sinan paused. "If King Richard will not ransom you, messire John of Oversley, then you will die."

I said again, a dullness I could hear in my own voice: "I am not worth the King's ransoming."

Sinan continued as if I had not spoken. "The Lord Richard shall pay. The debt, after all, is his." He got to his feet. Inclining his head, he bade me go in peace.

I thought as I went away of the Tree of Knowledge of Good and Evil and of the Serpent coiled around the Tree. Sinan was that Serpent and the Rule of the Calling and all the Assassin lore was the Tree.

I waited for days together in my cell, and one day was as much like another as the separate cold drips of water that fall in torture upon the victim's head beneath, and each was harder to endure. At last, silent as his own ghost, de Passy came to my cell. Though I hated him, or told myself I hated him, I babbled to him only half coherently, as I have heard travellers do who have been lost in the desert and found only after many days. He listened and was patient. Once more I was surprised to discover that he bore me no malice for the rebuffs he had suffered at our last meeting. He was too deeply concerned with himself, I could only suppose, to be troubled by anything I might do or say.

I ceased to babble and related what had passed between Sinan and myself. De Passy, too fluent in his turn, offered more than one explanation. " He is playing with you as he plays with everyone." And again : " His mind is not made up."

" Does Sinan need to decide as other men do ? " I asked. " Does he not always know in advance the next step he must take ? "

" With him everything is policy, or pleasure and policy mixed, that is true." De Passy was thoughtful for a moment. Then, suddenly, he said : " More than anything except his power over other men and their fear of him, Sinan loves gold. He may think your life so worthless he will not take it."

I admitted that Sinan had said as much.

" There is this also," de Passy continued. " It may tickle his sense of the fitness of things to pay his annual tribute to the Knights Templars with Crusader gold."

I repeated that no one would ransom me.

" It is unheard of," de Passy declared then, " that one of the King's company should die for lack of ransom money."

I reminded him : " I am no longer of the King's company."

He paused in astonishment. " What stiff valiant fools these King's captains are ! You could not deceive one of your own bullocks." He laughed very pleasantly at his own wit.

I was silent, a dozen furious answers whirling in my head, when he said again : " There is this in your favour also. I think the climate, one may say, has changed, for the Sultan Saladin is now certain, I believe, of coming to terms with King Richard and for that reason no longer seeks the King's life. Sinan may think it politic to curry favour with King Richard even though he has done his best a month since to murder him. For all these reasons it is possible that Sinan is sincere in demanding ransom for you."

I had no heart for conjecture. There was nothing, I thought, for me to say.

While I stayed silent, de Passy turned suddenly and said : " When you have won your freedom, will you ransom me ? "

I stared at him. He waited, his eyes on my face. " It is impossible," at last I said. As I spoke I could not—it was an old weakness of mine—from the confusion of my own thoughts look at him.

He continued: " I have gold and jewels stored away in the port of Alexandria with a rich merchant there. Half may be yours if you wish. With what remains I can still buy my life with a prince's ransom."

I asked him : " Who has paid you so well ? "

He hesitated. " Conrad of Montserrat, if you must know."

" You took Conrad's bribes and betrayed him," I said.

De Passy answered : " Conrad betrayed all the world. He betrayed even himself."

" So do you betray yourself," I returned.

" With Sinan," he replied, " I think I do."

I looked away from him again. "' I wonder that so much faithlessness could content you or any man."

He spoke courteously. " I admit it is wearisome to believe in nothing as I have done for so long. Like climbing a steep stair," he said, " for ever."

" Beyond Sinan's stairway the abyss lies," I said.

Half mockingly he answered that he believed he could find peace there.

I looked at him. " It is unbelievable that you of all men should speak of peace."

" Do you not know," he asked, " that men are apt to deprive themselves of what they most desire ? "

" You traffic," I said, " in too many words."

" I could not be plainer," he returned. " Men desire one thing, I say again. They seek as often as not another. There is no rule for man, I think, as there is for magpies and the stars."

" Surely," I answered, " we live by virtue and by God."

" When I was a boy," he said, " I wished most vehemently to be free, for I, who was only a piece of wreckage in the world, was in all ways shackled and bound. Therefore I sought an order and a law within which, after a due measure of obedience, I might be free ; I sought a rule in which I was not expected to believe, a discipline I was not asked to love. For just as I have never been able completely to believe, so I have never been able successfully to love. I grew up cloistered and brooding, loving only myself, myself my universe, my measure of all things. And yet, landless as I was, other men despised me. In order to live at all I must obey and serve, on my knees often enough. My masters were insolent and I despised them ; they humiliated me and I hated them. If, as you say, I have destroyed myself, I have destroyed many of those who so humiliated me. I have found pleasure and release in revenge."

I interrupted him. " How could you believe that Sinan would advance you ? "

He was silent for a moment. " I am no more to you," he said then, " than one of many other petty sorts of traitors ? "

" You are perhaps more gifted," I said.

He asked : " Why are you so certain that I have failed ? "

" I am certain," I answered stubbornly, " that in one way or another Sinan will finish with us both."

He spoke once more like a man emptying his mind. " I can mend nothing and I regret nothing. I had a great talent for deceit and treachery.

I have used my talent, and now I have come perhaps to an end, and the end, it may be, is nothing. But beyond that nothing, beyond the abyss, even for me there may be peace. I have heard the Arabians say—I do not differ from them, though I will not say I believe—I have heard them say that no part of the universe is different in kind from any other part, that there is unity everywhere in this created world of sun and stars and sea, of movement and stillness, of light and dark, procession and decay. Beyond this nothingness I would find this unity and be lost in it, and at one with the rest."

I looked at him.

He said : " I, too, would have believed if I could."

I was silent. We had not talked like enemies, I thought, nor yet like friends, nor even like men, but rather like spirits or angels, without feeling or strife.

He pleaded with me a second time. " You loved me once. Will you not ransom me ? "

" I loved others too," I answered. " They are spoiled, or blinded, or dead."

He reminded me again : " I saved your life by the pool."

" You have lied to me too often," I said, " for me to believe you now."

He stood off from me, white-faced and strange. " I believe that nothing can save you, or perhaps save me."

" I think I am past caring," I replied.

He jeered at me and, I think, at himself also. " To-morrow we shall see and know."

I was untouched by his jeers. " To-morrow then," I said.

He left me silently. Before long my cell, that had felt fever-hot before, grew fever-cold. Outside in Massiat nothing moved but the shadows ; in the heavens the stars danced in a maze of light.

10

TO-MORROW

THE to-morrow, of which de Passy and I had spoken, came. Once more Sinan's white-clad Fedavi lined the walls of Sinan's open audience chamber ; once more the plain chair and the plain canopy over it waited for Sinan. The day was like a holy day in Massiat : crimson and white banners hung on the walls ; the lances of the Assassin guards bore pennons of white and red, and a long carpet, gay as Sinan's garden, and full, like his garden, of singing birds and trees, and jugs of wine, and small wide-faced flowers, ran in a straight line from Sinan's footstool of ivory to the furthest wall. Again the sky was blue as the Virgin's robe, untroubled as her sculptured face ; again the birds sang, and from the abyss below the battlements came the steady hum of flies, as if the God of Flies held a different audience there.

Scarcely moving, we waited for Sinan. It was impossible in the silence not to be aware of one's own pulse-beats and the panic that could scarcely be quietened in every man's breast. No one spoke, no one looked at his neighbour ; no one, I believe, was concerned for anything beyond to-day. We waited still. The silence, I thought, was part of the torment that Sinan loved to inflict on other men. I saw faces sharpen under the strain, eyes stare more rigidly ahead. A Fedavi fell silently, two Assassins from me, an arm over his foam-flecked face. As silently the lay brethren carried him away. I eased my fingers ; my knuckles cracked as I did so.

Eleanour would have an ear for each crack of my fingers or her own. I remembered her cracking her fingers for sweethearts in our orchard at Oversley when the fallen apples burned red and rotten in the long darker patches of grass. " Only two," she had said. " Why can I not have five ? But I shall cheat," she declared. For one finger of the two had scarcely murmured. " I wanted five. I must have two. And not one like Raymond. Holy Mary," she had prayed, " not one."

I saw her again in my mind's eye : grey eyes, freckled nose, all the sensible candour of her face. " I wanted five. I must have two," I heard her say and I saw the pigs guzzling and the purple butterflies gorging delicately on the rotten fruit.

I moved. De Passy looked at me. He stood a distance of about six men away where Sinan's flowery carpet ran in a straight line from Sinan's footstool to the fortress wall. There was some sort of appeal, I thought, in his eyes. But I could not be certain even of this. Even to-day, when it was likely that one or both of us would come to an end, I did not know how much there was of falsehood in him, nor how much of truth. I looked away. To-day at least, I, who had always been sociably inclined, was content with my own company. I had no wish to be nearer him in fear or in thought. I know that fear was there in my mind, though wrapped in a blessed numbness of sense. I had looked as steadily as a man may at his own peril and in doing so I had fallen, as I had been confident I would, into a great calm. I looked away from de Passy, away from Sinan's rock and his guards and his orchards and all his encircling walls. In their place I saw our courtyard at Oversley again and our ducks, their bellies loaded, waddling engagingly towards our round pond, in a spring dusk that was velvety and soft and filled with gold, under a sky coloured

He turned away. He gave the signal twice. Two more Fedavi leapt, so swiftly and easily I marvelled, as I was meant to do, that any men should be so obedient.

Sinan rose and turned as though to go, then paused. Everyone waited with him ; the Fedavi stayed motionless at their posts along the walls. Only the pennons and the wind bending the tops of the trees on the edge of the abyss moved indifferently. Above the silence and the light movements of the wind I heard once more the steady drone of flies.

Sinan addressed me a second time and once again I held myself cruelly still. He said sleekly :

" John of Oversley, would you not wipe out a failure as a scribe smoothes a wax tablet he has spoiled ? "

" Sir Sheikh," I said, as quietly as any man could, " I think that that is just."

Sinan lifted a hand. There was too much drama here, I thought. If it continued a man might be moved to disgrace himself and weep or laugh.

Once more, and more deliberately this time, Sinan pointed a finger. It was Guy de Passy, relaxed and almost smiling at that moment and certain of my death, who took the leap, not I. I saw him turn. He turned so slowly, like a man surprised. I shut my eyes. I did not see him go or hear him fall. Only the flies disturbed shot up in an angry swarm ; only the place where he had stood at the end of the flowery carpet showed gaping and wide.

Sinan bowed to me. Trembling, for I had loved de Passy once, I bowed in return, most courteously. Sinan had not finished with me yet. It seemed to me that I had still to die.

I have often been glad that solemn moments do not always work out so solemnly. The moment, some days later, was grave enough. Summoned once more to Sinan's presence I did not know how to conduct myself nor what to expect. After so many hours in the dimness of my cell the whiteness of Sinan's inner Hall of Audience dazzled my eyes, a bluish pallor, almost a deadness, seemed to me to be apparent in Sheikh Sinan's face.

Sinan spoke—it was then that the pigeon sunk on the arm of his chair roused itself and winked at me. It was then also that I resolved, if ever I should live to return, to add a pigeon to our coat of arms at Oversley.

" You are mistaken, messire," Sinan began. " King Richard and your friends will ransom you."

I waited.

Sinan went on : " You shall have food and escort for your journey "—here the pigeon winked sleepily again. " Are you willing to set out ? "

"I am willing," I said. I felt confused and weak; my knees shook under me; there was a buzzing in my ears.

"It is now and then pleasant to be merciful," Sinan somewhat unctuously declared. He lifted a hand. Once more he bade me go in peace.

"In peace, I thank you," I answered. I bowed my head in greeting, and the pigeon waddled a pigeon's step or two away from us both.

Accompanied by three Fedavi, I set out from Massiat within the hour. The duty of my escort, they declared, was to collect the ransom which a party of Templars, come for my sake at old Sir Hugh de Winton's summons from their fortress at Tortosa, would deliver at the foot of the mountain, and afterwards return.

I listened and could scarcely persuade myself to believe a word. Their leader, who kept a firm hold on my horse's bridle, was the Fedavi of the hooked nose and ravaged face in whose company I had first travelled to Massiat after Everard's death and Robert's blinding. The faces of my other two Assassins were expressionless as eggs. Hashish-filled, hashish-consumed, every one of the three, I told myself, would take my life with pleasure, and sleep all the sounder afterwards. When I remembered our ambush and my escort's part in it I beguiled the long silent tedium of the way with thoughts, which I knew to be no better than day-dreams, of revenge.

Mine was always a careful rather than a sanguine temperament. So now, I did not dare to nurse any firm hope of freedom. So far as I was bold enough to rejoice at all I rejoiced only in this : that, suspect though I was, someone among the King's friends had thought my life worth the ransoming. I did not dare count on forgiveness yet, or rate my own chances of ultimate happiness higher than they had been. For caution's sake, during all the hours in which I rode silent between my escort of Assassins, I reminded myself of the many stories I had heard in Outremer, not of straightforward death from the Assassins' dagger, but of stranger, more secret killings by witchcraft or by poisoning. I called to mind Godfrey de Bouillon, the first King of Jerusalem, who had died of eating fruit sent to him by the Emir of Caesarea, though the Emir denied it ; and King Baldwin the First of Jerusalem also, who perished from witchcraft, the fish he himself had caught having poisoned him ; and William of Tyre, that honest Chronicler, whom poison slew also. I recalled the death of William Jordan, nephew of Count Raymond of Antioch, who died of an arrow shot mysteriously at night. Finally, with a sudden green shoot of thankfulness, I reminded myself of Raymond de Chatillon's fate, so much worse than mine, I recognised, and the many years of his captivity and what un-Christian hatred grew in him as the result of his sufferings.

All this in mind, I resolved to be watchful in everything until a party of Templars in place of my present escort of Assassins rode beside me.

The track I followed with my escort appeared both easier and shorter than the roundabout way down which my own fears had driven me in my earlier descent from the rock. It wound downhill by easy stages past boulders shining with tiny crystal particles, between juniper trees flattened by the wind, along half-dried water courses, to patches of hard thorny grass again. Here a profusion of flowers covered all the grey expanse of rock : lavender and mignonette, larkspur and anemone, willow herb and small fringed white daisies. I saw an eagle drinking at a spring ; I heard a shepherd in the valley piping to his flock, and suddenly, like a man coming into his garden after sickness, I was deeply glad to be alive. With joy fear visited me again. What, I asked, if the ransom money were not delivered ? What if no message were left on the flat rock called the Ransom Rock, which lay a day and a half's journey, or so I had been told, from the foot of the mountain ?

My escort and I waited within sight of the rock until noonday. Before the sun was at its height, before those flowers, which in my county we call shepherd's clocks, had closed up their dandelion-like heads, a messenger could be seen toiling up the slope. Undeterred by the sight of us, he came on, a white kerchief drooping from one hand. I fixed my eyes on the valley while he drew nearer. Streaked with water courses, it showed fertile and green. I thought I heard mules' bells and the shouts of drovers. I said nothing : I think I did no more than breathe.

The messenger, a Turcople archer in King Richard's livery, approached the rock. It was round like a wishing stone ; like a wishing stone also it was flat-topped and circled by a path. A skin bag containing the ransom money was set down upon the rock ; the contents of the bag were checked by my hook-nosed Assassin, and the King's messenger plunged once more down the path. Having pointed out the way which I must follow for the rest of my journey, my escort of Assassins took their leave.

That night I could not sleep. I heard the running of the streams in the valleys ; I saw the galaxy of stars in the high spaces of the sky and felt their cold and strangely piercing light ; I watched the sway of the trees, heard the night wind run like a fox over the shadowed earth. I thought the stars sang to me and the trees and the night-wind answered, and all their song was of never-ending life. Sleepless, I watched the dawn come in and sun and sky dwarf in their splendour all the quieter beauties of earth, and I was glad again, almost to shouting point, that I was alive yet, and whole, and that to-morrow, at the foot of the mountain, I might be free.

When day came I was hungry, and yet I did not dare to eat. I examined my bag of food for the journey and reminded myself once more of all the triumphant poisonings I had previously remembered. While the mists cleared I amused myself by throwing out a few crumbs to the birds, and afterwards forgot that I had done so. I fastened my girdle tighter and went on. Then I saw a little scuffle of feathers in a flurry of brown dust, and stooped, and picked up a small half-dead bird. I went on a pace or two and came upon another, wings outstretched and dead. I wondered what poison Sinan had used this time, and how much, if a crumb were enough to kill a bird, was needed to destroy a man ?

I reckoned that I had still a full day's journey before me. I resolved, therefore, not to think of food. But the torment of hunger consists in part of no more than this, that a man thinks constantly of food. I thought lovingly of rich steaks toasted on gridirons over the clear embers of a fire, of our home-cured hams broiled in cider or stewed in sweet wine, of mutton pasties and lamb's tail pies, and Christmas marzipan and simnel cakes, and cool draughts of mead tasting of honey and all the scents of the flowers. I thought of them until my mouth watered and my stomach turned. I sat down and drank water from a stream, and wished I could tickle trout with my bare hands. Straightway, so weak is the mind, I found myself in imagination in the Vale of Evesham again when Evesham apples, rosy as any speckled trout, were ripe.

On a different thought a fresh fear visited me. Could it be, I asked myself, that my escort had cast me woefully astray, that I could not follow this track upon which I was and within the limits of a starving man's strength arrive in time at the appointed place ? For a moment I touched panic ; afterwards I reasoned myself into sanity once more. There was no other track, my eyes told me, but this one that I had followed, that I followed still.

Even the suggestion that I might be late for my rescuers was enough. I started up in haste ; I set off running. Once more I could fancy that every rock hid an enemy, every tree cast too black a shadow. While my breath lasted, I ran on, fetching up at last at a most desolate spot where the track narrowed once more between giant boulders and rounded lumps of stone. To me, all my senses heightened by hunger and fear, there seemed a dead silence about the place, in which every sound echoed menacingly. A stone fell and went clattering, clattering down the track until it lodged at last against a larger stone. Even the flowers—and they were brilliant here—could not soften so much hard desolation of stone. Beyond was a greener, gentler slope. Thankful that it was day I made my way towards it. A light slither of stones followed me. I looked behind and saw a boulder detach itself, as it were awkwardly, from its bed on the hillside and advance in what appeared to be a leisurely way in my direction.

I watched and stood still : while I did so I thought of a hare, for the stone came loping along like a hare, hesitating and loping along again, as a hare does. Next I was reminded of a toad from the squat shape of the stone ; last, and almost too late, when the thing gathered pace and a kind of purpose, I remembered myself. I leapt to one side ; it rolled past me. Another followed from the same place, and another. I ran on ; and the deluge followed me. Before long Sinan's agent posted on the hillside, for I could not doubt this sudden avalanche was of Sinan's rather than of the Almighty's making, had set a large part of the hillside in motion.

I took shelter out of sight, I judged, of the hilltop within a circle of upright stones, and waited there. I was exhausted a little. While the light lasted, even though the mountain had grown silent again, I did not dare stir out. When the moon shone I decided I would make haste to go where boulders would not step out of their ancient places and fall upon me. I found on a greener slope a grove of thorn trees and lay down between them. In this quiet place, lamentably empty though my stomach was, I slept until the sun was up and piercing the interstices of the small leaves. For a moment, bound still in my world of sleep, I scarcely knew where I was, nor why I chanced to be so near the sky in this strange sloping far-away place. I woke and remembered that to-day I was bound for freedom or for nothing, and my soul, I hoped, for judgment or the stars. I looked out from my shelter of trees. I never saw, I thought, this side of England, so fair a morning, so lit with sun and dew, so full of small sounds of bees' wings and the flutter of birds, so full of stillness and the scents of flowers. It did not seem to me that, having passed so many dangers, I could chance to meet worse to-day among such a wealth of peace.

But every easy thought was vain yet, as I very well knew. I made myself as ready for Sinan's next attempt as I could. I tightened my girdle once more and my sandals ; I tried, and afterwards sharpened, my knife. And nothing happened. The day, as I had half-expected, grew broad and full ; my way stayed clear. I had been told to expect my escort of Templars at the foot of the mountain at noonday. I had been warned to look for a stream and a bridge of wood over the stream, and this side of the bridge a small grove of five oak trees. Having travelled so fast through the night I arrived within sight of the place before the appointed time. Not daring yet to show myself, I stayed where I was on a small thyme-covered shoulder of the hillside overlooking the valley and the stream. The water ran very pleasantly ; I was drowsy from so much starving and so much running and walking ; the sun was hot and I have always liked to sleep. I slept and dreamed. I dreamed I was in Oversley and my coverlet of otter skins had slipped from me and I was cold. I turned in my sleep. It was well for me that I did so, for I had a rude awakening.

The captain of my escort of Assassins, my Fedavi with the hooked nose, whom I had encountered twice before this, was here for a third and, I was certain, a final encounter with me. His dagger-thrust fell foul of its aim as I turned ; it missed my ribs, but caught instead the fleshy part of my left arm. He had his hands on my throat then, my ribs between his knees. He was stronger and taller than I was and at the moment better fed. I remember thinking so under the slow pressure of his hands upon my throat. I remembered also how my father while out hunting had once had a wolf at his throat and had killed the wolf. My right hand found my dagger : a good Assassin's dagger, I remembered. With all the strength I had I used it. My Assassin roared, or I believed he roared, when the knife thrust in. My senses half gone, I sickened again from the hot reeking death of this man. I had seen death in battle, but never so close and personal a death as this. My enemy's fingers relaxed about my throat, fell away as though reluctantly, one by one. I saw him by some last effort of nature or of will jerk his head once or twice, as if to escape the blade. Then, while I waited in horror and a kind of guilt, very quietly, and with a certain dignity also, he rolled off from me and, jerking no longer, lay still.

I bent over him. I took his dagger, which had fallen from his hand when his first stroke miscarried. It had, I noticed, and was for a second childishly glad of it, a jewel in the hilt. A dancing mist before my eyes, a warning buzz in my ears, I went on. It must be noon, I told myself, and at noon I must be free. I heard shouts ahead ; I saw figures on horse-back moving towards me up the track ; I recognised the white cloaks of the Knights Templars and the red cross on their shoulders, I heard the harsh cra-ak of a magpie on my left and the flow of the stream below. Who had spoken, I asked myself, of magpies and the stars ? I felt myself falling. At once the mist that had shrouded all my sense turned unmercifully to dark.

11

SEIGNEURS MALADES

I WOKE. Where I was I could not as yet be certain, since I had no recollection of what followed my meeting with my escort of Templars. The day appeared to be moving towards dusk, for the high white walls of the hall in which I found myself were smudged and darkening, and each bed cast its own pattern of shadow. Long windows of grey glass pierced the walls, round pillars of stone supported the arched and vaulted roof. All around me lay other men in other beds, small as mine was, cramped as mine was, and like mine spread with a black coverlet, and over it a white. There must, I think, have been a hundred or more beds in the length of the hall. Beside each was a bedside stand built into a niche in the wall ; over the head of each a wax tablet, upon which, I supposed, food and remedies were prescribed, hung suspended on a black cord. It was all as neat as the Courts of Heaven, and quieter also. I lay and counted the beards I could see : red beards, yellow beards, beards rusty-coloured, greenish-fair and brown. Since I lay so flat I could see scarcely any faces, only men's beards, and the long line of their bodies, and their splayed-out hands, and the twin ungainly promontories of their feet.

I heard the chapel bell ring for vespers and did not stir. " Seigneurs malades," I heard then, the voices of the choristers clean and fluting as those of some angels' choir, " seigneurs malades." I opened my eyes. The procession of choristers and of Knights Hospitallers stood twelve abreast in the body of the hall. The black cloak with the eight-pointed Cross in white upon it of the nearest Knight Hospitaller pressed against the foot of my bed. I was at Krak of the Knights, I realised now, the nearest Christian fortress to Massiat. Here, in the care of the Knights Hospitallers, I supposed I must stay until my wound was healed. I took note of the Master of the Infirmary at the head of the procession, and Garnier de Naplous, the Grand Master of the Hospitallers himself, beside him, and resolved to speak, if I might, to one or other of them.

" Seigneurs malades," I heard the choristers' voices again, " seigneurs malades, pray that God in Heaven may grant us His Peace on earth."

The sick men stirred in their beds as I stirred, and, hands uplifted, gave answer : " Lord God in Heaven, grant us Thy Peace on earth."

" Seigneurs malades," I heard, " seigneurs malades, pray for all pilgrims and Christians journeying by land or by sea, and for all those who have fallen into the hands of the Saracens."

Once more the answer came : " Lord, for all those who have fallen into the hands of the Saracens, and for all Christians travelling by land or by sea, we pray."

" Seigneurs malades," the boys' voices cried, so sharp now that I trembled, " pray for the kindly fruits of the earth, that they may be multiplied, and the people be strengthened and nourished by them."

" Lord God," we answered in chorus, " we pray."

So the Litany continued. We prayed for the Apostle of Rome and for all bishops and priests, and all Kings and captains and their fathers and mothers, that they might have peace ; and for Jerusalem.

While the Grand Master and all the rest with him were upon their knees, young boys, clad in white, brought tapers and lit, one by one, the candles in the high sconces. Presently, after the Lord's Prayer had been said and the Benediction pronounced, the procession moved away.

Later I heard the chapel bell toll softly for midnight. At this hour the Master of the Infirmary and the Grand Master were wont, I knew, to make their rounds of the sick-beds. It was now that I must speak to one of them. They came, bringing water for those who were fevered, medicines for the sick and cordials for those whose strength was failing them. Garnier de Naplous bent over me. I looked at him, but because of the suspicion that still clung to me I had no heart to speak. The Master of the Infirmary laid his hand upon my forehead. It was fleshy and cool : a priest's much more than a woman's hand. He held a branch of wormwood for protection against contagion on his other side.

" Sir," I said, " when may I continue on my way ? "

He regarded me intently before he spoke. " In two days," at last he said.

In two days I was indeed upon my way. From Tortosa, where my guard of Templars left me, I took ship to Acre, from thence I sailed to Joppa, and from there journeyed by land with all the speed I could to Beit Nuba and King Richard's camp. For all I knew I should be laid in chains, go in danger of my life at King Richard's hands and the hands of Master Moxon, a second time. I was the more astonished. As no one had witnessed my departure so no one, I believe, marked my return. The Marshal of the camp apportioned me a tent and a place without question. I sent word to old Sir Wisdom that I had returned and that I awaited his commands. I did indeed wait. I despatched a messenger also to seek out and bring to me if possible first Ambrose and Richard the Chronicler, so that I might know how matters stood with me, and after them, Giles and Brand. In truth, my fears apart, I longed to see them. Only men who have been captive and solitary among their enemies know what it means at long last to be in the company of a friend.

Ambrose and the Chronicler came. The Chronicler's grey eyes bulged with excitement, his ears glowed pink and familiar in the taper's light. Beside him Ambrose loomed shadowy and dark. But his voice when he spoke to me was as warming as the wine he poured. There was an eagerness about him also, an unusual fidget and restlessness about his long legs and hands.

Our greetings over, I looked at him. " You have news for me. Tell me now."

I heard what the two of them had to say and at first felt neither happiness nor relief. My innocence, it appeared, was as established as it could ever be. Bernard the King's spy had returned and had spoken in my favour.

How useless it was now, I thought perversely. How all but useless was any man's belief in me! I was aware of my friends' disappointment, almost of their incredulity as they watched my face. I declared, looking at the open palm of my hand: "Bernard the King's spy cannot vouch for me to the King. He cannot know."

The Chronicler grunted annoyance. He complained also—and this was the first time I had ever known him complain: "You are as thick-headed as any man can be."

Ambrose was gentler. "You have been in the company of the King's spy," he said, "and you have not known it."

"I thank you, but I do not care," I said.

Ambrose consoled me: "To-morrow you will feel differently."

"To-morrow," I said, "already to-morrow is too late."

In order to collect myself I asked hastily for news of Melisande.

I should see her shortly, they told me. There was talk of her marrying again.

I enquired next after Robert.

They answered me gravely. He had been ill and raving. He had raved of torment and burning. But Anselm, the King's chaplain, had spoken to him of Christ crucified and had quietened him.

My strength, husbanded until this moment, forsook me. I grieved, they said—even Ambrose reproached me—when I should have rejoiced.

I felt their bewilderment, and their vexation. "Forgive me," I said. "I forget my duty to my friends."

I looked at them and the calm I desired fled from me again. "But Robert of Kinwarton was my friend," I said. And then I knew why I grieved. I grieved for Robert and for him only. "I wish to God I had been blinded also," I said.

They became silent and busy. They filled me with wine and would not leave me. I was glad of their sympathy and yet I felt oppressed by it. Ambrose on one side of me like a long coffin lid, the Chronicler on the other like a soft bolster, I slept at last.

Brand and Giles came to my tent before the sun was up. Brand was accusing in manner and somewhat stiff. Giles was wooden and staring, determined, I could see, in all ways to resemble Brand.

Brand said stiffly: "Master, we came last night as you bade us and found you full of wine and asleep between the two scribes."

"Would you wish me to drown in sorrow?" I asked.

Brand's face cleared and shone. "Master, do you wish all that is past to be spoken of?"

I said, "I want only the next thing."

"Then," Brand said, and began to search in the inner pocket of his leather jerkin, " these should be better than wine, master." Breathing heavily, he thrust a packet of letters towards me.

" From the ship *London*," said Giles.

I cut the linen thread of the packet and scanned its contents while the two of them waited anxiously. The letter, written on both sides of the parchment in Father Andrew's close and clerkly script, told me a score of things, among them that my mother was well, my sister Eleanour recovered of the swine fever, that my mother had set up a sculptured monument in stone in the chancel of Alyncestre Church to my Uncle Raymond—here I paused to speculate for a moment as to how much of my revenues had gone to pay John Humble, the stonemason of Feckenham, for this piece of love and piety. No matter, I told myself then, provided I were not included (my mother being always frugal) in the same monument. I read on, only to find this piece of news sandwiched among many messages of love and greeting, namely, that Master Thomas Broadman, High Bailiff of Alyncestre, had drowned himself at floodtime for love of the skinner's wife, Marjory. I remembered this Marjory, a plump downy dame past her prime ; I remembered Master Thomas also, a ropemaker by trade, a large man who walked—he had need to do so, for he was most amorous— always very delicately. And now he had trodden water, I thought, not delicately enough, and was drowned. There was always a drowning or two in the town at floodtime, as if the river in flood knocked at the walls of the citizens' houses and said, " Come, come," and always one or more of them heard and answered.

I read on. The church tower, I read, was in need of repair again. When was it not ? I asked, and frowned, for this was no doubt a hint of what might be expected by way of alms from my mother and from myself. The starlings, Father Andrew added in smaller script, had ruined with their plenteous excrement the priest's new vestments left out to air upon the belfry chest. Well, now they had been limed as well as aired, I thought.

I continued with my reading, and this time was brought up short on a more serious matter. Brand's wife, Constance, Father Andrew wrote, had given birth to twins. Not by any means, he added unnecessarily, could they be charged to Brand. No, nor by any miracle, I thought, to Giles or me. Finally, at the tail of the letter came a message from Elfrida, in answer to earlier messages of mine, that set my blood tingling and put all recollection of monuments and falling towers, and drownings, yes, and twins and fallen wives also, out of my mind. Filled with a happiness of which I was partly ashamed, since it followed so closely on my misery of the night before, I laid the letter where it should lie, I thought, in lieu of anything better, next my heart.

" What news, master ? " Brand asked. His voice held a careful note.

I gave him all the news rapidly. "Your wife," I lied, "is well and greets you kindly."

Brand looked at me out of his little wise pig's eyes and said : "Not since she was twelve years old, master, has she been so long without a man."

Said Giles, jutting out his lower lip : "If my dame plays false with me I will have her ducked i' the pond. I have said so and I will."

"Will you make her clean that way?" Brand said. He sighed and was both cryptic and mild. "If you leave women you leave women," he declared. "They will do what they are minded to do ; they will do what they can, whether or no."

Ambrose stood beside me while the two of them took their leave. "Brand's wife has been adulterous," he said, "and you have not told him."

"I think he knows. I do not know if he cares," I returned.

I looked after Brand. It seemed to me there was indeed a droop about his shoulders, a heaviness unusual even with Brand about his feet. My mind misgave me for a moment, then straightway my thoughts returned to Elfrida again.

"I cannot help him," I said and could not keep the buoyancy from my voice.

The Chronicler pointed a sly finger at me. "This morning you are like a man who dreams of roses. To dream of roses is to dream of love."

"Last night I did not dream. Perhaps I dream now." I spoke gaily. "There is only this," I said. "She greets me. She is glad that I am whole. Therefore, Chronicler, I am twice as whole as I was."

Ambrose was looking at me smilingly.

I believed I read his thought. I answered it. "I am not changeable nor fickle. I am in love with her and with the image of her I have in my mind."

"And the reality?" Ambrose asked, still smiling but as though he would warn me if he could.

"When a man loves, what is reality? I do not know," I said.

"Nor I either," Ambrose returned.

They faced me. It was Ambrose who spoke. "Without kith or kin, saddle or bridle, we travel the world."

"But love is a country we do not travel in," the Chronicler sagely said.

I felt a kind of pity for them as I watched them go, and for all other bachelors who make a tidy emptiness of their lives and call it peace. I sobered then. If I were to live in my house I had still to build it ; I had still to come to terms with Robert and with all my world.

PART SIX

AND STILL THE SHADOW

1

BEIT NUBA

ON my first day of freedom I walked through the camp at Beit Nuba in search of Robert. If I could not be reconciled with him my freedom, I knew, would be incomplete. It was not that I felt any longer the same love I had had for him at first, for bitterness is a shrewd transformer of love. It was that he was a great part of my life and of all that I had thought and known, that without his friendship I myself could scarcely be whole or complete.

My heaviness of spirit increased rather than diminished as I went on. Only after the greatest effort on my part should we be reconciled. Robert —for there was both an inquisitor and a judge in him—would not, I was aware, advance one step in understanding towards me.

The morning was early ; the sun seemed never to have left the sky— I walked as though in an oven's slow heat over the burned-up earth, between the tents, through the drifting smoke of the camp fires of mule and camel dung, through the stench of burning refuse heaps. At this hour the camp was astir with sick and injured men. They came out in search of food, or water, or ease, creeping on their bellies, going on all fours, some of them jerking themselves along like sea crabs in a curious sideways motion I did not care to see. I could observe no other movement : men who appeared whole and well lay about, the morning's tasks undone, in a lethargy which appeared to go with sick bodies and sick minds. There was little sound. No one greeted me, no one whistled or sang or played any kind of tune. I wondered what deadness of spirit or what ferment of mind lay beneath so unnatural a quiet. I wondered but stayed indifferent ; for the torpor that appeared to be over all the camp was heavy upon me also.

When I had grown weary of looking for Robert at last I found him, leaning against a broken wall some short distance from the furthest limits of the camp. He had his lute within reach, a caged lark silent between his knees ; his face was upturned as if he were listening. I looked at him with anxiety first, and then with relief. His face was hollow and lined and burned to the colour of old leather from the sun. But there was a neatness about him, like a brave gesture to infirmity, that I was glad to see. He was shaven ; his hair, half its bright yellow bleached away, was combed and smooth. There was a burnt and ravaged peace about his face.

I came nearer. The Turcople guard who sat sideways to us, cross-legged upon a stone, cracking sunflower seeds between his teeth and spitting the husks tirelessly out again, stared, then spat once more.

Robert turned his head. He recognised my step and greeted me : " So you have come."

I dropped down beside him, for I was weary and the sun burned through the velvet cap upon my head. " I could not come before," I answered.

" And you are free ? "

I thought I caught an irony in Robert's voice.

" If you can call it freedom," I replied.

Robert did not answer. The lark fluttered blindly in its cage ; the Turcople guard folded his arms and seemed to doze. Because I could not bear to be silent I spoke again. " Robert, who tends you ? "

Robert smiled. " Brand." Even his smile seemed strange. Until that moment I had not known how much of a man's smile lies in his eyes. I shut my own.

" Am I not bright and trim ? " I heard Robert ask.

I was a fool, I told myself, to believe that he could be anything but ironical and indifferent, or withdrawn from me.

Nevertheless I tried to speak of the ambush and of all that had followed from it.

He cut me short. " What is all this to me now ? "

Since he appeared to accuse me in manner if not in speech, I defended myself. " I am as much a victim of circumstances as you."

He checked me a second time. " I do not blame you. Believe that."

For my life I could say no more. He rejected me, I felt.

He went on to speak not of me, nor even of himself, but of the army, and of Jerusalem, and the Cause, and of Count Henry of Champagne who had gone off to Acre in order to bring back the stragglers from the army. The Count had not yet returned, and the King and all his captains waited for him yet. " And Jerusalem is only two days' march away," Robert said. " Two days ! Why must we wait ? " He turned to me. " Have you heard Bertrand de Born's new jest ? It is that King Richard, like King Canute to the waves, has told time to stand still."

I replied sharply that I had heard too much of what was said of me in malice about the camp to believe anything his enemies might say of King Richard.

" There are times," Robert declared, " when I could blame not only the King but God Himself that our Cause should fail."

I waited, then asked Robert : " What will you do now ? " For I remembered our setting out and how I had told myself then that Robert belonged more to the cloister than to the world.

"I would turn monk if I might," Robert said. "But God, I know, must be served with eyes, if not with hands." He fumbled for the catch of the lark's cage, and, having found it, took the bird between the fingers of his one hand and fondled it against his breast. The creature half freed itself, then, neck outstretched, burst into song. I have often heard a grounded lark sing unseen and marvelled at the passion and the volume of its singing ; I have never heard a lark sing as this lark sang, all its life in its throat.

"They say a lark sings better when it is blind," Robert said, and he put the bird back once more into its cage.

I spoke of Father Andrew and of Alyncestre, and afterwards of Elfrida.

Robert said, so quietly I could not tell what he felt : "She is not one of those women a man can bind closely to him. She has her own life within that she must live."

"She shall go," I said, "into what kingdom of the mind she pleases if she will not go altogether out of my sight."

Only to speak of Elfrida was to make the estrangement between Robert and myself harder to bear. I pleaded with him then that he should not blame me for my friendship with de Passy, which I knew quite well had helped so much to change and spoil his life. "Think," I begged him, "how I also was deceived."

His one hand over his face, Robert said : "That is an old tale by this time."

I cried out to him : "At least do not blame me that you are blind."

He spoke with a dreadful slowness. "You sleep in the King's tent. You mount special guard over him. All men have orders to believe you. Will you never be content ? "

"The shadow of what I did will be over me for ever," I said.

"I have grown used to shadows." Robert turned from me.

I should have been silent, but like a woman I continued, like a woman once more I pressed Robert too closely with my love. "One day you will believe me," I declared.

He turned impatient. By stages he grew merciless also. "With me it is not a question of belief. It is that I see you now. I think you are one of those unfortunates who betray their friends without meaning to do so, and afterwards torment them with your sorrow and your love."

"There is no kindness left in you," I said.

"What is kindness to me ? " Angrily, with his one hand Robert shook the cage. "I am no more fit for life than this bird."

I was silent again. I would have left him, but, as if some faint compunction stirred in him, he went on : "I could have borne anything rather than to be blind. Only to feel now for ever, never again to see, to be left nothing but remembering." He faced me. "Father Anselm exhorts me : 'Forgive. Put sorrow behind you. Go straight forward !' I tell him : 'Wait. Pray for me. A man must get used to the dark.' "

It was then that Ambrose and the Chronicler came, followed closely by Brand and Giles. I greeted them stiffly, then, sick and heavy of heart, drew off from them while Ambrose and Robert played and sang in turns, now upon the lute, now upon the viol.

In the intervals between their singing the three of them passed wine to each other and afterwards to me. I drank, and grew thicker of head and more savagely morose.

Ambrose sang yet another song. I had heard it once before ; I was to hear it several times again. The verses, I was certain, were of Ambrose's own making. I remember I was pleased to curl my lip at the time and to feel satirical at so much melancholy making of songs and poesy.

Robert had sung :

> " *Men are most like shadows*
> *That move with the great sun,*
> *Show fair, and then do falter,*
> *Come and are gone.*"

Ambrose sang :

> " *O, the scars that life leaves,*
> *The tender heart grieves*
> *For crooked weaves*
> *Of the years' spinning.*

> " *O, the scars that life leaves,*
> *That only love receives,*
> *That love in turn bequeaths*
> *For pain of giving.*

> " *O, the scars that life leaves*
> *The gentle heart bereaves*
> *Of gust of living.*"

I lay apart from them all this while. Suddenly I was diverted. In a grieved voice close to my ear, Brand said : " Master, it would not be courteous even in a mule."

I had no need to look or to ask. The Turcople was urinating against the wall.

Robert raised his voice in vexation : " Tell him to go away."

The Turcople, still urinating, went.

The Chronicler looked after him and spoke mildly. " Poor animal !
He is bored with so much singing."

" And so am I," I declared, forgetting all courtesy. I left them and
went off on Brand's mule, Brand and Giles following sheepishly.

When we were on the outskirts of the camp Brand reproached me :
" Master, it is not natural nor Christian-grateful to be so out o' love
with creation."

I turned my head. " For me it is most natural."

Brand was inclined to argue with me. " Master, I would live heartily,
without moan, and die so."

" You are too hearty," I rejoined.

I might have been the better in a short while for his admonishment had
not a long figure stretched out before one of the tents upon a low Turkish
couch greeted me by name. He wore Saracen robes, a white turban
swathed his head, a jug of wine and an open missal lay beside him.

I returned his greeting. Out of ill-humour I halted beside him, and
drank his wine and listened to his bright tinkle of talk, while Brand and
Giles, under pretence of walking the mule, drew further and further away.

He had not, my stranger declared, in all the six weeks he had spent in
Beit Nuba, met one soul worth the talking to.

" Surely, sir," I answered, looking after Brand and Giles with more
than half a mind to follow them, " surely you may talk with whom you
please since you need no answers."

My companion blinked light lashes at me, but prattled on. He was all
perversity and all conceit. His hair was cut in elfin locks under his turban's folds, his nails were squared, his speech clipped and strange. I
grew more annoyed as I listened and more seethingly silent.

He was of Provence, he informed me ; he rejoiced that he was not so
brutish as to be of Normandy. What a country was Persia, he declared,
and laid a hand on his missal. Not one poet but a thousand dwelled there !
From Persia and wine and roses he progressed, grasshopper-fashion, to the
Sultan Saladin. Here he shot a question at me. What truth was there,
did I think, in the tales current in the camp that the King was about to
receive an envoy of peace from the Sultan's brother Saphadin?

I stared at him. How should I know ?

" For my part," he declared, running on, " the Sultan may have all his
fly-blown cities back again if I may return shortly to Provence."

" If King Richard should hear you, he would beat you about the
buttocks with his sword," I promised him warmly.

My grasshopper leapt to his feet. I was rustic ; I was impertinent.
I had been too careful, also, with my answers. Honest men, he protested,
were not so. " I do not believe in your innocence, messire John of Overs-

ley," he said. "I do not believe you, sir, even though the order has gone forth that you are to be believed."

I heard myself speak. I said thickly : "If I were not so full of your wine you should eat your Persian missal, page by page, so that you might become ever more Persian-poetical." I added that I was relieved to see him so angry since I had feared there was nothing left in him but malice. "Just as there is nothing left," I said, "to a rotting stinkhorn fungus of the autumn woods but a little jelly and a noisome smell." I made off from him after that, stumbling as I went in a kind of mist.

So this, I told myself, after all my hope of being believed, was where I stood. I was trusted only because the King had ordered it. And any parti-coloured strumpet of a thing could abuse me. Waist-deep and all but drowning in my own thoughts, I stumbled on.

A sergeant of mounted archers stepped out from the side and accosted me very civilly : "Sir, you are of the King's Company. Tell us, if you will, do we go on to Jerusalem ? "

Another time I would have answered him as civilly. This time, though I halted and listened, I passed on without answering and left him cursing. He desired to be home for the next harvest, he had said. Why, by God's robe, I thought, so do I.

Other men spoke to me to the same purpose even more anxiously. Their preoccupation fretted me ; I answered none of them. The camp was in ferment, both earth and air so dry they seemed about to burn. I heard the water carriers jesting grimly together, their pitchers no more than half-filled with water thick as mud. "My masters, when you come by this, you will find both meat and drink." I had no heart to jest. Every new sight seemed only to darken my mood. Jokes had a ghoulish ring ; faces appeared brutishly empty or filled with sourness and discontent. I heard a jingle of bells. The burial carts, emptied of their burden, passed me at a smart trot. I took note of the drivers' faces and believed I read both fear and excitement in their eyes. A man beside the track, unobserved by me until that moment, spoke quietly, nodding as he spoke : "You see, sir Esquire, you see, it is all death with us now, all death. A man, sir Esquire, bleeds at the nose, if it please you, bleeds at the mouth, it may be—all's one after that. The bloody flux has him and shortly, you see, he is dead. Tell the King."

Once more I went on. In order to shorten my journey I turned off the track by the tents of the washerwomen. Having no water for their trade they lay apart from each other, like fat sows in a dry orchard. I shunned them and hurried on.

From the quarters of the washerwomen I had no choice but to skirt the encampment of the pilgrims. They were busy, as always, over their prayers and their quarrellings and their cooking pots. They were louse-like but sober, I told myself. And then I saw one who sat by the way, pouring dust and ashes like a Moslem over his head and wailing Eastern-fashion as he did so : " God the Father is against us, the Holy Spirit is against us, the Lord Christ has departed from us."

I prayed earnestly for no more sights and travelled on, my cloak over my face. In my present mood it seemed to me that an evil fate did indeed follow the King and the Cause which he had made his own. Unseen Titans fought against us : sickness and the elements themselves, and all these in our own minds. We had suffered as much as any army yet had suffered. Our men had died in their thousands of camp fevers and rheums and scurvies and wastings, of dropsies and drownings, of wild beasts and scor-pions, of madness and the sun and the cold. We had perished of un-numbered ills and of the enemy. And now, out of his infinite store of evil death, God had sent us a fresh quick ending in the bloody flux. Those whom the flux did not destroy were so weakened as almost to be destroyed. The new death, like a plague of old Egypt, sprang from the water, the priests and the physicians declared. Though the water was foul our men still drank of it under the hot sun.

We had squandered Time, the greatest Titan of them all. Time mocked us now. Racked by illness, our men fretted and longed for home. The knights and captains were in no better state. Many of them had great possessions in Syria and wished to enjoy them ; others, even among the Knights Templars and the Knights Hospitallers, felt that the army had accomplished enough. All of us alike who lived by faith had grown tired. Among so many difficulties we had forgotten almost where we were, and why, and to what place we were bound. We had grown hollow from too much effort, from too long a waiting. The worms of the camp had in truth eaten our substance and our strength away. Of all our sacrifices, little but the memory of them, it seemed to me, remained. And in a year, in two years, even memory would fade. All was flux ; all was impermanence. We were shadows pursuing shadows. Nothing remained.

I reached the King's tent. Fever distorting my vision and my sense, I lay down upon my bed. The tent, half-closed for coolness, was dusky on two sides with shadow ; on the other the sun's fierce light burned. I remembered Robert's upturned face and the lark's singing. On the sunlit patch of tent before me characters assembled and took shape before my eyes. I could not decipher them at first and then I saw them plain :

> Men are most like shadows
> That move with the great sun,
> Show fair and then do falter,
> Come and are gone.

2

FATIMA

THAT night and all the day following the King held counsel with his knights and captains in the long tent hung with banners, set with trestles and benches of cedar wood, which served at Beit Nuba for a Council chamber. The clerks came and went, passionless as sea crabs and no less silent, their tablets in hand, their rolls of parchment under their arms. The knights sweated in shirts and breeches only, their armour and weapons hung up on poles outside the tent. Now and then men came out for air and went in again ; at intervals the waggons, laden with carved cold meats, with cut lengths of bread and flagons of wine, went round. The knights' servants were posted, two by two, beside their knights' armour. Behind them, beyond the silken barrier of cord set around the tent, the army and the pilgrims waited, and with every hour that passed the tension and the rumours grew. Fearful of a surprise attack, we who were outside the tent scanned the plain beyond the confines of the camp and the hills, beyond which Jerusalem and Saladin's army lay. No horseman showed ; no cloud of dust moved.

I have never, for all my long apprenticeship, been good at waiting. When my watch was over, since I judged the Council would go on until sundown I sought out Melisande. I did so all the more gladly since to-day the sight and even the odour of so much male flesh wearied me.

The old palace, where those ladies who remained with the army had their quarters, lay a stone's throw beyond the outskirts of the camp. Its half-broken walls of yellow stone still sheltered a garden of ruined terraces and ragged cypress trees. I found Melisande seated in the courtyard beside a wall hung with dried-up trails of clematis and vine. A tall orange-red lily bloomed in a blue Persian pot beside her ; the rest was desolation itself. She sat quietly, her needlework, a panel of tapestry, half-falling from her lap, her needle threaded with indigo idle in one hand. A casket of inlaid Persian work spilled its skeins of coloured silks upon the uneven paving of the floor and two raddled doves, coloured a dirty white, pecked at a few grains of corn around her feet. Her gaze as far away as her thought, she sat very still.

I stirred, and suddenly she looked at me.

" The knight upon your panel of tapestry," I said, and laughed at her, " is nearly complete."

" I have the hands to do yet," she said. She looked down at them. " I think I have forgotten how it is with a man's hands."

I spoke again as a man does sometimes to no purpose, my mind full of my thoughts of her. "Whose face is it you have outlined there in the figure of your knight?"

"I think the face of all the men I have ever known," she answered. "Except perhaps one." Here she looked at me, and I remembered all the talk I had heard of her marrying again. She was for ever marrying, or not marrying, I thought.

"The Marshal will leave you a widow a second time," I warned her.

"No, messire John," she returned coolly. "The Marshal will live, I am certain of it." She took up her work and began very swiftly to stitch at the girdle on the knight's gown. "The old live for ever," she declared, and held up her work, and looked at it, then turned to her stitching once more.

I would have spoken of Everard but she interrupted me. "I cannot believe any longer, I cannot hope any longer that Everard will return." She hurried on. "We were different, but we could have made our lives together and not grown tired. From that alone I know that he is dead." The colour bright in her cheeks, she stitched rapidly.

I reminded her: "He may yet return."

She looked at me. "To be a woman, messire John, is to be unsafe always, to walk under a burden and wait on a dark night for the stars. I am hungry from so much waiting."

"No state is poetical," I replied, "though it is fashionable to be poetical. Last night I told myself—and do not call me," I said, "pompous or solemn either—that a woman should have her heart full and her hands full and her mind full, and, if possible, her arms full also. Only then, it seemed to me, would she ever be content."

"I have had something of the same solemn thoughts," she said, "and at night also. By day they appear different again."

It was later that I told her of de Passy. She answered me simply: "He is better dead."

When she spoke of Robert her colour changed. "He has never forgiven me. I think he will never forgive me. I saw him and pitied him. I offered him my arm. Would I lead him on a chain, he asked me, as I had led Aziz once, as devils lead apes in hell?" She looked at me. Once more she spoke simply. "When I pitied him in truth I loved him also."

"Must you marry the Marshal?" I asked. "Why must you?"

She burst out at me. "So that I may be finished with marrying. So that I may be finished with desiring also."

She began moving her casket of embroidery threads, folding up her embroidery panel, unfolding it again, seeming to do both things at once, and at the same time rustling her skirts about her feet.

When I made as though to go she sprang up. " Do not be angry. You know that I am always tempestuous and unreasonable."

I took both her outstretched hands for answer, and kissed her fingers one by one.

I heard my name called but did not turn my head, so engrossed was I. Someone spoke my name a second time, a note of patience in his voice. Melisande took away her hands.

A blunt-faced fellow in a leather jerkin stood just outside the confines of the courtyard. He had a spade in one hand. From that I took him to be some sick soldier turned gardener who tended the walks and the terraces. His speech as blunt as his face, he said : " Sir, there is a tall Saracen stranger without who says that he must speak with you. I set the hounds on him ; they did but lick his fingers. He says that he has come far, that he must speak to you without delay. I was to ask you, sir, in proof that he is honest, if you remember the knife Fatima ? "

I remembered the knife Fatima. Truly, it seemed to me, life might be stranger and more packed with chance than any tale told in a ballad. My pulse beating too fast for comfort, I went in search of the stranger.

As I came up he turned toward me. I knew him at once, though from amazement I could scarcely speak his name.

He appeared embarrassed. He said : " I am not dead, though I think I should have been a score of times."

" Everard ! " I exclaimed at last. I both laughed and embraced him.

He drew off from me, moved as I was, but embarrassed still. " Careful, man," he said. " You embrace a host of camel fleas."

" And the knife Fatima, where is it ? " I asked finally.

He produced the knife. " My houri, do you remember ? " He chuckled and stowed the knife safely away once more. " What a tale, man ! " he declared. " What a tale to spin by my own fireside when I return ! "

" What tale ? " I looked at him in affection and astonishment still. I threw at him a dozen more questions. I asked on a sudden thought : " Will you not be suspect as I was ? " I told him something of the suspicion in which I had been held since my return.

" Why should I be suspect ? " He laughed at me. " I have not turned infidel. Do not think it. Nor married the Sultan's daughter. And I was never de Passy's friend."

I said : " Because of de Passy I have had you on my conscience grievously." I finished : " Not a soul who knew you but has sorrowed for you."

Straightway he related to me a tale of captivity and escape as strange as any I had heard. " I had the devil's own good fortune," he said. He had been rendered unconscious by his fall into the ravine. Having come to himself he had shammed dead. When finally he had got to his feet and gone in search of the camp he had been taken captive by a fresh band of Saracens. " I had no weapons," he said, " no wits left, no legs for running and scarcely a tongue with which to speak." He broke off. " Tell me, how did Robert fare ? "

I told him.

" And he is alive ? "

" Alive ? Yes," I answered.

" And de Passy ? "

" Beyond us for ever," I said. " Stone dead among cold stones."

" Pity," Everard said, and again, " pity."

He went on with his story. If he had not enjoyed his adventures at the time, he enjoyed them now. Taken prisoner by the Turks, he had been imprisoned at Khartfert. He had played chess with his warders and had avoided death by prolonging the game. Because of his height, he had been chosen to wait upon the emir at his table. He had set fire to the house during a Moslem feast and had made his escape in the confusion that followed, taking with him all the jewels that he could find. After twenty-four hours wandering in the dark he had found his way barred by a river, which, since he had been so badly bitten by tarrentes as to be unable to walk, he could not attempt to swim. Peasants whom he had partly bribed and partly cajoled had ferried him across on a raft of bladders. On the other side, hungry and unable to walk even yet, he had hidden near the bank among bushes and reeds. The same peasants had obligingly offered to bring help. He had not believed them, but presently, to his surprise they returned on the same raft, bringing with them figs and raisins and another peasant still. The newcomer was ready to help, he declared, but first he must kill his pig. He had a wife, the fellow continued, and one child, and an ass.

" You be my wife," he said. " You ride my ass."

Everard, while marvelling what this might mean, had agreed. He had eaten his figs and raisins and waited once more. Before long the peasant had returned, bearing with him a bundle of women's clothing and a child of some two months old. Dressed in women's robes, veiled and cloaked and holding the child, Everard had ridden off with the peasant towards Tell-basher and comparative safety. Within earshot of a band of Turks, the child had grown hungry and wailed loudly. " I gave him my finger to suck," Everard said and laughed. " And all I have remaining of the emir's treasure," he said, " is this." He fumbled again, and produced from a square of yellow silk a topaz set in a round filigree of gold. Having shown it to me, he wrapped it carefully in its piece of silk once more, and asked, after a moment's silence, " Is my Lady wed again ? "

I was ready for him. " Not yet," I answered.

" Who is it now ? " He sat down suddenly, cross-legged like a Turk, upon the sand.

" The Marshal," I said.

He rocked with laughter at that. " Old, but mighty," he declared. " Oh, Melisande."

" Whom did you think ? " I asked.

He was on his feet in the next second. " I feared you."

" I will take you to her," I said.

" I am not fit yet." He looked down at himself, longing and hesitation in his face.

We found Melisande in the courtyard still, the embroidery casket empty beside her, its skeins of silks, as though she had wished to tidy them, tumbled in her lap. I thrust Everard forward, then stood back a little way.

He took a few steps towards her, then halted and spoke her name questioningly : " Melisande."

She turned her head and for a moment did not speak. But the skeins of yellow silk she was holding fell from her fingers, the pink feet of the doves slid in sudden alarm over the tiles of the floor. I thought there was a look of horror and of something more, though what I could not tell, upon her face.

Everard came forward another step or two, then halted again. " I am returned and whole," he said, a stiffness and a trembling also in his voice.

She was on her feet, her body swaying and shaken as I have seen a sudden wind in March shake the daffodils.

He came forward another step. " Shall I go back," he asked, " and die again ? "

She ran forward. " Oh, Bogis, Bogis," I heard her say, her hands trembling and as though blind, touching his eyes, his lips, his face.

I left them then. They had found, I thought, what Robert had lost for ever, what de Passy had despised, what I had still to seek : a way perhaps that belonged to them only, that was wide enough for the two of them to take.

I made my way back alone to the camp and as I went pondered heavily, too heavily I am certain, upon what men term fortune or fate. Though I have never been a philosopher, I have always tried to follow where reason led. And yet, when I considered the varying strokes of fortune that had been dealt out to Robert and Everard, to de Passy and myself, I could see no reason but only a great irony in the world. For it seemed a cruel part of irony to me that Robert, who had seen everything in so sharp a light, who had lived, as it were, shrouded in a bright mist, should now see only with the piercing concentration of the blind ; it appeared cruel to me, though just, that de Passy, who had looked down always, as it were, from a mountain top upon a world in which everything except the mountain and the man upon it were to be despised, should have embraced a mountain for his private world and died despised. A harmony was here, and yet it seemed to me disquieting and strange, as if a man took ship and sailed beyond the vaporous unknown borders of the world to discover only chaos and mystery again.

I had not progressed far beyond the outskirts of the camp when all thought of Melisande and Everard, and all argument also, left me. The camp, as I rode in, was once more a camp of mourning. In my absence the King's Council had ended its sittings ; I had no need to listen to the distant voice of Philip, the King's crier, once more crying sorrow and woe throughout the camp ; the faces of all those whom I met, the scraps of talk I overheard, told me that what had at first been rumour was now truth. For another year we must give up all hope of reaching Jerusalem. After all that we had endured, another year seemed longer than the stars away. When we came for the second time to Beit Nuba, Jerusalem had been only two days' march from us ; once again it seemed for ever out of reach.

It was not difficult to find reasons for the decision of the King and the Council. I had heard the case for the army's retreat argued a score of times. Once more I went over it in my own mind. In imagination I heard the Earl of Leicester say in his thin voice : " The Sultan's new army is more numerous than ours and fresher. Where shall we on our side find so many new and unwearied fighting men ? " I heard another voice, a Templar's or a Hospitaller's voice, raised impatiently : " We have conquered all the ports upon the sea coast. Surely we have accomplished enough." I heard other, more general voices : " We will meet and fight the Turk. But the winter weather while we lay siege to Jerusalem is an enemy we dare not meet." Last of all, the Marshal's voice came to me, lisping and husky and oddly out of keeping with his vast frame : " The Sultan has poisoned the water courses and the wells. We die already of the bloody flux. Must we die also of thirst ? "

I heard no answer to all these questions in my own mind. There was only silence. I came nearer. It was then that I heard the notes of the heralds' trumpets, and the voice of Philip, the King's crier, crying the retreat.

3

THE WHEEL

NEITHER sorrow nor rejoicing continues on the same note for long. By the evening of the next day excitement and expectation had taken the place of mourning in the camp. There were to be other fluctuations of mood in the host before finally the retreat to Acre was begun, but never a reversal so sudden or apparently so complete as this. I marvelled at the change and yet was thankful for it. I was young; I was no Job nor yet a Jonah; I wished to be done as soon as was decently possible with lamentations and grief. There is something futile, after all, in over-much public mourning, since inevitably what men in the East call the wheel of life turns on, always, to the next thing.

So it was with me. All day a name that had gone tiresomely in and as tiresomely out of my ears since I came to Outremer was once more on my own and on every man's lips. Bernard the King's spy, I heard in every place. Bernard the King's spy, I heard again from Robin de Herdecourt in the King's tent. This Bernard, it seemed, had brought news to King Richard that the Sultan Saladin's great annual caravan of treasure would halt the next night at the Round Cistern, not more than an evening's hard ride from Beit Nuba where we still were. The news, and the hope of plunder that came with the news, for the time being thrust all mourning for Jerusalem from our minds and gave new zest to us all. What could be more heartening to us in our downcast state than the plunder of the Sultan's treasure and the enrichment of the King's coffers and our own? Smiles and radiant looks reappeared as suddenly as desert flowers; the armourers sang as they burnished up weapons for the encounter; the smiths shouted above the noise of their own hammers; the monks and priests were busy everywhere throughout the camp with intercessions and prayers; even the Burgundians and the French, ready the day before to slit all our throats, overflowed with amity.

There was no shortage of volunteers for the enterprise, only a sad shortage of horses. Ambrose had procured two fairly fresh mules for the Chronicler and himself, and, since we must ride out at night, the Chronicler and he spent a large part of the previous day in practising upon their mounts.

We were so beside ourselves with expectation when we set out that not even the need for silence could keep us from joking and laughing together. I remember that the Chronicler, in great fear of being thrown, rolled like a sack of grain upon his mule, and that Ambrose's mount was too mettlesome for him. I know that Everard sang softly all the way,

never more than the same line of the same song. " O Love, O Constancy,"
Everard sang suitably enough, and I had not the heart, for love of him, to
close his mouth or my own ears. The night was shining and still when we
rode out ; even the moon showed large as if it were made of gold. And
two strangers in Saracen robes mounted on Arab horses as milky-coloured
as the light of the moon rode out surprisingly to join us from the camp.

We saw the caravan, an array of peaceful shapes of men and beasts,
encamped at the Round Cistern around the covered tops of the great wells.
Men and beasts were so still they might have been asleep. We heard no
sound, saw no movement, saw only the glitter of the moon's light on the
lance heads of the Sultan's cavalry and on the Beduin guards' long spears.

All Christendom knows how we fought them, how the Sultan's horsemen, taken by surprise, fled at last before the charge of the King and the
knights ; how our men hoisted the treasure on the backs of the caravan's
own beasts and led both victoriously away. I remember that the camels
and the mules and the horses set up a loyal and protesting din and that
our men had hard comical work in mastering them.

I rode back that night with the rest in the small dew-laden hours, no
thought in my mind unless it were joy at our exploit, and relief that it was
over, and a pleasant anticipation of rewards to come. Suddenly a heavy
hand smote me resoundingly upon the back. Jerked into wakefulness
once more, I heard a fat rollicking voice I knew call me by name. I turned
my head. A burly fellow in Saracen robes accosted me. " Come share my
coverlet, boy," I heard. I looked at him. The stranger laughed, holding
his fat sides. I recognised him then, and though I had good reason to be
grateful to him I greeted him coldly. Even yet I did not care for his
voice or his manner of speaking. Nor was I pleased that he should choose
so public an occasion to renew our acquaintance. I feared, I suppose,
what de Herdecourt and the rest of the King's men might think or say.

I said : "You are my muleteer."

He clapped me on the shoulder once more and corrected me. " Messire
John, I was your muleteer."

I had been slow before ; I was quicker then. Here was my muleteer ;
here also, without a doubt, was Bernard the King's spy.

I stammered foolishly : " I believed you were an invention."

" I am, like other men, my own invention." Laughing at his own
joke, he rode beside me.

"You are the stout madman also," I said, " whom the two Assassins
encountered by the Tower of Flies."

Presently we rode side by side, a little apart from the rest, while the
King's spy spoke to me, as I had half feared and yet hoped he would, of
Guy de Passy.

" I had had warning of the Frenchman," Bernard said, " therefore I watched him while I could. To escape me he fled to Tyre ; from Tyre he fled again to Massiat. In both places he was in his own country."

I said : " I cannot believe de Passy was completely false."

" Tell me of someone who is all false, messire John," Bernard said. I felt his eyes on me. " This man was false by purpose and by inclination. For lack of greatness he bore a grudge against other men and the world. Both Sinan and Conrad used him as you are aware ; neither trusted him. Such men as de Passy," Bernard said, " leave themselves too small a world in which to live."

I did not speak. I remembered de Passy as I had seen him first. He had been arrogant, but surely he had not been treacherous then.

As if in justification of himself Bernard continued : " The Frenchman was a spy as I am. And a member of the Brotherhood of the Assassins also, which I am not, which I could never be. Know, messire John, I do not serve myself or any earthly power. I serve King Richard only and the Cause."

" If only that I might think better of myself I would not altogether condemn de Passy," I said.

The King's spy spoke quietly again. " Messire John, you must condemn him or condemn yourself. Such men bring death to thousands and ruin to great kingdoms."

" Surely," I said again, " surely he was too small a kind of traitor to merit so much blame."

" In himself he was nothing," Bernard answered, " but, like Sinan, he desired to be everything. He was the bastard son of a Saracen lady by a Frankish knight. As a boy he fled from the House of Cluny which had sheltered him and was joined by a member of the Brotherhood of Assassins, himself a renegade monk called Benedict."

" Who was bent of back," I cried, " who had served in the Turkish galleys and was sometimes mad."

" The same." Bernard continued : " This Benedict took de Passy to Massiat. There the Frenchman was trained in the Assassin creed. You have heard them and their deceiving quiverfuls of words." Bernard yawned, open-mouthed, then shot a quick glance at me. " I have known worse men than the Frenchman."

Seeing me still so silent, he mocked me : " You are too full of feeling, messire John." Full of coarseness and perceptiveness himself, he rode off.

In the blackness that falls on a man's spirit at the hour of dawn I thought how de Passy had left his mark upon all our lives and gone. It seemed to me then that the wheel of chance that had stayed stationary for so long was turning again, was coming almost to full circle. Soon Robert and

Everard, Melisande and John of Oversley, brought together so strangely by circumstance, might be scattered as strangely. For a moment mystery touched me with her cool finger. I shivered ; I confused one thing with another ; my mind seemed divorced from me and cold. The rim of yellow light in the east deepened in colour before my eyes, then ran like fire until all the eastern sky was ringed with light. While I watched, the sun came up, effortless like a round flower. And suddenly I wished that the wheel might turn faster and time change, that I might be quit of my vow to King Richard and be gone. I wished more impatiently in that moment than I had ever wished anything yet, that I might find my own place and my own peace. The wish was as foolish as any dream, I knew. My thoughts all of Elfrida, I rode on and did not pause once to reflect how strange a passion this was of mine that grew by thinking only and a message of two lines.

4

MONTJOIE

I NEVER see our great barn at Kinwarton, in which all my folk can sit down together at Harvest Home, without thinking of our night's work at the Round Cistern, without remembering, since memory like a bird in the air follows the same flight paths, that day we saw Jerusalem. I built the barn with my share of the Sultan's treasure, an esquire's share, which King Richard gave to me as my right and for which, one more reason among many, I loved him. I planned it piecemeal in my mind down to the last timber, and the pattern of iron nails upon the door, during the last desolate days of our stay at Beit Nuba where we lingered still and where, alone among all the host, only the King was undecided yet whether to retreat.

That day we saw Jerusalem I sat on one of the Sultan's flowery carpets within my tent building my barn, timber by timber, in my mind and polishing, though it needed no polishing, the eight-foot shaft for the King's lance, made of apple wood grown in the orchards of the great Abbey of Pershore, when Brand and Giles greeted me :

" A message, master, for King Richard from a Christian Beduin."

" What message ? " I asked. " And what Christian Beduin ? "

" He says you must come yourself, master," Brand declared.

I went out and took the message and delivered it again to King Richard: " Sire, the hermit of Mount Samuel bids you come."

"He is peremptory," the King said. He continued to turn a jewel in a filigree of gold between his fingers. Suddenly—all his movements were sudden in these days—he shot a question at me : "How can a man in two minds decide anything ? "

"Surely by the truth, sire," I said, "by the truth as he sees it."

"By the truth?" the King returned. "But I have come to believe that the Sultan's truth is equal to my truth, and that all men, whether Christian or Moslem, may be brothers."

I caught the drift of the King's thought. Greatly daring, though a man might dare anything in honesty with King Richard, I begged him not to treat yet for peace with Saphadin. I asked : "Will you not wait, sire ? "

"All the camp songs complain that I wait too long," the King answered, "and therefore that I am always late."

"Sire," I asked again, "must you care greatly what songs smaller men make ? "

"I will make another song if I live," the King swore, "that shall outlast all the songs of the camp. If I may not make a song of Jerusalem I will make one of Acre again, or of Beyrout." He leaned towards me. "I have dreamed, or I have been told it, that my eyes shall see Jerusalem."

"Sire," I said hastily, "the hermit of Mount Samuel would speak with you, perhaps of Jerusalem. His messenger still waits."

The King grumbled then. "He will prophesy woe again ; he will promise me everything that I do not desire ; he will give me yet one more piece of the True Cross, when the only piece of the Sacred Tree that I desire is that which Saladin has still and which after the fall of Acre he swore should be mine." He got abruptly to his feet. His hands tightening his sword belt, he said : "Tell this messenger I will come."

We set out that same night for Mount Samuel, or Montjoie, as it is sometimes called, the hill of Gibeon from whose summit crusaders and pilgrims may first set eyes upon the Holy City. Robin de Herdecourt rode with us and the two brothers des Préaux, and Everard, and Henry le Tyois, that other sweet singer, whom the King had that day made his Standard-bearer.

Together we talked of what might follow after to-night's work was done. On the following day, unless the King should decide differently, the retreat to Acre would begin. A few days after that we should garrison Joppa with William, Count of Châlons, as governor, and a garrison of 2,000 men. The many hundreds of sick and wounded would be left in Joppa also until the fleet could put in and take them away. And on the following day, I told myself while the talk went on, I should bid farewell to Everard and Melisande, since both, together with the Lady Isambeau—or so Everard told me—were for Joppa ; on the same day Brand and Giles and I, and

Robert with us, would go on to Acre. We should pass Arsur by the same road along which we had travelled not so long ago, and the dead bones of our men, I felt, would mock us silently from the sand.

I roused myself. The next day's events, for a few hours more, might wait. To-day's occasion was here; our shadows ran beside us, neck by neck, jostling each other upon the sand; the waning moon scudded between low clouds; we rode so hard I think we outpaced the moon.

We talked together in undertones again while the King stayed morose and silent.

Pierre des Préaux grumbled irreverently. "I am weary of hermits. They tunnel everywhere under this land like conies."

"When I speak with hermits I shut one ear and open both eyes, for they are great cozeners," Robin de Herdecourt blithely said.

"They stink of the excrement of bats, but they touch Heaven somewhere," Jean des Préaux declared heavily.

"This hermit has a gift of prophecy and will speak to us of Jerusalem," I said.

The holy man came upon us at our journey's end as suddenly as any sea monster out of his cave. He was short and squat, and covered, which was fortunate for him since the cave was cold, with a mat of hair. His beard was forked; grotesque as some old image carved in stone, he stood within the entrance to his cave. Behind him a fire of cedar branches burned and shot out fiery particles that were no greener than his eyes. An odour, unforgettable even yet, came from within, of human excrement and the excrement of bats, many layers deep, many years old.

Cap in hand, the King went down upon one knee and spoke as courteously as only he, when he wished to do so, could speak: "Sir Hermit, I am Richard the King."

The hermit mouthed painfully for a moment. Still mouthing, he beckoned us inside. We waited in the gloom and stench of the cave, in the heat of the fire. Having removed a stone from the wall the hermit produced a wooden cross of about a cubit's length and gave it to the King who held it in his hand—and this amused me—as if it were a sword. All of us crowding forward, the hermit, who had by this time recovered his tongue, prophesied at length, until the King, swinging the Cross impatiently, bade him be brief.

The holy man paused and was indeed brief. He addressed the King familiarly. "Richard," he said, "you shall win more and more victories, always, until you die, ever more victories, but never Jerusalem, never the Holy City or your heart's desire."

Holding the Cross by the head, the King answered harshly and briefly in his turn: "Sir Hermit, I think you lie."

Though the holy man turned a look of spite and power upon the King, he spoke calmly enough : " In seven days' time I, who have dwelt with God so long, shall at last speak with Him. Tell me, Richard Plantagenet, why should one who is so near the truth of the world lie ? "

The King's face hardened. He signed to Robin de Herdecourt and to me. We took hold of the holy man ; we left the lamp burning and the fire ablaze ; as courteously as we could we carried him away. Mounted on a spare horse and roped between the two of us, he made no protest, but all the while looked backward as we rode off until the cave and the glow of the fire burning within the cave were both out of sight. I looked at him and it seemed to me that there was indeed the strangeness of death upon his face, an odour of corruption about him above even the stench of the cave. Since the night air was piercing and cold, I cast my cloak about him for warmth. He thanked me with a sudden babble of words ; he blessed me with uplifted fingers ; I fastened the cloak more securely about him and we rode on.

We rode for a little while as it were between night and dawn, for our feet were in shadow, our faces, like the lower slopes of Montjoie, were touched and warmed with the day. The sun rose higher, its beams pierced the clouds, made a wide path of light from heaven to earth. A dazzle of sun blinded us for a moment, then fell away, and we could see. We saw Jerusalem then, like a city built of men's thoughts or a flower in stone, so insubstantial it seemed among the mists, so transformed in the beam of light.

The King paused as we did, looked as we did upon Jerusalem, but more poignantly. Then, casting an arm over his face, the rest of us dejected and silent, motionless upon our horses, he prayed aloud : " Suffer me not again, fair Lord God, to behold thy City since I may not deliver it from Thy enemies."

While we waited the sun rose higher and for another moment Jerusalem could plainly be seen. Covering his face with his hands now, the King wept. There was not one of us who did not grieve with him.

The sun's light dimmed as we rode on, and the day that had begun to break in such splendour was filmed with cloud. We looked back once more. Jerusalem, that city of peace, as if indeed it were made of nothing more substantial than men's dreams, dream-like, had once more dissolved away. In a few hours' time we were within sight of the camp ; in dejection and silence, the holy man nodding and muttering between us, we rode in.

5

FROM SUNRISE TO SUNSET

We had made our way back in safety to Acre, a city whose walls we had first destroyed and then rebuilt, whose streets we knew. And yet we found it changed and ourselves changed also. We had no purpose now in Outremer ; we were travellers only with no longer any purpose in travelling, travellers who waited to be gone.

I was alone. One of the Sultan's cushions under my head, a floor patterned with cool tiles under me, I half-slept in the King's palace at Acre. A lute strummed in the Ladies' Garden behind the high peach-clad wall; a black-and-white-barred butterfly lit on a leaf and stayed vibrating there ; a peacock from the walled garden pricked into sight, shot out a long neck, and stepped back again.

As I half-slept, so I half-dreamed. I was nothing and less than nothing, my mind went ; I was content to be so at last. I should never, it was likely, be dubbed knight, nor ride in to Alyncestre, as I had so often promised myself I would, with banners and green branches out for me in the streets. Instead, I should ride in quietly like a man coming home, and the life that I had left, that had gone on without me and had not changed, would close in on me again like a green wall. The house waited for me—so my mother sent me word through Father Andrew—the land needed my care (I doubted that) ; the house servants had grown slack since Raymond had died (that I did not doubt). She wrote anxiously : if rumour for once spoke truly, if King Richard were indeed coming home, what crops would I have sown, for example, in my forty-acre field ? Should it bear rye or leas ? And the gales, she added, had thrown down a walnut tree and two of our apple trees in the little orchard. Should she plant new ? Let it be rye, I sent word ; on my return I would eat rye bread again ; if I might, I would devour no more vile worms among sour biscuit husks. I would plant my apple trees myself, I said, and stake them, and a walnut tree.

Still half-asleep, my mind ran on. Thought runs on smooth lines ; thought flows free, never stumbling over any stone ; nowhere in the created world is there anything so satisfying as thinking and dreaming. I was nothing, I told myself again. It had taken me twenty years to hit upon so pleasant and so palatable a thought. Being nothing, I could make a bid for everything that I wished : Elfrida and my own manors, my own quiet. I had seen enough of wonders and battles to crowd my memory for a hundred years ; for the rest of my time I wished to see no greater wonders than I had turned my back upon—the growth, and change in growth, of all the common things I knew more familiarly than I knew my own hand or my own face : the unfolding of the myriad leaves in spring ; the thrust of wheat blades through the stoniest earth ; the opening and the closing of a rose. I was sick of hard skies and a harsher earth, of a world of men, so many thousands of them gone like shadows ; I was for substance again, for living men and beasts, for the wholesome stench— the dung newly spread—of my own earth. At Kinwarton, as he rode over his own fields or visited again his familiar places, Robert would find eyes once more, would see again.

So I assured myself. But suddenly the peacock screamed. The sound parted the sleepy air, sliced off, as a sword slices off flower heads, my dream. The peacock danced on his two feet before me and, sliding round like a French gallant at a court feast, opened his tail, wooing me as if I were a hen. I threw my cap at the bird for the insult and tweaked a long feather from his tail and went off.

Dreams apart, I had debts to pay, Saracen gold (my share of the spoils of the caravan) to change. Besides that, the King and the fleet, and John of Oversley with them, were for Beyrout in the morning. This was the new song in action the King would sing, as he had promised, in order to outdo all the songs of his enemies. Of all the towns upon the coast of Outremer only Beyrout remained in the hands of Saladin ; failing Jerusalem (the hermit of Mount Samuel had died meanwhile and Jerusalem appeared to be for ever behind us), the King would have Beyrout if he could.

I went out into Acre's streets. Awake, I was more sober than when I dreamed. All my desires waited, I knew, upon our assault on Beyrout and upon my safe return. I wondered as I went on why I had told myself that Acre had changed. Here before me was the Acre that I and all men knew. The pigs jostled in the heaps of refuse as I passed, or slept, as I had seen old men sleep after a night's debauch, blue, white-lashed eyes squinting and half-closed. The water in the harbour held the same oily gleam, the flies were no less numerous than before and buzzed at least as indefatigably.

I hurried on. Beyond the Tower of Flies the King's ships, white-sailed and freshly trimmed, rode gently on the green swell. The Customs House, whither I was bound, appeared closed for the night. Two rush-lights burned on the covered bench of the money changers, two more marked the place of Zimenes, the Grecian Chief of the Customs. But no one was there and the door to the Customs House behind the covered bench was closed and barred. I beat upon the bench and called.

It was Xerxes the Persian, though like Zimenes he had turned Christian for convenience long ago, who came out in his flower-embroidered Persian coat, rolling a little on his short legs and broad feet, and holding his great paunch before him with both hands. Grumbling and puffing between each word, he reminded me that the sun was almost set, that it was late.

I reminded him that though we should change my money by rushlight it was he who would cheat.

He answered that I had brought him from his woman and his wine ; to cheat, therefore, was the least that he could do.

He changed my Saracen gold, taking not more than a tenth over his due and talking ceaselessly while a Kurdish merchant—so I judged him to be from his long moustaches and high cap of fur—watched us from the topmost window of the Customs House, and chewed and spat.

" He will sleep on his bales of carpets, that one," Xerxes declared with a jerk of his thumb over his shoulder towards the merchant from Kurdistan. " For he arrived last, this Kurd, see you, and Zimenes would not come out. Why is he garbed like a buffalo in winter-time ? " Xerxes asked, jerking a thumb at the merchant again. " And he puts butter on his head. And it is rancid butter. It stinks, see you. He is a Kurd, I say. And you," Xerxes turned on me suddenly, " to-morrow morning, perhaps to-morrow noon, perhaps even this night, you go. King, knights, ships, horses, all of you, gentles and commons, will go. But not the ladies. To Beyrout ? You do not answer, but we know. The sailors talk and the ships themselves talk. Siege engines on board, more siege engines than food. More weapons than men. Where else would you go, eh ? " He picked his teeth and left my last bag of gold unchanged while he talked.

I thrust the bag towards him. " May it please you ? " I said. " See, the rushlight burns low."

" Then I shall cheat you twice, my friend," he declared, and went on : " There is but one place, I say again. It is Beyrout. Beyrout is strong. It makes all things of iron ; it is of iron also. We know what you will do and the Sultan knows also. Have his spies not been here, asking many questions, merchants with no merchandise looking all about them ? And are they not gone also, on swift horses with other horsemen ? But first they send off messenger birds with small rolls of parchment tied to their legs or held underneath their quills." Xerxes looked up, one finger poised, while I waited. " Your king is brave, we know. But the Sultan is cunning. And this land is cunning also."

" Do not be so flowery, Xerxes," I said, " for my grandfather was not a poet. It is a difficult land, but it cannot be called cunning."

" Every Persian's grandfather is a poet, and I have many grandfathers," Xerxes returned. Tipping the rushlight forward a little, he began to count the contents of my last bag of coins.

" Two hundred besants," I said, " and I will not take one besant less."

" It does not change, this land," Xerxes continued, counting and breathing stertorously as he did so. " It has always been the same since the first year of King Solomon. And before that. Come and go, always come and go, and men leave no mark. Egypt has gone, and Babylon, and Persia, and Israel has come and gone, and Rome also, and Mahommed and his followers have come and you Christians after them. You Christians have come and you will go. Deny it if you please, or do not deny it. I will always agree with you."

" I do deny it," I said.

The merchant from Kurdistan withdrew from his window and fastened the shutter carefully and slowly while continuing, I dare swear, to watch us out of one eye through the blink.

Xerxes shrugged. " Very good. As I have said, I agree. You stay. The West has no wisdom. Wisdom is where to stop, wisdom is when to begin." He paused to spread out both hands, then continued : "It is a big expense for you, this war. Your King is tired, your captains are restless. Other men take their lands and sleep, it is likely, with their wives."

" Indeed it is most likely." I made pretence of sighing.

Xerxes was much encouraged. " Your armies," he declared, " have dissolved. Like butter they have melted in the sun."

" I do not care for your comparison," I said. " The armies of the Sultan melt also."

" But he has much butter," Xerxes said. He thrust a final bag of coins towards me, but kept his hand upon it. " An Arab says Christians smell. A Christian says Arabs smell. It is all a matter of taste and opinion. My opinion is that you will go, that you will not return, and that you smell. How do you answer ? "

I did not answer, for in that second I caught sight of Brand and Giles running towards me. In the same instant I heard the trumpeters sounding the call to arms throughout the city. I snatched up my bags of coins and fled.

Xerxes, squat and immovable as a toad, called after me : " You go ? Yes ? "

" We return, Xerxes, we return," I shouted, and all at once (even Xerxes would not know why) I remembered what day it was. It was the twenty-eighth day of July, a day I was not soon to forget.

I ran on before Brand and Giles and called out to them over my shoulder as I ran : " What now ? "

" To Joppa, master," Brand answered, panting, and Giles echoed him.

I overtook Henry le Tyois, the King's Banner-bearer, and questioned him. Running beside me on thin grasshopper legs, he told me that indeed we were for Joppa as fast as wind or oars would carry us. For Saladin was laying siege to the city with his new and vast army and the garrison—so they had sent word—were surrounded and hard-pressed. Therefore the King called upon all his faithful fellows to follow him to Joppa with all haste.

That same night, the wind freshening, we set sail in fifty ships. Never was there a more hurried embarkation, never an enterprise upon which men set out with greater zest. We were a mixed company : English and Normans, Pisans and Genoese, but no Frenchmen. We were most oddly assorted and most unequally equipped : a King with helm and hauberk and sword, but without steel greaves or mailed shoes ; a hundred knights with no more than six horses between them ; a thousand or so crossbowmen and foot soldiers, and a Banner-bearer, newly appointed, in a herald's coat. At the last moment a party of armourers came on board, bringing with them a cask of Cyprus wine, at the sight of which our men cheered. At the last moment also, Brand and Giles, for whom I had been waiting anxiously, arrived, bringing Robert with them. The spectacle— perhaps foolishly, for Robert was his own master still—vexed me ; even the sight of my new long sword, which I feared had been left behind, and which Giles, not Brand, had remembered, scarcely restored my good humour.

I sat beside Robert at table in no better mood and carved his meat. The truth was that I feared for him ; I feared for myself also that I must spend time on board ship and in the battle in caring for him.

We did not speak, and yet he was aware of me, for when I could no longer bear with patience the nervous plucking of his one hand on his dagger hilt, he begged my pardon courteously.

I burst out at him in return far from courteously : " I am concerned for you. Why must you come ? "

He turned his head, and asked : " Is she not there ? "

When the meal was over I left him and leaned over the ship's rail. In the blackness of my mood Brand came to me. A rat had gnawed at my green surcoat where rich gravy had fallen from the feast of a night or two before. I spoke shortly : " Let the rat eat the rest." I heard him move heavily away and reproached myself once more.

I looked after Brand and became for the first time aware that the waves washed only lazily now against the ship's side, that our ship, and all the King's ships with her, most unhappily for our people in Joppa, were becalmed.

We were held in Caiaphas harbour for three days, while the King fretted and our men grew superstitiously afraid. The unseen witches of the deep clung to each ship's keel, our men swore ; great Sathanas himself held back the winds at the urgent prayer of his servant Saladin. The King's chaplain prayed fervently in our hearing : "A wind, O Lord, Gracious God, a wind." The ship's cook, who had a Cypriot dame for his mother, stole out at dawn and slew a cock and daubed its blood against the mast. But still no wind blew.

Last of all, King Richard himself on the morning of the third day thrust his chaplain aside. Down on his knees he went like any Templar, his sword held before him, and prayed more imperiously than cook or chaplain : "God, ha' mercy. Why dost thou keep me here when thou knowest that I am set upon thy service ? "

As every man on board, as even the King's chaplain himself expected, the wind from that time did indeed change. The colour of the water and the sky, the faces of the King and of all our men, the face of all earth, it seemed to us who looked on, changed as we sped out of Caiaphas harbour towards Joppa at last.

Late on the evening of Friday, the thirty-first day of July, we arrived within sight of the city. It was silent on its high cliff above us. We strained our eyes. In the thin summer darkness we could see only the close-packed army of Saladin waiting upon the shore. From the inner citadel on Joppa's hill no movement came, no stir of life. Our ships strung out in a long line, we waited with what patience we could for the light, while the wind that had followed us all this time, its work done, fell away. While we waited a sea mist came down and hid us from each other and from all those, whether enemy or friends, upon the shore.

At last day dawned. I never saw so slow a glory march across the eastern sky : tall clouds like ships floating over still lakes of amber and of pearl, and the great sun, as if he were God Himself, shining in majesty beyond. The mists heavy about our ships even yet, we continued to wait. Our men, lined up on deck, broke their fast with dry biscuit and cold bacon washed down by draughts of mead. They had been silent before ; presently they spoke in undertones. A few were for turning back, the greater number were for storming the citadel, whatever the consequences to themselves, and regardless of whether we should find enemies or friends within. The men murmured a little as time dragged on, but the King and the captains went about counselling patience. We were not here, the King said, to throw away our lives but to use them for the Cause and for Christendom ; we were too few to be rash, the Sultan's folk too many suddenly to allow themselves to be overpowered. "You know well," the King said, "that I am not one for waiting when the enemy is within sight."

While we waited in the warm mists our fears grew like mushrooms in the dark. We had no means of knowing the fate of the garrison. It might be, we agreed, that while we were delayed at Caiaphas they had been overpowered. It was possible also that the garrison had retreated to the citadel and were awaiting our arrival there. As the light strengthened it became evident to us that the Saracens were in truth in possession of the town. Their gait, even the tasks upon which they were engaged, were those of conquerors, it seemed to us, of conquerors also who went in small fear of attack. Our perplexity increased when in the early hours of the morning we saw the Sultan's cavalry ride out of the town and post themselves on either side of the outer gates of the citadel. Though we waited nothing further happened, and the citadel stayed silent. Quite suddenly the town came alive under our eyes. Drums and trumpets were sounded, yet though we strained our ears we could distinguish only the notes of Saracen trumpets, the roll of Saracen drums. Though the mists hid us still, the enemy, it seemed, were by this time aware of our presence. Their watchers peered over the walls upon us, signals were given, alarms sounded. Like children the Sultan's men blared defiance and battle at us with horns and trumpets ; like black and scarlet beetles they scurried busily to and fro, though what their purpose might be in so much scurrying we had no notion.

The morning wore on to noon. Men who had stood since dawn sat about the decks now and clasped their knees. When we almost despaired of both citadel and town, the news we had awaited so long came to us in the evidence of our own eyes at last. The Sultan's cavalry posted about the fortress gates closed their ranks ; fresh sentries with drawn scimitars were placed on either side of the gates. Presently the inner gate of the citadel which had been closed all this time was opened and our men began to come out. They came slowly at first, walking one by one. We counted twelve of them, each man bare-headed, carrying neither sword nor weapon, but only his shield.

In the hope of proving to them that help might be had, the King ordered every instrument on board ship to sound, every man to shout. The resultant din should have rent Joppa's walls ; it dislodged not even a stone. Only the seabirds, disturbed for a moment, left their nests and wheeled above us, ghostly and grey in the mists. We watched and were once more silent. Our people came on, slowly still. We counted thirty-nine of them. Presently women as well as men were to be seen.

The way was long from the citadel to the lower gate ; the descent, which was by numerous wide steps, was as steep as that from Heaven's floor. We watched, silent still, while the sun came out and burned fiercely upon the hill. The light of the sun in their eyes, our people came on, not faltering, not looking back. Even yet, though the mists had thinned and cleared about us, unbelievably no one looked down upon us, no one was aware of the burden of our thoughts.

The first knight had reached the outer gate where the Saracen swordsmen stood. Having delivered what we believed to be his ransom money, he bent his head as if he would pass through the open gate. He passed, in truth, for a sword swept once, impersonal and terrible and strange. We saw the procession of our people following him falter for a moment, then steady and come on. One woman covered her face ; another whose hand had flown for an instant to her throat dropped her hand once more against her side.

When the second knight died our men, silent until this moment, let out a deep groan. With the sudden movement and stir of so many bodies the King's ship shivered, the ship's timbers appeared to murmur as though in echo of that groan. A new fear plucking at me, I strained my eyes. Ten more of our people came out from the citadel, walking two by two, hand clasped in hand. Lastly a woman came. As if she felt no touch of death upon her she walked quickly. She seemed anxious, I thought, to finish and have done. She was not large nor tall, her gown that the wind ruffled and caught was blue-green like daffodil blades. She turned her head ; her hand came up in so swift, so familiar a gesture I was certain then. I cried out, an anguish sharp even in my own ears in my voice. She could not have heard, and yet there are times when thought overleaps space, when mind speaks to mind beyond the range of any ordinary sense.

Melisande halted. We saw both hands come up now and shade her eyes. It seemed to us then that she looked beyond the steep cliffs to the stretch of sea below where the long line of our ships lay. For suddenly she turned again, and tossed up an arm. The gesture, peremptory even at this distance, appeared to halt the procession of our folk. We saw them hesitate, then pause, then come as though instantly to life. In the same second the sun that had been against us all the day changed sides and mercifully hid his face. On King Richard's orders our ships closed up ; for the first time they were clearly visible to those upon the shore. At once all was turmoil within and without the citadel. Our people regained the shelter of the inner gate, while watchers from within, hidden from us until this moment, came out upon the battlements and ran to and fro distractedly, like moths within a glass, and the Saracen horsemen rode about angrily.

The King called the galleys together and held a council among them as to what should be done next ; whether, for example, to risk all our lives and the safety of our ships also, and attack ; or whether to abandon the remnant of the garrison and return. While we were still undecided a small shape no larger than a cannon ball was as though launched upon us from the battlements. We looked, and could scarcely contain ourselves from expectation and a kind of fear. Ridiculously upheld by his ample robes the figure of a monk could be seen as though flying like Elijah through the air. He fell and was half buried in the mud along the shore. While we let out a great shout of relief he was seen to pick himself up and, like a stout ungainly bird, take to the waves. We hauled him on board the King's ship and took him, burning and cadaverous between our hands, to the King. Shaking himself and emptying mud and sea from his mouth, he delivered himself pantingly : " Sir King, the remnant of your people are lost within the tower unless God and you have pity."

Though we had hesitated before, there was not one of us who could hesitate longer. To go on might well be folly ; not to do so was surrender and, for us, a special kind of shame. All the world knows what happened then : how the King's galley shot forward, how the King, still without greaves or mailed shoes, was the first to wade ashore, how the rest, without distinction of rank or office, followed: knights and archers, foot soldiers and esquires and servants, English and Normans, Pisans and Genoese. All the world knows also how we fought and how, within an hour, small though our numbers were, we possessed the shore, how afterwards we reached the citadel, the King leading us up the Templars' stairway from the shore. Once inside the tower the garrison came out to meet us ; together we turned against the Turks within the town. By sundown not only the citadel and the shore but Joppa itself was ours.

At the foot of the flight of steps where the Saracen swordsmen had waited, some of us waited also for those non-combatants who were left within the citadel to step down to safety. They came, the sick and wounded among them, the women and the children, hand in hand or leaning upon each other, or walking slowly. There were some who wept and some who were so calm as to appear almost indifferent ; there were others upon whose faces the strangeness of death still lay. I waited for Melisande. Her lips curved into a small fixed smile she carried—Lord knows where she had plucked it—between her hands a small stiff daisy flower. Trembling, she passed close to me. As I looked at her I loved her again ; we greeted each other though we did not speak. Behind Melisande came a woman with a child by each hand, both children weeping. Last of all in this small procession—shamefully I had forgotten her until this moment —came the Lady Isambeau, floating a white head-dress, a purple mantle, her bag over one arm, and dangling from it, inevitably, a grey stocking. Hare-faced and gap-toothed, she was gallantry itself. And for a moment, so moved was I beyond my ordinary self in chivalry, I was ready to love her also.

Since citadel and town were in our hands, we might have rested from fighting for the remainder of that day, but the King, all the old lust for battle alive in him, would not rest. Nothing would content him but that we should attack the Sultan's army which had withdrawn and was encamped in the fields outside the city. In this new assault we met even greater odds, suffered even fiercer shocks. Never, even at Arsur, had we faced so vast a cloud of arrows. What harm they did us I did not know nor greatly care, for the King's madness, if madness I may call it, was upon us all. To-day we were forgetful of ourselves ; to-day we were brothers once more ; again God fought for us, once again we could not fail. So, in this last encounter, faith was rekindled in us ; the magnificence and the glory, or what Everard and William des Préaux had once called glory, returned. Though I will not speak of glory, for fear of being dazzled by a name, I have been glad since that we burned out our strength that day and the day following. I shall always remember how the King, mounted on one of our six horses, and an indifferent horse at that for so large a man, drove the Turks before us like sheep, though they were by no means sheep, until by sundown all the fields around Joppa, and the whole of that stretch of land on which the Turkish camp had stood, were ours.

The fighting over at last, I sought for Robert and found him, his Turcople guard standing tranquilly by. I greeted him : " The two of them are unhurt, and she is well."

He turned his head. " I know. She stooped as she passed and touched my face."

A dull foreboding, I did not know why, plucking at my mind, I looked for Brand and Giles. I enquired for them here and there, always more anxiously—a crossbowman with a large nose, a serving man whose knees knocked. There were hundreds of their sort, it appeared, at Joppa in the King's army. While I hurried I remembered how much I owed Brand and Giles, and how solitary I should be if one or both were gone. I hastened through the camp ; half-despairing, I looked for them in the darkening streets of the town. Joppa was already deep in corruption and decay. Here in the streets—a grim Saracen joke, this—the carcases of dead pigs kept company with dead Christians ; upon their mounded bodies—a Christian answer—the bodies of many Turks slain by our own men lay. I fled the town and returned once more to the camp.

I came upon the two of them in a small clearing among the trampled grass and broken shrub-like trees, where a small trickle of water ran in a deep crack to the cliff's edge and a few reedy grasses grew, mixed with small bristling daisy-like flowers. Brand lay on his side, half-covered by his shield ; Giles knelt beside him. I went down upon my knees also ; I touched his hand ; if I might I would have cried out to him, " Oh, do not die." I wept ; I could not speak. Between cracked lips Brand spoke words I did not hear, which Giles translated for me : " Brand says, ' No matter, master, all is well with Brand.' "

I wept once more, and Brand, his head turned towards me, died, a look of half-comical surprise, perhaps that I should weep for him, upon his face.

We buried him, that good piece of my own earth, where he lay. They say bodies keep well in that hot sand. I would have gone then, for it was almost dark, but Giles, Brand's belt of ox-hide dangling from one finger, stayed and mourned :

" I shall have none to talk to now, master. There is none in this heathen country that do understand. For Brand could speak o' many things, o' sheep and men when he had a mind to, and a' always prayed at night for Holy Cross. A' was gentle and had no love of killing, though he could slay the heathen in a rage or when hard pressed to it. Well, 'tis done now, 'tis all over and finished. A' was a good shepherd, a' come a long way to lie in desert sand. So God rest him, Christ company him. 'Tis night now."

Together we made our way back through a darkness velvety as the first shadows of spring. Already the stench of carrion tainted the night air, and the dark was filled with bobbing wisps of light as men with torches went about, as I had done, to find their dead. And found them, I did not doubt. Under cover of the dark, unknown to Giles, or perhaps not unknown to him, I wept silently.

6

FULL CIRCLE

DURING the next four days the wheel of fate upon which Robert and Everard and I were bound was to turn full circle, and we three who had set out together were to come, each of us separately, to our road's end.

I had little thought of this in those first hot August days at Joppa, and yet a sense of mortality, of a man's helplessness before things unknown, sat with almost a physical heaviness upon my shoulders and filled my mind. I mourned for Brand, and although I knew he would never walk earth again I looked for him when the flap of my tent lifted suddenly, when whistling or heavy footsteps were heard, or when a group of men over a butt of wine gathered together to tell tales round the sergeants' fire. From oppression of spirit I grew irritable. Since Giles only was left to me, I should have cherished Giles ; instead, in mourning for Brand I came near to chastising him.

Giles himself reproached me in surly tones : " A man is not like his father, master, and I am not like Brand, who was not, indeed, and could not be, my father. Nor is Giles any match for him."

I excused myself. " I am melancholy," I said. " That is all."

Giles said : " I have had a brood o' nightmares visit me, master, since Brand died."

I had little time for melancholy. The good angel and the devil mixed in King Richard exhausted us in hard labour and upheld us also. The dead were left unburied, the most necessary tasks left undone, no prayers were said. From the first light of dawn until the first stars of night we toiled to rebuild Joppa's walls. Every man, every woman and every child also that was capable of labour took part, and King Richard toiled with the rest. Since we lacked lime and mortar, men from the Cotswolds and the Pennines came forward from the ranks of the archers of those regions and taught us how to build walls after their manner, stone locked with stone, the whole bound as it were with air and yet curiously strong. Our hands bled, our bodies all but cracked under the strain of so much unaccustomed labour. The colour of the stones, ochre-yellow and dusty red, burned itself into our brains, and the fearful stench of the slain came to us now and then like a blast from the charnel-house of Hell. Yet no man fell out from work upon the walls who did not fall out to die, and the walls rose, every hour another foot or so of wall between Christendom and Saladin's waiting army. I know that Robert toiled beside me, Giles aiding him with eyes and hands, that Everard, something over-anxious about him, kept beside Melisande. I know that of all that we endured in Outremer, both of dreams and nightmares, I could least bear to build Joppa's walls again. By the end of the third day the walls were built ; at nightfall we rested, having heaped great fires of brushwood before our tents, the smoke of which, we hoped, would shroud the stench of the dead.

The five of us, Robert and Everard, Ambrose and the Chronicler and I, talked round our fire while the sweet wine of Cyprus went round. There was not one of us who did not ache from weariness, and yet we talked as if we were in some cloister of Cluny or of Bury, as if books and minds were the only commerce that we knew. It was a relief to talk ; in doing so we fled from too great a closeness to the things we knew : the threat of to-morrow, the tenseness in our minds and bodies, our lost Jerusalem, the building of a fortress wall with naked hands.

Robert, his white cloak shrouded about him, sat quietly with an air of waiting before the fire. Giles squatted in the outer ring like a charcoal burner, his hands dropped between his knees. The Chronicler, unexpectedly rosy of face, stared peacefully at the flames : he had an empty flagon crooked absently over the finger of one hand. Ambrose faced me, long arms clasping his knobbed knees.

Everard dropped down before our fire and yawned into one hand. "Lord, I could sleep for an eternity." He yawned again. "Lord," he said a second time, "how we are all changed!"

"You are not changed, messire Everard," Ambrose assured him. "I see little change in you. But I have turned half-priest again, I that was never quite a priest. I have begun to ask questions again, I who have questioned nothing for years. Who can explain this world or the next? I ask. There is no dogma, there is only mystery, I say. The body dies and the soul leads on, but where? God ends, I answer, God begins it all."

"Who," Everard asked, "that was in his right mind would wish to understand everything?"

"I have not been in my right mind these three weeks," Ambrose said gloomily. "One thing above all others troubles me at this time, though before this I own I did not care. It is that we kill in God's name, for Christ's sake. Oh, Christ, I think now, is this not a mockery?"

"We should have died in Joppa then and spared your consciences." Everard got very pleasantly to his feet.

"That was not in my mind. Before God it was not," Ambrose said. When Everard moved away he went after him.

"Thought is always light-headed. Men forget that." Robert gathered his cloak about him and, one hand held out, moved slowly away, Giles stepping carefully beside him.

The Chronicler swayed to his feet. "Men should sleep more, and talk less."

"You are drunk, Chronicler," I observed.

"*In vino veritas*, friends," the Chronicler said, though only I remained. Presently I slept. Mine was a shallow sleep. I thought that Robert came and spoke to me while his Turcople waited outside the circle of my fire. "Forgive me," Robert said. Astonished at so much humility from him I awoke. No one was there.

Only a Genoese archer came running towards me, breeches unlaced, sleep and terror in his eyes. He mouthed a dozen words, of which I caught only a few: "To arms," I heard, and "ambush," and again, breathlessly, "the King." He ran from me. He ran so like a mad dog I thought him mad. And then I heard the thud of horses' hooves and Saracen cries. Mounted on a heap of rubble, I caught sight of the Sultan's cavalry moving in upon the camp, glimpsed the thicket of their lance heads and their tossing plumes.

On our side drums were being beaten, the alarm cried. The knights came tumbling out of their beds—laughably enough, if this had been a time to laugh—the Marshal of all England in his nightshirt, the Lord Bishop of Salisbury grasping his crozier but mother-naked in a white satin skin, the King of England cursing like King Henry his father, in body armour but with his great thighs bare, Ralf de Mauleon, who boasted a lion upon his surcoat, in his surcoat indeed, that was too short for him, and breechless beneath. There were Templars in their underwear—no Templar was allowed to sleep unclothed ; Hospitallers wrapped for coolness in no more than their great flapping cloaks ; men cursing and sweating, looking for arms and gear, every one of them like Adam without his fig leaf. I saw old Sir Hugh de Winton running, his great helm clapped upon his head, his sword in hand, but bare and rosy—I swear it—of behind. I laughed then. Mortal though our danger was, I stood and laughed. Such sights last longer in the mind than death or war.

Once armed, I ran to warn Robert. All the camp was on its feet, seeking arms, seeking captains and sergeants, fellow archers and companion knights. It was chaos, but out of the chaos order, as in the first day of the world, was being made. The King was armoured by this time ; the archers and their sergeants had formed themselves into companies. Though the cooking pots were overturned, and fires, half put-out, filled the air with particles of ash, men were forming themselves into line, and were standing and marching to order again. Moreover, now that the alarm was given, the enemy for the moment had turned back.

Having left Giles in charge of Robert, I hastened to take my place beside old Sir Hugh de Winton and Robin de Herdecourt and Ralf de Mauleon and all our company about the King.

I have heard of many warlike encounters, tales of Greeks and Trojans and the wooden horse of Troy ; I know how Leonidas fought, how the great Tarquin died ; I was familiar with the exploits of our own day, of Bohemund and Roland. And yet I think I am not partial when I say no men since the first sun shone fought a harder fight than our men did that day in the fields about Joppa. We were unfed, our thirst unquenched, wakened from sleep by sudden terrors and alarms, itself a fatiguing thing ; we were half-armed still and a quarter clad and, for all the order that we made in so brief a time, woefully disarrayed. We were no more than fifty knights, with six horses between them, and two thousand sergeants and men against a vast army, well-fed, well-mounted and well-armed, spurred on by the certain expectation of Paradise after death, and, if they should chance to capture King Richard, of fabulous rewards at the Sultan's hand in life. Except for our six mounted knights, I repeat, we were a handful of foot soldiers and knights fighting as foot soldiers against an infinitely larger host of mounted men. As I write, it seems to me beyond belief that we should have surmounted so many obstacles and gained so complete a victory. Perhaps that day we were, as men are sometimes, a little more than mortal ; perhaps the fire that burned with so unquenched a flame in King Richard that day fed a small spark also in us who fought with him. Whatever the answer, the King saw the one thing that it was possible to do at Joppa and did it, and we obeyed and aided him.

There must surely always be something simple in greatness, an element of the obvious in what at the time appears inspired. So it seems to me now when I think of our plan of battle then. What, after all, could be simpler than for foot soldiers to form themselves into a square, locked and interlocked on its four sides with men, in order to withstand the repeated shock attacks of unnumbered cavalry ? Behind a low barricade of wood from the camp, while the enemy still held off, King Richard arrayed us in lines and companies of a hundred men, to every hundred a captain who was either an esquire or a knight. I had my own company ; Robert—a signal favour, this, from the King—had his also, with Giles and a sergeant to act as left hand and eyes for him ; Everard was posted with Robin de Herde-court and Gerard de Furneval on our flank by the sea, hard by Joppa's St. Nicholas Church. My own place was near the centre where the King rode, and the enemy pressed hardest against our ranks. On every side of our square was a living wall of men, locked with shields, bristling with lance heads, and once more, as with our very different order of battle at Arsur, invincible, providing—no small proviso this—that every man stood patient and stood firm. In order to assist him to stand firm, every man, by the King's directions, had his right knee pressed hard upon the ground, his left leg lightly bent ; in his left hand he held his shield so that it covered his body ; in his right hand his lance, its eight-foot shaft fixed firmly in earth, its point of steel turned towards the enemy. Between every two men a crossbowman was posted, and behind him another, whose business it was to load for the first, or take his place if he were wounded or fell. In this manner we kept a triple front, for the enemy who escaped our arrows was forced to charge upon our lance heads. And as the enemy came on, the shower of arrows from our ranks did not cease.

It was well after midday, when discomfiture could plainly be seen among the ranks of the Turks, and when one more assault had failed, that a new confidence began to take possession of our men. We had been concerned at first only to fight and to endure—if the truth be told, we had not felt too confident even of so limited a success. Now, because we had fought and endured, and because we had taken the measure of all the powers opposed to us, we saw for the first time that even victory might be ours. The realisation bred a momentary impatience in us. We would have finished at once if we could. But King Richard, who in war was as intuitive as a woman is in peace, sensed the feeling that was uppermost in all our minds and rode along our ranks, laughing and shaking his head at us and lifting his sword. He possessed a voice that was oddly stirring to the dullest ear, at times mellow and warm so that it spoke to a man's heart, but in moments of crisis harsh and strident also, a ring of cruelty and pride in it that shocked and nerved the will. Even now, when the demons of pain come at me from the half-light as Saladin's cavalry came upon us in the first hours of that morning, I remember how King Richard spoke to us then, and my mind repeats a part of what I heard at that time : " Adversity sheds a light upon the virtues of men as prosperity casts over them a shade. There is no room for flight, no time for fear. Continue, therefore." He said more than this, but it is this that I remember.

He had scarcely finished when the Turks beat on us once more like a shower of rain. They broke against our lances and recoiled ; they sent their javelins and arrows against us in even denser flights ; they came on, only once more to fall back. Next, for they were cunning, they tried by feints and subterfuges to break the steadiness of our men and tempt them forth from the shield wall. They would charge, then check their charge and wheel, and counterfeit a sort of flight. But we were not deceived. So the day wore on. The felt and quilted jerkins of our foot soldiers were stuck as thick with arrows once again as a hedgepig is with quills ; King Richard himself had half a dozen javelin heads caught and broken in the meshes of his coat of mail.

When at last the Turks drew back and appeared to hesitate the King once more rode along our ranks. " Did I not tell you," he cried, " how it would be if you would stand firm and be patient ? Only continue and we shall have them yet."

He called for food and wine and ate and drank before us very merrily, while the Turks stood no more than a hundred feet away. Our men turned merry also and one or two of the most forward called to him : " Sir King, we wish that we might eat and drink also."

" And so you shall," the King cried and laughed back at them. " So shall we all eat and drink. By the Bread, brother Turks, how we Christians shall eat and drink after this day ! "

The King was merry and mad with it, and many of us feared for him. But, since he was never altogether unthinking, it is possible that he was reckless on this occasion for a purpose. For the Turks, who could see him well enough and some of whom could hear and understand his words also, began to grow angry almost to madness in their turn.

Their ranks moved suddenly ; they came at us now with redoubled strength. It was the last, the ninth and drowning wave. By might and violence our men were almost overwhelmed. King Richard, to his great grief, had Fauvel and one other of our six horses slain under him ; it was then that Saphadin, the Sultan's brother, more gallant than many a Christian knight, out of love for the King, sent him two more. The King took them and joked to us again : " I would take horses from Sathanas himself to help us through this fight."

The fight went on. For me it became a nightmare of sights and sounds, a blurred and double vision of Turks on horseback and riding Kings, of dark flights of arrows like long thorns, and hosts of steel javelins. Our old enemies, so old as to be familiar as friends, were present also : sunstroke and thirst and choking dust and blinding heat and sand ; there were other less familiar enemies in aching muscles and straining limbs, in eyes that burned between reddened lids, in mouths so black and swollen our faces seemed all burning eyes and mouths.

Just before sundown both sides paused once more, their strength almost spent. At this point Saladin himself harangued his men. They stayed sullen and motionless, and some of us, for their sufferings and ours were identical, pitied them. The sun himself, as if even he were weary of our hate, began to turn his back upon the day. The sky above us was dark, not with night yet nor with arrows and javelins, but with small crying birds coming from whence we did not know, going we knew not where. Our men watched them with bloodshot eyes and thought, it may be, as I did, of flocks of lapwings moving in slow dipping flight over the wet furrows, of hosts of swallows coming from the dark edge of the world or the deep pond.

We had had time to pause and take breath. Presently the Turks moved again. This time—and there was not a man who was not glad of it—King Richard, followed by the Earl of Leicester and one or two more knights, charged into the Turkish ranks. It seemed like folly and death to do so, but death itself appeared to retreat before the King. He was lost to sight one moment only to emerge the next ; always, when he appeared surrounded, it was the Turks who fell. The truth here at Joppa as elsewhere was that no man alive had so long a sword's reach as the King, nor such a giant's strength.

The ranks of the Turks, rent apart by the King's furious charges, did not close up ; the enemy were weary as we were and despairing by this time of victory.

When the garrison inside the walls of Joppa, who had waited in anxiety until this moment, saw that the Turks were almost beaten they, too, came out. Caught between the garrison and the King's own men, the enemy lost all coolness of mind and, brave and skilful though they were, fled.

A surprise by King Richard and a handful of knights only had become a rout. What had begun as an ambush at dawn in Joppa's fields ended as a Christian victory at nightfall. Yet, of the two armies, our men were the more exhausted. We should have pursued the Turks as they retreated, but we had neither strength nor will left. We stayed in the same spot, and, filled with an infinite but dull content, let the Turks ride away. Only when dusk began to fall could we bring ourselves to stir. We did so with difficulty, our limbs so cramped and stiff we were as though rooted to the one place. Slowly, in companies even yet, we moved towards our tents.

In command of my own will once more, I remembered Robert. I had seen him fall, seen him held up again by Giles ; I believed him safe. Though I made many enquiries I could find no news of him. Every man to-day was for himself and for all the rest : there were no other loyalties than these.

Before nightfall Ambrose came in search of me. His long robes flapping about him, he looked like a gaunt woman in the evening light. His face, even his long fingers that clutched at mine, appeared distraught. I guessed what he was about to say. He said : " Come. He is for the golden floor."

Feeling nothing at all of what I might have felt, I followed Ambrose. They were within my tent : Robert fevered and almost past speech, stretched out upon my bed, the Chronicler crouched and blinking in a corner, Giles nursing a wounded arm and hiccoughing and weeping in turn, but whether for Brand or Giles, or even for Robert, I did not know.

They left me ; I did not see how they went. The tent flap was open, and Robert stayed still, his face, as always since his blinding, turned towards the light. We seemed so quiet we might have been alone in some high place, and yet the camp was close around us and the traffic of men. I remember no sound, only the rustle of some small creature, a lizard or a mouse, on the floor. We were so quiet, time was like nothing too. We moved back in time : the confusion was no longer there, nor our long struggle and dispute. I bent over Robert ; the creature, lizard or mouse, slid away from under my feet. Robert's lips moved ; I bent lower, his hand between mine.

" Now I go to explore the mystery," I think he said.

I looked down at him. I loved him, and yet in this instant of time I felt no grief. There was greatness in him, I thought, and something fanatical as well which loved and yet rejected life. And so life, as life cheats us all, cheated him. He was dead ; he was one with the mystery. I went out of the tent. Then, indeed, for all the trembling of stars in the sky, then indeed it was dark.

7

ONCE MORE THE TITANS

THE little bells of the priests sounded throughout the camp as they had sounded every day since Joppa, ringing with the same plangent sound the dead into Heaven and the Evil One back into Hell. Even when they were silent they rang in my brain.

I closed my eyes ; I tried to listen to Giles ; they rang in my brain still. We had triumphed, but our triumph seemed likely to be short-lived. Once more the unseen Titans of sickness and dissension and despair stalked among us like monstrous shapes of mist. I had always had a heart for Pharaoh and his men stricken by the twelve Israelitish plagues. Since Joppa, our King stood in Pharaoh's place and our men died from a pestilence worse than any Egypt had ever known. As in Pharaoh's time the sun hid his face, the sky stayed overcast by dense thunder clouds ; even by night no cool wind stirred. Men turned superstitious once more from misery : the land, they swore, was accursed and God was angry. It was an old tale.

If the truth be told the cause of the pestilence was plainly to be found in our own ignorance and in the urgency of the moment that had obliged us to spend every instant of time in the rebuilding of Joppa's walls. For now, the dead still unburied, corruption past remedying filled the air, poisoned every breath we drew, tainted the water that we drank, the food we ate, sickened with mortal sickness our bodies and our minds. So the camp at Joppa was as foul as a half-dry pond and the sound of the little bells of the priests was the only stir in the air.

Giles repeated his question patiently. Dangling Robert's lark in its cage, he said : " It was his, master. It should go with him."

I looked at him. " Why ? "

" It is blind, master," Giles said. " Ten to one it will not live."

The little bells sounded again. " Set it free," I said.

Grumbling, Giles lifted the wooden latch of the cage. " Now I'll have to find another bird to take to our Motty," surprisingly enough, I thought I heard him say.

I clapped my hands and the bird, which had perched uncertainly at first upon the open door of its cage, was gone.

Giles watched its flight and disapproved again. " If you hadn't let it go free, I could ha' given it to our Motty, master. Ten to one the other birds'll peck the poor creature to bits, ten to one."

The lark went on soaring : something, I told myself, no lark could do in any cage.

" Master," Giles asked, " can I keep the cage ? Master, I have a word for you from Sir Hugh de Winton."

" I know. He is sick," I said.

" No more than the Bull o' Bashan when he is on his dunghill, master," Giles answered heartily, " or King Pharaoh o' Egypt when he whipped up his horses over the Red Sea. He is roaring aloud, master, and putting everybody to rightabouts. But the King's clerk is dead, and you must go, if you please, master, to the King."

I said wrathfully : " Could you not have told me so before ? "

Giles stared at me. " Why, no, master. Because of the bird, master. Because you would not ha' listened to me then about the bird." He went on. " It is the King that is sick, master John. He has thrown his sword through his tent, they say, and every man that likes who passes can see him in his scarlet bed wearing no armour at all." Giles paused breathlessly.

I got to my feet. " If I had ever beaten anyone I would beat you for a talkative mule."

Giles followed me, dangling the cage. " 'Twas always old Sir Raymond that thrashed me. And a' beat you too, master. But Lord, poor mortal, a' had no strength. ' Do but lie down,' Brand told me, ' and, Giles, you'll feel it no more than the tickling of your bum on a thistle patch when you do sit on it sudden and sharp after a swim.' "

I lost patience with his prattle. " You are a fool, Giles," I said.

" We be all fools," Giles answered, " that come to this place. And by the same light o' knowledge all that leave it would be wise men also if they depart quickly."

I asked carefully : " Who talks of departure ? "

" Why, every man Jack of us, master," Giles replied. " There's nought left for a man to do here but pray for himself and bury his friends." Giles paused, then went on : " They do say in the camp also, master John, that King Richard is sending to the Lord Turk, the Sultan's brother Saphadin, the one that gave him horses in the midst of the battle, and that they aim to speak of peace."

" Your ears are too long," I declared. I dismissed Giles ; I went on alone.

I was perplexed and heavy at what I had heard. I do not know what special part of pride it is that suffers when a man feels himself obliged to withdraw from some enterprise upon which he has set his heart. I only know that a defeat of this nature is both sour and bitter and does not sweeten with the years. Though I had joined King Richard's Holy War in search of adventure and gain rather than from reasons of Christian piety, though I longed for my own place as keenly as any man, the thought that we might now be about to make a Turkish peace was wormwood to me. I was angry, and yet in our present plight—our army dying slowly within two miles of the enemy—I realised that peace with Saladin might offer our only hope of retaining the conquests we had won.

I pressed on. A throng of pilgrims and soldiers was massed about the King's tent. I felt their eyes, hard for some reason and pitiless also, upon me as I came up. No one spoke. Unshaven and unwashed, the men squatted, hands hung between their knees, and stared at me, wooden and motionless as trees. I found the King, as Giles had warned me I would find him, prone on his scarlet bed in his surcoat of blue embroidered with the dancing leopards in gold. The flies trafficked noisily through the great rent in the canvas of his tent, and outside the rent a patch of sky, leaden as the grey canvas, showed.

" John of Oversley, I sent for you," the King said. His eyes shone sharply like blue glass ; his voice—I had not heard it since Joppa—was brittle and changed like his eyes.

" Sire," I said, and waited.

" I burn with fever," the King said. " Neither by day nor by night can I order my limbs or my thoughts. Neither the Knights Templars nor the Knights Hospitallers will follow me longer. Therefore, I have come to an end. Therefore, write now for me to the Lord Saphadin."

My mind worked slowly. I hesitated and could not speak or raise my eyes.

While I hesitated the King started up so fiercely I trembled. Even while I trembled I pitied him.

" Write," he commanded me. " Write now to Saphadin."

I wrote as the King directed me : " Richard, King of England, to the Most Noble Saphadin, greeting. Sir Knight, I am fevered and in danger of death if I am not refreshed at your hands. Of your love and courtesy, send me, I beg you, fruit and snow. And afterwards let me have word with you on what concerns both your brother, the Sultan Saladin, and myself. I will requite your courtesy with thanks a hundredfold."

I read out his words to the King. As I did so my voice trembled and almost fell away.

The King looked at me curiously. " You should be fevered as I am," he said, " messire John of Oversley, for fever burns up grief."

I gave the letter, as the King had ordered me, to no less a personage than the great Simon, Earl of Leicester, and left it to be sealed and doubly sealed at his hands with the King's seal. Presently I saw the Earl ride out towards the Turkish camp, Henry le Tyois on his right, carrying the King's banner, a de Montfort kinsman on his other side bearing the banner of the de Montforts.

I waited, as I had been directed to do, and heard the trumpets calling on all men in the King's name to come forward and serve him at his expense.

I saw our men's faces, clouded at first with doubt, turn half-eager and half-afraid. I watched the first handful of men step forward ; I waited while more men followed. By noon a thousand archers and foot soldiers, roughly a half of our small force, had handed in their names, but, except for the King's own friends, not one Christian knight.

The King had summoned Robert de Sabloil for the Knights Templars and Garnier de Naplous for the Knights Hospitallers to him. Though he had sent word to Saphadin it was clear he still hoped to win some support at least from these two great bodies of knights. In my presence he pleaded with them again : would they not, he begged, at least take charge of the fortresses of Joppa and of Ascalon so that he might go to Acre and be cured of his sickness ? And, being cured, return and begin again ? They were great men, famous in all the Christian world, but in this matter their minds were made up. They were courteous and brief. " Sire," they answered, " without you we will not. And there is no beginning again."

His head bent, the King let them go. I gave him, as Sir Hugh de Winton had commanded me, the numbers of the foot soldiers and sergeants who had volunteered to serve him. He listened, and when he understood that the knights had held back he cried out : " Fair Lord Christ, what is this Cross I bear ? Joppa my Golgotha, my place of skulls, this bed my Tree ! "

He raved for a moment, and then, half raving still, said : " Write this to Saladin. These are my terms of truce."

I held my parchment and my pen ready, but no words came clear enough for any man to write down.

" Ascalon," the King said. " I will never give up Ascalon, Syria's Summit, Egypt's Bride, which the Sultan tore down, which we built up again." I wrote " Ascalon," and waited.

The King only murmured now : " Ascalon, Ascalon. The Sultan will have Ascalon, but I will not yield it. We might have peace if it were not for Ascalon." I waited still.

His hands before his face, the King prayed and commanded in the same breath : " Fair Lord God, I am thy servant Richard. Let this sickness pass."

He took away his hands. He looked at me like a man again, though he spoke strangely once more.

" God fools me," he said. " God fools his Church. Sin is not black nor goodness purest white. Unbelief is not damnation but a difference. Now, in the person of these two men, Saladin and Saphadin, the devil tempts me. I grow tolerant, and what would the great Bernard of Clair-vaux say to that ? " He paused, then spoke quietly. " I would rather be mad or blind and go through darkness like a dream for ever than yield up Jerusalem to our enemies. And yet I must yield more than Jerusalem. If I am fevered, therefore, it is with too much thought."

I did not speak even yet, while the King mourned again : " If I had Saladin's wisdom, Saphadin's gentle courtesy, had I been subtle and temperate like William Longsword of Salisbury, my half-brother ! But I was myself, as all men must be. From being too much myself I have squandered the great hope I had. I might have dissembled more ; I might have taken the Lady Alois, King Philip's sister, for my wife and denied her afterwards. But that I did not wish to do. Poor lady, she had been shamed enough. I could have turned humble and walked softly and waited. But then would Philip of France have been less ambitious or Conrad of Montserrat more loyal ? I could have used time more wisely, and now my time is almost gone. What is left of my time waits here, John of Oversley, smiling like the courtier I am not, half-seen in the corner of my tent." Here the King pointed. " He wears a silken shirt, no armour. He bows, his hand upon his heart : ' Your servant, King. I am here for one hour only.' One hour, John of Oversley, between Richard of England and the Lord Saphadin."

The King looked at me. He went on : " I must always, my enemies said, go conquering. There is some truth in what they said. For splendour and fame must be mine always. A man can die and fail, I think, of too much fame."

The words beat over me. The priests' bells tolled still ; they seemed far away like sheep bells in a mist. More than once I believed I heard a stir outside the tent, and my pulse leapt, only to quieten again as the stir fell away and no messenger came in. At first I looked for comfort for the King. I found none. Instead, familiar images possessed my mind : of hosts of falling leaves, of flying shadows dark over smooth sand. I grew tired and prayed that the day might end.

I listened while the King raved again : " If I have failed here of the great plan I made I will not fail elsewhere. I will have all my castles and lands again, all my dominions. The King of France would have done better in the end if he had stood by his promises and by me." He paused. I kept silent still.

He went on : " If I have not made amendment in Jerusalem of the wrong I did my father, I will make it differently in France. If I live I will do it. By God's Eyes," the King swore, " by his Blood and his Pierced Feet."

He turned abruptly. " Will you fight in my cause ? "

" Sire," I answered as steadily as I could, " I would live in peace."

The King looked at me curiously. " Whose peace ? " after a moment he asked.

" My own peace," I answered. I said again : " Sire, I would marry Robert of Kinwarton's sister and care for her, for my own and for his sake."

"I have never found marrying a long business," the King said, and now he seemed surprised.

Another time I might have laughed. I might have answered him also. That day I kept silent. I did so for fear that I might be persuaded to serve him further out of a useless pity, for fear also that I might become one more among all those other shadows that in my mind's eye creep at night over the sand.

While I waited and held myself aloof there was a stir outside. Voices speaking in Arabic could at last be heard. I moved from my place.

The King raised his head and spoke quietly once more : " There is Saphadin."

Presently Saphadin and his emirs came in : spare, slight men, very quick and proud, stepping swiftly and lightly like Arab horses. William the Marshal followed them, yellow-moustached, red-complexioned, and slow, his large frame girt about with iron like a wooden tub. After him came Earl Simon of Leicester, with his flat lion's face, his quick tread.

I withdrew, and two blackamoors came in, rolling wild eyes under scarlet turbans and bearing between them a great crystal dish of snow. Two more followed, bearing fruit piled high upon a platter of silver most intricately wrought with gold.

From staring at them and their burdens I tripped, and fell upon my face. Someone—it was Everard—picked me up, and half-shaking me, asked roughly : " What, man, are you drunk or sick ? "

I was astonished that Everard of all men should speak in this fashion. I answered so loudly some other voice commanded me to hush : " For one day I have indeed had more than enough."

Everard bore me away from the crowd, which by this time stretched as far as a man could see before the King's tent. He spoke roughly and unlike himself again, as if, I thought, marriage had filled him for the first time with care.

" What is on foot between the King and Saphadin ? " he demanded. " I have been a prisoner," he said, " I have been shut up in Joppa ; I am not willing to lose everything."

" To-night, or perhaps to-morrow," I said, " I think we shall have peace with Saladin."

We waited and watched together all that night. William the Marshal and Earl Simon came out of the King's tent, and the emirs followed them while the King talked privately with Saphadin. We watched them troop back at dawn. We waited again while the stars faded in the sky and the moon waned thin and small. Finally, by the light of the new-risen sun we saw the Turkish horsemen ride away.

Everard looked after them and complained, tight-faced : " My God, why must there be this peace ? "

As if they waited for a miracle or a sign our people stared after Saphadin and his men. They looked in vain. The Turkish horsemen seemed to mass closer together, to ride faster. The sun rose higher and shone mighty and majestical as ever upon the world. The night and the messengers with it were gone. Here once more, changing all our to-morrows, was day.

8

AN END AND A BEGINNING

IT was October. At home—so I told myself—the leaves would be falling, first the yellow, then the red. The woods would be full of harsh fungus smells and the few leaves left on the willows would be streaming out in the wind. In the mornings the beech trees along our lane at Oversley would burn through the white autumn mists and the corn waggons creaking home for harvest would have left long trails of corn in the wild hedge. There would be dewberries, lustrous as blackamoor's eyes, to be picked at will on every waste. In Outremer the last of the day's sun lingered still.

Our men thronged Acre's streets waiting to take their leave of King Richard. He had made a truce for three years for himself and all the host with the Sultan Saladin. We were to keep the coastline of Outremer and all the sea ports from Acre to Joppa and the strip of land beyond. Ascalon was to be pulled down and given to the jackals and the crows. Christian pilgrims were to have right of passage without hindrance to the Holy Sepulchre. These were great things. But Jerusalem, that City of Christ we had come to save, was not ours, could never in our lifetime be ours, and our enterprise, to which we had vowed ourselves, must remain unfinished.

The King had summoned all his creditors to him and had paid them and overpaid them also ; at great cost to himself he had ransomed, as in honour and in affection he was bound to do, his friend, William des Préaux ; he had taken his leave of the army and of us all. There was no need, therefore, for us to wait. We waited nevertheless, though it grew dark, though no wind stirred the King's galley sails, though the sea stayed oily and smooth as an eel's back. While we waited the stars came out ; they shone brightly, trembling and thick as flowers in the sky. The wind rose, freshening upon our faces, bringing with it the foul harbour stench and a salt whiff of the sea ; the waves came knocking, gently at first and then more urgently, at the harbour wall. We watched a man climb the mast of the King's ship. Slowly he went up, slowly, like the moon indeed, he came down. Now the King's lantern that had guided us through the first storm on our coming out swung gently and burned once more at the masthead. At the sight the crowd murmured and stirred. We waited while torches were lit about the deck and dim shapes of men moved quietly about their tasks, while the oarsmen ground the sleep from their eyes and, straightening their bowed backs, laid hands once more upon their oars. Our minds tense, we waited still. And suddenly the trumpets sounded for the last time, unearthly, heart-piercing, and the King came out of the midst of the trumpeters and the torch-bearers and stood beneath the mast. His hand raised in farewell, he spoke to us, and the wind, I thought, contrary as all things were in Outremer, carried his words away. "Jerusalem, fair city of Christ, how I leave thee ! "—these, I learned afterwards from men who were nearer him and possessed of sharper ears than mine, were the words the King said.

As if the sight of the shore dazzled him, he turned away. I would have given all my hopes of my own peace to have been with him at that moment, so strangely solitary he appeared for so great a King. We waited while the anchor was weighed and the sails unfurled. Then, without sign or movement on board or any shouting from the shore, the King's ship, Alan Trenchemer at the helm, moved out slowly towards the open sea. The waves and the wind took her : she moved more swiftly. Only then did the pent-up sighs of many hundreds of men make themselves heard. Close about me many men wept, hard silent tears caught incongruously in the rough stubble of their beards ; one foot-soldier, distracted for a moment, climbed a rotting pole, white with gull's droppings, and cried un-availingly : " Return. Return." Some men were silent and hard-faced in grief ; others turned away angrily like men who feel themselves deceived.

There were others still who grimly said : " This is what comes of allies and of quarrelling."

While I waited in a strange isolation of mind and the crowd thinned and broke about me, a fat hand closed objectionably for a second about my arm ; a voice sugared as Christmas plums soaked in sweet cherry wine said : " You go. Did I not say so ? Do you return ? "

It was Xerxes the Persian. I was glad to change from grief to anger. I turned on him ; I flung off his hand. " We go," I said. " But by the Sepulchre of Christ, one day we shall return." And I dealt him for his insult, and for all the many times he had cheated me, a buffet on both cheeks.

" We return.   Do not doubt it," I said.   " So cheat no more.   We shall return."

Putting, as he was wise to do, a bold stomach upon my answering affront, Xerxes turned and began to make his way towards the Custom House, a section of the crowd following close upon him.   I also turned away, for by this time I disliked the plaudits of the crowd as much as a moment before I had disliked the Persian's jeers.

While I hung about still and gazed at the ships and wished myself aboard one of them, and pitied myself and all those other men whom King Richard had left, who were without any peace yet or safety, there was a stir in the crowd ; an impatient feeble clapping of plump hands could be heard, and voices.   Ready to be vexed once more, I turned and stared.

A portly and befurred outrider was punctuating his shouts with hand-clappings.   " Make way," I heard, " make way."   Memories so far off as to appear legendary stirred in my mind.   Half unconsciously I started forward only to see Melisande's blue and silver litter come into view, linkmen with torches riding before her, her servants and baggage following. As soon as I might I laid a hand on the outrider's bridle ; I called to Melisande.

She parted the curtains of the litter and leaned out towards me.   As always when I set eyes upon her unexpectedly my senses were strangely stirred.   Once more for a moment I had no wit to speak.   Her unbound hair fell over her shoulders, her face was fairer than ever now, I thought, it was so full of sleep.

We greeted each other.   " Now I see you as I saw you first," I said.

She spoke softly.   " No.   No.   Now I leave Outremer and all my folly."

My own folly in mind, I said :   " What profit is there in remembering ? "

" Who can help remembering ? "   She put her hand on mine.   " And forgetting also ?   I am for the *Great Joy* of Dover," she said, " and Everard waits for me."

" As always I shall follow you," I answered.   I kissed her hand.   I bent to kiss her cheek.

Her lips against my ear (which I did not much care for), she said suddenly, looking over my shoulder towards the open sea :   " I am afraid of this crossing of the Great Sea."

I drew away.   She could surprise me still.   I said :   " You used never to be afraid."

She laid a hand on the blue and silver curtains as she spoke.   " I am with child."

My voice harsh in my own ears, for who was Everard to be so blessed, I said, not looking at her :   " And now are you content ? "

" I may grow tired," she laughed at me, " of so much content."

The litter moved on. The outrider started his foolish clapping of hands and crying again: " Make way. Make way."

I went in search of Ambrose and the Chronicler. It was they, before I expected them, who found me. A procession of priests, bound also for the *Great Joy* of Dover, followed hard upon Melisande. They came two by two in their white vestments, chanting as they came. The torches shone on their smooth faces, the smoke from their incense burners was sweet in my nostrils, smarting in my eyes. Their chant came to an end ; their leader, who carried a cross of gold before him, raised an admonitory finger and addressed us all : " Woe unto him, king or priest, captain or man-at-arms, who delivers God's land to the heathen, who abandons Christ's Holy City to the unbelievers, woe and eternal damnation for ever upon those who betray their Lord. Woe, woe," he cried, striding forward, a stout man as fat as butter, striding towards peace and comfort and safety. We made way for him. He passed us arrogantly.

I spoke impiously out of the sudden anger that I felt. I spoke, I thought, for all the ranks of silent men about me who lived yet, who still might die for their own and this priest's dream. " Lord God," I said, " the arrogance of thy priests sickens me."

But Ambrose, whom as yet I had not seen, stepped forward and caught at my elbow to silence me. The Chronicler pulled his hood over his face and peered out from under it like a frightened mouse. " You fool," he said. " You fool."

Hot still, and beginning to regret my own boldness, I followed them while the crowd closed up behind us and the priests, chanting once more, passed on to where the *Great Joy* lay.

Late that same night, having consulted with Ambrose and the Chronicler and recovered Giles and collected our baggage, I sought out Harding the Englishman, master of the *Good Content*, also of Dover. He it was who had first brought me news from England while we were at Messina. In return for a part of what remained to me of the Sultan's treasure, some one hundred gold besants in all, he undertook to transport the four of us to England again. He was a good shipman, remote in manner, red-bearded, burly, with wide-set blue eyes ; grandson, men said, of that other Harding, also called the Englishman, who had spoiled the Turkish fleet in the First Crusade.

At dawn we moved out, silently, like a ghost ship. Giles stood beside me as we moved away from the shore.

He declared too manfully : " Master, I no longer fear the mermaids nor the serpents o' the sea. I fear nothing now."

" You have been drinking, or you would not be so valiant," I returned.

He sniffed first, then answered : " Master, it is true I have been drinking.

It is true I cannot bear the thought o' leaving Brand to lie among that mess o' foreign bones."

I left him hiccoughing. The hour was solitary and sour between the first streak of day, the last shade of night. I waited in an odd desolation of spirit while the first primrose-coloured shaft of day lit on the masthead and kindled all my face, and gradually once more the coast of Outremer, white and glistening, thinned and dissolved away.

Many weary days and weeks of travelling lay between us yet and safety ; many unsuspected dangers lay ahead. We lay becalmed off the Grecian isles, oppressed by clouds and mist through which moved, it seemed, like the wings of the Furies, only the giant wings of unknown birds ; off the island of Rhodes once more we fell into a great storm, a hundred times we believed that we were lost, a hundred times we were restored exhaustingly to life again. After about four weeks' sailing we came within sight of the coast of Barbary, where Mahommedan pirates lie in wait for Christian ships. Here, most wretchedly, we were once more becalmed, and afterwards, while we waited in the sea mists and the half dark, we heard the splash of oars of a pirate ship looking for us, and the sound of Saracen voices, and glimpsed the darkness of the pirate's scarlet sails. Off the island of Sardinia we were driven by a sudden squall between the Island of Falcons and the hermit rock. Dawn found us peacefully enough in a small bay, the falcons of the island that had screamed about us all night long sleepily settled upon every perch about the ship, and the hermit standing on the peak of his rock most perilously ringing his copper bell. We put into Marseilles for water : here the French would have stoned us and our ship, so much they loved us even yet. For that we fought them, venting in this manner some of our own resentment for King Richard's sake. We came away with water indeed, and horses, and certain kinds of loot, and, as well as a fair image of the Virgin covered in gold leaf, several small dagger wounds and broken noses and fine closed-up eyes.

On Sunday, the first day in February, we set sail for England and for home. With every day's journey that we made, to-morrow knocked more closely at our thoughts, and King Richard's Holy War and all that we had done fell behind like yesterday. I thought of high white clouds sailing like ruffled swans over our fields of green corn ; I heard the full flow of the river after the rains and the quiet rise of small fish in the willow-fringed pool ; I saw Elfrida walking in the fields. And Outremer seemed to me no more than a part of all the rest.

The winds kept fair ; we crossed the dreaded Bay on this side of France as if it were no more than a small choppy sea, and the ship sped on. Here the Chronicler made little bulky parcels of all his writings against a last-moment shipwreck, and stowed them about his person secretly. And Ambrose, in remembering England, almost forgot his verses. It seemed there was a girl named Ruth near Dover whom he wished to see, whom he might marry if he wished. Torn between the priestly vows he had cast off and the new marriage vows he had yet to make, he paced the deck in thought or hugged his knees. " Could we not put in at Southampton ? " he asked in sudden panic, and shot as suddenly to his feet. " From remembrance of her and terror of damnation," he declared, " my brow is damp."

We put in at Dover. While I waited on the quay for baggage and for Giles, Ambrose, who had set foot ashore earlier that morning, came towards me. His Ruth, it seemed, had died. " And now once more," he said, smiling only with his eyes, " without wife or child, saddle or bridle, I travel the world."

We blessed each other and parted. Ambrose went towards London, and the Chronicler, for this portion of his journey, went with him.

While once more I waited, struggling, as if I were a stranger in my own country, with the sense of desolation that invaded me, a great ship sailed in. I looked at her and scarcely dared to hope, then looked again, shading my eyes with my hand against the sun. It was the *Great Joy* of Dover.

I sought for and afterwards found Everard and Melisande. Together (Melisande and the child following in a horse litter), Everard and I, with Giles, rode home at last, part of a merry jingling company. We rode home, as I had dreamed we might, to April sun, and clouds, and the lift of buds against an April sky. The shadows were light and dancing that day, for there was more sun than shadow, changing and fleeting over the green meadows. There were wine-red gleams of light in the wayside brooks as we passed and raindrops glistening and pendant everywhere after the showers. Father Andrew, warned by rumour beforehand, came out to meet us and blessed us with uplifted hand while his choir sang a *Laus Deo*. They sang through their teeth still, I thought, but more tunefully.

I rode in to Kinwarton alone. The kingcups and the wild daffodils were out in the water meadows ; from the dovecot came the same sudden passion and stir of wings. I halted for a second. Robert is here, I thought, and is not blind. I rode on. And Elfrida came slowly towards me, over the wilderness between the birch trees, in a blue cloak over a rose-red gown. She had grown tall ; under the sun she showed satin-fair.

I waited, trembling from the love I had felt for her for so long and the high hopes I had. The river under the twisted roots of the alders made the same sound and song, and the swans, like full-rigged ships, sailed slowly past.

Elfrida came more quickly, her hands full of the wild daffodils. She thrust them towards me with an awkward grace, and said : " I did not think you would come so soon."

I laughed out in a gladness beyond all measure then and held her to me, and the daffodils, and all my world. " Oh, peace," I said, " my heart, oh, peace. I could not come too soon."